W9-AQR-271

BISHOP'S
PROGRESS

BISHOP'S PROGRESS

A NOVEL BY
D. KEITH MANO

HOUGHTON MIFFLIN COMPANY

BOSTON

Second Printing c

To My Father —

    Out of whose unremittent suffering
and patient endurance came the inspiration
for this book . . .

BISHOP'S
PROGRESS

MONDAY, AUGUST 14TH—

THE FIRST DAY

A BLACK CONVERTIBLE pulled up even with us. A little girl sat alone on the back seat, her blond hair streaming behind from beneath a green bandanna. I'm amazed now at how observant I've become. Our driver accelerated around a Volkswagen and then swerved dangerously into an opening between two other taxis—one yellow, one green. My lower body began to slide toward Michael's. I tightened my stomach muscles and, by their effort alone, managed to maintain balance. Since I can remember, I've been proud of my strong stomach muscles.

"Please," hissed Michael. "Please. There's a sick man back here." Michael's a priest. I'm still a bishop. The driver glanced backward, and I raised my hand in an ironic salute. I was the sick man, or so I'd been told just three hours before. A bulky manila envelope swung backward and forward from between my thumb and forefinger. X-rays of my chest. A great deal of gray on gray, on black. Misty ribs, translucent shoulder blades. And a thing—a whiteness seeming both flat and rounded. David Parsons said it didn't belong with the other whitenesses. "That," he said, scratching at a blunted triangle with the texture and the substantiality of a soap bubble, "that's your heart. This is very close to it. Maybe they're touching. I can't tell. If they are," he said, "well . . . well, anyway it shouldn't be there."

Lexington Avenue: The six of us had met near there—in front of the old Cherry Blossom Restaurant. With our white sweat socks showing between our penny loafers and our pegged khakis. Our hair was crew cut, our ties were thrown back over our shoulders and against the wind. Gentlemanly, one-punch street fights. Taxi races. Penthouse parties. *Virtute et fide* was inscribed in gold beneath the emblem on each blazer vest pocket. And yet, we sometimes forgot . . .

Our taxi came to a quick halt. The August heat caught us up: warmer, it seemed, than ever after its chase through the Seventies. A bus subsided, shuddering as it idled a foot from my window—putting out films of brown smoke like a great, terrified squid. In the bus there were sounds of little Negro boys playing siloogie with someone's cap. "Gimme Rufus. Kick y'teeth in. Gimme." No more siloogie for me.

And all the while Michael waited: he watched me breathe; watched as I scratched my thigh; watched as beads of sweat swelled for the descent of my cheek. Finding all these things full of portent, ominous, because he'd never had to notice them before. How observant we've all become. Michael's body swayed in the shadow of my body. Like a safety man waiting below a high-wire walker.

Park Avenue: The church where it had all begun. Where the Young People's Fellowship was heir jointly to fifty million dollars. Where I had held court twenty-five years ago—dancing and playing basketball and making very substantial love. "The chapel?" he had said. "Must be here somewhere. I know where the swimming pool is and the billiard room. No. The chapel . . . You better ask someone else."

A gray, shamefully worn suitcase stood between my knees. Contents: toothbrush (bristles caked and splayed); washcloth (stiff and slightly rancid); pajamas (too large and wrinkled); and my obscene, obscene slippers. Fifteen years old. A great comfort to me and, alternately, a great embarrassment. Drips of tea and toast crumbs; persistent athlete's foot; corns and in-grown toenails; nightly trips to the bathroom. The privatest things of a public man. But no wife wrinkled and stiff and splayed. Only Michael.

And a beautiful cat. A fat tabby, tastefully done in camou-flage paint. Brown, black, yellow; circles and butterflies and bull's-eyes. Exactly symmetrical along the spine as a Rorschach test. Favorite foods: fish (properly cooked or very raw and fresh); chicken livers and hearts and gizzards; milk with a raw egg yolk (beaten in well); chopped veal laced with a dash of cod liver oil; please, nothing that comes in a can. I'd made out a very long list for Michael to follow—although cats terrify Michael and Pious, as a cat will, makes the most of that. Scrape the box out every day. Fill to three inches with Kitty Litter. The scoop is under the sink. Drag the cat-nip mouse quickly across the floor—then let it climb slowly up the sofa until it is hidden behind the edge. Be certain that it is hidden. Make intriguing sounds. After Pious has leaped and pounced, begin the process again. He'll be doing it for your benefit, but he needs the exercise. Pious, my joy, what will I do without you? In Adam's fall we sinned all, but never once a cat.

Madison Avenue: I walked barefoot there with Nancy so many years before; and she was coffee-tanned and beautiful at three o'clock in the morning. I said I'd love her forever—which

was until Christmas when she came back from boarding school.
Her feet were brown and her toenails were painted pink. The
pavement of Madison Avenue's sidewalks held its warmth just
for us.

*Please. Please, my God. Let me have a private room. I don't
fear death, but I am unaccustomed to its presence. I may be
unpleasant. I don't fear death, but I do very much fear my own
nature. Forgive me, my God. Forgive me. But let me have a
private room.*

"Mike? Did you arrange for a private room?"

"Well . . ."

"Well?"

"She said . . . Why don't you put your suitcase over here?
It won't hit your knees then." I thought Michael was going to
cry, but it was only sweat welling up in his tiny eye sockets.

"I'm all right. We haven't far to go." My voice was deep
and serene. The way children imagine God speaks. Soothing
Michael, reassuring him. "The room?"

"She said they don't have private rooms. Not in the major
surgery ward—that's what she called it. Private rooms are only
used for post-operative care. She said she'd give you a bed in
a semi-private room. Four beds, but it's empty. This is the off-
season, she said. People prefer to take vacations." Michael
paused. "I told her your father knew Horace Cavendish
Senior. I said you made a very large annual contribution. But
. . . It got very unpleasant, I think."

"Doesn't matter. We'll make the best of it." I'll have to
make the best of it. *Quite right, my God. Forgive my asking.
Quite right.* The heat will be unbearable. I shall sweat, and I
shall open my pajamas. For the first time in twenty years,
strangers will peer at my nipples and the now gray hair on my

chest, and the blue veins bulging on my calves. *Forgive me.* But, after all, it's the off-season. People prefer to take vacations. A room with four beds might yet remain empty.

Fifth Avenue: Where Mary Anne and Judy and Candy Culver had lived, nestled in money. Walking next to the Park on huge, dirty bathroom tiles. Wearing Bermudas; leading intelligent poodles cut like hedges; looking away when the poodles went. Desultory talk of girls who had cut their wrists again or had taken sleeping pills again and were, unaccountably, still alive. On the West Side they killed each other. On the East Side we killed ourselves.

"It'll be all right," said Michael. And that really startled me. I was going to thank him with a smile and an inclination of my head, but he spoiled it then by saying, "It will, won't it?" And I knew Michael hadn't been trying to comfort me at all. Afraid to drag a cat-nip mouse up a sofa. Short and fat. Hair like the fuzz left in a hen's nest. A weak chin with almost a goiter beneath it. Eyes tiny as a doll's, sunk in the fat of his puffy face. Constipated, too, I think. Constipated and vaguely guilty about it.

"If the best doctors in the world can make me all right, I'll be all right. But, look Mike, anything can happen. We've got to face that. God hasn't set me apart." David assured me—he assured me—that Dr. Snow was the man. He said it might be touch and go, but Snow was a miracle-worker. He assured me of that. I have three more chapters to finish, and then the whole has to be rewritten. Three or four months of work left. No one in the history of modern surgery has surpassed Dr. Snow in imagination and sheer technical prowess. That's what David had said. "I'm prepared," I said, "whatever the eventuality, Mike. You've got to be prepared, too. I guess, in cases like these, there's always some slight—some negligible—chance of a mishap."

"But who will take care of—who will take care of Pious?"

"We'll find him a nice parish somewhere. A comfortable living, someplace where he has to preach just once a month and then only in a whisper."

Central Park: Where I lay under dirty bushes with Sesame one cold spring Sunday. She, naked to the waist and fifteen; I, fourteen and meaning to be ardent, while my nose ran with the cold, and my eyes searched out the policeman's feet, the spoked wheels of the sanitation cart, the legs of little children who played over our bodies as though we were part of some scrubby, Amazon jungle. I was proud that night—warm with my manhood and an incipient strep throat.

Michael tapped page three or four of the *New York Times*. Then he folded the newspaper and handed it to me.

BISHOP BELKNAP

TO UNDERGO

MINOR SURGERY

Whitney Belknap, Bishop of Queens and a controversial leader of the radical movement in the Episcopalian Church, will enter Cavendish Memorial Hospital today for minor surgery of an undisclosed nature. Michael Herbert, spokesman for the author of the best-selling *A God For Our Time*, said the operation was not expected to have serious consequences.

"That was yesterday," said Michael. "Yesterday you told me it wouldn't be serious."

"Never mind," I said. "That's just the right note. Won't worry anybody." No one must be worried. No one. There is nothing to worry about.

I looked out the window. Our cab was crossing Broadway, making its way west to the river. I wanted the streets and their business to distract me, but the West Side was another city—as unfamiliar as the noisome closeness of Middle European cities. A watering truck lumbered north on Broadway. The force of its spray pushed anonymous bits of trash up and over the curb. The sudden wetness drew a sickening, hot smell out of the pavement. I held my breath, closed my eyes. And, when I had done that, I found that the sounds alone disturbed me.

Then I saw the Hudson. It was the first thing I saw, when, at Michael's nervous insistence, I opened my eyes. The sun sat on the crest of the Palisades. The mote-filled air had turned it a scarcely luminous, luscious amber-red, and its glint lent the water a seeming texture of rippled ice. A tug, terribly alone in center stream, moved without apparent movement toward the George Washington Bridge. A massive, cleansing flow, sweeping away detritus from both its filthy shores—passing noncommittally beside Westchester opulence and West Side squalor alike. A lovely, uninvolved thing.

And, for a full ten blocks along the Manhattan shore, stood the gray massivity of Cavendish. Square upon square of symmetrical, uncolored reassurance. Surrounded but not touched by grass and flower beds and the raking hands of lawn sprays that fell harmless just in front of its walls. As noncommittal as the river—exuding only a terrific American competence.

After a while it reminded me of a tiny railway depot beyond Cincinnati. I had sat on just such a brown bench with the same gray suitcase between my legs. From midnight until past five I had waited with just such people, it seemed, as were now waiting with me. Waiting then for a train to take me home. Tense, tired, stupid. Sitting in the yellow half-light, unable to

sleep for the sound of the thing always coming. Stultified.
Made uneasy by an uncompromising anticipation.

In the admissions room prosaic questions were being asked
of frightened people. Name of father and mother: I have a
brain tumor, and I am no longer certain what my body does.
Occupation and place of work: There's a cancer in my lung
and beyond my lung; if the radiation works I may live another
year, seared like black toast. Any previous illnesses, accidents
—explain in the space provided: I am old and the fabric of
my body has come undone. In front of us a middle-aged woman
was reassuring her father. They, she anyway, would come every
day. He'd be home in no time or certainly for Thanksgiving.
And the middle-aged son-in-law watched the clock on the wall
as he swung the old man's shiny new suitcase with little, irritated jerks. How long, said the little, irritated jerks, how long
can any man hope to live?

I'm only forty-two. Much longer, thank you. The nurse at
the desk asked for "Mr. Belknap?" Michael jumped up—his
pants over his shoes, his stomach over his belt, his chin over
his collar. He spoke to the nurse for some time, but it was me
they wanted. Rejected, Michael waddled slowly back across
the reception room.

"No private rooms. I asked again. But the room with four
beds is definitely empty."

Referred to Dr. Snow by Dr. Parsons? Very lucky indeed,
she said. There was a smile on her face. Whatever my trouble
was. Very lucky. Dr. Snow was the best for anything at all.
Anything, but just this morning he'd left for a conference and
wouldn't return until Wednesday. A very, very important conference. Dr. Snow? The best. She knew a woman who—but
that was a long story. Room 714.

David wasn't certain what it was—he told me that right off.

"I'm not a specialist, mind you. But, offhand, I'd say it's pressing against the descending aorta. Could be a mediastinal cyst, I suppose. But that's a ticklish area, no matter what the trouble is. Then again—could be something wrong with the aorta itself. Whitney, if there's even a chance of that, you can't afford to wait. Snow's the only man, I think. He's right here at Cavendish. No money worries, I suppose?" No money worries. "He's a genius. A strange sort, but a certified genius. Get over there pronto and do whatever the hell he says."

At the second floor two interns pushed a bed into our elevator. The doors closed and, as they did, the ugly presence of the man on the bed closed in around us. He was waxen and without hair; the smell that rose from his bed became somehow associated in my mind with yellow embalming fluid. A bottle of glucose was suspended above, attached by a plastic tube to an artery in his white-blue instep. He was groaning. And then I realized that my heart, my strange, abnormal heart, was beating faster and yet faster. There were thumps at my neck and a tiny, terribly insistent knocking at my temples. I saw the gray-white outline of the thing inside my chest; I felt it swell, and the skin over my heart squirmed under the pressure of my shirt. The wax man groaned again. I wanted to scream at the very top of my voice, but a sign on the wall said *Quiet Please*. Then the elevator halted, and Michael fell against me. The jolt reconstituted the outlines of my external frame; with that familiar form came a certain calm. As I walked out of the elevator, I touched the ribs above my heart. Michael must have thought I'd reverenced myself, for, quite apropos of nothing, he made a sign of the cross.

It was a nice room: clean and bright and understandable. Two white beds on one side; two white beds opposite. And, nicest of all, an unobstructed view of the Hudson. I rested my uncertain chest on the windowsill and sought to regain both my composure and Michael's. My Michael is an emotional megaphone. If I scream, I scream through him a hundred times as loud; if I whimper, my whimper returns as a shriek. Below, a red tugboat pushed its furry nose into the current. It tooted. The toot echoed solemnly across a quarter mile of river. An eerie welcome. I wanted to toot back, but that would only have set Michael tooting.

Then a nurse, a very beautiful woman, tore into the room. She swept Michael, by his mere proximity to her momentum, across the floor and between the two beds opposite. She had short brown hair, blue eyes and a complexion compounded of all the colors that lie between white and pink. Three dimples were squeezed from the surface of each cheek by a determined frown. A green square, just over the slope of her left breast, said: Nurse *MacArthur*. Her hands were strong and unadorned; she held them slightly away from her hips as though they were little vestigial wings. A small, but very competent, cumulus cloud.

"Mr. Belknap? Father Belknap?" She frowned.

"Bishop—Bishop Belknap," said Michael from between the beds. Nurse MacArthur drew the curtain around the bed on the right nearest the window.

"Dinner is at six. You'd better undress and get into bed." I didn't move. "You are the patient?" She looked at Michael. He opened the drawer of a bedside table, as though it might offer an avenue of escape.

"Yes ma'am," I said. Nurse MacArthur frowned again, as if a special beam of sunlight were glinting against her vision.

"Well then, you'd best get into bed. You're not a well man."

"I'm not?" I said it with a certain amount of curiosity. But Nurse MacArthur wasn't listening. "No, I'm not," I repeated dully. She pulled the bed curtain entirely around, turned briskly and left. I walked behind the curtain and began to undress. Tentatively, Michael stepped out from between the beds, as a snail might after some small danger has come and gone. He found, to his own horror, that he wanted to peek behind the curtain. I'm sure of that. But I guess he decided it'd be enough to see me in my wrinkled pajamas; yes, and in my slippers. I decided to leave my socks on—so that Michael needn't cope with the curly dark hair on my insteps. I drew the curtain back.

Michael was leaning, as I had leaned, on the windowsill. I could tell that he was praying. Some force exuded from Michael when he prayed, like heat waves from a tin roof in the sun. There was so much effort involved. He turned away with his eyes still firmly shut, and opened them only when he was facing me. Yes, there I was.

"How do you feel?"

How did my heart feel? How did I feel wearing pajamas and tattered slippers? I said I felt fine, and that, in the face of medical evidence quite to the contrary, seemed to satisfy Michael. We stood rather stupidly for a moment, just staring at each other. Then the lovely-fierce Nurse MacArthur came back, and Michael was made to retreat to the radiator. She handed me a half-pint bottle.

"Fill this please," she said. Then she was gone again.

"What did she mean?" asked Michael.

"Urine sample," I said. I threw the bottle on the bed. I had several things yet to unpack. Books first. I piled them up neatly: some in the locker, some on my bed table. The Bible. Two copies of *A God For Our Time*, with my picture on the back. Saint Augustine, Calvin, Tillich. Bonhoeffer, too. Then the manuscripts. I lifted them carefully, enjoying their cu-

mulative weight. My next book to be. Thick manuscripts and
neatly piled books are a great comfort to me. Then I noticed
Michael was standing beside me; he was peering at the bottle
on the bed.

"Where will you get it?" he asked.

" 'By your fruits ye shall be known,' " I said. I'm used
to Michael's questions. Just then I was preoccupied: I was
wondering how I might avoid handing the urine sample to
Nurse MacArthur. I didn't want her to feel my vulgar inner
warmth on the palm of her hand. As I thought, I opened and
closed my tattered gray suitcase once more. Then I slid it into
the bottom of the locker. I hung my clothes up.

" 'For the time of the figs was not yet,' " said Michael. He
knew the entire New Testament verbatim. My Michael is a
genius of sorts, I guess. He once repeated the genealogy in Matthew I backwards and without a single mistake. He has almost
total recall, but, somehow, the things he chooses to recall are
never quite the proper things.

"You'd better go, Mike. Mail these letters as you leave. Be
sure you change the litter in Pious' box tonight. Distract him
if you can." I opened my billfold to the place where I kept
Pious' picture and set it carefully on the bed table. "And, above
all, keep people away from here. Everyone—no exceptions. I
don't care what you have to do. Got that?" He nodded. "Fine.
In any case, don't worry. Hold the fort and pray for me."

"I will. I will." He backed to the door. "Is there anything
you need?" I saw Nurse MacArthur pass quickly along the corridor.

"I guess," I sighed. "I guess I could use a new pair of slippers."

*

I should have been writing even then, but my experience in
the elevator and my new surroundings had unsettled me. For
some time I sat by the window, watching the sparse river traffic: a couple of conscientious tugs, hauling each a fat, yawning
barge; a buoyant tanker; a huge, white yacht. Darkness
seemed to be rising from the confused, dirty shadows along the
Jersey shore. I presumed, but could not distinguish, a feverish
activity there.

In time I passed into a semiconscious state, following, or sup-
posing that I followed, the configurations of a single ripple on
the water. I was withdrawing; I was tired. Tired of writing,
which I had always despised. Tired of being what even the
New York Times now considered a highly controversial figure.
Soon, I feared, the other beds would become occupied. Others
demanding to know what a bishop does in the face of a serious
heart condition. And so I sat by the window and watched the
river. Though my eyes were open and aware, I slept within
myself for a few blessed minutes.

At six a huge Negro woman with great, oily, tubular arms
brought a dinner tray into my room. I hurried to the bed, embarrassed, even before her, by the wrinkles in my pajamas. The
woman hauled my adjustable table into position with the edge
of her foot. Then she placed the tray carefully on my table.
Throughout I could hear her breathing heavily, heaving up
little whistling sighs. Her shoes, worn to slippers, scraped on
the floor. One pink heel showed in its entirety.

I smiled several times, but she made a show of being
too seriously intent just then to acknowledge me. Having
brought the table up to my solar plexus, she stepped back, her
fingers on her already smudged hips, as if to examine the effect.
I was hungry. I smiled and removed the aluminum cover

from a plate. She didn't move. I played with my knife and fork. Still she didn't move. I was hungry, but not hungry enough to spoil the meal by beginning it in her presence. And then a little breeze passed through her clothing. An ugly smell of rancid kitchen garbage rose up, over my tray. My nose, forgive me, my nose wrinkled.

"G'won. Eat it up."

Two gold teeth were set exactly in the center of her upper jaw. The lower jaw was empty, overflowing with immense pink tongue. Her hair was done up in a bandanna, tied, as only they know how to tie them, with little, hard knots. I smiled. Then I scratched at my nose, as if in atonement. She had no intention of leaving. After a moment I lifted the cover from my cup of soup: a distinct smell of over-saturated sweat, mingled now with the smell of garbage, poured out with the steam. I stirred at my soup. Two pieces of rice rose up and slipped back. But that was all. I had to smile again.

"Honest? You sure 'nuff a bishop?"

I nodded.

"That so? My, my . . . An' there's your Bible." She pointed to my bed table. It was there all right. And still I could find nothing to do but smile and agitate the little pieces of rice until they virtually romped through my soup. After just a short moment's acquaintance, she lifted a massive left thigh and sat ponderously at the foot of my bed. The smell of garbage billowed up under my sheets and poured into the sleeves of my pajamas. I am going to scream, I thought. I am going to scream.

> BISHOP OF QUEENS
> THROWS CHICKEN BROTH
> IN NEGRO ATTENDANT'S FACE

I'd never be able to eat now. The blessed peace of the last hour had dissipated utterly. Tense, angry, I smacked the balls of my feet together under the sheets. I was filled with revulsion, and only then did she put her hand on my covered shin.

"My husband—he in the same bizniz," she said. I would have laughed.

"Indeed?"

"In-deed. Yes sir. In fact, the deacon of the Harlem Tabnacle. On Lenox Avenue."

I saw it all with perfect clarity. A defunct liquor store or dry cleaning outlet. The front window splashed with yellow or pink whitewash. A crude cross or a lamb or a crown of thorns sketched in on top of the whitewash. And, here and there, a few pseudo-scriptural phrases: Are You Washed Brother? Is God Under Your Skin? A schedule of services sufficient to keep two cathedrals frantic. The smell of dry rot and insecticide and urine. The same business? Oh yes, indeed, the same business. *Forgive me . . .* The same business.

"What's wrong with you, Mistuh Bishop? What you in Cabbemdish for? Come on. Eat up like a good boy. You needs your strength. Don't let Sarah's big mouf keep you from eatin'." She squeezed my shin and laughed exquisitely— laughed at the freedoms she could take even with a bishop because she was a jolly, American black mammy. I buttered my bread and tore it in half. Then I tore the half in halves and jammed both quarters under my plate.

"My heart," I said, but my voice was tense and without body. "Heart," I repeated. "Heart has something wrong with it."

"Your heart. Oh my . . ." She made ominous clucking sounds inside her fat throat, and the skin from her ears to her chin took up the rhythm. "No sir. No sir. You don't fool 'roun wif a heart. Who's your doctuh?"

"Snow. Snow."

"Gunness . . ." She clucked again. "Doctuh Snow. He's somethin' else. Now don't git me wrong—he's a good doctuh an' all. One've the best, so I hear. Fix your heart up in no time t'all. Jes, he pretty tough on the kitchen staff. Believe me, I wunt be sittin' on your bed—an' you a bishop an' all—I wunt be sittin' all friendly like this, if'n I dint know Doctuh Snow away at a comfrunce. No sir. But he take care of hearts like nobody's bizniz. You don't have a wurry in th'world. He just ain' no fun like Doctuh Cone or Doctuh Smithuh."

I heard myself asking why. As much as I hated to prolong the conversation, I think I was even more curious to learn about Doctor Snow. Sarah leaned forward to whisper, and the smell and texture of a little, wheezy sigh reached out at me. Then she squeezed my shin—higher this time—and looked out toward the corridor.

"You give out with a whistle case Nuss McAwthuh pop by. She move so fast she make me dizzy. An' she don't like me talkin' to the patients—special not 'bout Doctuh Snow." She paused. Then she tapped the sheet with her forefinger several times. "Know what he say t'me? An' I don't care what anybody say diffrunt—it just ain' a nice thin' for a man t'say to a married woman. Know what he say?" I finally shook my head. "Well he say, 'Sarah Samson, you the most—what he say?—the most unhygienk thing in this whol' hospitul.' That's what he say. It just wunt kind, an' it wunt true neithuh. I wosh my hands evvy night—right afore I comes up wif the meals." She presented them for inspection, and their condition was so obvious I thought at first she couldn't be serious. But she was. She turned them from one side to the other—from blotched pink to brown to blotched pink again—and clucked as she did. "You a bishop—d'you think he's right t'say a thin' like that?"

"No," I said. No, indeed—he should've fired you instead. "No. But you must try to understand. After all, Sarah," always call them by their Christian names, "he must have a great deal on his mind. Maybe it's difficult for him to be as thoughtful as he'd like to be. You'll have to try and forgive him." And me . . . Forgive me, Sarah. I've allowed your presence to ruin my dinner. And I don't think your husband's in the same business at all.

"Yes sir. Wif all them hearts an' lungs an' mortibund people 'roun, he sure nuff must have a lot troublin' him—even if'n he don't show it right out. I can see that. Yes sir." She laughed. "Well, look here—here's a big, fat woman wif piles work t'do sittin' on your bed an' you a bishop 'n all." She got off the bed, but she knew very well she'd have *carte blanche* with the Pope in his own bathroom. We have treated the Negro shamefully, but we compensate in certain small ways.

"Come and visit any time, Sarah. I need your comfort. After all, we're both in the same business."

"Now ain' that the truth?" She nodded violently, and her shoulders and breasts took up the nod and deposited it in various corners of her body. "I married Samson 'cause I was called. That what he say. He say, 'I'm called Sarah, an' I'm callin' you t'marry me.' An' I did. Where the Lawd leadeth, I will go. An' I bettuh git on my way right now. You ain' gone eat that up?" I shook my head. "Well, don't you wurry 'bout your heart. Doctuh Snow take care of that. You read your Bible there an' hope in the Lawd an' evuhthin' come out fine. I'll have the whole congreegashun pray for you Thursday night." She took a step forward. "What's you a bishop of?"

"The Episcopal Church."

"Pipscopal? That's Christian, ain't it?" I nodded. She

smiled. "I thought so. We ain' Pipscopalians, but we is Christians. That's what counts. Right?"

"Right."

"That what Samson say all the time. He say, Sarah, we's all—"

"That'll be enough, Sarah. No one else has been fed yet."

Sarah put her hand to her mouth and pretended to laugh with me at her own naughtiness. But she left quickly, pushing her shoes before her. Nurse MacArthur took my pulse and temperature. Then she picked up the urine bottle, held it to the light and shook it. Instinctively, I closed my legs.

"You didn't eat much," she said.

"I'm sorry. I wasn't hungry."

"Would a tranquilizer help?" I said no. Then I leaned over to the bed table and tapped at my Bible.

"I have one, thanks," I said.

"Yes? Oh, yes." It was a pretentious, silly gesture, and I felt ridiculous almost at once. "Well, that's fine," she said indulgently. "You'd better get some sleep. Tomorrow's a big day. You're down for X-rays and an angiogram in the morning. I'm afraid you'll have to go without breakfast."

"Did you say X-rays?" She nodded. "I brought some with me. Doctor Parsons took them. I left them with the nurse at the desk downstairs."

"Oh, those? These are for Doctor Snow." She went to the window. The river was a deep brown. Lights on the slope of the Palisades had begun to show in clusters. Nurse MacArthur pulled down the shades.

"What's Doctor Snow like?" I asked. Nurse MacArthur shook her head.

"He's at a conference just now."

"Yes, I know. What sort of a person is he?" She began to crank down my bed. I held my sitting position as the bed fell away from me.

"He's a surgeon, that's why," she said.

"Why what?"

"Let's see. Would you like a Seconal? Sodium Amytal? That's the best I can do for you until Doctor Snow prescribes."

"No," I said.

"No? All right. But you'd better try to sleep." She seemed tired. As she tired her movements, as though perversely, became swifter and more efficient. "By the way, Mr. Belknap. Please don't encourage Sarah to talk. She'll get in trouble, and you wouldn't want that, would you?" Dismayed, I shook my head, my mouth open in a silent protest. "Fine then. You'd better put out your light. You're not a well man."

"I'm not a well man," I repeated it after her, but Nurse MacArthur was already gone.

I made ready for sleep. The room was silent, but for muffled footsteps in the corridor, and an occasional metallic sound. The three other beds seemed to imply the existence of people who were not yet. I moved my feet under the sheets, and the movement comforted me. I was tired, but not afraid. Interested, but not afraid. I was alone, but, with my God, quite self-sufficient. I leaned up to turn off the light. As I did so I saw the face on the back cover of *A God For Our Time*. I thought it smiled at me.

Lord God my Father, I thank Thee for this Thy gift of physical weakness. Thou hast taken my human pride and subdued it by violence, and I am grateful. It is in the nearness of death that we truly know humility.

Oh Lord, I pray only that Thou grant me time and strength to complete my task here on earth. Let the words that I write by Thy words. Dedicate me that, in the days to come, I may write as did the inspired servants of Thy Gospel—always and only to the honor and glory of Thy Name, through Jesus Christ our Lord.

THE SECOND DAY

IT WENT into my arm; it probed deep inside the vein. I heard, or thought I heard, the sounds of little, soft, wet things being crushed. Yet, even at that, I remained perfectly still. I looked only ahead and upward, vision concentrated on the under-surfaces of my eyelids. I was determined not to show pain, for he had angered me—standing there with the needle nicely balanced in the palm of his hand: weighing it, drawing my attention, willing me to anticipate its enormity buried in the flesh of my arm. And then the pain settled in. It welled up into my elbow-pit like hard, icy water. I could imagine the entire mechanism of my elbow, and there was a terrible sensitivity, a terrible friction, wherever I thought skin touched tendon, tendon touched bone. My fingers hung loose, unable to ball up a fist. But I only stared straight ahead and yawned.

"One cc. diodrast please, Miss Black." The 1 cc. was injected. Miss Black took my head between her cool, brown hands and twisted it several degrees on my neck. Then Dr. Crecy pushed at my knee until my legs were closed, dangling over the edge of the X-ray table. I could have done that my-

self. I could have turned my head; I could have moved my
knee. My empty stomach made sounds as of crumpling wax
paper. I knew my breath was foul: a fetid sourness rose from
my throat up, into the back of my nose. One of them—I'm not
certain which—took my unviolated arm and put it someplace.
I continued to stare straight ahead, but this time I couldn't
yawn.

The X-ray apparatus hung suspended in front of me like an
aged and quizzical voyeur. It was the same color as Miss Black,
and it moved as she did—gliding easily along certain familiar
tracks. She had the thing even with my chest now. I sat there
seeing only the top of the machine, the top of her head. Miss
Black's eyes were illuminated by a vivid, lemon-yellow intensity of purpose, but that purpose, I sensed, was very specific,
very clearly defined. Circumscribed.

"Well. That will do. He doesn't seem to be dying." Dr.
Crecy looked at his watch. He was a small man, at least half a
foot shorter than I, but there was undeniable strength in his
wrists and forearms. Not once while we were in the X-ray room
did he stop moving. His fingers palpated the air, searched at
themselves, dug into things—faster, I thought, than ever mere
sensory perception could register. His tongue prodded at his
lips, the upper, the lower, so that, one after the other, they protruded. He was French, I think. His phrasing was monotonous
and artificial; it frustrated the nimbleness of his little body.

I'd come to dislike Dr. Crecy instinctively and at once. Perhaps I felt he was trying to humiliate me before Miss Black.
But, if that was so, Miss Black seemed not to care. She hardly
looked at me. Instead she stared at Dr. Crecy, anticipating, af-
firming, helping. They worked very well together. I thought
then that Dr. Crecy was having an affair with her, and I ima-

gined, with jealous disgust, that he was monstrously efficient in bed. But he, too, agreed that Dr. Snow was a genius, and I was grateful for that.

"And now, Bishop Belknap, the time has come. I must ask you to help us." I brought my eyes down. When I saw the thing sitting on, in my arm, I started involuntarily. I recalled a foot-long model of the anopheles mosquito we'd once made in high school. Out of yellow plastic and thin, sharp wires. Dr. Crecy smiled: half because of my start, half because of the equally involuntary annoyance that followed it.

"What do I do?" I said it almost angrily.

"I'm going to inject a certain substance into your vein. The substance has a bitter taste. When you taste the bitterness, I want you immediately—that is, at once—to raise your free arm. Do you understand? Immediately." I nodded. "Decholin, Miss Black." Dr. Crecy attached another syringe. "Miss Black, you will time his reaction from one half second after I make the injection. Are you ready?"

"Yes, Dr. Crecy."

"And you? Are you ready, Bishop Belknap? Good. Try to relax your body. Yes. That's it. Breathe naturally. Now let your arm down. Fine. I'm going to count to three. At three I will inject. Now. One . . . two . . . Please! Please! You must not move!"

My heart leaped. I looked around, up, down, in confused uncertainty. He had screamed, actually screamed, at me. I was as frightened as I had been when Mrs. Morse caught me cheating in the third grade. Dr. Crecy stood back; he was shaking his head. Miss Black was sympathizing.

"I'm sorry," I said. Yet I couldn't remember having moved.

"Well . . . You must try to control your anxiety. Shall we

try again? Miss Black? Bishop Belknap?" He got into position. "Breathe evenly. And remember—as soon as you've tasted the decholin—at that very moment—raise your free arm. All right. We will begin again. Now. One . . . two . . . three . . ."

I felt nothing. My eyes returned to their accustomed position. I waited. And then I found myself wondering how I could taste what had been injected into my arm. Into my arm . . . It dawned on me that the stuff, the decholin, was even now making its way through the most secret channels of my body. What had been in Dr. Crecy's hand was now in my shoulder. Now swirling around in my heart . . . And then I tasted it, smelled it rather. Deep and bitter like the residue of vomit. I raised my arm.

"A little over three point one seconds, doctor."

"Yes. That sounds right. Let us say a little over two seconds for the left chambers and the aorta. Start the camera at one and one half seconds after I have begun injecting."

"Is there more?"

"We haven't properly begun yet. Patience, please."

I'd begun to feel sick. My arm, suspended and bent, was shaking perceptibly. My empty stomach had bound itself into a tiny knot and was floating crazily inside my abdomen. I think it was my heart. Every other part of me felt it straining, beating—indignant before the alien substances oppressing it. My hands, my stomach, my eyes wavered in sympathy and, perhaps, in fear.

"The machine is in position, Dr. Crecy."

"Fifty cc. diodrast." Dr. Crecy took the syringe and raised my arm to a forty-five degree angle. "Breathe easily, Bishop Belknap. That's correct. Yes. Now try to steady your arm. I'm going to ask you to exhale and then to hold your breath. Then

I will ask you to inhale deeply. At that moment I will inject the contrast solution. Do you understand?"

"I'm not feeling too well, Doctor. I think I—my heart is beating terribly fast."

"Please. It's only natural. Your heart is already weak—now it's undergoing a terrific strain. What else could you expect? We have a two percent mortality in angiograms."

"Two—two percent mortality."

"Yes. I, for one, am surprised it isn't higher." I remembered then what the word mortality meant. The joints in my arms and legs went dead, so very dead that there was an echo of my beating heart inside each of them. Two percent from one hundred is . . . Zero borrow one is ten, minus two is eight. What eight?

"Exhale, Bishop Belknap. Hold. Hold."

I held. My head swam. Intermingled circles like the surface of greasy soup ran over the wall.

"Inhale!"

I felt it in my arm this time. A great deal of material, lead-like, running up my vein and into my heart. The X-ray camera machine-gunned. I felt a warmth pouring into my chest, into my neck, my head. The hairs on my body rose on little hillocks and swayed in waves. Heat radiated into my face from my lower body, collecting in my nose and eyes. *Our Father who art in* . . . I began to slide backward. I remember feeling the needle come loose. And I remember hearing Dr. Crecy say, "Dypsnea, hot flush, faint. Take that down, Miss Black."

A little white Band-Aid crossed the crook of my arm. It was just the sort of Band-Aid my father might have put on a scraped knee or a cut finger, and, as such, I found it reassuring.

I touched it with the fingers of my left hand. I was able to distinguish insensible sterility from soreness; the fingertips from the Band-Aid; the Band-Aid from the skin of my inner arm. My elbow itched, and I scratched it. All these things were reassuring.

I sat up. For just a moment ruddy streaks colored my vision, but soon again I was able to see the day. It was overcast and cool. Rain had fallen during the night. Throughout the early morning hours I'd heard the morose sounding of foghorns—very much like the lowing of great, gentle cows. The beating of my heart was regular now. Regular, but, in the tiny pauses between each beat, the continuity of my existence also hesitated, irresolute.

My lunch came. I let it lie on the table, enjoying my hunger and the prospect of its satisfaction. I had never imposed mortifications on my body. Fasting made me irritable: it led only to the mortification of those around me. All Belknaps appreciate good food and the most lavish of physical comforts. That, in a sense, is what we are. And whenever I experienced guilt, an article would appear commending my various self-indulgences as some sort of radical religious innovation. The very thing, they'd say. The very thing a God who is *really* for our time would sanction. And so I continued, unperturbed, to abstain from fasting.

I had rested comfortably for about five minutes—looking out on the river, my arms behind my head—when I realized that someone was watching me. My first instinct was to turn quickly to the door, but we have an inborn dignity that censors sudden movement. Instead I turned very slowly, shaping a smile that implied complete foreknowledge of the event. My smile fell on Dr. Crecy. He was leaning against the door jamb, his right arm bent behind him. After a moment in which nothing was gained or lost on either side, he smiled and came toward me. His right arm, I noticed, was still bent behind his back. A little yellow square was pinned to his lapel. It said, *Dr. P. Crecy.*

P. Crecy stood at the foot of my bed, balancing himself precariously first on one foot, then on the other. I found him repulsive. I pulled the adjustable table up close to my chest. Then I pulled the lunch tray toward me. P. Crecy said nothing. There is a certain species of mole with a handful of tentacles protruding from its face in place of a nose: as if smells are to be snatched and felt. P. Crecy's nose was prehensile. It held odors and pulled them to shreds. Odors that my body gave forth against its will.

"Have I disturbed your meal?"

"No. Not at all. I hadn't begun." For some reason I took my Bible from the bed table; it was as though I had a passage to quote him. Having done so, I was embarrassed to explain the gesture. I left the Bible on my chest.

"I thought you'd want to know— Dr. Snow called in this morning. He'll see you at ten o'clock tomorrow."

"That's wonderful."

"Indeed it is. You're very fortunate, Bishop Belknap."

"I know. Do you think he'll operate?"

"Do I think?" He shook his head. "I am Dr. Snow's eyes and ears and fingers. Yes, and sometimes his nose." He tapped his nose. The nose seemed to relish P. Crecy's tribute, as a cat does when it is scratched behind the tail. Pious, my Pious. Do you miss me?

"You must forgive me, Dr. Crecy. I carried on like a woman this morning. I hope you don't think I faint very often."

"Only natural. A heart is like an eyeball. No? Think enough

of its softness, its vulnerability—and it becomes impossible to look at sharp, pointed objects. Only natural. A great stress." His hand was still behind his back, but, even so, I could see that it was moving. I took the aluminum cover from one of my plates. A little steam escaped, and it startled me. There was silence. P. Crecy stood at the foot of my bed, rising, falling, prodding at his lower lip. I wanted to eat, but a sliver of lamb was twisted into an intestine, and the creamed onions, I knew, would resist my fork as an eyeball resists a pin.

"I'm not too familiar with angiograms—what will it show?"

"Many things, Bishop Belknap. Many things. The size of your pulmonary arteries, the height and size of your aortic arch —the abnormality that causes a shadow to appear in your X-ray. Dr. Snow is a genius. Once he has looked at an angiocardiogram—" He raised his hand in a fist. Then he opened the fist quickly. "Nothing escapes him."

"I see. How long have you been associated with Dr. Snow?" I picked up my fork, and sat upright over the meat. I could see black-gray seams in the lamb. Veins where blood had flowed. Fatty tissue half-dissolved and fallen away.

"How long?" He smiled and looked out at the river. "Quite some time now. But you'd better eat. Your meal is getting cold."

"Yes," I said. But I could no longer see the food as food. I played with my soup. At least its relation to living things was less tangible. I touched it with my spoon. And then P. Crecy spoke.

"You will excuse me, Bishop Belknap. There is one other thing. Dr. Snow requires one other thing." He took his right hand from behind his back. In it was a dessert cup and a very long plastic spoon.

"What's that?" I said. I lifted my fork toward it. I could only suppose it was something else to eat.

"A stool sample. You'll please to give me a stool sample—as soon as you have eaten." He waved the cup in the air, his fingers covering imaginary woodwind stops. I stared at the thing, transfixed.

"A stool sample?"

"Your excrement, your reverence." He gave both pairs of words the same deferential emphasis. "After you have eaten."

"Yes, I know quite well enough what a stool is." My voice became tense. "But am I to . . . who will—?"

"You, your reverence." He shrugged. "Who would you have do it?"

"No, of course not," I said. I swallowed some of the saliva that was flooding my throat. "But how?" I asked.

"The spoon is sufficiently long, I think. And you, I imagine, are sufficiently dexterous. We need only a teaspoonful. No hurry. After lunch will be fine." He raised the cup in the air and brought it down between the broth and the stewed prunes. The stewed prunes . . . Then, I think, he turned and left.

I stared at the cup, and my throat began to constrict. I was both angry and distressed, and I could think of nothing but what I would have to do. Pores opened simultaneously over the whole expanse of my body. My thighs, my neck, my back became wet. It was white and deceptively clean. I saw it and only it. My hunger, my concern, my whole intellectual reference disintegrated before the cup and its white, long tongue. I took it up in my hand.

Lord God my Father, we are dust and we will return to dust. Thou dost well to remind me. Thou dost well to remind me.

Thou dost well to remind me. Thou dost. I dust. Thou dost.
I opened my eyes. My fingernails had left perceptible im-
prints on one side of the cup. I recalled then that my father
had come in while I was sitting there. He said words that were
sounds, and then he shook his big finger at me. I pushed the
adjustable table away. Without taking my bathrobe or my
slippers, I ran out into the corridor. When later I returned to
my bed, I found the lunch tray gone. That was just as well, I
think.

Whenever I managed to fall asleep, they shook me awake to
make polite requests of my body. A little blood; a little skin;
a little more blood; a bit of sputum. When I asked, an intern
admitted that my blood was to be used in research not even
remotely related to my own case. Then I was allowed to sleep
again. There was nothing else I cared to do.

Michael happened to arrive while a blood sample was being
taken. He assured me that he had "left something outside."
Then he put the tips of his fingers to his mouth and disappeared. When he returned, Michael seemed subdued and
miserable. For ten minutes he sat by the side of my bed, watching me watch the river, peering from the corners of his eyes at
the crook of my elbow. He was cheerful only once: when pre-
senting me with my new slippers. They were preposterous, of
course—garish red plaid hung with big, white pompons and I
had to put them on and walk around the bed before he was
satisfied.

We talked of Pious. Michael didn't share my interest, but he
said that Pious was fine. I believed him, both because Pious is
a sturdy cat, and because there was a vivid surface scratch down
the length of Michael's nose. Very soon after that, however,

it became time for Michael to leave: he had neither hope, nor
emotion, nor anything beyond minimal desire, unless he could
derive them from me. And, at that moment, I hadn't the patience to satisfy or even to understand his demands. We said
good-bye.

By then it was late afternoon, and I knew that the time had
come for me to write. I made much of the preparations. My
pens, my ink; the first draft manuscripts in neat piles on my
left; my Bible, books of reference on my right. I tried to com-
pose myself. For several moments I watched a barrel as
it bobbed on its end in the river. And then, as usual, I found a
reason to hold *A God For Our Time* in my hands. A little pile
of reviews slipped out from under the front cover. I had underlined several passages in red ink, compiling what my critics had
said, as an index of the task yet before me. *A God For
Our Time* . . . I let the title interest me. Simulating innocence, I opened the book and turned to my own preface.

The tide of our religion is at low ebb. I am a bishop of
the Church, and I find that this is so. It is not a pleasant
fact to have to admit and, perhaps, as some have suggested,
it is not a bishop's place to do the admitting—but no one,
I think, would dare to deny the truth of that fact. The
tenets of "organized" religion are no longer credible in an
age which has turned so much of what was recent reality
—natural reality, psychological reality, spiritual reality—
into the most irrelevant of mythologies.

And yet I firmly believe that the problem is chiefly one
of presentation. We of the Church—out of a mistaken
sense of what is sacred—continue to present Christianity
in terminology that dates, at best, from the Middle Ages,
at the worst, from the first century after Christ. The world

view implied in that terminology is quite simply preposterous. No man—atheist, agnostic or devout believer—
could possibly relate his life to it.

This little book asks whether that terminology and that
world view are a necessary part of Christianity. It
asks whether, in fact, they only succeed in rendering Christianity incredible to anyone who possesses the common
sense and the scientific prejudice of the Twentieth Century. It suggests that our religion is more deeply based in
God's truth than ever mere external forms—absent or present—could ever injure or destroy. It suggests that the time
has come to acknowledge the brave, new world in which
we live for what it is: a valid and important part of God's
plan. Finally, this book suggests that it is time, high time,
to recognize Christianity as the religion of all men, and not
merely as the private preserve of a tiny, "religious"
minority—a minority to whom the words, the standards
and the superstitions of an ancient way of life are not utterly beyond belief . . .

I liked that. I liked the urbanity of the style. Curious, I
turned the book over to see just what manner of man had written it. I was impressed by the face. And then, in order not to
be too easily swayed, I picked up the pile of criticisms. Knowly
Patterson in the *New York Times* Sunday Book Review:

I'm afraid the most significant things about *A God For
Our Time* are: first, that it was written by a bishop of the
Church; second, that it was subsequently made very available in paperback editions; finally, that several important
and frightened men within the Church managed to make
the book controversial by attacking the Bishop. Too, the

style is very simple, very sincere and, I suppose, very appealing. But the ideas themselves are shamefully unoriginal. Most of them are veterans of countless theological wars. Now, however, they've been rejuvenated: given a most direct ecclesiastical sanction by an influential member of the Church. And they've been placed where the average lay reader can conveniently get his hands on them . . .

. . . I am tempted to say that Bishop Belknap has betrayed his own cause—and quite unnecessarily at that. But I will refrain from doing so, for I suspect the Bishop knows all about that. And if he is, in fact, sincere, he's going to have problems enough with his own conscience.

Harold Lamb, writing in a conservative organ:

To put it bluntly—the Bishop of Queens has a hell of a nerve. Without so much as a by your leave, he has usurped the Lord God's power and secured the salvation of the damned. And he has done it in the most high-handed manner: that is to say, by bringing Christianity down to the level of the atheist.

Christianity need not be perverted—at the price of its consistency, its magnificence and its truth—because the population explosion of the last hundred years happened to produce chiefly unbelievers. Christians have been in the minority before. That is, after all, the glory of faith. Let us not extend socialism even to sacred realms; let us not take the very lowest common denominator in human nature and make that the minimum requirement of a Christian existence.

Conrad Haupt, a classmate of mine in college and still a close, personal friend.

I was disappointed, first and foremost, to find that
Bishop Belknap—heretofore considered the sole imaginative force in our episcopacy—had said so very little in his
much over-publicized *A God For Our Time*. On the other
hand, I was alternately amused and disturbed by what he
so studiously avoided saying.

For instance, it's all very well (though, of course, it is
not) for a bishop of the Church to say: "Must we insist on
a Christology which maintains that Christ was both man
and God, separate and yet indistinguishable? Must we
demand of faith that it believe in an immaculate conception, when such a doctrine renders modern men skeptical,
unable to accept even what they may long to accept
in Christ?" As I suggested, it may be all very well for a
bishop of the Church to say this—but can it be quite right
for him to say it without once mentioning Christ's miracles,
His Resurrection, or His subsequent appearances to men?
Certain parts of our Christology might conceivably be
"played down" but, without the evidence of the miracles
and the Resurrection, what is Christ more than any other
great, good man? And with the Resurrection, the miracles
and the later appearances, the Christ saga is, I'm afraid,
very supernatural indeed . . .

Yet, for all Bishop Belknap has not done, he has still, in
point of fact, done a great deal. He has given ground. He
has broached questions—unsuccessfully and with obvious
hesitation—which others, less scrupulous than he, have already proceeded to take much further. Because he is a
bishop, because he is—without question—a good man,
even his hesitating answers, his half questions, will become
full sanctions to others, who read the book only superfi-

cially or who read it only as it sheds freedom on their inhibitions.

The Church can neither disown the bishop, nor fully accept his views. The limb is subtly diseased and it threatens, in time, to infect the whole body. No one dares amputate it, and the limb itself seems very happy where it is.

I liked that, too. Conrad always wrote with a likable easiness. I was both warmed and amused by the little personal kindnesses he had injected into his criticism. We had met in a Freshman Composition class. At the end of the year, it was I who was awarded the fifty-dollar medal, although Conrad had considered it his from the first day of class. Yet one more competition . . . I put the criticism down. There was another, a tiny clipping, beneath it. This was from a small Protestant magazine, and it was simply initialed *H.K.* It was the best of the criticisms. The only one that had ever bothered me.

Love, love, love says the plausible Bishop. And not one of us dares question his right to say it. But where, I ask, is all this love so suddenly to come from? Is not man's inability to love the whole meaning of the Crucifixion story? Was it not the greatest penalty exacted from Adam at the Fall?

And I say to the Bishop, pride, pride, pride. Can it be that he is speaking from personal experience? Are we to think he is so full of love that never the shadow of hatred darkens his mind? He is not. No one is perfect in love. No one will ever be perfect in love, but by God's ineffable Grace. Christ died on the cross to expiate sins committed in selfish, imperfect, human love.

I, for one, would not trust love—not the passionate, confused love that men, even at their best, must feel. God
only loves. He alone can grant us the power to love as He
loves, perfectly, deeply, wholly. I'm afraid Bishop
Belknap has prostituted his great eloquence. He seeks to
convince men that this titanic love is in themselves, in their
petty personal relationships. He persuades them that if
only they "truly love" the powers of darkness will fall before them. This, as Bishop Belknap must know in the
depths of his human and fallible heart, is not only un-
Christian—it is also stupid and dangerous and vain.

I unscrewed the top of my fountain pen. Then I underlined
the last phrase of the criticism thoughtfully and with a very
straight line. I was thinking, but nothing in my thought was
specific. I made little boxes. I put circles inside them. There
was something wrong, but the indictment was too vague to be
really damning. I was glad of that. I could no longer distinguish between the needs of my great purpose and the demands
of my own ego; between the validity of the poem and the
validity of the poet as human being. And then there were all
the good reviews—the reviews that hailed me as a healthful
revolutionary, a breath of fresh air, a twentieth-century St.
Paul. There were many of those. Very, very many. After a
little while, I took up my manuscript and began to write. As
I did so, I realized that a disturbance, yet distant along the corridor, was proceeding swiftly toward my empty room.

"Don't run, Jimmy!"

"Jimmy, please!"

"Oh God in heaven, he's running!"

"Jimmy's running!"

"Please walk dear! Mommy wants you to walk!"

A little boy ran into my empty room. He noticed me before he had crossed halfway to the window, and my presence, I saw, confused his enthusiasm. He halted in the middle of my room. Then he took a flat, brown baseball glove from under his arm-pit, as if he meant to give it me in lieu of shaking my hand. Instead, he smiled and said, "Pleased to meet you, sir." I smiled reflexively and rustled my manuscripts in order, I think, to plead preoccupation. And all the while I heard myself saying, "Not a child. Not in this ward. Not in my beautiful, empty room." But by then he had claimed the bed opposite mine. He was sitting on it, pressing the tips of his fingers into the webbing of his glove. There was a warm tan on his face and a blue baseball cap on his head.

He was followed almost immediately by a considerable entourage: a mother carrying a large black pocketbook and a string of lollipops; a father carrying a small suitcase; what I supposed to be an uncle staggering under an immense pile of children's games; what I supposed to be his wife staggering under an immense pile of comic books; a teen-age sister holding a portable radio; a teen-age boy holding the sister's hand. Each, in turn, halted before the little boy on the bed and then looked critically at the room. My room. The boy began to jump up and down on the bed, pounding his fist into the glove.

"Don't, Jimmy."

"Think of your mother."

"Think of me, Jimmy."

"Sit still, Jim."

"Have a nice candy."

Jimmy sat still. The mother saw his stillness and began to cry in a very practiced manner. The sister looked up at the boyfriend. The aunt shook her head, put down her pile of

comic books and leaned her forehead on the uncle's shoulder.
The uncle put down his pile of children's games without unsettling his wife's forehead. The father had some difficulty
opening the suitcase and sat on the bed with his back to his son.
The boyfriend reassured the girl by squeezing her hand.
Jimmy picked up his baseball glove and began tentatively to
make fists at the pocket. The mother kissed him on the forehead, smoothed his crew cut with her left hand, and subtly removed the glove with her right. Jimmy twisted away from her.
He looked toward the window.

"Think the game'll be called off?" he asked.

"No, Jimmy."

"Hope not."

"Saw the sun a minute ago."

"I hope Mickey Mantle hits a home run," said the mother.

"Mantle's got a broken ankle," said Jimmy. "He's not playing."

"Oh," said the mother. She began to cry again.

"See, Jimmy," said the uncle, "you're not the only one in the
hospital."

"Mickey Mantle, too," said the aunt, as if Mickey Mantle en-
dorsed hospitals.

"Yes," agreed Jimmy thoughtfully, "he's always in the hospital."

The father, after a moment's indecision, began banging
Jimmy's suitcase on the foot of the bed. The aunt turned the
uncle a ninety-degree angle so that she could cry unobserved.
The boyfriend squeezed the sister's shoulder. She touched his
hand lightly. I let my head fall, my manuscripts go limp. I
began to breathe as I imagined I did when I slept. Against my
breathing I heard the polyphony of the mother's crying and

the aunt's crying and the banging of the stubborn suitcase against the metal bedstead.

"See if the portable works, Uncle Joe," said Jimmy politely. Almost immediately the radio began to blare. Uncle Joe turned the dial all the way up before he discovered how to turn it down. I added snoring noises and dream reactions. Then the mother dropped her pocketbook on my foot. I sat up in anger, caught myself, converted my anger to sleepiness, and then converted all to a benevolent smile. *Lord God, my father, forgive me. Forgive me. I am a hypocrite. A hypocrite.* And even that's an effort.

"I'm so sorry," said the mother. When she was certain of my attention, she cried at me. Her tears said, "He's so young. He's mine. He's so young. Why couldn't it have been yours instead?" Though inarticulate, I found it shallow and monotonous. I have never had a very high threshold of tolerance for agonizing mothers. Jimmy, now in nothing but tight underpants, was standing on tiptoe by the windowsill.

"Lookit the tug," he said. "Two, four, six barges."

"Bet she's got a red smokestack," I said. "Red smokestack usually comes upriver about this time."

"Sure. It's red." Everyone crowded around the window to show interest in the tug and the barges. The mother maneuvered Jimmy's arms and legs into a set of light blue pajamas. Jimmy said, "Lookit" several times, unaware, it seemed, that he was being dressed. The others said, "Yes. Oh, yes," and "That's a tanker, Jimmy, it carries oil all over the world." Or, "That's Palisades Park, Jimmy. Right across the river. Daddy'll take you there soon's you get better." The radio blared louder in a fit of spontaneity, as though humans were not to ignore it for tugboats. I gave up hope. I put my book

in a neat pile on the table. Then I put my manuscripts in the
top drawer. I was receiving.

"Why're you here, sir?" said Jimmy. He had his baseball
cap on again.

"Well—seems there's something wrong with my heart."

"Me, too." He said it with unmistakable pride. Then he
pounded his fist against the left side of his chest. The aunt
grabbed at her breasts in empathetic agony. "Do you play
baseball?"

"Of course he doesn't, Jimmy," said the mother. I was insulted.

"I used to play ball in college," I said.

"What position?"

"Third base."

"I play third base, too—when I got nothin' on my fast one.
You a Yankee fan?"

"Certainly."

"I thought so."

"Got the son of a bitch open," said the father.

The mother was measuring me. She shooed Jimmy over to his
own bed. The father was arranging the son's clothing and toilet
articles. The aunt had borrowed the uncle's handkerchief. The
boyfriend squeezed the side of the sister's breast under her armpit. She ran her hand expertly over his thigh, from the groin almost to the knee.

I smiled at the mother. She smiled and made signs of worried
hesitation. Then she pointed to a chair. I nodded. She drew
the chair up near the head of my bed. I saw that her hair was
dyed henna; blackish roots were visible. Probably with so much
trouble, she didn't feel right in going to the hairdresser. She
blew her nose. After she put her handkerchief away, there was

still a stringy piece of gray mucus in the middle of her upper lip. Erratic tears had cleared a network of ways through her mascara. Her lipstick was smeared. I noticed all these things because I was prepared at once to dislike her. To dislike her because she was a middle-class woman who cried too easily; to dislike her because her son was ill, and she had dared to bring him into my precious empty room.

And I quote: "Christ must exist in our lives, in our personal relationships, and not merely in isolated moments of religious meditation. These latter have their place, but Christianity is, first and foremost, a real, operative force in day-to-day existence It becomes valid only through love, for Christ was love—love in all relationships, love that obviates all worldly considerations." And I knew I was perfectly prepared to dislike the father, too.

"May I speak to you?" she asked. She wrapped her fingers around my wrist, knowing full well that a worried mother is permitted to do such things.

"Certainly," I said. The word in my mouth extended mere certainty beyond the moment to the eternity of the world. Certainly. Certainly.

"I couldn't help hearing—I mean, I hope you won't think I'm prying. I hope you won't. Are you having a heart operation?"

"I'm not sure yet . . . I think so."

"Who is your doctor?"

"David Parsons. But you mean here—Dr. Snow."

"Dr. Snow, too." She brightened. "That's Jimmy's doctor. We've been told he's wonderful. Real wonderful. Really wonderful."

"Well," I said, "certainly everyone I've spoken to here agrees with that. Ask Dr. Crecy, for instance—Dr. Snow's

genius has made a tremendous impression on him. In fact, ask
anyone. Doctors don't get to Cavendish on their bedside
manners, and Dr. Snow is chief surgeon here. Think of that."
She increased her pressure on my wrist. I could feel my own
pulse along her fingers.

"But even at that," she said. "Even at that. It's so serious.
Did you hear him talking about baseball? Did you hear?" She
sobbed. "If you know of anyone else, please say so. Money is
no object. Not with us."

"No," I said. "There's no one else I know of. After all, I've
put my life in Dr. Snow's hands too. And," I added, because
I knew it would comfort her, "money is no object with me
either." She smiled.

"I like you. You know—right off I could tell you were a good
man. I didn't know you from Adam, but I knew you were a
good man. Isn't that funny? Your children must love you very
much."

"I have no children."

"Oh, I'm so sorry," she said. Her eyes dropped from my face
to the area of my thighs. I sat up as though I'd been goosed.

"No need. No need. I'm not married either."

"No?" She thought for a moment. She wanted to know why
I hadn't married, but she realized it wasn't the proper time for
such matters. "You see," she said, "we're a little worried. We
wanted to get Jimmy into a ward with boys his own age, but Dr.
Snow wouldn't hear of it. We're afraid Jimmy'll be out of place
here. He likes to listen to baseball and . . ." I put my hand
on her shoulder.

"I like baseball. Really. And I was going to ask someone to
bring me a radio."

"You are kind. Kind. I saw that right away. I knew it the
minute you told Jimmy about the tugboat." She started to cry

again. Then she decided to press her advantage. "Jimmy likes
to play games. We'll be here as much as we can, but—but he
may get bored, and then, you know, the poor thing might start
worrying. I know it's a terrible interposition. I know that. But
maybe you wouldn't mind playing him a game of Tactics or
Clue or Monopoly. He likes Monopoly. Just now and then."
She sighed. A heavy, powdery perfume rose visibly from her
bosom when her breasts heaved together.

"Please. Say no more. After all, Mrs.—"

"How stupid of me. Lopopulo. Rose Lopopulo. And this is
my husband. Alfonse. Alfonse, come over here." She made a
beckoning gesture. Alfonse crossed the room, a surly, bothered
look on his face. He hulked over me. It wasn't hot, but he was
sweating, and a thin powder on his skin made the sweat seem
viscid.

"What's wrong?"

"Nothing. Nothing, Alfonse dear. I want you to meet Mr.—"

"Belknap. Whitney Belknap."

"Mr. Belknap has offered to play games with Jimmy. Now
and then, that is."

"That's real nice, Rose. Real nice." He presented a gnarled
hand. The lines along the back were filled with a certain white
substance. "You can call me Al. Short for Alfonse. How's about
I call you Whit? People in trouble gotta stick together. It
was Whitney, wasn't it?"

"That's right."

"Fine then. What line you in, Whit? I do a bit of contracting myself." He held my hand all the while. I could feel the
liquid texture of his palm and the horny sides of his fingers.
I was indignant. His assurance irritated me. I very much enjoyed telling him just what "line" I was in.

"Actually, Al," I said, "I'm a bishop of the Church."

Alfonse let go of my hand. Then he began to wipe his sweaty palm on the back of his coat sleeve. He looked at his wife. She looked at him. The Lopopulos were Catholic, and they were horrified. You don't glad-hand a Catholic bishop. You don't call him Whit or even Whitney. And Catholic bishops never play Monopoly or listen to baseball—except in the movies.

"The Episcopal Church," I said. "Diocese of Queens."

"Oh," said Alfonse, "that's Protestant, isn't it?" I nodded, but Alfonse was still uncomfortable. "I'm sorry if I come on too strong, your reverent lordship. It's just I'm awful upset. This is a terrible thing. Comes right in my busy season, too."

"Forget it," I said. "How the hell could you know? I'm not exactly in uniform." I thought my "how the hell" set just the right tone. After that, all I had to do was relate myself professionally. I did so. "My father was Harold Belknap of Belknap and Collins Hardware on Warren Street. Maybe you know it?"

"Sure. Sure. Big gray building. Do a lot of construction work don't you? Builders' hardware?" I nodded. "Now ain't that something? Small world. Right now I'm up to my neck in work. Housing project on hundred fifty-fourth street. Hell of a job." He waited to see how his "hell" would be received. When I nodded sympathetically, Alfonse decided that he could finally relax. "It's real nice. You helping to cheer Jimmy up, that is. We'd appreciate anything you could do."

"Certainly," I said. Certainly, Mr. Lopopulo. I may be dead this time next week. And that table you've put your big hand on—yes, that one. Well, in that table is the manuscript of a book. A book, my friend, the importance of which to my religion and your religion is probably incalculable. I don't know how much time I have left. My mind is incapable of the simplest logical processes. I haven't eaten in twenty-four hours.

I feel my heart swelling and distorting inside my chest. My pajamas are wrinkled, and my slippers are either tattered or hung with ludicrous, white pompons. Certainly, Mr. Lopopulo. I should be delighted to count tugboats and play Monopoly with your son. Certainly. Certainly.

"Excuse me?"

"I was just wondering, Whit—would you like to meet my people?"

"Certainly." I thought then that if I heard myself say "certainly" just once again, I'd tear the sheets from the bed and dance lewdly around the room in my underwear.

"This is my sister, Angela. And this is my brother-in-law, Joe De Nucci."

"Very pleased to meet you both."

"Don't mind my hand," said Uncle Joe. But he gave it to me anyway.

"This is my daughter, Maureen."

"Hello, sir."

"Her . . . friend. Sidney."

Yes. I had sensed something was wrong. The boy was Jewish, and Mr. Lopopulo didn't like it at all. Sidney was tall and dark. His face was both handsome and intelligent, though his features—especially the nose and mouth and ears—were heavier than they should have been. I could see, too, that Sidney was arrogant. He stood above and, somehow, all around Maureen. Anyone could tell that Maureen loved him passionately. She had to, I thought. He wouldn't have tolerated her otherwise. Probably Sidney could do anything he pleased with Maureen. Probably Mr. Lopopulo sensed that. When he said the word "friend," little smiles appeared on the faces of all in the room who feared they might betray the tension.

"Very pleased to meet you all."

"Mr. Belknap is a Presbyterian Bishop," said Mr. Lopopulo. He said it chiefly to Sidney.

"I didn't think there were such things," replied Sidney. I guess Mr. Lopopulo thought Sidney had insulted me. His eyes widened, and the mounds of his shoulders moved one after the other. He wanted to strike Sidney. He wanted to strike him for me and for Christianity and for the hand that lay negligently near the top of Maureen's left breast. Uncle Joe moved past Aunt Angela so that he could restrain Mr. Lopopulo if the need arose.

"Episcopalian, Alfonse," said Mrs. Lopopulo. Then she smiled at me, as if to say, "What do all these silly words mean anyway?" I smiled as if to say, "Nothing, nothing at all."

"I said Episcopalian."

"I'm sorry. Must've misheard you," said Sidney. He made little searching movements along the nape of Maureen's neck. It was infuriating: Sidney's tactfulness had put Mr. Lopopulo at an excruciating disadvantage. The shoulders moved heavily again and again. Sidney's fingers continued delicately to titillate the skin on Maureen's neck. She leaned away from the heaviness of her father, and her father, almost in fury, watched her go soft under the power of Sidney's fingerings.

"Well then," I said, "you must be in Bishop Hanrahan's territory." I thought a little inter-denominational banter might help to clear the air.

"Well I—" said Mr. Lopopulo.

"I do," said Mrs. Lopopulo.

"When?" asked Mr. Lopopulo, in genuine surprise.

"Quite regularly," said Mrs. Lopopulo, avoiding his eyes. "Both Maureen and Jimmy have been brought up as Christians."

"Yes. That's right," said Mr. Lopopulo. "We're all Christians." He looked at Sidney. Then he added, "From birth."

"Ah, food!" I said. I forgot that Sidney was Jewish, and that all the Lopopulos were Christian from birth. Sarah was standing in the doorway of the room with my dinner tray balanced on her huge forearms, and at that moment I realized just how hungry I had been all day. Desire of any more complex sort became irrelevant.

"There you are, Mistuh Bishop. How you this lovely evenin'?" The crowd around my bed made way for Sarah.

"Fine," I said, peering at my tray.

"I see you has all your friends wif you this evenin'. A lovely family you got here, Mistuh Bishop. Lovely. Lovely." She stood back as though to take a group shot.

"No," I said, perhaps too quickly. "No. These are Jimmy's relatives." I pointed across the room. Nurse MacArthur was speaking to Jimmy. He seemed to be listening very carefully.

"That so? That Mistuh James Lopopulo, what I got a nice tray for? You stay right there, 'n I bring it to you." She waddled quickly out, trying, I thought, to impress Nurse MacArthur with her immense competence. And then I noticed that Uncle Joe was lifting the covers of my tray, one after the other. Instinctively, I took up a fork to defend my food. But I put it down again.

"Food looks swell, Jimmy," he said.

"My! I do envy you," said his wife.

"Only the best for my kids," said Mr. Lopopulo, again chiefly to Sidney.

"Is it really good?" asked Mrs. Lopopulo in a conspiratorial undertone. Aunt and uncle came closer, inserting their heads into the aromas that rose from my tray.

"Mmmmm. Buttered carrots," said the aunt.

"Mmmmm. Vegetable soup," said the uncle.

"That looks like pork," said the mother. "Is that pork?"

The meat question was too much for him. Curious, Mr. Lopopulo, too, peered at my tray. Together they looked at the food as if it were something obscene that I had done. The uncle said, "Hope y'don't mind?" and lit a cigar. Some powdery perfume puffed out of Mrs. Lopopulo's bosom. Her husband put his cracked hand on the table. They looked, and the pork—if pork it was—became a disgusting, shriveled thing.

"Pork did you say?" asked Mr. Lopopulo.

"Sarah's brought Jimmy's tray," I pointed out. "It's right over there."

"Try it. Do. I'm dying to know," said the aunt.

"Yes, do," said the mother.

"Got an ashtray?" said the uncle, after the horse had gone.

"Jimmy's eating," I said. "He must have the same dinner."

"Sure he does," aid Mr. Lopopulo. "Only the best for my kids."

"I'll just use this water glass," said the uncle. "If you don't mind."

"Go on," said Aunt Angela. "Have a bite. Tell us. Don't you think pork would be fattier, Rose?"

"Looks like pork to me."

There was no way out of it. I had to pick up my knife and fork. I had to taste the vulgar, distorted thing. But it wouldn't cut. I turned the knife over and over. Still it wouldn't cut. Still they watched me. I panicked and began pulling, ripping at it. I tore the meat apart. Mashed potatoes slid off my plate and onto my pat of butter. I picked up my fork. The fibrous thing tasted like excelsior. I had to take a sip of milk to get it down. And all the while I "mmmmed" and smiled and made gestures of surpassing satisfaction.

"Veal," I said. For all I knew, I had eaten my own lower lip. I sat back carefully. If I moved too suddenly, I knew I would have to vomit. But they weren't really satisfied.

"I could have sworn it was pork," said Mrs. Lopopulo. "Are you sure it's veal? Pork and veal taste pretty much alike."

"Pork isn't Kosher," said Mr. Lopopulo to no one. "We can eat it, though."

"See you tomorrow evenin'," said Sarah. Nurse MacArthur had her firmly by the shoulder. Uncle Joe left my bed and went over to see Jimmy.

"Was it tough?" asked Mrs. Lopopulo. "Seemed you were having trouble there. You pay enough in this hospital. At least the meat should be tender."

"Fine. Fine," I said. "I was just cutting against the grain. It's fine."

"Say!" said Uncle Joe, "Jimmy has no buttered carrots."

"No buttered carrots?" Mr. Lopopulo looked at Jimmy's tray for the first time. "That's right. Bishop Belknap has buttered carrots."

"Maybe Jimmy isn't supposed to have buttered carrots," said Aunt Angela.

"Nonsense," said Mrs. Lopopulo, "they both have heart conditions. The nigger just forgot Jimmy's buttered carrots. Ring the bell."

"Have mine," I said. "Have mine. I'm not really keen on buttered carrots, and I've had a large lunch."

"Really?" said the mother. "You wouldn't mind? No, we couldn't."

"We couldn't do that," said Mr. Lopopulo.

"We couldn't."

"Please."

"Well, if you really don't want them . . ." Mrs. Lopopulo had already taken my plate—and my bread pudding spoon to scrape them off with.

"I already ate my carrots," said Jimmy indignantly. "I always eat them first. I hate them."

"Now Jimmy—" said his father.

"It's true," said Sidney. "He had quite a few carrots. Didn't you see them?"

Mr. Lopopulo's eyes widened again. This time he took an aggressive step forward. Sidney didn't move. Mrs. Lopopulo quickly brought my plate back. The buttered carrots were hanging off one edge; the mashed potatoes were hanging off the other edge. Mr. Lopopulo was going to hit Sidney, and I was going to throw up. Maureen tried to shield Sidney with her body. Uncle Joe moved past Aunt Angela once again.

"Sidney—just tell me why you didn't say Jimmy had buttered carrots. Just tell me."

"Now Alfonse—" said his wife.

"No, Rose." His voice got louder. "No, damn it, the time's come. We're gonna have this out once and for all. Come on, kid. Why didn't you tell us before?"

"I thought maybe Jimmy'd want some more."

"That's it. You see, Rose? You see, Joe? Always out to get something for nothing. Trying to cheat Mr. Belknap. A bishop. Feeding off decent citizens and their children. Just like leeches. leeches. You're just like leeches, all six million of you."

Uncle Joe put his hand on Alfonse's shoulder. Alfonse shook him off. Sidney stood his ground. The tension was terrible— terrible because there was nothing Mr. Lopopulo could do, beyond pushing his brother-in-law aside. Nothing. Sidney had already educated Maureen to think less and less of her father, and every violent movement of his shoulder was sending her further and further away from him. *Lord God my Father, Thou dost afflict me. In the mist of my affliction, Thou dost afflict me. And I cannot love.*

"Come on, boy. Look me in the eye. What d'you want from her? Answer me, or I'll knock the answer out of you." I closed my eyes. It was the kindest thing I could do. As I did so, I noticed that Jimmy had already closed his eyes. At that moment, Nurse MacArthur stepped into the room, a hypodermic in her hand.

"Does anyone need a shot to keep them quiet?" She furrowed her brow as she advanced on Mr. Lopopulo and brought the point of the needle up near his solar plexus. Mr. Lopopulo retreated. The tension turned to mere embarrassment, and then the whole business was suddenly ludicrous. There was a nervous laugh, but only one.

"Sorry. Sorry. Didn't know I was raising my voice. Sorry. It's just I'm awful upset. This is a terrible thing. Comes right in my busy season, too." He pointed to Jimmy. Jimmy didn't look like a terrible thing.

"I understand that. But I think you could take a lesson from your son." She began to use the hypodermic as a shovel. "Now it's high time you all went home."

One by one they apologized to Nurse MacArthur. Then they apologized to "poor Bishop Belknap," and to Cavendish Memorial in general. Even Sidney. When Sidney apologized to me, I felt Mr. Lopopulo's eyes widening as he stood in the doorway of the room: the argument wasn't finished. And, while they were apologizing, Nurse MacArthur removed my tray. I had eaten one forkful of veal since lunch on Monday.

Then we were left alone. Jimmy piled his games neatly on

the table. He smiled shyly at me several times, but he didn't
try to speak. I was thankful for that, yet, even so, I couldn't
bring myself to continue writing. It was nearly eight o'clock.
Jimmy would turn on his radio, and what remained of my concentration would then be forfeit. Jimmy got out of bed. He
put his left slipper exactly even with his right. Then he climbed
back into bed. He covered his waist with the sheet and took up
a comic book. I was amused. His nose tilted upward and, in
doing so, it took his upper lip with it. He seemed to be smiling
satisfaction at everything. After a moment he rang the bell.
When Nurse MacArthur entered, he asked where the bathroom was. Nurse MacArthur came over to my bed.

"You haven't eaten much, Mr. Belknap."

"No. No, I haven't. Just off my feed, that's all."

"Would you like a tranquilizer?" She looked at her watch in
an attempt to minimize the implications. She thought I was
afraid.

"No. Not yet," I said.

"I think you'd better have a sleeping pill." I looked at
Jimmy's radio and nodded.

"All right," I said. I couldn't eat. I couldn't write. I couldn't
think. Sleep only was left to me. Nurse MacArthur took my
pulse.

"Did you have your angiogram this morning?"

"Excuse me? Yes. Yes, I did. Quite an experience, you know.
Dr. Crecy isn't too charming, but I must say he's amazingly
thorough. I don't know what happened to me, though. I
fainted. Silly. Womanish green sickness."

"Dr. Crecy? Is he new here?" Her brow furrowed and her
hands, held open and away from her sides, became alert.

"New? I wouldn't know. He's a little, wiry chap with an

accent. French, Belgian maybe. First initial is P. Don't you know him?"

"I should. I've been here long enough. Crecy? How do you spell that?" I spelled it for her. She shook her head. "No. He must be very new."

"Funny. Said he'd been Dr. Snow's assistant for some time. At least I think that's what he said. Miss Black seemed to know him quite well."

"Black? No. That can't be. She's only been here since Monday." Nurse MacArthur began to arrange the things on my table. She chewed the inside left corner of her mouth thoughtfully as she did so. I sat forward in excitement when she picked up *A God For Our Time*. She looked at the picture on the back; then she looked at me. "Did you write this?" she asked.

"Yes. Yes, I did." There is nothing more wonderful than acknowledging a book, printed and compact and beautiful. And my little book had sold half a million copies in five languages. Nurse MacArthur was a woman, and I recognized the pride I felt for what it was.

"I haven't read it," she said.

"Maybe you'd like to borrow a copy. I have an extra." I was too eager.

"No. It's not the sort of thing that interests me. But Dr. Snow has read it. I know that. I heard him mention it to Dr Smither. He was . . . impressed."

And, at that moment, my estimate of Dr. Snow became intricately involved with my estimate of myself. He had been . . . impressed. Impressed by *A God For Our Time*. I was proud beyond Christian conscience. I wanted to question Nurse MacArthur, but she had left then to get my sleeping pill. Impressed. That was good. Then he would have to understand what was at stake. He would take good care of me.

I took *A God For Our Time* into my hands and squeezed it. The shiny covers felt smooth against my fingertips. The compressed green sides of the pages were hard and square and logical. I ran the book against my face. I turned it over. There was a blurb about my life and works, and there was the picture. It was superb. A delightful warmth about the eyes; just the suggestion of a smile. I was graying at the temples even then, and my hair was combed straight back. A face to be trusted. The nose gracefully shaped, the forehead high and intelligent. Only the comforting timbre of my voice was absent, and even that was implied. I smiled at the picture. Then Nurse Mac-Arthur came in, and I had to shove the book quickly under my sheet. Jimmy had returned. He was putting on his radio.

"Sir?" he asked. "Would you like to listen? Or should I keep it low?"

"Don't worry about me, Jimmy." I swallowed the sleeping pill she'd brought me and lay back, my hands folded across my stomach.

". . . Batting seventh and playing shortstop, John Kennedy. Batting eighth and playing third base, Charlie Smith. And the pitcher, going for his fourteenth victory of the season, Mel Stottlemyre. Now our National Anthem . . ."

A tug, its superstructure hung with soft, yellow lights, moved slowly up the river. Somewhere a foghorn intoned a somber question. An answer came from far down the river. The question was asked once again, and there began a solemn litany that lasted long into the night.

Lord God my Father, support me in this, the time of my trial. Purge me of fear and weakness. Dedicate me only to Thy

*will. Let Thy words be my words. Let them ring out through
the world.*

"... Pepitone takes ball one. Pepi batting just over three
hundred since early August. Grant gets the sign. He looks to
first. Now he steps off the rubber ..."

*Lord God my Father, let not the demands of my fearful
body make me proud and willful. Teach me to love: Let the
spirit of Thy Son Jesus Christ inspire me with tender understanding, that, though I have been entrusted with the unfolding
of Thy greatest message, I become not overbearing and vain.*

"... Pepi takes ball three. Three and O. We'll have to see
whether Joe has the go ahead. The Twins not shifting on
Pepi with men on first and second. Now Joe steps out, rubbing his hand on the pine tar ..."

*Let Thy protecting Spirit descend on all those in this place
who are faced with sickness and sorrow and loss. To the healers
grant wisdom and compassion. To the suffering, strength and
patience. To the dying, knowledge of Thy Grace and hope of
life everlasting. And especially send Thy Comforter to little
Jimmy Lo—Lopopulo, that even in his youngness he may know
that Thou art ever with all men. I ask not this for my sake but
for ... but for ...*

Soon after that Jimmy, I think, quietly crossed the room.
He turned the light off over my bed.

WEDNESDAY, AUGUST 16TH—

THE THIRD DAY

I awoke in sweat—the viscous, unhealthy sweat drawn by hot sunlight from a sleeping body. Wherever my skin reached out to touch itself—at the groin, the armpits, between the fingers —there was a tacky, elongating join. My pupils misted and cleared and misted again. It was half past nine. Little white stalactites were strung from the roof of my mouth. I could feel the heavy clumps of dry hair as they stood uncertainly upright on my scalp. One of my feet hung, bared, over the edge of the mattress. Tufts of hair, I knew, grew on the backs of the toes; the heel and the ball were discolored with yellow callouses. I sat up. I put my face in my hands.

"Good morning, Mr. Belknap. You missed your breakfast." Jimmy smiled at me. I tried to smile back, but the corners of my mouth were painfully inelastic. Jimmy was moving little colored tokens across a board. A layer of tissue paper was spread on the table. It was there, I think, so that the rolling of his dice would not disturb me.

"Sleeping pill last night. First time . . . Went out like a

light." My stomach shifted uneasily within me. It seemed to undulate; then it dropped away as I brought my knee up to my chest. "Why—why didn't they wake me?"

"They tried to, sir. One of the nurses shook you hard—real hard." He didn't look up. "Excuse me, sir. What's a Pious?"

"A Pious? Oh. Pious is my cat. How did you know?"

"I guess you must miss him, sir. You said his name over and over again in your sleep. All night long. I miss Tommy, too. And I've only been here one night." I yawned. "You must've been awful tired, Mister Belknap." He was absolving me of the sin of sloth, and he contrived to do so without once looking up from his game. I was thankful for that. My episcopal dignity does not wear well through the night. I yawned again. I should have asked Jimmy who or what Tommy was, but I don't think I really cared.

I rang for the nurse and asked her where the showers were. She said I was a big, fat sleepy-head, who ought to have been ashamed of himself. I agreed. Jimmy rolled his dice apologetically. My pajamas were black with sweat at the throat and in the armpits and groin. The surface of my left eyeball was coated with a gluey substance that diffused the light into meaningless grays and yellows. I picked up my towel and walked to the window. The air had gone limp. There was just a suggestion of haze over the West Side Highway and the river. The night's coolness had trickled away. Heat waves shimmered off the asphalt, wriggling, confounding themselves. Even the water seemed hesitant. A great, structureless ship was being urged downstream by two tugs, but everything, even the urgers, seemed reluctant to move. My eyebrows filled with sweat. When I drew my arm across my forehead, they ran like sponges into my eyes; then, as my eye-pits filled, tears of sweat dribbled slowly down my cheeks. Standing there, I said my morning prayers.

    There was an accumulation of hair in the shower drain. I cleared my throat and spat heavily onto the tiles. As it left me dropping away to the shower base and yet still part of me, I remembered the subway car and the man I had so unceremoniously left there. I was no more than sixteen years old at the time. I remember it was past three o'clock in the morning, and I was wearing beautifully cut evening clothes. I had immaculate, gray gloves on my hands. Gloves on my hands . . . When I am impeccably dressed, I cannot tolerate dirt or any sticky substance on my fingertips. I could, I think, if I were naked and bathed to the neck in filth. I would commit myself wholly then. But I cannot bear the contrast between that which is clean and that which is not.

    I crossed my legs. The crease in my trousers angled itself at the knee and ran precisely true to a point above my instep. I took a book from my pocket. I opened it tentatively, as if the characters might otherwise slide into my lap. I have never once broken the binding of even a paperback book. And as I stood in the shower, the water pressing at my chest until the grayness of my hair seemed the grayness of my skin, I could remember just how happy and confident I'd felt that night. In the afternoon of that Saturday I'd won a football game with a last half-minute interception. And, just a quarter of an hour before, I had escorted the lovely Tansy Lipton to her home. At the door of her apartment, she'd said, quite spontaneously, that she loved me. I didn't have it in my heart to blame her.

    There was a crashing sound and then another. The door at

the end of the car opened suddenly, and a figure stumbled
through. He tried to close the door behind him, but it
held fast, ridiculing, seeming to anticipate, his disordered ef-
forts. Then, when the car swayed violently, throwing him
against the wall, the door closed smoothly by itself. He stared
at it. His back was toward me, he was the length of the car
away, but even by then I had closed my book. The car was
empty except for the two of us.

Having judged the sway of the train with his knees, he
launched himself violently into the current and fell, staggered,
more than half the length of the car. For a moment he hovered
uncertainly. Then he collapsed on a seat across from mine
and a little to the left. I saw his face. It was swollen and
hectic-spotted. A sparse, gray growth of beard mildewed his
cheeks. There was a great smear of grease diagonally across
his forehead. It was shaped like an exclamation mark and the
right eye, round and black, seemed somehow related to it. His
left ear was entirely gone. Blood, now black and clotted, had
run from his scalp down his neck. His shoes were splintered.
He wore no socks. The torn pockets of his jacket hung down
like tongues of overheated dogs. I put the book in my pocket.

He leaned over, he balanced uncertainly for a second, and
then, with an effort, he spat. But the saliva was so thick
it wouldn't come loose. It hung from his mouth, waving lazily
with the motion of the train. He shook his head; he worried it;
he tried to bite it off. Then he gave up. The string of saliva
seemed to have a life of its own. It thickened and thinned,
waved, shook and reached out dumbly downward. We watched
it. Then the bum raised his head: what was left of his spit
floated on the air and fell against the front of his jacket.

He wiped at his mouth with the back of his sleeve, and, as

he did so, he saw me. He saw me, and he saw me. And when
my presence had fully impressed itself on his consciousness, he
smiled. I could see no teeth. I saw only, with anxiety, that he
was trying to rise. I uncrossed my legs. The bum went to one
knee, then he dragged himself upright. He came toward me
—still wearing that mockery of a smile—and I clenched my
fists. He came closer. Just six inches from my lap, he halted,
swaying uneasily at the knees and the shoulders. Then, in one
gesture, he wiped his face and touched his crotch. As though
he were crossing himself. As though he were making himself
presentable.

He brought his right hand slowly up to my face. It had four
fingers. Then he let the hand fall, holding it flat and palm-
upward between us. The hand flexed uncertainly under our
scrutiny. I wanted to ignore him; I willed myself to ignore
him. But there are things in life that correspond immediately
to one's most abhorred fantasies. This was such a thing, and
I was fascinated, transfixed. There was liquid at the surface
of his eyes and nostrils—in the tiny corners of his mouth. Now
he was trying to speak. His tongue began to play coquettishly
with his gums. His lips puckered and relaxed. He seemed to
think he was expressing himself perfectly. But, against the
roar of the train, I could hear nothing.

I drew my head back, but I was powerless to move my body.
I looked away, and yet I could sense his presence out of the top
of my eyes, swaying there, impending over me. And then I felt
it—something had touched my knee. My legs splayed apart
instinctively. Saliva. It had come again through his idiotic
smile. There was a little puddle on my knee—a puddle that
was attached to his mouth by a thin, tough strand.

I heard savage, growling sounds within my own throat. I
rose up, and, as I did so, I hit him full under the jaw with my

left—a left which had all the momentum of my rising body behind it. I felt his rough stubble through the gray knuckles of my glove. Then he fell from my view. I turned and ran the length of the car. Only when I was pulling at the handle of the door did I look back. I saw his head—I still see his head—rolling backward and forward, as if it were attached to his body only by an insubstantial stalk. I pulled off my left glove—I struggled manfully, it seemed, with my own hand. Then I threw the glove between the cars . . .

I knew I was sweating in the shower. The water carried my perspiration away before it was formed, and yet the sensation was there. That man was mine. Mine. Only in my later years did I attain sufficient perspective to know it in those terms. But he was. From that night onward, driven, I think, by the urging of fear, I began—I have been in process of beginning ever since —to turn away from certain things and turn toward others. That was the first time. With the water pouring on my shoulders, I knelt properly to God above the clotted drain.

And then I was looking at the back of my own head. But for that—but for the fact that I had surprised my own body in an entirely different moment of time—nothing in the room had changed. I heard the wet towel fall heavily over my feet. The sound troubled me. My heart faltered, registering its uncertainty in insistent monosyllabic questions. And still the back of my head remained bent over Jimmy's bed—bent because I am over six feet tall. I stepped back toward the corridor. I ran my hand against my pajama front; buttons lodged clumsily between my fingers. I knew my face had gone pale. Jimmy looked up at me and away from what was also me. Then the back of my head turned around.

It wasn't me: I knew that because he wasn't sweating. Yet

the nose was delicately carved, and the hair at the temples was graying just slightly. A man with an unsymmetrical face seen in a mirror: everything is the same, but the composition is wrong—wrong and yet so nearly right that the effect is deeply disconcerting. The sides of my stomach slapped together in a spasm. My knees buckled but held. "One, two? One, two?" asked my heart. And then the one was louder than the two, and then both were louder than either had been. The heat pressed me down at the neck and at the knee joints. I was dying. I stumbled forward, the wet towel tugged limply at my ankles. I held desperately to the foot of an empty bed.

"You okay, Mr. Belknap?" Jimmy's feet were already over the side of his mattress. I took my hand from the metal bedstead and waved him away. Then the bedstead began to stretch and buckle at the center. I watched it, willing it into hardness again. When at last it solidified, I put a hand on my thigh and leaned the weight of my upper body on my own leg. I began to breathe in a rhythm just slower and then slower than the frantic pulse of my heart. Jimmy's feet still dangled uncertainly over the edge of his bed. The other figure hadn't moved.

I stood erect. The top of my scalp to my eye sockets went numb. A drop of sweat hung from the tip of each of my fingers. My bed was six paces away: three for my right leg; three for my left. I began to walk, my hands flying out for balance. The other man disengaged himself from Jimmy's bed, but he made no effort to help me. He was watching. I felt myself passing under his eyes, and, as I did so, I observed my own body with a strange objectivity. I watched myself fall on the edge of the bed; I watched my hand squeeze the remaining button through the buttonhole; I watched as I shook off my right slipper—a red plaid thing with white pompons; my left slipper

—a brown, tattered thing. One foot, evidently my left, in the grave.

"I'm Dr. Snow. I'm afraid I've been waiting some time now." A voice, too, like mine.

"I'm sorry," I whispered. My voice caught on each of the vowel sounds. I meant, I think, that I was sorry for myself. With exaggerated carefulness, I leaned back on my elbows, yet, by that time, I was already feeling almost secure. As the beating of my heart approached its normal rate, I leaned forward at the waist and put my hand flat over the left side of my chest. As though in pain. He was watching. I think I wanted him to be concerned.

"No," he said, "no need to apologize. I'd hoped to have more time with you, that's all. Now I'll have to be rather abrupt."

I looked up at him. A questioning glance appeared on my face—the glance, I imagined, by which all persons who are in great agony signify their separation from the real world. And again the likeness fascinated me. I tried, for a moment, to rearrange his features, but the difference was so subtle that I could neither measure nor define it. He was leaning back on his hips, his hands nestled in the front pockets of his white coat —as if he were enjoying the palpation of his own abdomen. He was looking down at me, and yet he was not. Dr. Snow's eyes, I thought, are very strange: they seemed to have false surfaces like large, opaquely gray contact lenses. Dr. Snow's eyes looked without looking, as a blind man's eyes look. My eyes, I remembered, were a lovely and limpid blue.

"I've heard a great deal about you," I said. I contrived to speak, as though speaking were still a dangerous effort.

"And I of you," he replied. Dr. Snow picked up my

little book. "You keep a copy on your table, I see. Can't say
I really blame you. I don't imagine a more important book's
been written since—no, not since Luther nailed his theses to
the door." I have sought praise all my life. Yet, when it has
come my way, all I've ever been able to do is bow at the waist
and say, "You're too kind."

"You're too kind, Doctor," I said. I tried to bow while sitting
upright. Dr. Snow raised his eyebrows.

"You disappoint me. Too kind? Really? No, I don't think
so. I don't think you find me too kind at all. Humility is fine
in its place, but here—here it's more an insult to my intelligence than anything else." He held the book in front of him—
in both his hands and higher than necessary. He weighed it;
he caressed it; he externalized his admiration. Yet, though
ostensibly he was concentrating all his attention on my book, I
found it impossible to follow his gaze. His pupils seemed eyes
within eyes. They watched behind themselves.

"I'm sorry. I didn't mean to sound patronizing. The book is
important. Lord knows, I've had that brought home to me
often enough."

"Important. Yes, indeed. Earth-shattering—" He looked
toward me. "Heaven-shattering? I don't know. You've a pretty
big following here—in the hospitals, that is. Did you know
that? No? Until this moment, I don't think anyone of your sort
has been able to speak through to us. Doctors have developed
—how should I put it? A peripheral guilt complex. It doesn't
keep any of us awake nights, but still the implications are always present. Too much knowing. There were seeds in Eve's
apple core. We planted them and pruned them, crossed them,
fertilized and harvested them. Very successfully, I might add.
And such success is intimidating. Everyone's a bit too awed
even to hate us."

I don't know what I said then. "Interesting." "Glad to know that." "I wouldn't have thought of it in just that way." Something. I was thinking of Dr. Snow's intelligence, and the wonderful way in which his praise was magnified by it. My body was rigid with the effort required to suppress all visible signs of my satisfaction.

"You're writing another book?" He pointed to a manuscript page. "In the same vein? Yes?"

"Yes," I said. "I hope to take things further. In six months I received over five thousand letters. I'd say forty percent wildly critical. The other sixty percent enthusiastic, but rather obviously confused. If what I'm saying is to have any real validity, I think I've got to consolidate my position. The new book has to be logically unassailable. Of course, that means it'll be more, quote, theological. A lot less popularly appealing."

"Five thousand letters . . ." He seemed to be whistling, but there was no sound. "Amazing, but predictable. If you attack any halfway vital establishment, the establishment must necessarily retaliate. Especially when the attack comes from within."

"Wait a minute now," I said. I think I wanted to make every aspect of his praise acceptable. "I'm not attacking any establishment, least of all my own. That's largely where my critics go wrong. It's my task to preserve the establishment by compelling it to adapt gradually to a new, an unavoidable environment. I'm a conservative in the deepest sense of the word."

"Yes and no. Yes, you are a bishop. Yes, you may think you're a conservative. But no, this book was not written by a bishop. Only a free mind can write an imaginative, forward-looking and—I have to add—emotional book like this. And a free mind is elastic, unpredictable, dangerous, no matter what doctrine he may subscribe to superficially. You, Whitney Belknap, Bishop of whatever it is, involve the establishment in perceptions and emotions that are frighteningly unfamiliar to it. You don't attack the establishment. By force of personality you move it, so to speak, outside its defenses. You make it seem human. You make it vulnerable. An establishment cannot be subjective."

"Well, perhaps . . ."

"Perhaps nothing, I'm afraid. But, be that as it may—I hope this hasn't intimidated you." He put my book down. "Whatever you do, don't recant—don't go back on your statements about God. It's at that point that you begin to talk sense to people like myself. People like Dr. Abrams and Dr. Zito." He quoted from memory. " 'God isn't here or there. Up in a heaven or through in another dimension. God is deeper than any spatial concept, no matter how subtle.' It's there that men with no aptitude for religion begin to listen. Personally—beyond generalizations about its historical or social impact—I want you to know your book moved me deeply. It left sealed doors ajar. Only ajar, mind you. But even that little bit is significant. It unsettled me."

I said nothing. Dr. Snow was tempting me, and I knew better than to show eagerness. The mechanism of conversion is like a wooing: it's the coy ones who do the shaping. I raised my eyes. Dr. Snow seemed to be staring at the ceiling. His neck, at least, was tilted that way. I remember admiring his profile with an almost vicarious enjoyment. Then he took his hands from the pockets over his abdomen. He held them high as a praying mantis is wont to do. They were beautiful things, long and brown and supple. His mouth moved as if he were calling them each by name. Then he returned them to his pockets. He had decided, too, to say nothing further. It was a stalemate, but there was yet time.

"Damn. I'm sorry, Bishop Belknap."

"Call me Whitney, for goodness' sake." He nodded.

"Forgive me. My time is very short. I'm afraid I've got to go." He smiled. "Just lie where you are. No need to see me to the door."

Dr. Snow was halfway to the corridor, before I'd understood the significance of those words. I sat up suddenly, my hands pushing at either side of the mattress. Just lie where you are . . .

"Dr. Snow—" I said. I almost shouted it.

"Yes?"

"The tests. The angio—the angio thing. What do they show? I mean, how should I be feeling these days?" I said it lightly, but I didn't feel it that way. I turned my eyes away—so that he could speak freely, I think.

"You're fine," he said cheerfully. "Fine." The answer was so unexpected that I did a double-take. My neck cracked audibly. Dr. Snow was examining his right hand. He flexed its fingers. "Fine, fine . . ." he said again. A thing burst in my throat, and I knew that it was joy.

"I can leave then?"

"Leave? Who said anything about leaving?"

"Then—?"

"Relax, Whitney. Just leave everything in my hands." He cupped his right hand, as if to show me how it might be done.

"Of course, certainly. Of course. You're the doctor."

"I'm the doctor. That's right. You find the food satisfactory? You don't?" I nodded stupidly. "You do. Good. The service is excellent. The nurses, I know, are attractive. And just look at that view." He looked at it. I looked at him. "What more could you ask for? Costs a bit more than Grossinger's, but the idea's the same. Relax. I'll be around to see you soon. I might even—who knows—I might even swallow my pride and ask your advice about some things." A shy smile extended itself over his lower face, but the eyes were blind and it went nowhere. Dr. Snow turned to go again, and this time the word leaped, flew from my mouth.

"But my heart? Dr. Parsons said time was very important."

"How philosophical, the doctor. But don't worry. Probably he meant that Dr. Parsons was important. Different thing, you know. Don't worry about it. No sweat like." He used the colloquialism uneasily. "I really have to go now. Take it easy, Whitney, and remember—you're my special patient. I've a very real interest in what you're doing. Trust me. Have faith. And try to get some writing done."

"It's so hot," I said. I fell back onto my bed.

"Is it?" he inquired.

"Believe me, Dr. Snow. I wouldn't—not for one moment—presume to question your judgment. I don't know about these things. I'm just a little worried. Concerned. All this is new to me."

"I understand. But you must have patience. You've got to believe in what we're doing here. That's half the game right there." He smiled. "I'll get around again as soon as I can."

He left. I stared into the empty doorway for some time. I felt that I'd somehow left myself behind in the bed and gone away. Then I remembered Jimmy. I looked to his bed, afraid that he had known the anxiety in my voice for what it was. But Jimmy wasn't there. I leaned back and hot air, almost as substantial as steam, puffed out of my pillow. A few minutes later Jimmy returned. I couldn't remember having seen him leave.

*

A bead of sweat inched down between my ribs. I lay motionless. The tickling hesitated and fell, hesitated and fell. Then it was gone. Sixteen in an hour. They were waiting for me to move: the heat and my hunger. The one was without form until I moved against its endless surfaces. The other was jagged and heavy and painful only when I disturbed the equilibrium in which it hung balanced. Eighteen in little over an hour.

Jimmy was very busy. He managed to personify all the tokens on his Monopoly board simultaneously. Politely asking himself in behalf of himself if he might have this or that. Making neat piles of things; making the piles symmetrical in relation to one another. I watched him. He held a comic book as though he were afraid to break the binding. But comic books don't have bindings that break. At Jimmy's age I was already reading Shakespeare. Pretentiously, perhaps, but still it was Shakespeare and not Batman. I watched as he put the game away. The money neatly piled; the cards neatly piled and in proper order. One bankrupted token stood alone and neglected behind a glass where he could not see it. I waited. The cover on the box; the board beneath the box. Jimmy got up and put the game in its designated place among the other games. He returned to his bed. Then he saw the forgotten token. Without apparent irritation he rose, took the Monopoly box, opened it, replaced the token, replaced the lid, replaced the box. Then he climbed back into his bed. I smiled inwardly. Twenty-three. Twenty-four.

I thought of Dr. Snow. As I did, an image of Martin Luther —sandals on his feet, hammer in his hand—presented itself to my mind. I liked Dr. Snow. He was intelligent and scrupulously honest. I wanted him to be my friend. I wanted to do all the things he would ask me to do. In return for my life, I had already planned to give him still greater things. Still greater things . . . And then I saw my own self standing, quite ridiculously, before the great door of the church—sandals on my feet, hammer poised in my hand. Thirty-three at a little before noon.

A nurse brought Jimmy's lunch. I sat up and began to prepare myself with pathetic eagerness. Already I could smell the food on Jimmy's plate. I watched his fork and, as he tasted and drank, I tasted and drank. Now that the prospect of its satisfaction was virtually before me, I was glad of my hunger.

"What've we got, Jimmy?"

"Excuse me, sir?"

"What's that? What's for lunch?"

"I'm sorry, Mr. Belknap. It's roast beef." He held up a reddish piece on his fork.

"Yes. Roast beef. That's nice."

"Yes sir. I don't like it really. But Mommy said she was paying good money for it. So I have to eat it all."

"Yes. Roast beef. That's nice."

Footsteps and a sound of crockery approached down the corridor. In order not to betray an unseemly desire, I turned my head toward the window. My fingers rapped an excited rhythm on the mattress. I was very fond of roast beef. I heard the nurse as she approached. I prepared to smile and say, "Can it be lunch-time already?" Then a strange and singularly hollow sound tapped lightly at my ears. I turned. There was a cup of tea on my table.

"What's this?"

"Your lunch. Doctor's orders. All the liquids you can drink, but no solids."

"No solid food?" I began to stammer. "Why? For how long?"

"Don't ask me. Usually it's just for a day or so. Doctor probably wants to clear out your stomach and bowels. For X-rays, you know."

"My stomach and bowels? I have a heart condition. My heart." I pounded my fist against the left side of my chest. "My heart. That's what I'm here for. There must be some mistake."

"There's no mistake. We don't make mistakes here. That's what Dr. Snow ordered for you just after eleven o'clock today. It's down in black and white on your chart."

"Dr. Snow?"

"Isn't he your doctor?"

"Yes. Yes, he is. But he was just here. He didn't say anything to me."

"Oh, didn't he? Isn't that too bad?" She laughed and made little ticking sounds with her tongue.

"But—but he even asked me if I liked the food here." I threw my head back angrily onto the pillow.

"Now don't get yourself upset. You're a big boy now. You're not going to die. A man your size can live off his own fat for weeks."

"Yes. But, you see—you see, I haven't eaten a thing since I entered. Not since Monday afternoon. This is Wednesday afternoon."

"Well, I don't know anything about that," she said suspiciously. "Your chart says you've had three meals a day."

"I know. But I—I haven't been able to eat until now. Now I'm very hungry."

"I'm sorry," she said. "I tell you what. I'll bring you a nice glass of grapefruit juice. How's that?"

"Please."

She left. The disappointment, even more than my hunger, had upset me. No solid food. The heat threw me an ugly caress, and I tossed my head in irritation. Why hadn't Dr. Snow prepared me? No solid food. I heard Jimmy's fork scrape lightly over his plate. A buttered carrot? No, he ate them first. I was in a frenzy of hunger.

P. Crecy stood at the foot of my bed. Now and again he would rise up on his toes, as if he were trying to see down inside me. I pretended to be asleep. P. Crecy smiled and nodded his head. His tongue pushed at his lower lip and, as it did so, little muscles rippled and surfaced in his throat. He didn't try to wake me. He intended, instead, to stand before my bed until the knowledge of his presence became intolerable. It became so. I coughed, gagged, opened my eyes and saw him, as it were, for the first time.

"Sorry to disturb you, Bishop Belknap. A blood sample, please."

"I don't think I have any."

"Of course you do," he said. P. Crecy delighted in taking what I said at its face value. "Without blood you are dead. Even a bishop. Without blood a bishop is not a bishop. He is dead." He came around to the right side of my bed. I looked at Jimmy. He was asleep, his head back, a comic book disordered on his chest. My stomach hissed. P. Crecy rolled up my sleeve and began poking at the veins in my forearm. Then he took a rubber cord and wrapped it tightly around my bicep. It pinched the hairs on my arm. My wrist, my fingers began to bulge with blood. P. Crecy dabbed the pit of my elbow with alcohol. I knew perfectly well what he was doing. Even so, the coolness confused my nerves. My body tensed.

"Not yet," he said. "We are only cleaning the arm. Only alcohol. But surely you expected that, Bishop Belknap? It's the heat, no? You're a little bit nervous. Perhaps I should order you a tranquilizer."

"No. No tranquilizer. Food is what I need. Your Dr. Snow has put me—oh!" He jabbed the needle into my thickened elbow. "Your Dr. Snow has put me on a starvation diet."

"Has he?" P. Crecy jerked the needle out of my arm. "Sorry. The vein wasn't where I expected it to be. I must try again." I dug the nails of my left hand into the mattress. The discomfort infuriated me. My stomach pushed out a high whistle that died slowly away—as though it had given up and was deserting me. Sweat trickled along my sideburns and over the lobes of my ears. I wondered how often P. Crecy missed a vein.

"Why did he do that?"

"Do what?" He squeezed my funny bone, and the fingers of my right hand danced helplessly to the tune that he played.

"Put me on a starvation diet."

"You are allowed liquids, are you not?"

"Yes, but—oh!" The needle went in again. This time there was a little sucking sound.

"Then you are not on a starvation diet. Liquids are very nourishing. Very nourishing." P. Crecy was making painful adjustments in the vein of my elbow. I slapped at a bead of sweat as though it were alive. The pain had begun to make me nauseous.

"Whatever you call it. Why can't I have solid food?"

"Bastard," he said. I turned angrily toward him, but, of

course, he hadn't meant me. The needle was jerked out again.
It was empty. "I'm afraid the vein has burst. I'll have to try
the left arm."

"Again?"

"Yes. Again." He took the rubber cord off. The last length
jumped from between his fingers and nipped at the skin of my
bicep. I snarled. P. Crecy apologized in an undertone. Then
he moved quickly around to the other side of my bed. I tried
to seem unconcerned, but the muscles in my neck had become
so tense that my whole head vibrated with my pulse. I didn't
want to feel the needle again. I was afraid of the pain.

"Why can't I have solid food?"

"Why? It's hard to say. There could be many reasons. Dr.
Snow has methods of his own."

"What methods?"

"Hmmm—how shall I say? Stretch out your arm, please."
The rubber cord went on again.

"What methods?"

"Well . . . Sometimes before a serious operation Dr. Snow
decides to test the patient's constitution. The body may seem
strong, may, in fact, be strong—but the will, that's quite
another matter. The stress. The pain. The anxiety. The
shock involved in such an operation is often intolerable.
I tensed again. He was cleaning my left elbow. "Then, too, Dr.
Snow may merely want a few intestinal X-rays."

"What is this blood for?" The needle sunk in as I said it. I
whimpered.

"An important survey we're making. Your blood may someday save many lives." He waved the red tube in front of my
face.

"But not this life—not my life, I suppose." He shrugged.
"It has nothing whatever to do with my life."

"The ways of medical progress are not always understandable or strictly fair. But progress is the only thing. The only God. Sacrifices—" I cut him short with a violent motion of my arm. Then I sat up, my head close to his chest. I was so angry that, for a full moment, I couldn't see his face.

"Get this straight once and for all, Dr. Crecy," I said. I directed my voice viciously at a point just below his Adam's apple, whispering so that Jimmy would not be wakened. "I'm damned sick of the little games you've been playing for the past couple of days. All of you. Don't give me any nonsense about important research. Two days ago Dr. Parsons told me that my life was in danger. I was led to believe that, without immediate surgery, I was as good as dead. Well, I've been in this wonderful hospital since Monday. I've had my blood drained out of me, my crotch X-rayed, my excrement carefully scrutinized—but no one's once mentioned my heart, not even in passing. Why I'm not dead now, I don't know. But one thing I do know. I'm not used to such cavalier unconcern for my health, and I'm damned if I'll put up with it."

P. Crecy's fingers danced on the tube of my blood. His eyes widened until I thought the lids were no longer there. So extreme was his agitation that ugly guttural sounds came uncontrollably from his throat. I think he wanted to hit me.

"Is that all you have to say, Bishop Belknap?"

"Yes. That's all."

"Then—with all due respect, your reverence—I, too, have something to say. I am a doctor, yes. But I am nothing. A mere talented flunkey, no more, no less. It is nothing to insult doctors like me. Do it—do it as often as you like. You're an important man. But please, Bishop Belknap—please, for your own good—never make such a mistake with Dr. Snow." He paused, for it was becoming difficult for him to speak. "This is

not your world, Bishop Belknap. There are more factors involved in a major heart operation than you could possibly ever
dream of. Don't try. You're helpless here. A child. And you
must—I repeat, you must—have the faith of a child. There is
no one—no one in this hospital with time on his hands. We
can't allow you to have an operation, if the operation will kill
you sooner than the disease. An inner heart operation? Do you
know what that means?" He put his hand up to stop me from
speaking, but I had nothing to say.

"I know you don't want my opinion. I know you don't like
me. Yet I will tell you what I think. I think you're spoiled,
Bishop Belknap. Spoiled and ungrateful. Do you know what
Dr. Snow is? Do you have any idea what he can do? Let me try
to tell you." Spittle had begun to drip from the corner of his
mouth. He wiped it back with his sleeve. "In an hour
or so there will be a third person in your room. A Mr. Farbstein. Five days ago Mr. Farbstein had an artificial valve put
in his heart. Let me tell you about Mr. Farbstein. He is almost
seventy years old. He has diabetes. He has asthma. The prob-
ability of survival for such a man after such an operation is ridiculously low. Only perhaps three doctors in the world would
have dared to operate. Dr. Snow did so. Five days now have
passed. Mr. Farbstein grows stronger every day. He will recover."

"On the day after the operation, I myself informed Mrs.
Farbstein of the results. Mrs. Farbstein is an old woman. An
intelligent woman. A woman used to great respect. But this
Mrs. Farbstein went that very afternoon to Dr. Snow's office.
She got down on her knees and crawled—crawled across the
floor—to Dr. Snow. 'You are a God,' she said. 'You give life.
You are a God.' I know how it upset Dr. Snow. But she was
right. Dr. Snow is a God. He is, Bishop Belknap. He performs

miracles every day. I have seen them. I know. I know. And I will not have the man or his methods criticized by the likes of you. You, whose life depends on Dr. Snow. You." He stopped. He could barely speak. After a moment he went on. "I think you had better understand this. You are a powerful man, a rich man. But there are men and women all over America—all over the world—who are begging at this very moment to have their mothers, their wives, their children accepted into Cavendish. Yes, to have their blood drained out and their excrement scrutinized. Be grateful that you're here. And please—please, for all our sakes—don't ever betray your feelings to Dr. Snow, as you have betrayed them to me."

When he finished, there was a light as of the highest inspiration in his eyes. P. Crecy said nothing more. He merely turned and left me. He left me with my hunger and my sickly heart and my growing sense of shame. I was only thankful that Jimmy had not wakened.

Michael arrived at three o'clock. By that time I thought that I had separated out the merely tangential, personal elements. Not relevant were P. Crecy's antagonism and my own anger at finding my will subordinated to the will of others. Understandable, yet still not relevant, was my increasing fear of pain. These things were unfortunate, but only superficial. Significant alone was the margin remaining between the time before my death, and the time yet necessary to complete my work. Only the book and what it represented could justify my continued existence. For that reason alone, I would have to trust in Dr. Snow and in his surrogates. Already I sensed that he was somehow, inevitably, involved in the doing. For the greater glory of Christ it was intended that I bear humiliation.

Lord God my Father—Thou who dost ordain that joy will grow out of sorrow, and sorrow out of joy—I thank Thee that Thou hast brought to the greatness of my work, a healthy sense of my own miserable stature. Grant me only the physical strength to endure, the moral strength ever to abase myself. Dedicate me anew to Thy purposes. Remove from me all cruelty, impatience and bitterness. That, as I begin to die, I may have new and increasing life in Thee—to the honor and glory of Thy name, through Jesus Christ Our Lord.

Michael brought at least fifty letters. I took three at random and sent the rest back with him. There were two reviews of a night-long television program on which *A God For Our Time* had been discussed. A few reviews, too, of a new book by Bishop Grant entitled, rather too obviously I thought, *A God For All Time.* Then there was a letter from my publisher inquiring whether the manuscript of my new book would be ready before I "underwent minor surgery." They were concerned for the half-million-odd copies of my next book. I left them to be concerned.

Michael didn't look well. When he worried, he compensated by eating sweets—sometimes several whole chocolate cakes at a sitting. On such occasions his skin tended to break out in a very adolescent acne. It wasn't a pleasant sight.

"How's Pious?" I asked. Michael swallowed and seemed to shiver.

"He—he's not well."

"Not well? What d'you mean, not well?" I sat forward in the bed. "Speak up."

"Diarrhea. All over the house." Michael paled. Not that I could really blame him.

"Well . . . Other than that. How does he look?"

"Look?" The question confused him. "He's . . . He looks like a cat."

"Like a cat? That's a good sign. Diarrhea, in itself, isn't much to worry about. Probably it's the heat. Don't feed him fish any more, it goes bad too quickly in this weather. Did you leave the air-conditioning on?" Michael nodded. "Has he been exercising?" Michael nodded. "Does he seem to have an appetite?" Michael nodded. "Good then. But keep an eye on him." Michael compounded the nods with a larger nod.

"People are getting anxious about you. I put them off, but soon, I think, I'll have to tell them something."

"Not yet. And keep them away from here. Whatever you do. Tell them I've got a rare and communicable disease. No, don't tell them that. Most of them are leper lickers, anyway. You figure something out. I've got enough on my mind just now."

Michael wiped his forehead with a wrinkled handkerchief. It seemed as if he were sweating more than any man blessed with just a normal amount of pores could sweat. He virtually glistened. Beads of sweat sparkled among the thin hairs on his scalp. Sweat had soaked even through his jacket, making the black still richer. As I lay there, I thought I could actually hear him seeping, oozing. But now Michael was trying to smile.

"I've got some presents for you," he said.

"How nice."

He handed me two bags. One was squarish and white. The other was brown and vaguely cylindrical. I opened the white bag first. In it were a crossword puzzle book, and a little pocket volume entitled *Fun in the Hospital*. Between rather conspicuous parentheses it said, "For Seven- to Ten-Year-Olds." I beamed at my presents.

"That's swell, Mike. Very, very thoughtful. Just the thing to take my mind off my troubles." He grinned and nodded eagerly. Wet spots rained on my sheet. "And what have we here?" I took up the brown paper bag. My hand explored the opening. Then I gasped. It was a superb ham hero sandwich with lettuce and tomato and huge gobs of butter. My breath exploded in a curse. I put the sandwich down. Even so I couldn't help touching the soft bread with the tip of my forefinger. My stomach roared as though a great crowd were voicing its appreciation.

"That's very nice, Mike. Very nice. But I'm not allowed to have solids. I'm afraid you'd better take it away." Michael's face collapsed. He bent over to pick up the sandwich.

"Are you sure this is a—a solid?"

"Yes, Mike. Yes, it's very much a solid."

"Can I eat it then?" Michael always shopped for me as he would have shopped for himself.

"Of course," I said. I heard a crunching sound. "Not here, damn you!" I yelled. Michael jumped. His arms flew apart. The top of the sandwich fell off onto my chest. I picked it up between my thumb and forefinger. Michael, staring fearfully, took it into his hand, butter-side down. Now grease marks were superimposed on the sweat marks already on my pajamas. Michael stood there, his mouth full, uncertain whether he'd be allowed to swallow. Finally he did. Then he put the top back on the sandwich, the sandwich in the bag.

"I didn't mean to yell, Mike. Sorry." I thought I'd take his mind off it by giving him something to do. "You might buy me a new pair of pajamas." He nodded and began to write on a little pad. "You know my size. And nothing in red plaid or blue plaid or anything like that." He wrote that down, too. I tried to remember if I'd ever seen pajamas with pompons. Then I decided it was safer not to mention pompons at all.

There was a subdued commotion in the corridor. The bed opposite me and to my left was quickly removed by an orderly. Then two nurses and two interns entered the room, leading a bed between them. I remembered what P. Crecy had said. This, evidently, was Mr. Farbstein; the man who, just five days before, had undergone a miraculous heart operation. I sat up and peered forward.

Mr. Farbstein was groaning. He groaned in a most distressing manner. "Oh, oh, ohhhh!" he went. "Oh, oh, ohhh!" Again and again he groaned, and each groan, it seemed, corresponded to just that amount of air remaining in the room. It was terrifying. Mr. Farbstein was a little man: white and gray and yellow. He had a tiny, trapezoidal mustache; large tufts of gray hair protruded from his ears. A mesh of bluish veins lay just beneath the skin of his neck and forehead. Mr. Farbstein's mouth gaped wide. His right hand rose and fell, grasping convulsively at the air. A nurse and an intern moved his upper body onto a pillow. "Oh, oh, ohhh!" said Mr. Farbstein. He began to choke. This—I said to myself—this is a completely successful inner heart operation. Jimmy, too, was watching. His dice were in his hand, suspended in the middle of a throw.

"I'd better go," said Michael.

A dwarfish old woman huddled inconspicuously against the door jamb. She watched intently as an intern adjusted two bottles—one of glucose, one of saline solution—that hung above Mr. Farbstein's left shoulder. As he worked, the woman nodded her head and made ineffectual, helping gestures with her hands. The intern examined the limp plastic tube where

it entered Mr. Farbstein's inner arm. Mr. Farbstein groaned.
The woman pressed her fingers into the surface of her black
leather pocketbook.

"I think I'd better go," said Michael.

I realized then that the woman at the door was Mrs. Farbstein. Surreptitiously, I turned my attention toward her. Mrs.
Farbstein was well dressed, but her clothing hung on her
stunted frame, as a heavy fall of snow might overlap the outlines of a broken roof. She, like her husband, was chiefly white
and yellow: yellow skin, white eyebrows, white hairs on yellow
warts. And yet, for some unaccountable reason, she had painted
her lips a glaring orange-red. They stood out from the rest of
her face. Then, momentarily, the image presented itself to my
mind: Mrs. Farbstein crawling, falling forward on her knees
in front of Dr. Snow. I let Michael draw my attention away.
Certain things, I thought, are too disturbingly pathetic.

"Really," said Michael, "I think I ought to go. Really."
Michael had turned his back on Mr. Farbstein, but, in my
mind's eye, I could see his ears flattened back as an alert cat's
might have been.

"Don't forget your sandwich."

"Yes. Yes. My sandwich," he said. I had to point it out to
him. Michael took the bag and stuffed it into his suitcase. Then Mr. Farbstein began to scream in a quiet and spiritless manner. Michael made an answering noise of sheer animal
fright.

"All right. Keep Pious happy and—" But Michael was already halfway across the room. I called out after him, "Don't
forget the pajamas." He seemed to wave. Then he was gone.

The arranging, the preparation lasted a full quarter of an
hour. In time, however, the nurses and the interns disappeared,

and the room was quiet but for Mr. Farbstein's emphatic
breathing. He seemed to be more securely asleep. Less and
less often now did his breathing manifest itself in vocal sound.
Mrs. Farbstein sat, perfectly immobile, her hands in her lap,
her eyes hovering at the level of her husband's chest. Jimmy
pulled with his teeth at the cover of a comic book. I rolled my
head restlessly from one corner of my pillow to the other. The
man's influence was oppressive. Again and again I found myself rehearsing, half-aloud, what P. Crecy had told me. This is
an old man, I said. He has diabetes. He has asthma. You're
young yet. You have great physical strength. I said a prayer
for Mr. Farbstein only.

My hunger began, once again, to assert itself. I pulled my
torso upright and looked impatiently out over the river. The
late-afternoon heat floated in the air like powdery cotton; it
wadded itself into my nostrils and eyes and mouth. The wind
which normally pours off the Hudson was baffled by two wings
of Cavendish that jutted out at ninety-degree angles—forming
a U, at the center of whose base stood my bed. On the New
Jersey shore, smoke rose in mystic, brown streams that were
decapitated as they crossed the rim of the Palisades. Boats
wallowed busily in their slips. A smoke-writing plane formed
the last letters of a word whose first letters were already indistinguishable. So much wind, I thought; so little coolness.
So much activity; so little sound. So much time; so little time.
I leaned forward and pushed my books to the far corner of my
table—that they might no longer accuse me.

"Would you like to play some Monopoly, Jimmy?" I asked.

I enjoyed playing Monopoly. The two tokens, mine glob-
ular and yellow, Jimmy's green and sylph-like, became, for just

a moment, the sum of reality. As we moved in vague circles on
the square board, my concentration, like a tightening spring,
excluded more and more of what was beyond. I felt happy.
Once, when I rolled just the right combination, I let out such
a spontaneous sound of joy that Jimmy seemed both startled
and suspicious. He, on the other hand, was politely restrained
in his play. Yet, if he deferred to me, he gave no quarter. I
was bankrupted very convincingly.

Sarah brought Jimmy's tray, and I was driven back through
the heat to my own bed. Throughout the game my hands had
shook with embarrassing insistence. I lay, dispirited, on my
bed, thumbing through one of Jimmy's comic books, trying to
reject the sounds and the smells that elicited spasms of dis-
sent from my stomach. Mr. Farbstein showed no interest in
his cup of broth. The two bottles—the yellow and the transparent—dripped conscientiously down and into him. Now and
again he seemed to come awake. His eyes opened hugely, but
they were without character and the pupils remained fixed.
His wife was no longer there. In the time she had been, Mr.
Farbstein had not once opened his eyes.

"Man gotta have nurshment. What's Doctuh Snow care?
What he care?" Sarah stood before me, a cup of tea in her hand.
"But Sarah's not like that. No sir. Sarah looks after her friends.
I got a big sur-prise for you, Mistuh Bishop. You never guess.
G'won an' guess. No sir, you never guess. G'won an' try." I
shook my head.

"Can't guess."

"G'won an' try."

"Well. Let's see—"

"You never guess."

"No. No, I probably won't. A chocolate cake?"

"No sir. Better than a choklit cake."

"Two chocolate cakes?"

"Wrong again, Mistuh Bishop. You never guess—'less maybe
I give you a hint." She came close to my face and whispered.
"It's somethin' religious."

"Something religious? Something religious . . . Hmmm
—what could that be? Something religious. Let's see—no. No,
Sarah. I can't imagine what it could be. You better tell me."

Sarah laughed. Then she took from her left vest pocket
what I'd thought was the outline of a monstrous nipple on a
monstrous breast. The thing dropped out of her hand and
hung, swirling on a dirty cord. It was furry. It was filthy. My
head snapped back on my neck. I pretended that I was far-
sighted, that I had to have distance between my eyes and the
things I saw.

"What is it?" I asked.

"What is it? A lucky, blessed rabbit's foot, that's what. You
puts it round your neck like this—" Before I could protest,
she had pressed her hands flat against the sides of my scalp. I
felt the cord as it rolled over the sweat on my neck. "That's all.
Now you're protected from all evil. The devil can't touch a
hair on your head."

"Sarah, I couldn't. That's awfully kind of you. Awfully—"
I couldn't shake the thing off. It nestled, soft with little, hard
nails and bones, in the hollow of my throat. A frog clouded my
voice. I cleared my throat violently, and the thing seemed to
stir and then settle where it was.

"That's no ordinary rabbit's foot you got there. No sir.
That rabbit's foot has a history. That rabbit been dead a long,
long time. Samson's great gran'daddy shot that before the
Civil War. He's a minister. Before he die, he give this rabbit's

foot to his son. He's a minister, too. Now four generations of
ministers have worn that rabbit's foot."

"Sarah, I couldn't—"

"Now, Mistuh Bishop. You see that? You see the tears in my
eyes." I couldn't see them. "Don't make me cry. If'n you know
what I gone through t'get Samson t'give it me. But he finally
say yes. He say, 'The Bishop's in bad trouble. He need that
bunny's foot so he can walk through the valley of the shadow.'
That's what he say. I'm gone t'be a sick woman 'less you promise t'wear that every minute 'til you git home. Don't make me
a sick woman, Mistuh Bishop. Promise?"

"I promise, Sarah."

"Okay. The word of a Bishop gotta be trusted. Thursday's
my night off. We has prayer meetin' Thursday. But I'll
be roun' t'see you come Friday. Promise now?"

I nodded. Satisfied, Sarah slapped at her thighs and walked
proudly out of the room. I lay back gingerly. By then the skin
on my neck had become unnaturally sensitive. I could feel the
foot as it sedulously scraped at and explored my throat. It terrified me. I subdued my breathing in order not to disturb it.

And then it was too much. I began to laugh. I laughed and
I laughed, and the rabbit's foot danced on its bony toes over my
neck. Hunger and heat; shots in the arm and stool samples;
old groaning men and Monopoly games. Bring on the next, I
said. Bring it on. I'm waiting. I'm ready. I submit.

The Lopopulos left early. They entered our room smiling
and waving gifts, but soon Mr. Farbstein's terrific breathing
had oppressed all their petty enthusiasms. When he groaned
they froze suddenly and silently in whatever position they
chanced to be; they stood like thieves waiting for a sleeping
victim to turn over. After a moment Mrs. Lopopulo came to

my bedside. She asked what Mr. Farbstein's trouble was. When I told her, she put one fist to her mouth; the other she rubbed briskly over my forearm. I told her about Mr. Farbstein's age and his diseases. I even told her of Mrs. Farbstein's dramatic homage to Dr. Snow. As an afterthought, I told her to pray for Jimmy. But I don't think she heard. She smiled down at me.

"I don't know what I'd do without you," she said. "You're such a sensitive person. You understand. Poor Alfonse. Oh, I'm sure he feels something for Jimmy. In his way, I'm sure, he feels a great deal. But, you know—he doesn't understand."

After a while, Alfonse came over to my bed. He said, "Rose, let's get out of here. I can't stand this place any more." His wife looked at me. Then she took him by the hand and led him away. Mr. Lopopulo did seem out of his depths. Sidney wasn't there. Whenever Mr. Lopopulo looked at Maureen, she stared at the place where his hat would have been, had he been wearing one. Perhaps, indeed, Mr. Lopopulo didn't understand. Certainly no one was going to explain anything to him.

It was full night when Nurse MacArthur came into my room. The heat had turned even her competence into sodden deliberation. Everything she did, and I watched everything, seemed strangely detailed. When finally she came to my bed, she stood there for several moments, looking across my legs to the window.

"I met your Dr. Snow this afternoon," I said, deliberately breaking the silence. She looked toward me for the first time. Before she said anything, though, she began carefully to arrange the books on my bed table.

"How does he look?" she asked. I thought it a strange question.

"How? You mean physically?" Nurse MacArthur frowned irritably.

"Is there another way?"

"Yes. Well . . . He looked fine, I guess. Healthy. Of course, I'd never seen him before. Funnily enough—since you mention it—I rather thought he looked like me."

"Like you?" She seemed surprised. "How could that be?"

"Well. I mean—we're about the same height. The same age —uh . . . There are obvious differences, of course. He's hardly my twin . . ." I trailed off there. The look that momentarily crossed Nurse MacArthur's face distracted me from what I had meant to say. A look, I thought, of painful confusion.

"No," she said. "No, you're not twins—and now he's put you on a liquid diet. I saw it on your chart."

"Yes. He just did it. I mean, he didn't consult with me beforehand. He didn't even tell me. Actually it came as something of an unpleasant surprise. I haven't eaten too much since I entered. As you know, of course." She nodded and began to take my pulse. "However, I'm determined to bear with it. I'm sure Dr. Snow knows what's best." She put my wrist down delicately.

"You'd better take care of yourself," she said.

"How do you mean?"

"Take care, that's all. You're not a well man, you know." She left very soon after she'd said that. I began to wonder if she knew more about my condition than she cared to know. It was serious. There was no doubt about that. I felt between my ribs. Mr. Farbstein groaned. Serious. I lengthened the word. I emphasized the first syllable. Sere. Sear. I thought of sizzling things. Then I shook my head and turned the light off over my bed.

"Goodnight, Mr. Belknap," said Jimmy.
"Oh. Goodnight, Jimmy."
Mr. Farbstein groaned.

Lord God my Father, forgive me. Forgive me that, out of morbid concern for my own body, I have ceased to labor in Thy way. Dedicate my will, that I may write as forcefully for Thee, as I have written before.

I thank Thee that Thou hast seen fit to give me—in the person of Dr. Snow—a master worth the serving. May I be able to accept humiliation in body and pride and will—that, in obeying him, I learn better to obey Thee.

My God, let Thy Love ring out in my writings. Let it show forth in my life. Thou knowest me. I have dedicated my labors to Thee, and yet my way is not an easy way. Something has always stood between. I know not if it be pride or fear or an excess of zeal. I know not if it will come to pass. Help me. Let me become, as Thy Son became, a perfect witness of Thy Truth . . .

THE FOURTH DAY

I ATE my sips of orange juice. Thoughtfully, I shaped little cubes and spheres and cylinders between my tongue and the inner walls of my mouth. Then I chewed into them, imagining a substantiality that didn't pertain. Mr. Farbstein had a large, yellow bowl of oatmeal. The oatmeal was brown, I knew, and flecked with crisp, white sugar. There was milk to pour over it. But Mr. Farbstein neither poured nor ate. He only stared upward, his eyes unblinking and inert. The bottle above his shoulder bubbled gently. I watched Mr. Farbstein as a cat watches nature: only that which moves can hold interest. And so, inevitably, my eyes were drawn to the bottles—as though life were flowing into them and not out.

Surfaces glared. Beyond my window, each car on the West Side Highway caught the sunlight on its windshield and then, at a certain point, dashed it into my eyes. The water was a mosaic of countless, dazzling, polygonal looking-glasses without handles. Windows in an entire wall of Cavendish were the portals of a white-hot blast furnace. I turned away. Jimmy was trying to read, but, too often, I found him toying listlessly with

his comics. He scratched at their covers; he rolled them into
spyglasses; he used them as fans. Jimmy seemed dispirited. It
was as if Dr. Snow's miracle, life in death, had surprised his
youth and taken it unawares.

And now the miracle was groaning. I slammed my Bible
shut. Mr. Farbstein groaned again. "Shut up, damn you," I
said politely. The Bible slid off my chest and onto my wrist. He
groaned again—louder now and, seemingly, with more complete satisfaction. "Quiet. Quiet. Quiet," I said. "Keep quiet,
you old bastard." Again the Bible slipped off my chest and onto
my wrist. I slapped it back across my abdomen with a hollow
sound that surprised me. "Oh, oh, ohhh," said Mr. Farbstein.
"Ohhh, oh, oh. Oh? Oh? Ohhh." Subtle, infernal variations. I
wanted to strangle him. I wanted each of his moans to be at my
pleasure. And I quote, "Prayer, love, meditation, the 'things'
of religion must no longer be relegated to a few Sunday morning hours. We pray only as we live. Our religion is the culmination of an active, secular love. Christianity is not a thing of
special and very circumscribed moments. It is willing involvement. Engagement in the lives of others. Love."

There is *eros* and there is *agape:* the one is selfish and the
other is a special gift of grace. There is Faith, too. Faith in
Christ's Resurrection, in Up-thereness, in the potentially
miraculous, and, finally, there is Faith in Grace itself. I had
Faith, you must understand that. It was only Faith's vocabulary
that I questioned. The thees and thous; the primitive sup-
positions; the naïvetés that the devout alone could overlook.
The wonderful, useless excrescences. These things—though
reluctantly—I doubted. And so, for the sake of Dr. Snow and
his contemporaries, for the sake of our own self-esteem and our
God's esteem—more as an exercise of taste than of dogma—we

made those concessions. Hesitant, often illogical, always somewhat belated, we made them. All of us. All of us, that is, who
were being heard in these times. And I most of all.

"Oh? Oh? Un-huh?" said Mr. Farbstein. He began to mum-
ble thickly. His right arm hung, bent in an uncertain arc; the
fingers of his hand were gnarled, talon-like, above his shoulder.
I smiled at him, and the teeth at the back of my mouth ground
against each other. Mr. Farbstein did not return my smile; instead, he clawed slowly at the air. "Huh? Huh?" he said. And
then I realized that he was trying to get my attention. It was
his pillow. It had slipped down behind his back. Mr. Farbstein wanted me to help him. I looked quickly toward Jimmy,
but Jimmy was asleep. I looked at the ceiling, at the walls, the
window. I made my face an uncomprehending thing. And I
remembered the dreadful time when my father already knew
that he was dying. When he had said, "Use your strong hands,
Whitney. Massage my back." I had almost said no. There is
a law in the Jewish religion that a child must not see the naked
body of his parent. Standing there, kneading the heavy flesh
above his buttocks, I had understood.

I considered ringing for the nurse. But, challenged as I had
been, there were no suitable compromises. "Here's a nasty
piece of involvement," I said. "You'll like this." Then I was
standing barefoot beside my bed. I blinked my eyes so that Mr.
Farbstein's body would lie distant and in an impersonal haze.
I crossed the room. He wasn't looking at me now. He mum-
bled. Once I thought that I'd heard him giggle.

From the first attempt it was a nightmare. Mr. Farbstein
couldn't help me. Whenever I moved the pillow, he groaned
and struck out at me with his hand. I was afraid that the
violence of his movements would tear the nourishment from his

arm. Again and again an antiseptic, yellow odor caused me to
gag. Then I saw the last inch of his incision, a little mouth,
grinning from beneath his bandage. A black thread hung ob-
scenely from the corner of the mouth. I wanted to pull that
thread, to tear Mr. Farbstein open from side to side. But instead I bit so deeply into the inside of my lower lip that I could
feel little, hard lumps under the tip of my tongue.

"Immamash. Mash. Oh?" he said.

I stopped. I put my ear close to Mr. Farbstein's mouth, but
I couldn't make out what he was saying. Probably, I thought,
he can't speak English very well. The corner of his pillow
caught on the food tube, and had to circle the bed to disen-
gage it. But finally, urged on by an obstinate need to mortify
myself, I succeeded in making Mr. Farbstein comfortable. He
didn't look at me, but his mouth moved, and, at first, I thought
that he wanted to thank me. Again I leaned close to his face,
and again all I could hear was the same foreign phrase.

"Immmamash. Immamash."

"Do you want me to call a nurse?"

"Im—immamash," he said.

Then I realized that there was something beneath his right
wrist. Mr. Farbstein wanted me to look at it. I lifted his hand
and drew the thing carefully out from beneath the sheet. It
was a color photograph—a photograph taken evidently from
a plumbing catalogue. There were pictures of joints and
lengths of pipe and great, steel valves. And then, for the first
time, Mr. Farbstein was smiling.

"I'm a machine," he said.

The tips of my fingers and the ball of my right thumb looked
yellow in the early afternoon light. I knew that, if I smelled

them, I'd find the color imbedded in my cuticles, under my
fingernails. I got out of bed and walked to the sink. I washed
my hands thoroughly with a cake of green soap. Then I took
a glass and poured cold water over the back of my neck. I tried
to do it a second time, but the pressure from the faucet knocked
the glass out of my hand. It didn't break, though the sound
startled me terribly. I hurried back to bed.

Steel valves. There was another Farbstein—Nathan, I
thought his name had been—who had worked in my father's
office for nearly thirty years. Another white and yellow old
man, at least at the time that I'd met him. My father employed
several Jews in his office—Jews, he knew, were clever and competent—and yet no occasion ever arose for their advancement
at Belknap and Collins International Hardware. They were
exploited consistently and in a rather obvious manner, but my
father had a way of inspiring loyalty even in those he very pa-
tently detested. Henry Belknap was himself an Episcopalian:
chiefly so, I think, because he was neither a Catholic nor a Jew
nor an atheist. He never spoke of God. His beliefs, in general,
were not very clear. But he was implacable when it came to
matters in which he would not believe. Whatever remained
was right—presumably because it asked the least of his time.

When I was eighteen, I met a Jewish girl at a Barnard lawn
party. She was small and very brown, and she often wore her
hair in a thick, whip-like braid. Her legs were slim, with the
tiny, muscular calves of a trained dancer. There is a certain
Oriental Jewishness—unblunted by the coarsening effects of
middle-class complacency—which moves with a ghostly litheness. This girl moved as though moving were a simpler matter
than stillness: an easy accommodation of the air. She sang—
aloud, under her breath—when music was played, but, more

often, she remained quiet, lending a definable significance to all things around her. Her name was Naomi Moses, and she was a devout Orthodox Jewess.

I played baseball and basketball and football in college. And yet, despite the practice schedule, I managed to graduate Summa Cum Laude without serious difficulty. All the fraternities at Columbia, but one, invited me to join. I pledged because my father thought it a good thing, and I became, inevitably, what we used to call a BMOC—Big Man on Campus. Naomi was, of necessity, a very different person. She remained by herself. The rules of her orthodoxy created many barriers, and, by extending those barriers, she was able, when she felt the need, to isolate herself completely. Her father had a great deal of money, but her father's money was different from my father's. It brought different things. It was the differentness, I suppose, that first attracted me.

Naomi was doubtful at the outset; perhaps she was even vaguely offended. But I persisted for several months, and, in time, I imagine, I became enamoured of my own persistence. After that awesome first evening of her submission, I allowed Naomi, for more than half a year, tacitly to influence everything I did. That quiet influence, in the short time that it lasted, was perhaps the most beneficent force I have ever experienced. There was an assurance in everything Naomi said, an assurance derived, I thought then, from three thousand years of racial memory. And her orthodoxy fascinated me. I examined its laws as an eager and impressionable child watches the hands of a magician.

I had not told my father. It was a convenient omission, made feasible by years of formal distance. Through the father of one of my fraternity brothers, however, he eventually learned of

our relationship. And, one spring evening, he asked me
politely to come into his room: it was a thing he never did except in matters that required severe disciplinary action. I was
a good son. From the very beginning I had believed in an angry
father God. Not for some time had my father asked me into his
room.

My father was a large man, by that time grown rather ponderous. He was fast becoming bald; a massive pair of black eyebrows protruded from his high, bare forehead. He had the deep
and penetrating voice that all male Belknaps have, or soon find
it necessary to acquire. Never once had I seen him angry; but
then, I suppose, he hardly even had need to be. My father
could phrase a command with a real or assumed simplicity that
was devastating; those simple commands still come, in various
guises, into my dreams.

Before speaking, my father removed his glasses with exquisite
deliberation. He knew that his eyes beneath the impending
brows were far more impressive without them. He loved that
measured, pointing gesture; he used it whenever he wanted to
say something only once. And, when he replaced his glasses,
further communication of any sort was abruptly cut off, and the
discussion, such as it was, came to an end.

My father was sitting behind his desk. It was a little desk—
little, I think, because it stressed his hugeness. I stood before it
in a characteristic posture, my shoulders straight, my fingers
wrenching at themselves behind my back. My father smiled.
Then he removed his glasses.

"I'm disappointed, Whitney. I thought we'd taught you a bit
more discretion."

"To what are you referring, sir?"

"You've become—I think the word is 'involved'—with a

young Jewish girl. That's unfortunate. It's one of the less admirable features of Columbia. Things weren't always like that." He began to unfold his glasses, as though there wasn't much left to say. "I don't blame you, Whitney. I'm sure she's attractive in her way. Temptations are always strong, and you are, thank God, as virile a son as I could wish for. But now that you've had your fun, try to terminate this business as quickly as possible. It has already—I know this will distress you—it has already caused me considerable embarrassment."

My father put his glasses on and bent, or seemed to bend, over his papers. The room began to go slowly out of focus. I looked at the top of my father's balding forehead. The light from the desk lamp was reflected from two high points on his brow—another pair of eyes. Watching. Only one force is effective in the face of unreasoning fear: another unreasoning fear. I had come, unfortunately, to depend on Naomi—so much so that I was compelled to do what I never again did before or after. My father's guard was down; years of submission had made him complacent. And so I spoke to him. I spoke to him, though he had his glasses on, and there was nothing left to discuss.

"I don't think I'll do that, sir. I love her."

My father looked up. I think he was surprised to find I was still standing there. He sighed. Then, with a gesture of restrained impatience, he took off his glasses once again. He looked at them. He looked at me. Then, in the slowest, most deliberate manner, he spoke to me.

"Whitney. That's nonsense and you know it."

"I intend to marry Naomi Moses, sir. I'm afraid that's final." My father seemed to meditate. He seemed to be showing a certain amused interest in what I had said.

"Naomi Moses . . . Naomi Moses. Moses. Is that it, then? Well, before you marry Naomi Moses, I suggest you remove everything that's yours from the house. Do it as quickly and as quietly as you can. Your life is yours, Whitney. Far be it from me to interfere. If you want your children to be half Yid, half Goy—well, that's fine. But they won't be my grandchildren." He put on his glasses. "Please leave my room now. I certainly hope you'll reconsider. I love you very much. But, then, this is no longer any business of mine. Good-bye, Whitney." I began to stammer. I moved my mouth and my arms and my hands. I stamped my foot. But there was no sound. I couldn't be heard. I didn't exist. I turned and ran from his room.

I called Naomi as soon as I had reached my own room. The line was busy. I had a yellow bedspread covered with little brush-like tufts, and, when I heard the signals, I began tearing at the little tufts in time to it. One after the other, I tore them out, and, all the while, I heard myself saying, "She loves me, she loves me not, she loves me, she loves me not." When, finally, Naomi answered, the bedspread was in tatters. "Hi, honey," she said. And then I told her that I had given everything up for her, that I was an outcast in my own home. And she said I was speaking too fast, and would I please repeat what I had said. Very slowly and distinctly, as a madman will, I repeated it all. Then I said that I was coming over to see her. A man without allegiance, I said, must hurry to acquire new loyalties. She told me that I couldn't come over. I hung up while she was speaking.

As I passed the door, I heard my father gargling in the bathroom. My father gargled every night before going to bed. That sound, I realized, would be the last that I would hear in my own home. I ran out the door and down the stairs. Eleven flights, fourteen steps in each flight. Loves. Loves not. Loves. Not. Loves. Loves, loves, loves. The doorman threw a bullet pass at me, but I didn't pretend to catch it, as I always did, running, my hands cupped over my shoulder. I hailed a cab. Naomi lived only ten or fifteen blocks from our apartment. I had never been to her house before.

Naomi was alone. When she opened the door, she stepped quickly back, her liquid eyes wide with fear and, I hoped, a certain sort of love. I said I didn't care if my children were half Yid, half Goy, as long as she was their mother. Naomi backed yet further away from me. I called my father a dirty bigot. Naomi put out her hand and waved it, as though protecting herself with a sacred gesture. I said I would renounce him as he had renounced me. I slammed my fist into the wall. A little painting in a large frame fell off the wall and onto the sofa. There was silence.

"Don't you love me?"

"I love you," she said.

"Then why don't you say something? I need you now. I need you. Why don't you try to help me?" I sat on the sofa. Then I fell forward, my forehead pressed against the cool surface of a glass coffee table.

"I'm afraid," she said.

"You're afraid? You? What've you got to be afraid of? If you'd only seen my father—"

"I'm afraid of you. For you."

"Well, don't be. I know where I'm going now, and I've burned all my bridges behind me." I made a fist at the world. Naomi was silent for a moment. Then she smiled very sadly.

"No, you haven't. You haven't burned your bridges at all. You'll have to go back. There were never any bridges ahead of you. Not here." My heart leaped once. Then I didn't notice if it beat again.

"You don't love me," I said. "You don't love me. After all

I've been through, you don't love me. You never did." The tears of a childishness not long past surged into my eyes.

"I do love you. But I—who am I?"

I heard the front door open. Naomi spread her hands, palms upward, and held them before her. I saw that they were empty. She raised her right hand to her eye, as though in a little fare-well salute—then she was running and crying. Then she was gone. I tried to rise, but now there was a little man standing before the coffee table. A little, pink man with a fleshy face and colorless, thick glasses. The little man dropped his overcoat in front of him. Without looking down, he stepped onto it, as though it were a platform on which he intended to speak. Then Mr. Moses removed his glasses, and I thought that I was going mad.

"How do you do, sir. I'm—"

"What're you doing here?" he stammered. "What're you do-ing in this house?"

"Sir. I came over to speak—"

"Get out of that chair!" He screamed, and I jumped up. Mr. Moses came up close to me. I towered over him, but, even so, I felt his little body in the lower parts of me, working away at the things that held me upright. His face was on fire; his fists clenched and unclenched. He was stamping furiously on his own overcoat.

"Sir. I'm sorry if I—"

"Get out of here. I know who you are. I know what you want. I know how miserable you've made my daughter. Go home to your own kind. Why don't you leave us alone?"

"Sir. Naomi and I—"

"Shut up! Shut up! Shut your mouth!" He rose on his toes, his shoulders hunching at each phrase. Suddenly he bent and picked up a heavy metal ashtray. I put my hands up to protect my body, but he only pointed to the coffee table. "You touched that?" he asked. Before I could answer, the ashtray smashed down through the glass top. Splinters of glass fell into my shoes. "And I'll do that to anything else you've touched," he said. "Get out. Get out, before I kill you."

I left. I left and I walked the whole of the night in Central Park, tempting danger. But the violence that inhabits there avoided me, as though misfortune had rendered my body sacrosanct. The dawn came, and, filled with apprehension, I returned to my own bed. But, of course, Naomi had been right. My bridges were never burned at all. My father lived only a few years after that, but not once was the incident recalled.

And so I learned that my father was a bigot, but he was my father; Mr. Moses was a bigot, but he was a Jew. There are invariable laws even in prejudice. For every Jew or Negro or Christian who is persecuted, there is, somewhere, a Jew or Negro or Christian who is persecuting. Loyalty is a good thing, but bigotry is born of loyalty. And it is the alternation of love and hate, of the latter in the name of the former, that makes the world go round.

I slept. A black shadow settled over me and against the sun. Consciousness intruded on my dreams, and there it became a sort of fantastical awareness. I remembered impending cliffs, heavily leaved old trees, giant waves at sea shuddering as they crested. And then I remembered the skeletal, black-robed Death of my childhood. The shadow moved and sunlight, for just one moment, reddened the translucence of my eyelids.

Something curled itself around my right wrist. My heart shrieked aloud; my body tensed, subsided, lay unresisting. The thing was not warm, but it was pliant and very moist. I remembered Mr. Farbstein. I imagined that it was his hand, that he had crawled across the room—his food tube slithering behind him—to paw at me, to beg me to arrange his pillow. The thing began to pull gently at my wrist. Gradually and against the concerted strength of my apprehension, it drew me out of sleep. The shadow was Dr. Snow.

"Sorry," he said. "I had a few moments. I thought I'd drop in." He withdrew his hand from my wrist. Silhouetted, as it was, against the window's light, Dr. Snow's face was dark and featureless. Only his eyes were visible: pale gray and as persistent as a radium watch dial at night. I blinked and made questioning sounds in my throat. Dr. Snow's fingers were threading themselves at the level of my face—a mesh of small, brown vipers. He looked at them. They unwound themselves reluctantly; his hands dropped, motionless, at his sides.

"Excuse me." I cleared my throat. Then I held my hand up as a shield against the glare. "Glad to see you."

"Good. I have about ten minutes, maybe fifteen, while they're getting things ready upstairs." He turned and, gradually, half his face became illuminated by the sun's afternoon light. "Do any writing today? No? I'd be careful, Whitney. This inertia's easy and it's attractive. It's a tangible threat. A loss of attention; a capitulation. An approximation—more or less pleasant —of death. I think you'd better try to work."

"That's not so easy—what with the heat and this new business. In fact . . . I've a bit of a bone to pick with you." I hesitated: the image had caused me almost to salivate. "How can I work without food? I'm so weak now, it'd be a positive pleasure to stop breathing. I wish at least you'd prepared me for it."

"You haven't eaten?" He seemed surprised.

"Of course, I haven't. Good grief—don't tell me it was all a mistake?" I sat up. "You did put me on a liquid diet? You did, didn't you?"

"Yes—but I've been told you went over my head. Yesterday, someone saw you with a large hero sandwich. Ham, I think she said."

"That? My secretary brought it, but I didn't eat the damn thing. I didn't touch it. I sent it home with him."

"Oh," he said. I thought, unreasonably enough, that Dr. Snow didn't believe me.

"It's worse than that—I haven't eaten since I came in here. Not since lunch Monday. Monday afternoon to Tuesday, Tuesday to— That's almost seventy-two hours without food. My teeth're beginning to atrophy."

"Seventy-two hours? Really? Why couldn't you eat in all that time?" I hesitated. I couldn't tell Dr. Snow about Sarah Samson's smell, about my revulsion before stool samples, about the collective unpleasantness of the Lopopulos. Yet, when I looked at him, I thought that probably he knew.

"Various reasons. Ah—things just seemed to interfere. But —whatever the reason—the fact is, I'm starving now. Can I have dinner tonight?" Dr. Snow shook his head. I fell back onto my pillow, disappointment unconcealed.

"Have patience," he said. "There's a reason for this. Try to work. Don't dwell on it."

"No solids?"

"No. No solids. Of course, with your resources, Whitney— well, I don't suppose you'd have too much trouble turning a stone into a loaf of bread." I raised my hands, palms upward, in front of my chest.

"If there's a reason, and I'm sure there is, I won't eat until I get the word from you."

"Until you get the word from me . . . I see. Good. Now

here's something that'll interest you—take your mind off your troubles." Dr. Snow's left hand disappeared. Then it reappeared, suddenly, in front of my face. In it was what seemed to be a great white grub. The grub was plastic; it bulged at the middle and then tapered to about half its greatest width at either end. A smaller white tube protruded from the hump on its spine. There were thin wires, antennae, attached to what I supposed was the head. The huge larva lay curled in Dr. Snow's palm. His fingers were motionless, and yet I knew that he was somehow caressing it.

"What is it?"

"It's a heart. Part of a heart. Hold it." I took the thing into my hand reluctantly. It was about eight inches long and deceptively light. But the shape and color, the thin wires, repulsed me.

"Part—part of a heart?"

"Yes. An artificial ventricle. We took it out of an old woman just three hours ago. That thing you're holding kept her alive for more than eight days."

"She's dead?" He nodded. My hand began to sweat. I considered putting the thing down, but I didn't want Dr. Snow to suspect my revulsion.

"Yes. She's dead. Kidneys went, I think. We haven't done the autopsy yet." He seemed morose. "Compassion—not mine —dictates that we experiment only on hopeless cases. It's unfortunate. It clouds the issue. It leads to bad publicity. But still, we're making progress."

"What's it made of?" I tried to hand the ventricle back. But Dr. Snow made no move to take it.

"Silastic. An inert plastic. So far as we know, it doesn't traumatize the blood. So far as we know. Give me five years,

Whitney—ten at the outside—and I promise you, I'll replace any human heart that's weak with age or broken down before its time."

"With this?" I turned the thing over, and a wire antenna scratched at my wrist. My hand quivered. And my heart, as I had feared it would, began to thud.

"No. This is primitive. It's obsolete already. I have a device in my office now—but that's for the future." He looked toward the window. "The future . . . No more heart failure. A life span probably double what it is now. After that? Immortality, I think. I don't think even immortality is beyond us."

"Immortality?"

"It's in your hand. Take a good look. Except for the brain —the liver, perhaps—I doubt if there's anything we can't replace." I tried to show interest in the ventricle, but the phenomenon that really interested me was Dr. Snow. I found his enthusiasm hypnotic. His eyes were alive, though the light that illuminated them seemed strangely remote and impersonal. His hands, too, were agitated. I acknowledged our physical resemblance once again; quite irrationally, it made me proud.

"Immortality? You mean—when the last organ is replaced, the last body juice synthesized. When men are made entirely of inert plastic?" Dr. Snow smiled.

"That's a normal reaction. It doesn't disturb me. I guess immortality of my sort wasn't meant to make bishops more comfortable in their profession. Death is, after all, your chief patent fear."

"I wasn't thinking of that." I said it honestly.

"Then do. You'll find it an interesting proposition."

"I suppose so," I said. This time it was I who smiled. Dr.

Snow turned to the window, leaving me with the ventricle clutched in my hand. I stared at the back of his head for a long moment. Then a textbook picture, in red and blue, appeared in my mind. Ventricles and—I couldn't remember what the other parts were. Ventricles, anyway—like the things in my own body. My own body . . . I dropped the ventricle and pushed it the length of my arm away.

"You're right, of course," said Dr. Snow. He walked slowly back to my bed. "We've a long way to go. Right now, frankly, some of our problems seem insurmountable. If we hadn't already solved so many insurmountable problems, I might be pessimistic. Look, we've duplicated the action of one ventricle. The woman died, but I don't think it was our fault. We have a long way to go. We'll have to perform a miracle—nothing short of that. And, in the absence of supernatural forces, we have only patience and courage and human ingenuity with which to achieve it. But we will achieve it. I give you my word for that."

"I'm afraid," I said, "that my enthusiasm, my admiration hardly merit the giving. I know nothing about hearts—heart disease. Nothing about the obstacles you'll have to face. But, for what it's worth, I'm spellbound, literally, by the things you've told me. This is almost as magnificent as the act of giving life itself." I wanted to encourage him. To make some sufficient gesture—my hand laid lightly on his. But, though Dr. Snow wanted my admiration, I knew full well that it would never be necessary to him. And, for that reason, I withheld it. Dr. Snow was silent for a moment. He seemed to be waiting. Then he began to smile.

"You're wondering why I've told you all this. No—I don't want you to double your contribution. You and your father before you have done a great deal for us. I'm afraid it's rather more trivial than that. I just happened to come across something in your records this morning. Something that intrigued me. You went to St. Michael's Prep, didn't you?"

"That's right. Why d'you ask?"

"You played football?"

"Yes."

"I played cornerback for Winchester Academy. I was a junior when you were a senior."

"Let me see. Winchester. In my senior year. Yes, in fact, I remember the game very well."

"You ought to. You scored three touchdowns. The first one you took on a look-in pass. You went forty-five yards on that one. The second—am I right?—the second was on a sort of Z-out pattern near the sideline. The third—and I will never forget this—the third you took over your shoulder going straight away. I'll never forget it, Whitney, because you body-faked me at about the fifty yard line, and then you outran me all the rest of the way. No one ever did that to me. Not in prep school, not in college. It was a beautiful pass. The quarterback was the nephew or the son—some relation—of Horace Vanderburn. I forget which now. His sister came out with my sister."

"Clarence Vanderburn. His son. You were number thirty-five then?"

"No. Thirty-seven. Thirty-five was the left cornerback."

I could, indeed, remember that day. I remembered it often. That may, perhaps, sound childish, but it is seldom in any life that a moment of unalloyed triumph occurs. Tansy was there with her parents. The scouts from ten or twelve colleges were there. My father was there. He had brought three business friends to watch his son play football. Afterward—after I had,

singlehandedly, won the game against a team that hadn't been
defeated in two seasons—my father had come to the dressing
room, and put his big hand around the bulge of my shoulder.
And now Dr. Snow had brought it all back. He had been number thirty-seven. I couldn't remember number thirty-seven, but
I very much wanted to.

"It's a small damn world," I said.

"Yes," said Dr. Snow, "and I'd like to keep it that way."

"You had one hell of a team that year."

"Yes," said Dr. Snow, "but we lost." He seemed no longer
interested in football. Suddenly, he said, "I've got a surprise
for you, Whitney."

I could detect no indicative show of emotion in his voice. It's
the angiogram, I thought; they've found out. I sat forward. Mr.
Farbstein said, "Oh, oh. Oh, oh." As if he knew something that
I couldn't possibly know. Then he said, "Oh?" as though he
were no longer quite certain. I tried not to notice the agitated
pulsing of my heart. I smiled innocently. I made a trite remark,
but I couldn't even hear what I had said.

"Yes," said Dr. Snow. "I've arranged for a private room."

"A private room? But I thought they were only for—"

"There are special cases. You've been a good friend to us,
Whitney. And I know just how you feel. In a time of crisis,
privacy is damned important. An unpicked lot of strangers—
good God, they can drive you out of your mind." He gestured
toward the beds opposite me. "Farbstein and Lopopulo. No.
Not exactly the sort of people we'd invite to cocktails of a Saturday evening. I'm sorry about it. But I was away until Wednesday."

A private room. A private room . . . Mine only, the circles
of sweat beneath my armpits. Mine only, my yellow feet tufted

with graying hair. Mine only, the mindless lethargy, the empty staring at my cuticles, the back of my head shaping a bowl inside my pillow. I'd no longer be embarrassed by Jimmy's fastidious innocence. Mr. Farbstein would no longer moan with erratic and diabolical insistence. And again I quote, "God is love. Organized religion tends to set men apart, but Christ didn't choose to set his Word apart—He extended the gift of Grace to all men. If we restrict our teaching to the 'religious' few, Christianity will die of interbreeding and impoverishment." Neither the joy of love, nor the many satisfactions of malice have ever been my portion. A private room. A door to shut. No. I would be involved. And I would hate every man in his turn.

"Thanks anyway," I said. I was trying to suppress my irritation. "I'm fine right where I am. The view is lovely. I'd rather not put you to all that bother."

"No bother. All the paper work's done already. And the room I have in mind has an even better view. I'll have you moved after dinner."

"No. Really. I'd rather not."

There was a pause during which I found my breathing an embarrassment. Dr. Snow looked at me; his tongue swelled in his cheek. Then he cupped his hands in front of him and across his abdomen. I knew he was angry. He stared into his cupped hands for a long while. It upset me. I didn't want Dr Snow to be angry with me.

"A man of the people. I'd forgotten. Forgive me—in my simple way, I thought you'd want to be alone. It took some doing to clear it for you."

"I appreciate what you've done. Really. It's just that—well, I'd prefer to be with people."

"I envy you," he said. "Born into the same environment, and yet—what's that?" He pointed to my neck. I reached up, and then I pulled my hand away in immediate revulsion. I had forgotten about it.

"It's a rabbit's foot," I said.

"So I see. So I see. Mind you, I'm just curious. I may be wrong but . . . Your concepts of radical Christianity, with which I sympathize—that is, insofar as they are radical and not Christian—would seem to rule out a belief in such things."

"One of your staff members saw fit to give me this. It was a sincere, if rather misbegotten, gesture. I thought best not to refuse her."

"Sarah Samson. She continues to make a nuisance of herself. Well, this is as good a time as any. I intended to fire her two months ago. I'll see about it now." He turned to go.

"No," I said. "Please. She doesn't bother me."

"This is nothing. She's slow and she's dirty. But, unfortunately, I have to be careful about firing Negroes. If I'm not, I find CORE parked on my doorstep. But enough is enough. Just look at that filthy thing."

"Don't fire her now. I'll—she'll think it was my fault. I couldn't bear that."

"Couldn't you?" He hesitated. "Well. I suppose I can hardly deny you anything. What did you do the hundred in, Whitney?"

"Nine-nine was my best, I think. Why?"

"Isn't that strange? I did the hundred in nine-eight several times. Why couldn't I catch you? Was it a special moment of power? Did your God grant you a sudden burst of superhuman speed?" I laughed. His assumed naïveté amused me.

"I hardly think so. I wasn't much of a Christian in those days. It was late in the game. I kept myself in pretty good shape."

"That could be it. Well, I have to go now, Whitney. I've already outstayed my little time. I still can't convince you to move? No? As you please." Mr. Farbstein groaned. Dr. Snow turned toward him, and Mr. Farbstein's eyes closed, as a doll's eyes will when the doll is placed on its back.

"No solids?"

"No," he said. "I'll come tomorrow. I think by then—who knows—I may have decided to ask you some difficult questions. If you don't mind."

"I don't."

He nodded. Then he left. From the several tones of his irony, I knew that Dr. Snow was disappointed in me. And then an odd thought presented itself to my mind. Was he trying to punish me for what had happened those many years ago? Frightening me? Tempting me? Starving me into submission? It was a fantastic idea, but I had experienced even stranger things in men. The thought unnerved me.

I sat up, my head bent inward against the heat. Jimmy began to stir, and Mr. Farbstein opened his eyes once again. When I leaned forward, I felt the thing dangling against my body— seeking communion with the hairs on my chest. I cursed. Without thinking, I lifted the dirty cord over my head, opened the drawer and threw it in. Yet, in time, I realized I'd let Dr. Snow intimidate me. I sat up. Then, as a compromise, I took the rabbit's foot from the drawer, and left it almost in plain sight amongst the books on my table.

I remained on the edge of my bed—sitting, my shoulders hunched forward—long after Michael had gone. My elbows were balanced on the insides of my thighs. My hands hung limply down between my knees. I noticed, with indifference, that my fingertips were shaking; they vibrated in a quick, ir-

regular rhythm that soothed my attention. Now and then I
would look from the tops of my eyes toward the corridor beyond
our door. I had turned my back on the window. The glare of
the sun, the city's seething activity had begun to oppress me
hours before.

Michael had tried to be brave. I, in my turn, had exhausted
myself in an effort to seem cheerful. We talked seriously about
the woman in Michael's life: his landlady, an unsubtle mother
figure without—as far as I could tell—the slightest sense of
shame. Then we edited a sermon entitled, "Our Friends in
Tanganyika." Michael had never been to Tanganyika, and, indeed, the sermon seemed more relevant to the subject of "Ur-
ban Life and the Threat to Innocence." The text, if that is ever
an indication, was taken from the Genesis description of Noah's
Ark.

Had he forgotten my pajamas? No. No, indeed. Michael
handed me a beautifully wrapped, damp box. I opened it. My
new pajamas were pale blue and covered with baseballs and
bats and catchers' masks. Somehow Michael had found pajamas
intended for a species of giant child. But they weren't plaid,
and so I had no right to complain.

Pious was fine. He had run after his tail in the bathtub.
Then, as an encore, he had shinnied up Michael's leg. Michael
rolled up his pants leg in order to show me the red welts on his
fat, white calf. He doesn't miss me, I thought. He won't, as long
as the food keeps coming. But I knew very well that he did
miss me. Pious never sat on my lap. He slapped his tail on the
carpet whenever I dared to stroke him. Yet, in the mountains,
where I sometimes rented a cottage, he would accompany me
on day-long walks through the wooded foothills. He would
weave in and out of the forest; at times he would disappear for

so long that I was tempted foolishly to worry about him. But always he would appear again. He would spring suddenly out of a low bush, make a feint at my legs and then dash away. Sometimes I would find him sunning his fur on a rock at a turn in the path. Then Pious would stare up at me, his pupils paper-thin slits, as though to inquire what had kept me for so long. At those moments, tears of joy welled up in my eyes. But I knew better than to demonstrate my feelings. Without looking to the side, I would march past Pious at a good pace. Then he would pull himself up with a sort of assumed irritation and rush ahead— ostensibly to make very certain of the way. It was a Laurentian relationship, and it made me inexpressibly happy.

I watched as Mrs. Farbstein hobbled out into the corridor. The blades of her shoulders seemed abnormally rigid and prominent—a pair of embryonic humps. Through her thin blouse, I could see the straps of a pink brassiere. The thought of her wizened breasts sickened me—humps and warts, all the excrescences of old age, hung each in a tiny, pink sling. When she had left, I opened the front of my pajamas and blew down amongst the hairs on my chest. I blew, and a globule of sweat hunched itself fearfully. Damn, I said. Mrs. Farbstein had come back. I smiled and covered my chest. She picked up a pair of glasses. I waited, tense and uncomfortable, until she had gone.

A private room? No, really. I'd prefer to be with people. *Lord God, my Father, forgive me. Even now—even as I come to terms with my own death—it is only with hypocrisy that I can conceal my hatred. I have believed in Thee and in Thy Son— in the miracles He performed and in the joy of His Gospel. Why then, am I still so very far from Thee?* A private room. What had he said? "I envy you. Born into the same environ-

ment, and yet—" And yet the same. A father, a school, an un-
questioned image of the good and the beautiful. No, I thought.
You can't make a sow's ear out of a silk purse.

I locked my fingers together on my knees. Sitting there, I let
my neck go slowly limp—until my chin had settled into the
hairs on my chest. Something bubbled in my lower abdomen;
hunger, half an ache, half a longing, swirled inside me. I took
a deep breath. Two circles of pain appeared around my eyes,
as little red dots eddied on the surfaces of my eyeballs. I had
begun to capitulate.

A remote and strangely repetitious sound reached out toward
me. I listened. It seemed to be coming closer. "Hello, hello,"
it said. Then more clearly, "Hello, hello." A low-throated,
cheerful sound, almost a warble. Again, "Hello, hello." Closer
yet. A nurse passed by my door. She was walking quickly, pushing a wheeled rack on which swung a yellow bottle. The plastic
tube stretched rigidly behind her. Then a man appeared. He,
too, was walking quickly, for the plastic tube was sunk into one
of his nostrils, fastened there by a white bandage. He was
wearing a green nightshirt that drooped to the level of his
shins. His feet were buried in immense, furry slippers. His
hair was gray and very curly. Each of his features seemed out-
sized. I recalled distinctly the hugeness of his earlobes. He
turned to me, lifted his hand and gave me a wide, masculine
wave. "Hello, hello," he said. Then he was gone.

I turned toward Jimmy. Both he and Mr. Farbstein were
asleep. I think I wanted to share this apparition: man in his
second embryohood—secured by a thin, plastic tube to his
source of nourishment and forced to follow, at a good pace,
wherever it led. And yet, he had seemed quite cheerful. A
mature and virile enthusiasm was seated in his gray, curly hair.

I remembered his smile, struggling upward despite the plastic tube that depressed his lip.

"We believe in a stern post-operative program. The human body heals most efficiently when placed under stress." P. Crecy was standing in the doorway. I hadn't seen him enter.

"And if he can't keep up with the glucose—then he dies, I suppose?" Though we were some distance apart, his voice carried to me, as though borne on an electric current.

"It's not quite so austere as that. The nurse, after all, doesn't walk very fast." He came toward me. P. Crecy never walked on his heels—or, rather, his heels seemed to be where the balls of his feet ought to have been.

"I hope you're feeling better today," I said.

"Me? I? I'm always well."

"Fine," I said. "Fine. You'll be out of here in no time." He halted in his tracks.

"Oh," he said. "You are joking. Yes, I see. A joke." He laughed, and I found the sound he made most disconcerting. A tiny watch mechanism gone eccentric in its ticking. But I controlled my revulsion and spoke to him as I had planned the day before.

"Dr. Crecy. I hope you'll forgive me for what I said yesterday. I think you're probably right. I'm a bit spoiled—in a sense it's an occupational hazard." I smiled. "Please forgive me." I felt an immediate sense of relief. P. Crecy shut his eyes; it was as though he were embarrassed.

"Please. Please. You mustn't. I was also unnecessarily— what do you say? Carried away. You and I and Dr. Snow, we are all on the same side. We work together. You're new here and sometimes it's hard to adjust. But, believe me, Bishop Belknap, there is nothing to fear. From the beginning I have known

—known—that Dr. Snow takes a very special interest in you. It is, I think, because of your book, which I—I am ashamed to admit it—I have not yet read." He bowed his head. "I came for that very reason. Have you a copy to lend me?"

"Yes. Yes, of course. I have a copy right here. Take it. Do, by all means. It's only a little thing. A man of your intelligence can knock it off in an hour or two." He picked it up timidly.

"Thank you," he said. "Thank you. I have so little time to read. Dr. Snow is a perfectionist. He works everyone unmercifully. But it is strange: I am glad to be a doctor—I wouldn't be anything else—yet, I am in awe of men who write books. Always, since I was a student. Strange, don't you think?"

"The grass is always greener," I said.

"Greener? Yes? I don't see."

"In someone else's yard. That is—something you're not familiar with is always more attractive."

"True. Still, I am almost reverencing a writer as important as you are. They tell me hundreds of thousands of people have read this book."

"Closer to half a million."

"Fantastic. You must have extraordinary influence. Extraordinary. Turn over and remove your pants."

"Excuse me?"

"Please turn over and remove your pants."

The tone of his voice modulated so radically that it threw me into a state of confused alertness. I was embarrassed—my movements became awkward—but I managed to do what he had demanded of me. I wanted to ask P. Crecy to pull the curtain, but he became immediately so busy somewhere behind me, that I was afraid to do so.

"What is this injection for?" I asked.

Then an immense and terribly undefined pain rose up from the region of my groin. I shrieked into my pillow. I had prepared myself mentally for a hypodermic, and, when I correlated that with the area of contact, a monstrous image appalled my imagination. I tried to look back over my own shoulder, but I was pinned to the bed.

"What was that? What? What was it?"

"An enema. You shouldn't have tensed. It becomes unnecessarily painful."

P. Crecy had finished with me. I lay rigid and exposed. The bones in my neck crackled painfully when I put my head down. The pain had become an aggressive soreness. I would have been ashamed to ease it with my hand. But I said nothing.

"In a short while, I think, you will feel the need to evacuate."

"Yes—thank you." I tried delicately to inch my pants up. "Evacuate? What in God's name can I have to evacuate?"

"We shall see."

"What d'you expect to find—a ham hero sandwich?"

"Pardon?"

I didn't answer. I was preoccupied both with the exquisite nature of my suffering, and with the magnificence of my resignation before it.

"What is that?" P. Crecy was still standing beside my bed. I leaned forward on my elbows. He was pointing at my bedside table.

"What?"

"This. It would seem to be a rabbit's foot."

"It is." I picked the thing up and hurled it quickly into my open drawer.

"They are good luck omens, no?"

"Yes. But it's not mine." P. Crecy smiled and looked at his

little finger. "A friend of mine left it. Good grief, Dr. Crecy, you don't think I believe in the efficacy of rabbits' feet?"

"It is, shall we say, a bit incongruous."

I would have told him the truth, but I was reluctant to make yet another enemy for Sarah. I think, too, that I hated to acknowledge even the minimal influence she had over me. I knew I didn't have to explain myself. But P. Crecy was watching me: his eyes, his fingers, the nodes on his throat were gossiping in little pulsations.

"Dr. Crecy. Someone expressed a kind concern for my health. She may have done it a bit crudely, but I could hardly question her sincerity. Even as a bishop, I have to respect—damn!" Something wet had begun to run down between my thighs. I looked at P. Crecy. His face expressed nothing with such absolute determination that I was mortified. Michael's new pajamas and the baseballs and bats and catchers' mitts. "Excuse me," I said. I ran out, my thighs pressed together. As I passed out of the room, it seemed strange to me that neither Jimmy nor Mr. Farbstein had awakened.

"Sir? Excuse me? Did the Yankees win last night?" Jimmy was whispering. I turned to the sports section of the *New York Times*. Jimmy hadn't dared put on his portable radio—not since the terrific rhythms of Mr. Farbstein's breathing had begun, the day before, to calibrate everything in our room that was done or said or contemplated.

"They did. Seven-five."

"And Chicago?"

"Chicago. Chicago . . . They won. Do you want to look at the sports section?"

"Can I? Don't you get up, sir. I will." Jimmy came quickly across the room. I appreciated his concern. Now, when he ate, he swallowed his food hastily, as though it were something he had learned to be ashamed of. I noticed, too, that Jimmy sat nervously on the edge of his bed, whenever, on rising, I groped awkwardly for my balance. Still, he hadn't begun to let me win at Monopoly, and I was grateful for that. Jimmy sat, his legs crossed, on a chair near the head of my bed. He opened the paper only a few inches. Then he peered cautiously into it: as though there were degrees of reading intensity; as though too severe a reading were impolite. I knew that I'd have to make some effort to reciprocate.

"How many games are we out?" I asked.

"Two and a half. But it's only one now in the loss column, and Mantle should be back in a week or so."

"Where d'you play?"

"Me?" He seemed bashful. "My father's got a team. I mean, his company sponsors us. We won the trophy three times in five years. 'Course, I only got old enough two years ago."

"Pretty good. What d'you call yourselves?"

"Gee, Mister Belknap. Why'd you have to ask that? It's not our fault. It's the mothers. They made it up when they were sewing the uniforms. They don't know nothin' about baseball."

"Come now. It can't be that bad."

"It is, Mister Belknap. It is. All the other teams kid us about it." I couldn't help smiling.

"Tell me."

"Gee. Well, y'see my father's name is Lopopulo—Lopopulo Construction Company. So they call us the Lollipops. Lopopulo's Lollipops. It's awful. We play the Tigers and the Panthers and the Pirates. All real swell names." I laughed out loud. "See," he said. "Everybody does. They say they're gonna lick us, and the big guys do funny things with their tongues."

"But you win?"

"Yup. We got a big game with the Panthers a week from Saturday. They're tough. I hope the guys win." He was silent. It had been a mistake to bring up baseball. I realized that. And so I proceeded to compound the mistake.

"You'll be back next season."

"No sir," he said. "I don't think I will. I guess I'll be real lucky if I'm alive." He said it as if he were reading a filler from the *Times*. No immediately apparent self-pity explained his remark. The crew cut, the handkerchief folded in his breast pocket, the crossed legs, the opened newspaper—each seemed enormously calm, enormously reasonable.

"Nonsense. The human body is—well, a body as young and resilient as yours heals very, very quickly. Who knows? You might be in even better shape. Take my word for it. I don't think you've got anything to worry about." Jimmy looked at me. Then he folded the paper and laid it across his knees.

"I'm not worried, Mr. Belknap. There're more important things than baseball." He smiled as if he, too, were aware of the strangely sententious way in which he had said it. "Guess I wouldn't know what they were. But there must be."

"Do you believe in God, Jimmy?" He grinned. I realized then that Jimmy had been expecting me to say something very like that. I looked away from his eyes. A child, the mention of death: I had said it without thinking—almost spontaneously, but for the fact that my words were as rigorously conditioned as the response to a catechism. I had betrayed myself too easily; it annoyed me. But Jimmy didn't mind. It all seemed very fitting to him.

"I think I do. Sometimes it feels like there's no ceiling in my room and there's something soft and warm and—you know. Like my big feather comforter, when I get all the way under on real cold nights. Only it's sky-high—way up there."

Up there. Way up there . . . Sky-high God. Yes, I thought. Yes, quite obviously a case of pernicious medievalism. Nor, I thought, is God to be likened to a large feather comforter— even on the very coldest of winter nights. I smiled and nodded as though I understood—as though I felt a kinship, vital and profound, with what he had said. And, of course, I did.

"My father and mother don't go to church much. I mean they're real good people—but I guess they should go a lot more."

"Why's that?" I asked. Jimmy seemed uncertain.

"It's—it's good to go to church. Isn't it?"

"Why is it good?" Smudges of newsprint, little, grayish-black ellipses, had darkened his fingertips. While he was thinking, he wiped them clean with a piece of tissue. His fingernails were immaculate and very exactly pared.

"They're real good to me," he said. There was silence while he allowed me a moment in which to contradict him. "Real good. But, I mean—there are a lot of things—things like Sidney and Maureen. Like me when I'm real stupid. Things that make them angry. Then they do a lot of things they shouldn't do. I guess they can't help it. But, if they went to church, God could forgive them, couldn't he?"

"He could," I said. "He would." Jimmy smiled, as though he had been vindicated on a very doubtful point.

"I think I'll go to church when I grow up. More, I mean." Jimmy's miniature gentility fascinated me. I smiled. But then he said something that caused me to turn my eyes quickly away, to look intensely out onto the shining river. He said, "What—I mean . . . What exactly is death, Mister Belknap?"

Once I had delivered a sermon—a terrifying sermon—on the subject of man's mortality. Other sermons on the same subject had succeeded it: each a degree less terrifying, a degree more moderate. But not once, as I straddled the whole diapason of stresses and intensities, had I discovered a balance in which fear and understanding could coexist without the one dominating the other, without either exactly canceling the other out. And nowhere was there an equation that led directly from the contemplation of death to a single act of Christian resolution. Now —as I imagined myself standing at the foot of my bed, my voice rising and falling in tremolo, the black circles under my armpits gaping like auxiliary mouths—I saw that Jimmy was patiently waiting for my answer, his hands folded in his lap.

"I don't know," I said after a moment. "I don't know. I can only tell you what I believe. There was a time, Jimmy, when God wasn't way up there, sky-high—as you said before. When men—you and I and your parents, all of us—weren't down below, far away, as we feel we are now. All things were one and that was good. But somehow—there are words for it, but they don't really matter—somehow through a fault that was very much our own, we became separated from God, our Father and Creator. When Jesus Christ came into the World, He brought with Him a reconciliation, a forgiveness—that any man who believed in Him need never again despair of being close to God. When we die, if we have tried to close the gap, we will be allowed to return to Him. To God. Everything will be as one, we will stand with God—sky-high and never again alone."

"Then it's good to die?"

"Well, yes—it is good. But not without life. Life is like the

tests you have to pass before you're promoted. Do you see?"
Jimmy nodded. He seemed to be thinking.

"I don't think I'm afraid of death. No matter what Dr. Snow
says."

"What do you mean?" That startled me. Just before Jimmy
said that, an abstracted image of Dr. Snow—more the natural
phenomenon than the man—had unaccountably presented itself to my mind.

"I don't know. I don't understand what he says all the time."

"But he must've said something."

"Yes. No. I'm not sure." He paused. Then he decided to
tell me. "He said I wouldn't want to die. Ever. At least I
think that's what he said."

"Wouldn't want to die? Why?"

"I don't remember so good. He was feeling around on my
chest. Listening to my heart. Looking at me. The way he does.
I don't like him, Mister Belknap." Instinctively, I frowned and
brought my chin in against my chest. Jimmy seemed not to
notice. He wanted a confirmation from me. He expected it, I
think. But I, on the other hand, couldn't understand why he
mistrusted Dr. Snow. And so I made righteous noises. I think
I lowered myself in Jimmy's estimation.

"You don't like him? I'm surprised at you, Jimmy. Do you
know Dr. Snow? No, you don't. Shame on you. I grant he's a
bit distant—he has, after all, many, many things to worry about.
You and me, for instance. Do you realize that, if it weren't for
Dr. Snow, I wouldn't have a hope in this world? Do you realize
that?"

"Yes sir. I know he's a real good doctor. My mother and father wouldn't let me come here if he wasn't. But I don't like
him. I don't think he likes you, either."

"You see," I said with childish triumph. "You see right there how wrong you are. Dr. Snow likes me a lot. I know that for a fact."

"Then why won't he let you have anything for supper?"

"I think we'd better change the subject. Whatever Dr. Snow has decided, you can be sure he's decided for a very good reason. I'm going to go along with him. I'm sure your mother and father would want you to do the same." Jimmy nodded.

"You want to live very much, don't you sir?" It was inconceivable: I couldn't attribute malice to a boy of Jimmy's age. I paused in order that his question might fall into proper perspective—the brown eyes, the freckles spattered on nose and cheekbones and forehead; the tone that almost imitated a mature inquisitiveness. And, in spite of all these things, I was irritated.

"Yes," I said. I said it very evenly. "Yes, I want to live. There's nothing wrong with wanting to live. Nothing. Unless you do something sinful in order to stay alive. Don't you want to live, Jimmy?"

"I guess so," he said. "I wish I knew as much about it as you do, sir. I wish I did. But dying isn't such a bad thing. Unless it hurts."

"You mustn't talk about death, Jimmy."

"Why not, sir? I think about it all the time. I know I can't talk about it when my mother and father are here. I know that. But you and me're different."

Different. My intestines sputtered. I rose from the bed without answering him, and, when I did, I felt the uncertainty of my body in each of my joints. Different. There was death in my heart and nothing in my stomach. I kicked on my tattered, brown slippers, made a gesture of apology to Jimmy and

tottered toward the lavatory. I stumbled as I stepped out into
the hall and had to hold with both my hands to the brown bar
on the wall. Different. I was dying just a bit faster, a bit more
certainly, than the rest of God's Creation.

I stood in the doorway. An intern pushed past me as I stood
there, an empty glucose bottle and a roll of adhesive tape in
his hand. No, I said. No . . . The last bed had been filled. To
the left of my bed and directly opposite Mr. Farbstein lay a man
the color of cheap, aged paper. He was groaning, pulling convulsively at his plastic tube, as though he wanted to bring the
rack and its bottles down on his head. He turned toward me.
I backed out into the corridor, gesturing down the hall with my
head, pretending that someone had hailed me. Another yellow, dying man. Another pillow. Another soul for which I was
both ultimately and, now, particularly responsible. I moved
quietly into the room, my eyes fixed uncompromisingly on the
windowsill. As I did so, his lips puckered and exploded outward in little, moist bursts.
    "God damn heat—unnngh. God damn, dirty, mother-
humpin', son of a bitch. Dirty—bitch," he said.
    I could see that he had no teeth. The loose flesh around his
mouth ballooned out with each breath; then it fell suddenly
into a shriveled hollow. The rest of his body squirmed
sensuously from side to side—his torso was bare. A rectangular,
white bandage stretched from his solar plexus to the elastic of
his undershorts. He cursed again—with such violence that I
turned involuntarily as I passed the foot of his bed. Our eyes
met, and I was left with no alternative: I walked unsteadily
over to his bed.

"I'm Whitney Belknap. Anything I can do?"

"Christ. Grab that little, prune-titted nurse. That one. The one that just went by. Tell her to get me another shot. Pain's —unnngh! Damn. What time've you got?"

"Six. Little after."

"God damn. Two friggin' hours to go."

"Shall I ask?"

"Shall you? No, forget it. Y'gotta get tough. You're too nice a guy, Whitney. That the name? No—good. Buncha frigid little hookers. Don't give two farts if you die."

He rolled rhythmically from side to side, his knees pressed together, his groin puckered. His fingers scratched spasmodically at his scalp above the temple, and, as they did so, I saw that the top of his right ear had been neatly sliced away. There were little circular patches of yellow-white stubble under his sideburns, low on his cheeks, at the sides of his mouth. Once his face had been oval, swollen—now, like a rotted pumpkin, it had begun to collapse.

"Let me try."

"No. No, forget it. Waste of time. You got the window open?" I nodded. "Crotch-rottin' dirty heat. Name's Artie Carson. Pardon my not risin'." For several moments he closed his eyes and began to chant a sort of litany under his breath. "Son of a bitch. Son of a bitch. Son of a bitch. Bitch . . . Bitch . . ."

"Must be something I can do?"

"God damn. No use kiddin' around. I don't go big for pain, and I don't care who knows. Got a butt?"

"A cigarette? No—no."

"What good are you?" He smiled grotesquely. His gums, too, seemed to be gone. "What good is anybody in this prison?

Can't get a smoke. Can't get a drink. Hey, push my pillow up behind my back."

"Private room," I said, and I swallowed my own saliva with revulsion.

"What's that?"

"Nothing," I said. I staggered around to the other side of his bed. Artie alternately cursed and moaned behind me. His bare back was covered with fleshy acne scars and yellow, bristly hair. Sweat, in large, turgid droplets, hung from the hairs. I shoved the pillow tentatively up beneath his scarred shoulders, but he hadn't meant to let me off that easily. I pushed farther and then farther—until, finally, I had to touch his body. I'd been breathing through my mouth all the while; when I leaned forward, saliva ran out onto my chin.

"Try to sleep," I said. "They'll be bringing dinner soon."

"Food? You can shove it. They make me eat, but my guts can't take it. Not now, not before I had this thing." He pointed to his bandage. "You don't eat, you die. That's what they tell me." I moved around the bed. "Thanks for the pillow. What're you in for?"

"Heart."

"Yeah. That's bad, too. But at least it's all over one, two, three. You don't have to watch the flesh droppin' off your body —like you was rotten before they put you in the ground."

"Good God," I said. "That beats all. It really does. You've had your operation. You may be a bit uncomfortable now, but at least you're out of the woods. Now, I—" He began to laugh. The sound rolled and gurgled, trapped in his throat. Then it escaped from his lips in great, wet pocking noises. A thin spray of saliva drifted toward me. My throat tightened. I knew that Jimmy was watching both of us, and I resolved at that moment to use my influence with Dr. Snow to get that vulgar, degenerate man out of our room. I wouldn't stand for it. Not with Jimmy there.

"Operation. Operation." He tried to laugh again, but by now the pain had caught up with him. He was very silent, very still for a long moment. Then he began to speak quietly, his lips barely moving, from somewhere deep in his throat. "Had my operation? This was just a look-see, friend. Exploratory. They were too damn curious to wait for the autopsy. That's all. That's all."

"What did they find? What was there?" He smiled.

"Everybody's curious. Sorry. Snow said something about a cyst. I didn't ask for details. No thanks. I like surprises."

He closed his eyes. I straightened up. Then, quite all at once, something changed in the atmosphere of the room. I turned around. Mr. Farbstein was sitting upright for the first time, and he was staring, his eyes wide and furious, at Artie's obscene body. The man's intensity was appalling. It paralyzed me. Then, just as violently, his eyelids shut down and, as though a vitalizing current had been turned off, Mr. Farbstein fell back limply onto his pillow. Artie and Mr. Farbstein went to sleep. Their bottles of food winked as the sinking sun played lightly over their shiny glass sides.

No one ate. Artie and Mr. Farbstein watched their trays, as if expecting them to accomplish some very clever trick. Jimmy played with his food; he was guilty, I think, before my hunger. And I was very, very hungry indeed.

The heat had crystallized into a solid, intractable mass. Great, nasal "unnnghs" rolled up from my left, from the direction of Artie's bed. Then I would smell—or think I smelled—

a heavy and unhealthy odor of bodies. Artie's sheets hung limply to the floor. He had only his undershorts on: the full length of his bandage and the dark foreshadowings of his pubic hair were plainly visible. Now and then a barely audible stream of monotonous, indifferent curses would challenge the heat's supremacy.

Mr. Farbstein, too, was groaning—but not so self-consciously; rather as a grotesque elaboration of his breathing. Several times he had wakened suddenly, as a troubled sentry might. At those moments he would peer forward until, seemingly, he had comprehended the whole of Artie's diminished being. Mrs. Farbstein returned. He spoke to her for a few moments, raising and lowering the catalogue page in his hand. Mrs. Farbstein nodded and smiled. Then she put her hand subtly, but quite firmly, on his wrist. The page struggled, fluttering. Finally it ceased to move. Soon after, Mr. Farbstein went to sleep.

The Lopopulos entered, making cheerful noises, noises of resolute enthusiasm. They carried colorful toys and books and things mysteriously wrapped. But Artie at once increased his already elaborate show of pain—until the noises were dulled and the books and boxes hardly colorful at all. His lewd, half-naked body had an instantaneous effect on Mrs. Lopopulo. When his placket bulged open, she took Maureen by the armpit and led her to the solarium. Since Tuesday's altercation, Sidney hadn't made an appearance at Cavendish.

Jimmy asked if I'd like to join his family. I said I was too tired. The bones in my hands were sprinkled with little, blue pains. I lacked strength to expend on simple coordination: several times I strained myself in carrying out the most inconsequential movements. Moreover, I had begun to think of breathing as a conscious and voluntary physical process—the in-

flating of the lungs, the pushing upward against my ribs, the
almost stifling collapse—each a separate and decisive effort.
Mrs. Lopopulo came in to repeat the invitation. I was thankful
then for my exhaustion.

Expressions of breath—painful, resigned, questioning, bitter.
Expressions of breath measured out the evening. A fat tanker
moved irresistibly downstream, confident in its own buoyancy.
Row after row of lights flashed on across the river in New Jersey. The night became thick with industrial smells. I compelled myself to watch the coming of night. I knew—though
as yet I couldn't believe—I knew that, but for Dr. Snow and his
art, my days and nights, dawns and sunsets, were growing swiftly
together, becoming a single, homogeneous thing.

"Please keep your shorts up, Mr. Carson. There are other
people in the room." Nurse MacArthur took Artie's waistline
firmly between thumb and forefinger and jerked it up. Artie
groaned. Then he said something suggestive that infuriated
me.

Nurse MacArthur was gone again. Gone and back. Gone
again. My sleeping pill was on the table, and I hadn't had a
single chance to speak with her: to tell her of my fast-growing
allegiance to Dr. Snow, to make her understand that I, at last,
was one with them. I took my pill and turned out the
light above my bed.

*Lord God my Father, have mercy upon me. Tear me, mortify
me, humble me—not only before Thee, but also before those
here about me. I begin to wonder—wonder that I just now
begin—what validity my writing can have. Where is the source
of its truth? Not here. Surely not within me.*

Send, I pray, Thy Comforter unto all those here who are in sorrow, need, sickness and suffering. Not for my sake, but for the sake of Thy Son, Jesus Christ, who rose from the dead—who rose from the dead—for our redemption. And especially I ask Thee to shed Thy Grace and Love on little Jimmy and Mr. Farbstein. And on Artie—Arthur Carson . . .

I suppose I dreamed it. Once, late in the night, it seemed that I started suddenly awake. Instinctively, I turned my eyes toward the blackness beyond my window. There, disembodied in the glass, I saw a shrunken, laughing head. P. Crecy's head. All that while he had been looking deep inside my sleeping body. I closed my eyes. I capitulated.

FRIDAY, AUGUST 18TH—

THE FIFTH DAY

"Is THAT so? Good. Fine. Eat it yourself, then. It smells like camel dung t'me—camel dung. Y'ever smell camel dung? No? Well, y'missed something. God-damn smell's made me sick twice already. Get it off my table. Now—now, friend. I know when I can eat, and when I can't eat."

I woke up. I woke up after rotating for days on a huge and circular white marble smorgasbord. Chained there, I think. And all around the circumference—grouped like silent mourners at a wake—lay gravely interested piles of food. They were friendly; they were compassionate. The quizzical, bloodshot eyes of eggs *a la Russe*. Brownish-yellow frogs' legs standing upright, splayed and torsoless. White celery implicit of succulent sounds. Thick roquefort dressing and mustards; black caviar and horseradish. Camel dung . . . And I was awake.

"Stupid woman. Stupid, Puerto Rican bitch. It's no skin off her tits. 'What's this, Mr. Carson. No breakfast today? Shame on you. Shame, shame. Don't you want to get better? All that nice food.' Nice? You know what that egg smelled like? Rancid butter—I mean rancid—like on the inside of a garbage can cover."

"Good morning, Mister Belknap."

"Jimmy," I said. I nodded and cleared my throat. My jaw was tilted upward at an uncomfortable angle: the moist heat that radiated from my throat, from my chest, had been making my eyes water. The mattress design had begun to appear through my sodden sheet. My arms quivered beneath the weight of my torso. I had to let myself down on one shoulder, my back turned against the vivid glare of the morning's light.

"It's all like that." There was silence. "It all tastes like dung. Hard and soft. Sweet and sour. It's all like that. I got nothing to live for. I'm so thin—when I chew, I eat my own lips. I got a big sore on the side of my mouth. Here."

"What did you have?"

"A sore. Here." He stuck his forefinger in his mouth.

"No. For breakfast."

"Usual stuff. Cold toast. Cold egg. Cold coffee. Usual revolting mess. How come you sleep in this black hole of what's its name?" He stared at the ceiling. "Damn gnawing pain. Right here." He squeezed his left lower rib cage and the area immediately beneath it. "Right here. Night and day. Night and day. I lay on my side, and I lay with my legs up. No dice. It's not even here, where they cut me. That feels pretty good. Unnngh. Unnnnngh. Damn. Friggin' heat is terrible. Terrible." He made a vulgar sound as breath burst through his slack lips.

There was a hair on my tongue. I took my thumb and my forefinger and plucked furtively at it. Then I sucked the insides of my mouth in onto my tongue. Still there. Artie was watching me. Jimmy was watching me. I tried to ignore the hair, but I couldn't. With what I imagined was a graceful, an offhand gesture, I pinched my tongue. It was still there. I paused for a moment, I pretended that my pillow case needed rearranging, but Artie and Jimmy were full of patience. Finally I took the nail of my forefinger and dug it painfully down the length of my tongue.

"Got a hair on your tongue, huh?"

"Uh," I said. I took a tissue from my box on the table.

"I wouldn't use that," said Artie. Ignoring him, I wrapped my tongue in the tissue and then pulled downwards. The tissue disintegrated into wet shreds that stuck to my tongue and lips.

"See. Can't use Kleenex for that. Not strong enough. Use the bed sheet, something sturdy. Hair on your tongue is Goddamn annoying. But you can't get it off with Kleenex."

I lay back and began to work shamelessly at the inside of my open mouth. What had he said? Cold toast. Cold egg. Nice, cold egg. I chewed a piece of tissue, and my stomach, teased to wariness by the motion, spat like an irritated cat. I wiped the sweat from my throat, and then sucked the salt avidly from the tips of my fingers.

"Think I'm gettin' a bed sore. Damn sweat makes my ass slide down. Can't sit up right." He cleared his throat into a piece of tissue. It wasn't sufficient; phlegm poured through his fingers. "You havin' trouble breathin'? Oxygen. That's what we all need. Oxygen's the stuff in this heat. No sense wastin' it on me, though. A year maybe, that's all. No more than that. A year."

I smiled at Artie, but he hadn't been looking at me just then. I was grateful for that. My smile degenerated into an expression of disgust. I followed the bandage as it rode giddily up and down on his yellow stomach. I saw the patch of hair under his arm open, close, open like a little fan. And all the while he talked. Sometimes he would waken suddenly in the midst of a confused sentence; sometimes he would answer "yes, yes," to no

apparent question. I folded the hot, wet pillow up over my
ears. I pretended to doze.

   John Titus Porter . . . Once, soon after I had been ordained
—the first November after, I think—he had cupped my elbow
in his hand and said, "This you must see. It'll do your heart
good." I'd been warned about John Titus, but I was trying to
be very patient in those days, and so I went with him anyway.
"He'll get you there," said Duncan Worth, who was my mentor
in all things for about a month. "He'll get you there. And you
won't feel compassion for anyone but yourself."
   John Titus' sister, Claire, operated a nominally Christian
soup kitchen not far from the junction of Hester and Elizabeth
Streets in the Bowery. The sister's face, as I remember it now,
had been etched at some time by a vicious case of acne.
She hadn't been beautiful before: Claire's was a face that hung
exactly poised between that which becomes a man and that
which becomes a woman. There was a thin mist of black hair
on her cheeks and upper lip. The line of her jawbone un-
balanced her face as a modern frame might disconcert a
medieval painting. When she grasped my hand, I instinctively
took a step forward to relieve the pressure. Then Claire
smiled. Her teeth were a fence of glossy Chiclets, and the front
two were separated by a large gap. Yet it was both grotesque
and really pleasant. She smiled, and I knew from the way in
which that ugly gap revealed itself, that the smile was meant
as a smile and nothing more.
   Claire set us to making soup in a little cubicle at the rear of
the store. "Put the roaches on a separate plate," she said.
"They make great *hors d'oeuvres.*" Then she slapped her hands

together noisily and loped out to the front. John Titus shook his head in an emphatic show of disbelief, but I couldn't see what had made him so incredulous. Claire was nervous. She was on intimate terms with her own ugliness; she knew very well that John Titus had brought me down as a prospective gentleman caller. I felt sorry for her. And so I laughed about the roaches, and chopped the potatoes and the onions, and pretended I didn't know why I'd been brought there.

Claire said it was time to go in. John Titus and I lifted the heavy, steaming cauldron between us and staggered out to the front. As we entered, I heard a creaking and a sort of thickened sigh—ten or fifteen degenerates were rising uncertainly from folding chairs and boxes. I helped John Titus place the cauldron on the table; then I stepped backward. The far side of the longish room was fronted by a shattered plate-glass window that had been patched with squares of cardboard. I could make out the letters Y CLEAN where the glass remained whole. They posed a valid question. Claire had swept up as well as could be expected, but there was yet need of paint and plaster and light. The smell of alcohol and urine, not, evidently, a transient guest, compelled me to run my hand thoughtfully up and down over the bridge of my nose.

Claire had begun the serving. She was lifting huge spoonfuls of soup from the cauldron with an awkward, semicircular motion. John Titus had gone to the rear of the store to get the first of the tall piles of bread that we had prepared. The sounds of working, toothless mouths reached my ears—a host of invisible insects rubbing together soft parts of their bodies in sensual satisfaction. The room was dark but for two naked bulbs that straddled the table. I stood, tall and uncooperative, in the shadows—watching as Claire's great, good shoulders swung soup from cauldron to plate, from cauldron to plate; watching, as she spoke with undiscouraged cheerfulness to one after another of the abysmally uncomprehending faces.

And then a subway passed, rumbling beneath the store. My knees vibrated and buckled, so that I wondered how the rotted floor and walls could withstand the tremor. "Damn earthquake," I said, and I laughed—but no one seemed to hear. On and on the subway rumbled, its sound in my ears and in the bones of the mastoid behind my ears. My stomach contracted and rose up behind my ribs; I became terribly nauseated. And yet, no one else seemed to notice; the bums came to the table, they received their bread and soup and moved away. Sweat appeared on the backs of my hands; it filled my clenched fists. I knew then. No subway. No subway at all.

Claire turned to me once and smiled. John Titus returned with another plate of bread. As he put it on the table, he glanced surreptitiously from Claire to me and back again. My legs had worked themselves into another spasm of instability. I hoped that Claire wouldn't see them. John Titus smiled, then he winked. This is the woman for a priest, he seemed to be saying. And the insect bodies rubbed their parts together harder, louder. Dirty fingers made sucking noises when held against moist, cracked lips. A tiny dripping sound: without apology, a bum urinated into his pants leg as he ate. I couldn't breathe. My senses deadened themselves defensively. I pressed my arms to my chest, my hands into my abdomen, my eyes to the floor. My circle of reference began to contract. It sealed out the bums; it sealed out Claire; it sealed out John Titus. And, over and over again, I repeated to myself, *"Oh Lord, make clean our hearts within us and take not Thy Holy Spirit from us. Oh Lord, make clean our hearts within us and take not Thy . . ."*

"Whitney? Would you get that last plate of bread? If

we don't watch, the roaches'll get it. Four of them to a slice. It's the ugly truth. One at each corner. I've seen them do it."

I nodded stupidly and then hurried out through the door. There was one tall stack of bread left, and it was wavering backward and forward in a vaguely circular motion. "It's going to fall," I said. "Good God, it's going to fall." I almost wept at my own helplessness, but the stack of bread wasn't wavering at all. And, instead, I fell forward onto the stool in front of the table. I sat before that stack of bread like an idolator before a strange and awesome idol. Then I bowed my head and gripped the edges of the table, until I felt tiny splinters of wood edging themselves beneath my fingernails. I bowed to the idol and swore that nothing on earth or beyond earth would make me enter that room again. *Lord God my Father, strike me dead now. Now. Now. Now.*

"I see. You've decided not to bring my bread." There was a hand on my shoulder. I took my mind by the corners and folded it one way and then another way and then another. And when I was precisely sure it would fit into the palm of my hand, I turned slowly toward her.

"No," I said. "I'm not going to bring it. They're too many for me."

And then, with sounds of astonishment, I began retching on the floor. Her feet and my feet suggested a little square into which my yellow vomit spattered. I sucked air in, I bit my mouth closed, but I could not control the convulsions. And so I shrugged my shoulders and retched again, banging my fists against my knees as I did. Claire carried the stack of bread into the meeting room. She returned at once, closing the door behind her. Then she got a mop and a pail. I was bringing up only tiny mouthsful now, but to the tune of great, shameful, hollow sounds. Claire pulled the plug out of the sink, and the drain accompanied my grotesque agony.

When I had done, Claire set about cleaning up my mess without a word. I made a few gestures of apology, but vomit held no great mystery for Claire. As I watched in inarticulate misery, I realized that I was deeply thankful for Claire's ugliness. I would have been shamed beyond redemption before any other woman. Claire poured disinfectant onto the floor. She got down on her knees and scrubbed it in with a rag.

"What can I do?" I said. "It just comes. I can't control it."

"Do? What about, Padre?"

"They disgust me, Claire. They smell, and I don't like things that smell. Damned rotted faces. Damned scaly skin. What can I do?" She laughed.

"Nobody'd blame you much, I guess. They're a pretty revolting bunch, if I do say so myself. I wouldn't worry."

"You wouldn't. No. But I'm in the wrong profession, and I'm in it under false pretenses. That's only too obvious." I put my head in my hands. I wanted her sympathy.

"Take a look at me. Please. Over here." I raised my head. Claire was grinning. Her untractable hair hung in wild and rigid coils about her forehead. On the left side, her ear was clearly visible through the wiry mesh. It had a tremendous lobe, and I could see that the lobe had been pierced at one time. But there was no earring: her one adventure in affectation had left only a rubbery, ugly hole. "Can you see me? Poor kid. A guy I once loved said my face was an emetic. Pre-med student. I didn't know what emetics were then." She raised her hand. "But you were going to say, 'Beauty is only skin deep. People love you, Claire. Your soul is great and pure.' Well, maybe. Only, if it's great and pure, it's great and pure because

I was born looking like a horse." She came over and sat easily
on the table's edge, both feet flat on the floor.

"Why—why say that?"

"I'm not fishing for compliments. There's a moral. I hoped
it'd help you—otherwise I wouldn't have gone and embarrassed
you this way. I have embarrassed you, haven't I?" I shook my
head, but she had. There was still some of my vomit on the tips
of her shoes, and I was afraid she'd get it on my pants cuff. I
moved my leg. "So I'm good with revolting people? Is it any
wonder? I used to keep toads when I was a kid. By the time I
was six or seven, I'd caught on I wasn't going to be a raving
beauty. A bit later I knew I'd be a mess. Guess I didn't want
to be a mess. Who does? So I set out to find pots that wouldn't
dare call the kettle black. And I found them. They're all over
—it wasn't hard. I'm at home here, but I find nothing to be
proud of." She was silent for a moment. "John's proud for me,
but he wouldn't believe it, if I told him the truth. He says it's
God's love. I don't know. Maybe it's more God's stomach.
God's cowardice." She flicked her finger at a lentil that lay on
the table.

"No matter," I said. "Whatever you say—and I don't believe
it either—whatever you say, it won't exonerate me."

"Why not? Why the hell not? Look at you. Just look. You're
beautiful. The best-looking man John's brought down here yet.
And he's brought down a whole hope chest full. What have you
got to do with those things in there? Nothing. Nothing at all.
Forget about it."

I shook my head, but not in denial. Claire placed her hand
across the middle of my back—a great, squarish, heavy weight
like that of a flat-iron.

"I guess those poor souls in there are pretty spectacular.

Really impressive—like nuns gulping down swodges of phlegm. I suppose, as a priest, you figure they're your special business. I don't think so. Like all spectacular things, Whitney, they're the least important in the long run. Most of our Protestant Christians are in a lot better shape, I should hope. They're the ones who can still do things. They need your guidance. For the rest, soup is enough."

"But I don't care for any of them—clean or dirty. Respectable or degenerate." She laughed.

"But you seem to be worried about it, Padre; so maybe there's hope for you. Whatever you do, don't push it; stop testing yourself. Tiptoe up on your problems when they haven't their wits about them. It'll work itself out. Come on, let's take a walk."

And so, for more than an hour, we walked round and round the block. Claire clapped her arm over my shoulders in a particularly boyish manner. She was nearly as tall as I, and her breadth of shoulder was immense. The conversation was pointedly innocuous. She didn't want me to think her arm was drawing warmth and hope out of my back. And I matched her tone exactly—though, secretly, I wanted to say, "Claire, there's disgusting, dried vomit on your shoes." Then, in reaction, I would decide to make a pass at her when again we reached the corner. But I didn't. Claire had comforted me by saying everything that I had hoped she would say, and, for that reason, I think, I was both bitter and suspicious.

John Titus, in the time we were out, had smoked at least a dozen cigarettes. He was filled with good humor: evidently, he thought Claire and I had hit it off famously. In one sense, I suppose, we had. In the other and more important sense, I knew that I would never see Claire again, that John Titus and I would drift further and further apart. And so it was. That night I walked home alone. Behind me I left a test that I had failed finally and forever.

Mr. Farbstein was having his hair cut. He was sitting upright, a white towel wrapped cloak-fashion around his shoulders. His eyes were dull and immensely protuberant, his skin the color of flaked, yellow callouses. But, by then, I had come to have more faith in Dr. Snow's miracle. The picture lay in his lap. Whenever hair from the scissors showered onto it, Mr. Farbstein would worry the paper until it was clean again. After a moment he said something to the barber, a coffee-tan Puerto Rican, and the barber leaned close three or four times in order to hear what he was saying. Evidently he was unsuccessful, for he turned to Artie and made a circular motion near his own ear with the closed points of the scissors. Barbered, Mr. Farbstein had begun to look like a stupid little boy, and the smile that pushed irresolutely at the corners of his mouth was, I thought, a smile of mindless mischief.

Jimmy was arranging his things, as, it seemed, he did every morning. He had just taken a shower. Little drops of water, augmented by the sweat that was already forming, made sudden forays out of his crew-cut scalp. I smiled when he turned his back. Then I smiled at my own secret approval. Jimmy stood solemnly, one hand gripping the lapel of his bathrobe. He put a yellow comic beneath a green comic, fulfilling an order known only to himself. After a moment he nodded, as though acknowledging the justness of that order.

A blowing sound. Another. Another. Artie addressed a question to the room. Jimmy turned to face him, but Artie didn't

seem to require Jimmy's ministrations. I deliberately kept my
head turned away from his bed. Artie disgusted me; perversely,
moreover, he refused to notice my revulsion. Each time our
eyes met, I was compelled to speak to him for whole minutes—
those were the rules of our unpleasant game. I was determined,
the next time I met Dr. Snow, to have Artie transferred out of
our room.

An orderly brought the newspapers. I opened the drawer of
my bed table and, as I always did, took out fifteen cents for the
New York Times. I lay back wearily with the newspaper,
square and barely heavy, across my abdomen. As I lay there,
regular patterns took form, one after the other, in my mind: a
garden with flower beds; a window with twelve panes, three by
four; a row of teeth. But one of the teeth was missing. And, as
I thought back, I realized, with a growing sense of apprehension, that one of the panes of glass, too, was gone. The garden
. . . The garden was my bed table drawer. I sat up and threw
the paper aside. Pious still sat in his picture; his tail was still
curled around him. It was the drawer. Something that wasn't
in the garden wasn't in the drawer.

I smoothed my hair. I pressed it down. I released my foot
from the folds of the sheet. Then I leaned over the edge of the
drawer. A wallet. Two handkerchiefs. A tube of toothpaste.
I put the cap on the toothpaste. A sample bottle of hair tonic.
Three ball-point pens and a pencil. A book of crossword puzzles. A book of hospital games for pre-teens. Some change.
Two paper clips. The manuscript of a book . . . I closed the
drawer. Then I lay back on the bed and put my hands over my
face. I think I said, "Good God in heaven."

It was gone. I pulled the drawer open again. Quickly and
then more quickly, I drove my fingers through its meager con-

tents. Nothing. I looked amongst the books on my table.
I grabbed at my throat. It wasn't there. I said it out loud then.
I said, "That God-damned rabbit's foot is gone."

"What's that, Whit?"

"Nothing, Artie. Nothing." You'll suffer for this. Mark my
words. You'll suffer good. You'll wish you'd died two weeks
ago.

"Say, you never told me. What d'you do for a living?"

"I'm a bishop." Sarah'll come with a cup of tea, and you'll
have to tell her it's gone. Gone. Then she'll shake all over and
melt on the floor like chocolate pudding, like a vampire in the
sunlight. There'll be a terrible smell. Oh, you'll suffer good.

"A pisser? I'll say you're a pisser."

"No. Not a pisser. A bishop. Churches and things, you
know." How could you let it happen? Four generations of black
priests fought a civil war over that foot. And you had to lose it.
You came along after four generations and lost it. Oh,
yes. Your suffering will be an exquisite thing.

"A bishop?" I knew, without having to see, that Artie had
pushed himself up on one elbow. "A bishop? You gotta be
pullin' my leg."

"No, I'm not," I said, but, far inside my mind, I was wringing my knuckles and screaming in long, even shrieks.

"Hey? You hear what I said?"

"You took it, didn't you?" I hissed. I made menacing gestures with my fist and my teeth.

"Holy Cow. Holy Jesus cow. Don't do anything you'll regret.
I apologized. How could I know?" He whined. "Nobody tells
me nothin'. How could I know, Whit? Huh? Huh? Be fair. I
can't take it back. I apologized—it's the best a man can
do. Don't get outa bed. Don't. I'm a sick man."

"What, in the name of confusion and holy chaos, are you gib-
bering about?"

"Look, Whit—I'm sorry I been talkin' like this. I didn't
mean no disrespect. You gotta believe that." He lay back, as if
it were the last apology he'd ever make. "I got a damn filthy
mouth. If it's any consolation, it used to drive my father nuts,
too. He'd give me his high, hard one just about any time
I opened my trap. My brother never talked that way. You still
mad? Christ o'mighty. If I'd known you were a bishop—hey!
You're smilin'. You're puttin' me on, ain't you? You *are* a
pisser, you old son of a bitch. You had me creamin' in my pants
over here."

"Mister Belknap is a bishop," said Jimmy, as though he had
just made me one.

"No foolin'? A bishop? Hey kid, is he mad at me?"

I had been very distressed. I had taken the rabbit's foot from
the table—I had held it in my right hand—and then I had
thrown it into the open drawer. I remembered clearly, because
P. Crecy was watching, and so I, too, was compelled to watch.
Perhaps, though, I had missed the drawer . . . I hung over the
edge of the bed and looked down through the springs. Nothing. It was nearly mid-day. Only five more hours until Sarah
brought my cup of tea.

"Drop something?"

"Nothing. No." I fell back, my biceps and fingers numb
from the strain.

"Don't you get nothing to eat, Whit?"

"No."

"Special diet?"

"Yes."

"Hungry, huh?"

"Yes."

"Look. Tell you what—I can't get food down nohow. What say, I pass you a few things? Just to tide you over?"

"No. Thanks."

"On your honor, huh?"

"On my honor."

"Gotta watch the cholesterol, huh? Tough. Okay, Whit— whatever you say. It's just, you look kinda down in the mouth. Piss cuttin' heat don't help. Ain't it somethin'? Me, I can't eat. Tons of food. You, you're starvin'. Nothing. That's the way they run this friggin' place."

Lord God, my heavenly Father, Father of all the world, let me not cause anxiety to yet another of Thy children. And then I thought that, weak heart or no weak heart, I would leave Cavendish rather than face Sarah. I would leave the hospital and walk crosstown on Seventy-Ninth Street in my wrinkled pajamas and red, pomponned slippers. The world came, with a smile on its face, and poked into my little corner. It involved itself with me, and then it was dead. At that moment, God forgive me, I thought of telling Dr. Snow to fire Sarah before five o'clock. I am a sinner and I am a coward—but, after all, he intended to fire her anyway . . .

I saw him at once. I saw him before he entered our room. Dr. Snow waved. It struck me as an incongruous gesture even then. He nodded to Mr. Farbstein and winked playfully at Jimmy. Jimmy frowned into his lap. Artie hailed him, and Dr. Snow spoke with sympathetic interest for several minutes. Dr. Snow was wearing glasses for the first time. I thought he looked weary as he came toward me. The gray at his temples seemed a manifestation of age, no longer of awesome dignity. Standing before me in his long, white coat, he resembled nothing more substantial than a tired high school biology teacher. But, even so, I sat up immediately, my muscles—especially the muscles of my face—setting themselves in expectation. I pulled the wet sheet up over my lap.

He didn't speak at once. Dr. Snow stood near the window, his head bowed—as though he disapproved of what he saw, but was impotent before it. And then, as the sun glinted across his right temple, I saw that there were drops of sweat, like little warts, above the dark frames of his glasses. I announced that fact to my consciousness: Dr. Snow is sweating, I said. I found the thought oddly disturbing.

"How are you feeling today?" His eyes seemed disciplined, docile behind the frames of his glasses.

"Well. I'm hot and, even more than that, I'm hungry. The rest, I hope, you know better than I do."

"Yes," he said, "it's hot."

He raised his eyebrows for permission, and then sat on the edge of my bed. In deference, I moved my legs far to the side of the mattress. Dr. Snow's lovely hands were buried in the pockets of his coat, but I could see the backs of his fingers rippling beneath the white material—as though they were being forcefully subdued. An unpleasant coolness daubed my face at the nose and the temples and the cheekbones. As it did so, I became instantly alert. Dr. Snow was going to tell me something—something he had difficulty articulating. I knew what that was. My heart exploded softly in my chest. Dr. Snow was about to pronounce my imminent death.

"Dr. Snow . . ." It was a preface to nothing. He looked up at me, and I saw in his eyes such abysmal depths of despair and, I think, fear, that I almost tore the sheets from my legs. But

Dr. Snow was sitting on the sheets. Sitting, his hands now
balled into fists inside his pockets. Slowly they subsided into
flatness.

"I know how difficult it is, Whitney. By now you must be
nearly desperate."

"That's nothing. But my heart—I mean, I have a responsibility to others. I've got to know what plans to make.
Whether to finish my book now. Whether to prepare my office
for someone else. Whether to make my peace . . ." I trailed
off there. Now Dr. Snow was watching as his fingertips rose
against the lining of his pocket—like bubbles in thick soup.
"My peace," I said.

"What am I to do?" he asked.

"That's up to you, of course. I'm not interfering or trying to
pressure you—far from it. I only ask to know, if I might, what
you've decided. If you haven't decided yet—well, of course,
that's an entirely different matter. Entirely different." Dr.
Snow sighed.

"You don't understand. You're worried about your heart.
Of course. I know how it is. We've put you at a terrible disadvantage here. Two on one. You're confused, aren't you?" He
put his hand on my knee: perhaps he found a reflex; perhaps he
merely surprised me. My leg jumped, and we both smiled.

"Confused? How do you mean?"

"Let me try to tell you. I'd like to change places with you for
a while. To try, anyway. I need some help. At least I think I
do."

I had to believe him. After all, I'm a bishop, and many kinds
of men have sought me out in their need. Dr. Snow's forehead
was wet; his right hand was cupped over my shin just below the
knee; perspiration had caused the lower portions of his lenses
to mist. He had, quite effortlessly, become an object of pity.

"What can I do?" I asked. Dr. Snow hesitated. I thought he was uncertain whether or not to trust me. Then he took his hand from my leg and balled it into a fist.

"It's a little matter of intolerance, Whitney. Not exactly in your line. Still interested?"

"Yes."

"You don't mind? I've got to warn you—I'll probably be very unpleasant today, tomorrow, the day after. Whenever the reaction sets in. I don't like to lose the upper hand."

"You've lost nothing," I said. "But go on." I lay, a pillar of strength, waiting to understand and to forgive.

"I will then. I think you probably suspected something yesterday—when I tried to make you change rooms. It was a test. Forgive me. I think I wanted your tacit complicity in my intolerance—for whatever that was worth. I'd just read your book. It disturbed me. I jumped at the chance to experiment in less theoretical circumstances. And you passed. As far as I can judge, you passed my test with the proverbial flying colors. Why? That intrigues me. Why? There is, after all, a certain parallelism. Why should you have patience? Why should you be kind to people—inferior sorts of people—when I can barely bring myself to speak to them? And Sarah Samson, too—she most of all. Why? We're the same age. We went to the same schools. We were brought up on the same side of the city. We're of the same religious and national backgrounds. We both —I think you'll agree—we are both extremely attractive men, and all that that entails. At any rate, it puzzled me, still puzzles me. But, so much for my bad manners of yesterday."

Artie spat thickly. A private room; a test. It had been a close thing. I dug my fingers into the mattress. So much for the firing of Sarah Samson. So much for Artie Carson's transfer. The face on the back of my little book smiled down at me. I took the smile and presented it, intact, to Dr. Snow. Dr. Snow accepted it without question. Then he was speaking again.

"There's a passage in your book—" He took up *A God For Our Time* and found the page he wanted almost immediately. " 'Material progress is gained, it would seem, in a direct ratio to the amount of outworn illusions destroyed. This has been the experience of the last hundred years and no one, I think, much doubts its validity. We have learned that there is nothing in human life that cannot be questioned—not physical laws, not personal autonomy, not, most certainly, the existence of God. Indeed, the question of whether God exists or not has become rather remote of late, and fewer and fewer minds are interested even in considering it. Those who consider and accept are at a loss to communicate. They wonder, with far more candor than the Jews of the Old Testament, why they have been chosen as God's so very special people.

" 'There is one thing, however, that cannot be questioned—and that one thing is Love. Love in lower case and love with a capital L. It's possible to doubt the existence of Love in specific circumstances, but it is not possible to doubt its efficacy, its loveliness as a concept, or its immense potential for good. Love can be questioned, but only in the act of spiritual self-annihilation. There is, I'm well aware, a great deal of difference between selfish and unselfish love. But the former—the love of a mindless infant, of a lonely teen-age girl, of an ego finding pleasure in the contemplation of itself—is real evidence of the latter and greater manifestation. Evidence that the very lowliest of us is intimate with; evidence that, in spite of its meanness, leads to a universal whose purity cannot be questioned. Whether or not we can call it, happily enough, the Love of God—it is still the be-all and the end-all of any significant life. And there is, I think, no one on earth who doubts that this is true.' " Dr. Snow put my book down. "I'll grant you that premise. It's granted. But, tell me, you who are blessed with the ability to love up and down the ladder—what do the rest of us do? Yearn? Eat our hearts out? What?"

Whitney studied hard, she said. And Peter, standing in front of the class, watched as she tore up his paper. Whitney did his studying. He's first in the class because he's curious and imaginative and hard working. And, sure as anything, you stole from him. You ought to be ashamed of yourself. And I looked stealthily at Roger St. Cloud from whose paper I had copied three answers and part of a fourth, while Peter, unbeknownst to me, had been copying from my paper. I want you to apologize to the class, she said, and I want you, most of all, to apologize to Whitney. Peter came, broken and afraid, to apologize. And I forgave him. With a good grace and a winning manner, I forgave him.

Dr. Snow paused. He expected me to say something, but I had been better trained than that. Specifics. Personal specifics. I didn't want to distract Dr. Snow before he had committed himself decisively. Then I could afford the inevitable polemics; the seemingly plausible, seemingly unassailable arguments that are available to even the least capable atheist. And so I merely stared at him with an interested and slightly ironic expectation. Finally he spoke. I will make you fishers of men.

"Let's face it, Whitney—surgery militates against any simple and sentimental sense of human dignity. You know what a heart feels like? No? Well, let me tell you, beauty is only skin deep. I have difficulty considering anyone as more than just a complex of organs. It's not a morbid reaction—in fact, I think it's rather abstract. It arouses my sense of the ridiculous more often than my disgust. But here I am—like a man who knows how all women look when they get up in the morning. Only worse. Much worse." He smiled sadly. Then he was silent for a moment. "What can I do? I'm asking you because I feel you're a special Christian—a scientific Christian. One who understands me as a necessary outgrowth of the age. One who isn't horrified by the mere fact of my existence." He raised his hand. "And please, Whitney. Nothing about your Jesus Christ or your penitence or your God's great mercy. I'm not ready for that yet. I wouldn't want you to disappoint me."

"Have no fear," I said cheerfully. "I know better than that." I lay there, silent again, goading him with my complacency. The secret, I knew, lay in never becoming either indignant or impressed. The effect, then, is miraculous: contrite sinners rally to the defense of their sins; they dredge up their worst acts—acts often merely contemplated and then only once; they exaggerate and they embroider; then they present them strictly for their shock value. And now Dr. Snow was watching my face. He seemed uncertain whether to let his left hand rise out of his pocket. He decided not to. I was excited. I found my breath coming in short, hard puffs.

"I'm in a unique position, Whitney. You'll understand what I mean in a minute." Dr. Snow took off his glasses and wiped them clean with a corner of my sheet. Then he ran the sheet across his forehead and readjusted his glasses. He seemed uncomfortable with them on. "In case you hadn't heard, I'm one of the three or four greatest surgeons in America. That's considering technical prowess alone. Beyond that, I'm, without serious exception, the most influential intellect in medicine today. When I die, if I die, I'll have an obituary five pages long in every medical journal in the world. As you might expect, my

services are in demand. As you might also expect, I can ask my
price. I do ask my price." He paused. "Now, tell me, what's
your idea of a good doctor? A man who charges only according
to means? Makes house calls in the slums? Licks lepers? Op-
erates for nothing? No opinions? Very tactful, I must say. Well,
then. Let's see—maybe you'd be surprised to know that I've
never once operated out of compassion. Never once, and I
doubt if I ever will. I have a set fee and, if that fee isn't met,
I won't even consider operating. Farbstein met my fee.
Lopopulo, too, though I think," he nodded with patent satisfaction, "I think the operation will probably break him. And
that derelict? He's got a rich brother who's trying to buy off
his conscience. I've done my best by all of them. And my best,
Whitney, is very good. There are things I can do that no other
surgeon on earth can do."

Dr. Snow's voice was still subdued. He spoke with a gentle-
ness that belied the context of what he had said. I found that,
in spite of my resolve, I was becoming indignant. I didn't want
to say anything. I knew I was on uncertain ground. My silence
implied a secret complicity. I rearranged my hips, and that
strange coolness came again to touch my face.

"Not shocked? Not even impressed? You're an interesting
man. I guess I don't really understand you." He paused and
then took a deep breath. "Well, then—maybe I can go a bit
further. Would you be surprised to know that I've never once
—never once—operated on a Negro? Never once even examined a Negro? I operate on Jews. Yes, I do. But I'm not happy
about it. Most of my colleagues are Jewish, and anti-Semitism
doesn't sit well with them. But take a Jew with money and a
Wasp, like yourself, with money—give me the choice, and I'll
always take the Wasp. Always. Why not?" He was challenging

me. He said, "Why not?" again, and then he stood up. He
towered over my head. I think he knew by then how cautious
I was being. He wanted me to say something, anything. And
I did. It came out as nothing more than a question, certainly
not an indictment. A question. But that was all he needed.

"You can't control your emotions?" I said. "So? I wouldn't
worry. You're not exactly the first man who's discovered that.
What gets me—and, no doubt, it's because I'm not a doctor
—what gets me is that you have no compunctions about opening up a human body. I, for one, would find that more revolting than a man's skullcap or his black skin. After all, if you can
put your hand into any man's bowels, you should be able to put
a hand into a black man's bowels. If not out of compassion,
then out of indifference—out of the most abstract sense of
justice."

Dr. Snow nodded and smiled. Then he removed both hands
from his pockets. They flew out and upward like a pair of caged
birds, and, in each, there was an envelope. Dr. Snow put the
envelopes on the adjustable table in front of me. Then he removed his glasses, and put them in his pocket. Somewhere in
the basement, a great machine began working, perhaps the hospital generator. A low, dull vibration rumbled up through the
floor.

"I'm glad you said that. Would you mind very much if I
made you judge in a semi-hypothetical situation? A situation
I have to face—in one form or another—every day of my life?
I'm curious to know how a sophisticated Christian would deal
with it. Are you willing?" I nodded, but my nod was
only barely perceptible.

"Good. Well, then—let me give you all the facts. To begin
with, I'm a very busy man. I'm up at four every morning. I

work on my papers until six. By six-thirty I'm here at the hospital. After that, I operate or prepare to operate for literally hours on end, with three rooms working simultaneously—assistants doing whatever work doesn't require my special attention. So far today, for instance, I did three endarterectomies; three valve replacements—two aortic, one mitral; two abdominal aneurysms; and one mitral commissurotomy. Six more operations are being prepared at this moment. After I've finished operating I have letters to dictate and calls to make—endless calls. I'm chairman of the Senate Commission, chairman of the Cardiac Research Society of America, president and founder of the American Foundation for Surgical Research, editor and publisher of *Surgery Symposium*—to mention just a few. I keep five secretaries constantly at work. Each operation requires a week to two weeks of preparation and extensive study. I can work no harder than I am working at present. I can accept no more patients than I have. Time. There's the problem."

Dr. Snow hesitated. Sweat hung from every projection on my face—my nose, my chin, the lobes of my ears. I had difficulty breathing. The heat had transformed the air into a gaseous suspension containing tiny, harsh grains of some unknown substance. And yet I knew I'd have to remain alert. I looked up at Dr. Snow, and, when I did, my hand closed violently on the fleshy part of my thigh. I almost said it out loud, "He's stopped —he's stopped sweating."

"All right, then. Let's suppose—again for the sake of our hypothesis—let's suppose that a prospective patient suddenly drops dead. As a result, Operating Room C is freed for a certain period of time on a certain day. These envelopes contain two letters taken at random. At any given period of time there are anywhere from thirty to fifty such applications. But two, I think, are sufficient to make the point. One," he picked up an envelope, "is from a male Negro in Seaford, Maryland. He has an aortic deformity which limits his ability to work—he moves things. He has six children and no money. But you can read that for yourself. The other," he hesitated, "the other is, I think, from a little girl. Perhaps it's her mother—no, I remember now: it's the little girl writing about her mother. A melodramatic gesture. I doubt if it's the first time they've approached me. I forget what the mother's condition is, but she, too, is without funds. You can be sure of that." Dr. Snow stared out of the window for a moment. His hands performed an intricate maneuver, and, as they did so, I imagined that the generator's hum had deepened.

"Remember now. There's only one vacancy. Another won't appear for at least two weeks. I don't deal in emergencies—at least not in the conventional sense. These operations are too complex. I've got to know exactly what I'm doing, and that means X-rays, angiograms, biopsies, whatever. Already the problem is complicated. You'll note that either patient might die if an operation is not performed. Another competent surgeon might be found, but it's not likely. Complicated. Complicated. But that's only the beginning." He smiled, and his eyes took the smile and dissipated it. Thumbs dug into the pits beneath my throat and at the sides of my neck. I thought I was strangling. I looked to Artie and to Jimmy and, finally, to Mr. Farbstein. They were asleep.

"Now. Imagine. Just as you're weighing the situation, a telephone rings. A New York doctor. Someone you know. He tells you of a man—he happens to be a bishop—who seems to require a heart operation. What do you do? Is the Negro or the mother any more likely to die? Probably not. Are their cases more attractive? No—more poignant perhaps; some people find poverty poignant. But death is death, and, indeed, the bishop is likely to do more with what time you might give him. I'm prejudiced, I know. I'm bigoted. I chose the rich, Protestant bishop. But if I'd chosen the Negro, the girl's mother would have died. Damned perplexing, no? But you don't have to worry. You're in the works now. Even if we find your condition inoperable—and that's always possible—it would be too late to replace you. The problem is interesting but only academic. Read the letters, Whitney. Tell me what you would have done. I like to think of it this way: if I have to play God, I'll play God with the same magnificent arbitrariness that he displays. I don't get all that much satisfaction from it. I wish I got more. Unrelieved power is monotonous. I'm hoping you can help me—vindicate me, condemn me. I don't know. At any rate, I can't think of anyone more qualified." He looked at his watch. "I've got to go now. My assistants were ready ten minutes ago. See you soon."

And he was gone. The generator—whatever it was—sighed to a halt. There remained only a silence punctuated, from left to right, with four sets of breathing. I looked at my hand. I made it into a fist. Then I brought it down on my thigh with the full force of my waning strength. I heard myself cry out in pain. I took the adjustable table in both hands and shook it, as if I could close off its source of life. Then I picked up the two envelopes and, without looking, I pushed them deep into the back of my drawer.

The sun slanted down through the window panes, projecting a pattern of warm squares across my chest and legs. You, I

said, you, the bishop of Queens County, are a hot waffle. Then
I thought of waffles and butter and marmalade, and I was
hungry again. Hungry and black now—with muscles used for
moving suspended like raw sausages from my neck and back and
shoulders. There were children around me whimpering, their
thumbs and fingers prying at their belly buttons. Around each
black-brown neck was a lucky rabbit's foot. A lucky rabbit's foot.

I shoved my body to the edge of the mattress. Then, as they
found purchase in the sheet's slack wrinkles, I let my legs slide
gradually down to the floor. My knees cracked—first one then
the other—as they touched the rigid marble. I had to wait, my
chin propped on the mattress, until my breath and my sight had
wholly reconstituted themselves. Then, on all fours, I prodded
with scrupulous thoroughness beneath the bed, beneath the
table, into my two pairs of slippers. There was nothing, and
time, I knew, was getting short. Sarah was almost due. Again
I extended my arm beneath the bed. There was nothing but
the dull sheen of daylight against the marble.

"See my uppers?" I was so startled by Artie's voice that my
body tried to leap backward. But it couldn't. It made a feeble
show of surprise, and then it sagged.

"Excuse me?" I said after a long moment.

"My upper choppers. Teeth. They fell under the bed last
night." I looked behind me. Yes. Half a grin peered coyly from
behind a leg of Artie's bed. I studied Artie's sunken mouth.
Those were his teeth.

"You want them?" I asked.

"Yeah. If you could. I keep tastin' floor in my mouth." He
laughed. "You see them?"

The nails of my right hand cracked as I forced them against

the floor. The gums were unnaturally brown—like the gums of a dog. Artie's teeth . . . I crawled forward on my hands and knees: cautiously, as a kitten might approach its first toad. Hair and fluffy bits of dust adhered to the back molars. As I got closer, a loathing of all things artificial enveloped me—glass eyes, plastic food tubes, the valve that opened and shut silently inside Mr. Farbstein's heart. A little insect, its wings folded behind, crawled rapidly over the gums and down between the front incisors.

"Where'd you go? Whit? Huh? You got them?"

"I got them."

Artie's arm came over the side of the bed and dangled, groping, to the right of my hand. I had no alternative. I pinched the teeth between the thumb and forefinger of my left hand. They were stuck to the floor, and, when I pulled, they made a little, ticking sound. I gagged and closed my eyes. As I did so, I thought of ancient, brown chewing gum scraped from beneath church pews. Then I pushed the teeth into Artie's outstretched hand.

"Thanks. I'll just drop them in the drawer. I don't use 'em much—never did. The fit ain't so good, make my gums bleed." He coughed. "Probably won't need 'em again—ever. Not unless they start makin' hard Jello."

I sat on the floor, disappointed. I had wanted to see Artie with teeth. Mr. Farbstein sat upright. The catalogue picture was still clutched in his right hand. His empty eyes were fixed on Artie; his body seemed a caricature of alertness—strangely stiff and as though at attention. He seemed to be expecting Artie to do something: something heinous that he alone could anticipate and avert. I was vaguely grateful for his concern. Artie belched.

"Artie?" I said.

"Yeah?"

"Do you like Negroes?"

"Yeah. Why'd you ask? Negroes? Sure. One of my jobs, back when I cared to have a job, was fight managing. Had about eight, ten Negro boxers at one time. Good guys. Most of 'em can laugh—laugh, you know? And the women—man, y'don't have t'show them what to do. Not when it counts. Y'get what I mean?" I began to crawl back. "Hey, Whit. Whit. Don't get mad. I'm sorry. 'Course you don't know. Sorry. I got wrapped up in my memories. Don't get pissed at me again."

"Forget it," I said. "Just forget it."

Lord God, my heavenly Father—forgive me. Thou sayst, greater love hath no man but that he lay down his life for another. And what am I?—what am I—that my life should be preserved at the cost of another's? What am I? A bishop . . . I begin, my God, to weary even of despising myself. Leave me not, whatever my fate, in this futile round of self-condemnations. If I have failed, if now there is no recourse, let me at least know the cause, the necessity of my failure. For once. And, most of all, help me, my God—help me to talk to Sarah Samson.

Mr. Farbstein cleared his throat: a bitter, terse comment on Artie. Jimmy replied candidly in his sleep, counseling moderation. Artie was telling me about a certain Negro welterweight who could make all the moves. Or was it the Negro's wife? They ran together in my mind. The heat pressed its sinuous and heavy body against my chest. There was nothing remaining. Nothing I could do. Nothing further I could suffer. I turned to the wall and became, as best I could, an inanimate thing.

*

Michael arrived: I knew immediately that something was wrong. He stood at the door, reluctant, it seemed, to cross the room. His face was sheeted with sweat; it reflected light as a pale jelly apple might. When Artie saw Michael, he said, "Son of a bitch. He is a bishop." Then he groaned so horribly that Michael, in dread, drifted backward to the foot of Jimmy's bed. Artie was the *genius loci* of our room: no one could enter without first acknowledging the spirit of suffering and death.

"Is he all right?" asked Michael. "He won't be sick, will he?"

"You should be so healthy," I said. He peered cautiously at Artie.

"You sure?" I nodded. Michael was encouraged. He turned his back bravely on Artie. Then he sighed. "You're not wearing my pajamas."

"No. I had a little accident. You might buy me another pair."

"A little accident?"

"A little accident. I spilt something on them."

"What?"

"Some—some soup. That's all. Not blood. What've you got for me?"

Michael had some letters, but they weren't really important. I wondered why he had brought them. He seemed to become uneasy when I discarded them. Michael didn't want to speak to me. He drank copiously of my ice water, then he wiped his sleeve across his sodden forehead. As an afterthought, he wiped his sleeve with his handkerchief, and then refolded the handkerchief with meticulous care. For a few moments, he stared around the room, a thing he ordinarily avoided doing. Artie waved at him—Michael turned to me in horror, as a very young girl might after a strange man had smiled at her.

"Mike? Is something wrong?"

"Wrong? What makes you say that?" He smiled. Then he grabbed his front teeth between his thumb and forefinger. There was a moment's silence as his head wilted slowly on his neck. Gradually, though, honesty got the better of him. He began wringing his hands convulsively. They made wet, squeaking sounds. "Yes," he said. "Yes. Yes, there's something wrong."

"Get a hold of yourself, Mike. Take a deep breath. Take another. That's it. Don't start panicking, whatever you do. It's nothing we can't beat if we put our heads together." I sat up wearily. My stomach popped, as though, inside, someone were ripping stitches out of leather. Michael smiled when I said that. He depended on me.

"You think it'll be all right?"

"Well—most everything works itself out. Of course, it'd help if I knew what was wrong." Michael nodded. But, even with my best comfort, he hesitated to speak. That was unusual. I, too, began worrying.

"It's—it's Pious," he said. I sat forward so suddenly that the letters flew off my bed and onto the floor.

"What's wrong with Pious?" Michael looked at me. Then he realized that, after all, things would not work themselves out so easily. He began to shake his head from left to right, from left to right. But it was already too late for him.

"He—he's gone."

"Gone!" I thought I'd go mad. "Gone! What the hell d'you mean? Speak up, man. For God's sake, speak up."

"Hey," said Artie. "Don't take the Lord's name—"

"You shut your mouth," I said, without looking toward him. "Answer me, Michael. Damn it. If you've done something to Pious, I'll kill you. Do you hear?" Michael's body swayed from side to side. I wanted to jump from the bed and throttle him.

"Hey. Take it easy, Whit."

"Mind your own business, damn you. Tell me, Michael." I spoke slowly. "Get hold of yourself now. Now. Do you hear? Tell me what happened."

"I don't know," he whimpered. "I don't know. I don't know. I don't know. Maybe somebody stole him. I don't know. I don't know." He spoke through his hands. Jimmy was watching me; he seemed afraid. Artie was up on one elbow—I thought, ridiculously enough, that he was concerned for me. Mr. Farbstein alone refused to be distracted. He stared with undiminished intensity at Artie's head. Michael shuddered: I knew I could calm him only by calming myself. Pious. Pious, my joy. What have they done to you?

"Michael. Mike. Just tell me what happened."

"I don't know. Oh, God. I went in this morning to make his food. Then I called him. He usually comes right away—he frightens me. I called and I called, but he didn't come. I looked all over. All over. It was terrible."

"What was terrible? What? What?"

"Nothing. He just wasn't there. That's all."

"Are you sure, damn it?"

"I looked all over." He was nearly shrieking now. "In the closets, under the beds. I crawled on my hands and knees. He's not there. He's just not there." My mind took up the chant: not there, just not there, not there.

"Think, Michael. Please. Was the door locked yesterday?"

"I—I think so."

"You think so? In the name of all that's holy, aren't you sure? Didn't you lock it? Didn't you lock it, you Mongoloid idiot?"

I think then that I got up to look for him. I remembered slid-

ing off the edge of the mattress. I remembered hearing Artie
and Jimmy and Mr. Farbstein as they screamed, Pious, Pious,
Pious, in an angry chorus. Then the sound shut off with
a click, and I saw a warm, golden sky rocket fall from the heavens. It was scattering little, warm, golden sparks. Then there
was dark silence and anticipation—and a coldness hard against
my right ear.

". . . You took a beaut. You should've seen it. Man, what
a header. Like a tree goin' down. Wham. Just like that. You're
a big boy, Whit. Real big. What—six-two, six-three? When
they tried t'get you up, it was like the Marines on Mount Suri-
bachi. Me? I thought you was dead. No crap. Dead. What
with all that blood—and that thonck when your head hit the
floor. Son of a bitch, I ain't never seen such a nose-dive . . ."
I was conscious. I heard the inner ear drone that serves as a
background to all sound. I sensed the bandage on my right temple. I smelled food, as it approached down the hall. And in my
mouth there were things like hairs from the legs of night crawl-
ers. But that was all.
". . . I don't wanna say nothin', but it's crazy. A little
strange, don't you think? Huh, Whit? I mean, a guy your age
goin' berserk over a cat. Pious, that the name? Crazy. I don't
know. Butcher store where I lived always had a bunch of
cats. Crawlin' all over. New litter every couple weeks.
Unnngh. Bastard pain. My stomach's fallin' apart. You think
anything's in those needles? Just water, huh? That's what I
figure. And this heat— Ninety-five degrees since Wednesday.
Oh, you mother . . ."
My eyes crossed. Mitosis took place, and Jimmy's body split

into two bodies, joined strangely at the shoulder. I heard
Artie's voice, but I couldn't understand what he was saying.
My fingertips touched my fingertips and were satisfied with a
certain silent comradeship. But that was all.

". . . Like I was saying. I go into this butcher store once—
my old lady got me t'do all the shopping in those days. I quit
school when I was fifteen, and I wasn't so quick t'get a job. You
bet I wasn't. My brother, Albert—he was different. He's always the big cheese. Already he's goin' at night to City College. Anyway, I'm standin' at the counter, waitin' for the meat,
when this little, black kitten—I mean little, two-three weeks
maybe—come out from under the counter. Surprised me, I
guess, 'cause I jumped back. It's like I stepped in a big cow
pat. Just like that. There was this other kitten—I forget what
color—right behind me. Must've crushed its head with my
heel. Died right away. No pain; nothing. But I didn't feel
too good about it—you know how it is. The butcher don't
care, like I said the place is crawlin' with cats. But there's this
old lady in the store really give it to me good. That's the way
old ladies are. Just an accident, though. Not like what I seen
some kids do to cats—on purpose, I mean . . ."

I lay quietly—a man first operating the simplest of machines.
A touch of sound. ". . . Now, if it was a dog, I could understand. My uncle had a Doberman Pinscher stood . . ." A
touch of sight. Slowly the left-hand Jimmy oozed out, melting
into the right-hand Mr. Farbstein. Together then. A touch of
sound, a touch of sight . . . The simple machine short-cir-
cuited with an acid, white flash. Throbs of pain ran up and
down my nose, behind my eyes and round and round my skull.

". . . That fat friend of yours. What's with him? You can't
tell me he's all there. No how, brother. He took a good one—

right off the deep end—like a little kid. I ain't never seen a
grown guy carry on like that. Tell me truth, Whit—can he
manage for himself? I mean, can he function okay, can he put
on his shoes and socks in the morning? He run outa here with
his hands over his face. Just disappeared. You shoulda seen
him. I figured he's gonna go right through the wall. And that's
a priest? I mean, Whit—I mean, he gives people advice, and
they listen to him? Boy, what a laugh . . ."

My eyes licked themselves with their lids; rubbed against
them in narcissistic delight. I heard Artie speak and my ears
became strangely jointed and alive. My tongue hunched itself down in my mouth and waited, swaying from side to side,
in anticipation of a pounce. Below, my fingers nursed up and
down on my own stomach, stretching and tightening, preparing the soft material. But that was all. The things around me
communicated, and I was no longer compelled to understand.

". . . do for sex, you guys? I mean—well, hell, it must be
piss frustratin'. No wonder he's so crazy. I don't wanna talk
disrespectful—I don't know about these things—but, seems
to me, if you guys layed into a nice, greasy one now and then
. . . Well, hell—make you feel good all over. Who's to know?
They check around? Huh? Hey, kid. Kid. Jimmy. I wake you
up? Sorry, kid. That window open all the way? Sure? What
I'd give for one cool breeze—uhoh. Son of a bitch. Here it
comes. Here it comes. Knew I shouldn'ta moved. Unnngh.
God. God, that hurts. God. Whit. Hey, why's he givin' me the
evil eye? The old guy. He ever say anything? Huh? Makes me
nervous."

I sat on the bed and watched the dusk begin to thicken; the
sunlight fall back defeated from shadowy corners. My eyes
opened, and my face became wonderfully sensitive. A deep

and primeval desire welled up within me. And I considered the others in their otherness, encumbered by their opaque involvements, prying hideously into each other. I made no judgments. I watched only things that moved, and I watched them only for their movement.

And then she came in.

"Mistuh Bishop—I heard everythin' what happened. I heard all about your poor pussy cat an' everythin'. That Doctuh Snow . . . Lookit your head. Just lookit. Man don't fall down if'n he got proper food inside him. No sir." She put the cup of tea on my table. I remembered the Buddhist maxim, "it is the emptiness that makes the cup useful." But the cup was full of tea.

"Hello, Sarah."

"You poor man. I know just how you feel. I got one them big German Shepherd dogs—name of Goliath. If anythin' happen t'him, I just don't know what I'd do." My father used to say, "Jews have Negro servants, and Negroes keep big dogs." And so the world goes round—in a great, descending spiral.

"I don't see how come it happen. I don't, Mistuh Bishop. Not after I give you Samson's rabbit foot. It don't seem right." She stopped. Then she took a step forward. "Mistuh Bishop —Mistuh Bishop, where's the rabbit's foot? You promised t'wear it. I don't see it round your neck. No sir. I don't." She searched the top of my bed table. "I don't see it. You shouldn't put it away. It gotta be round your neck, otherwise this wouldn't happen t'you. Why's it people won't listen t'me?" She opened the drawer of my bed table.

"It's not there, Sarah," I said.

"Where you got it, Mistuh Bishop?"

"I haven't—I haven't got it. I don't know where it is." Sarah raised the backs of her hands up to the level of her breasts. Then she spread her fingers wide.

"Now Mistuh Bishop, I'll ask you about that rabbit's foot again. You tell me the truth this time—you don't say it's gone. You hear?"

"Forgive me, Sarah. I don't know. I just don't know where it is. Maybe somebody stole it. Maybe—I don't know. I put it right there in the drawer. Now it's gone. Believe me, I'm heartbroken about the whole thing. Heartbroken."

"Hotbroken, yes sir. That's the word." She began to search frantically through my drawers, throwing things aside, placing them precariously on the edge of the table. My toothpaste fell onto the floor, and the little, white cap came off, rolling. A handkerchief. Then my two pens.

"It's not there, Sarah. It's not there. I wish I could make it up to you somehow."

"Hotbroken," she said. Then, with a terrific suddenness, she fell forward onto her knees. The mass of her weight jiggled from thighs and biceps and breasts. Sarah began searching under my bed, pushing deeper and deeper, until only her immense buttocks and thighs were visible. The bed began to rise perceptibly from the floor, as she forced the base of her spine under it. I held desperately to the mattress—like the captain of a longboat being stove in by a whale.

"Hotbroken. Hotbroken," she said.

"That'll be enough, Sarah. You've gone too far this time."

Nurse MacArthur had dragged Sarah out from under the bed. Sarah struggled uncertainly to her feet; there were wet marks on her cheeks. Setting her lips, Nurse MacArthur took Sarah by the collar and pulled her great body toward the door. Nurse MacArthur was angry. The collar ripped, and Sarah turned once to speak to me. But Nurse MacArthur pinched the fat above her elbow and drew her, by that painful hold, out of our room.

"This place. Man, it's a God-damn loony bin. I mean it. Priests and Niggers goin' hysterical. You crackin' your skull over some stupid cat. That old guy starin' at me all day long. Tell you, Whit, I'm gettin' a bit nervous. Hey, that MacArthur wench is some piece of ass, ain't she? Tough. She tossed that fat blackie outa here like she didn't weigh nothin'. An' she weighed plenty, believe you me. What the hell was that all about?"

"I'd rather not talk about it," I said.

"Don't mind me. Just nosey. Hey, Jimmy—your people comin' over tonight?"

"Yes sir."

"That's nice. I get no visitors—nobody. Even the under-taker'll beg off. Your whole family comin'? Yeah? That's nice. Man, sure is piss hot in here." He tugged his underwear down until the upper half of his groin was entirely exposed.

I dreamed of paws, of tails held high, of sleek backs arched and curled. The unfamiliar ache over my temple startled me into intermittent awareness. I stared beyond my bed. Nurse MacArthur chided Artie; she plumped up the slumping Mr. Farbstein. But not once did she approach my bed. I could un-derstand that. I stood, unchanged, in a world intent only on progress and growth. Then a hand cupped itself around my el-bow—a hand arrested momentarily in my single spot of time. It was Mrs. Lopopulo.

"Oh, I'm sorry. Were you asleep? You poor, poor man. But I just had to tell you. It's next Thursday."

"Excuse me? What—what's next Thursday?"

"The operation. Jimmy's. We just found out. Oh, I pray—
I pray to God he'll be all right."

Mrs. Lopopulo clasped and unclasped her hand prayerfully
around my left elbow. Then she raised her chin toward heaven.
I felt the dull points of her fingernails. I saw the jutting protu-
berance of her considerable bosom. I smelled her over-ripe
sweetness. Her chin came slowly down. Mrs. Lopopulo hung
hugely over me, her bosom just above mine, her hands still
pressed into the flesh of my arm. Now she was sobbing. I rose
up on my elbow, and, with my right arm, I sketched a blessing.

"He'll be all right, I promise you that." It was, at the very
least, a presumptuous prophecy, but Mrs. Lopopulo seemed willing to accept it.

"Of course. Of course. God wouldn't punish a child—he
wouldn't punish my little Jimmy." She paused. Then she
brought her face close to mine. "You're a wonderful man. I
don't know why it is, but I believe in you more than I believe
in Dr. Snow. Take care of yourself. Please. You mean so much
to—to Jimmy, to all of us." She looked quickly toward Artie.
"We'll have to go to the solarium. Maureen shouldn't have to
see that. Disgusting, disgusting man. We tried, but we just
couldn't get a private room for Jimmy." She shook her head.
"Sleep. That's what you need. I'll come back and tuck you in."

She rose and went across to Jimmy's bed. Her husband said
something, but I could tell, from the set of her head, that she was
ignoring him. Jimmy picked out a game, and the three of them
followed him out of the room. As they passed Artie's bed, Mrs.
Lopopulo threw her body vindictively between Maureen and
Artie's prostrate figure. Then they were gone.

"Damn good looking kid," said Artie.

"Jimmy's a nice boy."

"Yeah. No—but what I meant was his sister. Whadda they call her? Huh, Whit?"

"Maureen, I think."

"Maureen, Maureen," he said. Then he turned over.

Lord God, my Father, protect him. Alone. All alone this night. I am not worthy to come unto Thee in prayer, yet—protect him. Thou who hast ever stood watch over the innocent, look down in kindness on this, the very least of Thy creatures . . .

I understand, my God. Never fear that. I don't question the justness of Thy retribution. There is Sarah; there is Michael; there is Artie. There is reason enough. In the name of Thy Son, Jesus Christ—mortify me, strengthen me, forgive me. And yet, let him not be the means. Let him not suffer. Please . . .

I don't know exactly when I first heard it. The rhythmic sounds—the creaking of the springs and the soft tapping of the headboard against the wall—they raised me gently into consciousness. I looked toward Artie's bed, but the room was dark, and I could see nothing but an amorphous whiteness. I fell back onto my pillow—and then I heard the words. They fell into rhythm with the other sounds—a whispered, frantic chant. "It's gone. It's gone. It's gone," they said. "Oh God, it's gone."

I knew what was gone.

SATURDAY, AUGUST 19TH—

THE SIXTH DAY

SEVEN O'CLOCK. By that time we knew—each of us—that this would be the hottest day. The air that burrowed into the membranes of our nostrils had the consistency of hot, powdered glass; mouths began to hang slack, like grotesque flowers pried open by the sun. We stared down the lengths of our bodies, into the chinks between our toes. We lay. Our patient resignation was unquestioning and absolute.

Artie gasped—breaths taken like tentative sips of hot coffee. And each gasp was an echo, an elaboration, of the last night's sounds. I hadn't looked at Artie yet that morning, but, though he disgusted me, I could feel no anger. Artie belonged to the ritual of my temptation. I understood that. I saw that it was good. Artie wasn't a human entity with vices that emperiled his salvation. He was an outward and visible sign of my mortification.

And Pious . . . That, too, was understood: my hatred impotent, my love yet pernicious and virulent. A cat. Uncertain, terribly excited, lost—and referring his fear, as indeed he might, to some secret sin of mine. That morning one of the

nurses had phoned a neighbor. He, too, had searched. But
Pious was gone. In our room, disguised as a sort of breathing, a
litany of loss was being intoned. And yet, almost from the beginning, I had seen that it was just.

I had tried, an hour before, to hold a wash rag, heavy with
water, to my sweating forehead. Now I dreaded the inevitable
call of my bladder. Starvation had wasted the vital strength
from my joints; my arms and legs hung lifeless, like pennants on
a windless day. Only the ache in my temple remained vivid. It
distracted my vision; my left eye would not follow my right eye.
I lay inert—a mind matured in evil, tabernacled now in the
body of an infant. But I felt no bitterness.

. . . My text for this morning is taken from the forty-first
chapter of the book of Job—"Canst thou draw out Leviathan
with an hook? Or his tongue with a cord which thou lettest
down?" God, as we know, is here speaking to Job from out of
the whirlwind. Job the righteous; Job the best of mortal men.
Job, sorely oppressed by a terrible and arbitrary act of God's
will.

We sympathize with Job. Our liberal reflexes are aroused
instinctively by injustice, and the story of Job was intended as
the pre-eminent myth of injustice. Moved by the very dramatic
narrative of Job's suffering, we are compelled to insist that a
God who allows—nay, causes—such suffering, cannot be a just
God; cannot, therefore, be worthy of our great reverence. Such
a reaction is perfectly natural—it is also perfectly wrong.

We are told, in this same book of the Bible, that, "A fear of
God is the beginning of understanding." Omnipotence— I
wonder whether human comprehension will ever approach
the enormous implications of that word. Omnipotence. Hear

the word. Hear its bigness. Who are we to ascribe good or evil,
height or depth, justice or injustice, to a God who created our
whole world, the entire limit of our speculation, in a solitary
moment, "when the morning stars sang together?" To a God
who can, indeed, draw out Leviathan with a fish hook? This
thought represents the culmination of Job's understanding. It
should also represent the culmination of our understanding, for
there is not a man, not a woman, in this chapel even as little
worthy as Job was.

Human existence soon teaches us that its very substance is injustice. Negroes and Jews are persecuted; little children die of
dread, painful diseases; the evil prosper in the very ecstasy of
their sensual delight. And we say, from the pinnacle of mortal
pride, "How can there be a God?" But there is a God. Yes, my
friends. And He is more mighty, more awesome, than all the
hymns of all the evangelists might serve to suggest. So mighty
that our evil becomes His good; our unfairness becomes his benevolence. So mighty that every mortal hope, every mortal
creed and value is sent spinning, senseless before His will. So
mighty that He encompasses each twitch and each thundering
alike of this, the only world we will ever know.

This is a God to be feared. And we, who are rational, it would
seem, only that we may be sinful, have the very most to fear from
him. Learn this and learn it now—there is no man or child of
man who deserves one jot less than the most dreadful calamity.
No man who has not, in the course of his humblest daily existence, called down upon himself the final and consuming wrath
of God.

No. None of us can hope for redress. None of us can, of
ourselves, expect an act of divine mercy. And yet this God—
who made all things and waits only to unmake that all—this

God, this omnipotent God, sent His only begotten Son to suffer death upon a cross for our redemption.

I see men here. I see women here. Most of you, I think, have brought children into the world. In turn you've nourished them, loved them, seated all your hopes in them. Think now— any of you who loves a son or a daughter—think what a terrible sacrifice that is. To lead your only child not only into death, but also into an agony of suffering. For someone else. For someone else. The Bible says, "Greater love hath no man, but that he lay down his life for his brother." I doubt that. I doubt if it is strictly true. Which of you would not—would not gladly —lay down your own life that your child might not suffer? Which of you would not? Think again. Is there anything, any cause, any person or group of persons, for which you would allow your child's hands and feet and chest to be pierced through and through? For which of you would willingly, joyfully, allow your child to perish in an excruciating torment?

I think not. Yet God, who has endured our scorn through millennia of sinful unbelief, who is omnipotent, whose will is irresistible—yet this God sacrificed His only Son for our miserable sakes. For us. You and I. Look around you. The immensity of that sacrifice is enshrined in the face of every child here. Yes, so God loves us, to such an extent—to such a terrific extent.

Remember this. God gives, with his love, not hope of an easy life and a bounteous existence. No. Nor a dream of worldly eminence. God promises us salvation from our sins and hope of life eternal—life eternal with Him, in Him, of Him. And this glorious hope derives from no intrinsic merit of our own. For, of ourselves, what merit have we? None. Such merit as we have is derived only from Christ and from the loveful sacrifice of His body and His blood—through a constant communion with

God's only Son. True: we are enjoined to do good works. True.
We must do them. They are healthful. But good deeds in themselves—make no mistake—good deeds in themselves are meaningless. "If you have sinned, what do you accomplish against
him? And if your transgressions are multiplied, what do you
do to Him? If you are righteous, what do you give to Him? Or
what does he receive from your hand?" He, God, receives nothing.

Someone says, Progress. I don't think so. In the things that
matter, we have not progressed. Death still comes, and we are
as weak before it as Job, as Adam. And for the rest—the frustra-
tions, the miseries, the injustices—we must accept, we must endure. This life is relevant only as it prepares us for a greater
life. Lest we swell with foolish pride, let no man ever say, "I
did not deserve this." We deserve; we will always deserve misfortune. Let us pray only that, in those times of tribulation,
God grant us strength to persevere, and a faith that remains forever unshaken. For the rest—it is God's will . . .

I still remember that sermon. Dean Oxpaugh took me aside
afterward. He was pulling at his nostril hairs; he did that whenever he wanted to seem friendly and offhand. "Whitney," he
said. "We all admire Jonathan Edwards. All of us. But this is
the golden age of liberal man. If you start talking about God
first—well, men may stop listening. A word to the wise, Whitney. A word to the wise." God forgive me, I've always wanted
men to listen. I never preached that sermon again—nor ever
one remotely like it.

Two fat, sizzling flies spiraled round themselves near the
ceiling. We watched. We approximated their spirals with
our feeble necks. Now a tiny, erratic sound accompanied the
heat; the compounded effect was extraordinarily irritating. The

lewd buzzing began, ceased suddenly, began again, sputtered, died, sputtered. No one in the room possessed either the strength or the coordination to destroy the flies. To each, in turn, the torment was presented. Some struck out wildly; others lay resigned. They fell from the ceiling toward Artie. I heard, with satisfaction, that he had strained himself in trying to kill them. Then they left Artie's bed to settle brazenly on my forehead. Patiently, I endured, as their prickly bodies lay in the sweat of my brow.

Jimmy was sprawled motionless on his bed, armpits and groin ajar. His pile of games was no longer neatly squared off; a comic book lay open on the floor. His pajama shirt was unbuttoned in a diagonal that ran from his neck down, across his left nipple. Like an incision. Poor kid, I thought. That's probably what he's worried about.

"Jimmy," I said. He sat up immediately, his eyes alert. I found it repugnant to have caused even so much movement in that heat.

"Yes sir?"

"Why—why not drag yourself over and talk a while? If y'can move, that is."

Jimmy leaped from his bed even before he had properly replied to my invitation. But, before he crossed the room, he put on his slippers, and even, I saw, contemplated wearing his warm, plaid bathrobe. It was too hot, however, for a formal visit. He compromised by buttoning his shirt front and folding his handkerchief neatly in the pocket over his heart. It was next Thursday . . . I think then I would have liked—actively liked —to have known that Jimmy would be all right.

"How d'you feel today, sir?" I placed the palms of my hands on my stomach and worked the skin as though it were a bellows.

Once already that morning I had found myself without breath sufficient to articulate even a few necessary words. Now I expressed myself in telegrams.

"Not feeling at all this morning . . . Improvement right there." Jimmy misinterpreted the movements of my hands upon my stomach.

"Gee. You haven't had anything to eat in days. Have you, sir?" I considered: would it be more debilitating to say no or merely to shake my head? After a moment I decided to shake my head— "That must be awful, sir," he said. "I bet, if you'd had somethin' to eat—I bet you wouldn'ta fallen down. Gosh, that was scary."

"Wish I'd been there . . . Must've been something."

"Dr. Snow oughta let you eat."

"Well . . . No sense talking. He knows best." I wasn't going to entertain a subversive discussion—not when both our lives depended on obedience. Jimmy deferred once again.

"You heard anything about your cat, sir? I think I dreamed about him last night. He was all right. But I guess that don't mean much." I wanted to conserve my energy, but, even so, I had to smile at that.

"Good sign. Maybe." Jimmy seemed interested.

"D'you believe in dreams, Mister Belknap?"

"Dreams . . . No, not really."

"Ghosts?"

"Ghosts?"

"You know. Spooks and supernatural things. Dead people comin' back to haunt. Witches an' devils. All that stuff. My father says there's no such thing. But he says it so I won't get scared. I don't know if he really believes—"

*

. . . The snowflakes flashed down through the long beam of
my light and then into the stream. I sat uneasily on a jagged
stone, listening to distant crowds imprisoned always in the sound
of water on the rocks. The sky was overcast; behind me, the
snow sizzled as it spread itself over the dead, frozen leaves. It
was cold. An icy wind slapped me again and again between the
shoulder blades.

I was twenty-two then. The night was New Year's Eve, and
I was far from the half-dozen parties to which I'd been invited.
Alone, with my watch in my pocket, that the new year might
come unheralded to the mountains. Snow had collected in my
collar; it formed a white, uneven circle on my head. The wind
reeled against me like a drunken celebrant. The silence crackled
and gurgled, but still it was silence. Alone and cold, but very
glad, I sat upon my jagged stone.

Every new year of my life, since that time, I have doubted
what happened there. It is hard now for me to remember; it
is hard now for me to believe. I was young then, and I was filled,
for reasons best known to my youth, with a wonderful self-pity.
Perhaps what happened was the product of heightened emotion—perhaps there was nothing. But that nothing or that something—whichever it is now or was then—altered forever my relationship with the eternal. I have never spoken of it. We,
especially, mistrust these things.

I snapped my flashlight out and stood up. After a moment, I
began making my way back along the wooded path by the light
of the fallen snow. I remember looking up once, as I turned
from the stream, and I remember thinking then that the moon
had suddenly made an appearance in the heavens. But I didn't
look again. I walked slowly along the path, pausing and pausing
again to fix moments of natural silence in my ears. The trees

were outlined dully against the white of the snow, and once I thought I saw a raccoon move quickly up the far side of a great oak. But perhaps it wasn't a raccoon. For then the very brightest thing was a shadow, the very loudest sound only an echo of some greater sound that had gone before.

I started and then stood very still. Water—it was almost warm water—had begun to run down my forehead, down into the sockets of my eyes. The snow that had collected on my head was melting: I could feel it searching deep along the pathways of my scalp. The wind, too, had ceased; striking still, but striking now at some outer bulwark far beyond me. A moment passed, an absolute and autonomous moment, a moment in which the past and the future stood unbridged by any present. And then I knew—it was the light. The woods were no longer lit only by the cold phosphorescence of the snow—the light was color now and warmth. The trees, I saw and my heart leaped, the trees were casting each a shadow. Suddenly I began to tremble—a sense of visionary power, a sense of mighty impending brooded over me.

I turned around. Above me, yet even above the trees, was a light—blinding white, and yet, implied within it almost to visibility, all the colors that are white. I stood upright, transfixed. My shoulders and my forehead rose to meet the light, and then it was upon me. The ground fell away from beneath my feet; I no longer felt the need to breathe. Within me— through every organ of sense and along every nerve and passage that leads to sensation—there burned a terrifying joy. And then, as though in the process of a mighty inhalation, it was gone into me.

I was on my knees. Around me the snow had already begun to fill a perfect circle of brown earth and leaves and twigs. I

said the Lord's Prayer. And when I said, "Thine is the kingdom
and the Power and the Glory," I knew what Glory was, and I
was astonished. I prayed for dedication and assent welled up
frighteningly within me. I think that I was terrified; I know
that I was happy. The sounds of the forest, like skittish animals,
came slowly close again. I knelt there until the wind and the
snow had rewoven whiteness around me . . .

"No. No such things. Your father's right, Jimmy. You've
been reading too many horror comics."

"No?" He sighed. "Guess I didn't think you'd say so. People
don't come back from the dead, huh?"

"No. They don't. That's all silly superstition." My stomach
growled with an embarrassing audibility. "Our primitive ancestors believed in those things because they didn't understand
nature. When they saw the lightning—things that frightened
them—they made up spirits and devils. They couldn't understand otherwise. But we know what makes the lightning." I
smiled at him. "It may be boring—not as exciting as your
comics. But it's the truth." Jimmy frowned. He cleared his
throat as though he intended to speak. Then he thought better
of it and took out his handkerchief instead. He ran it over his
forehead and cheeks. He seemed disturbed.

"But," he said finally.

"But what?"

"Did our ancestors write the Bible?"

"Yes. They did."

"Didn't it say—in the Bible, I mean—didn't it say that Jesus
came back from the dead?"

"Yes. But . . . That's different."

"Why?"

"Well. Jesus was the Son of God. He wasn't a man."

"So he didn't die?" Jimmy frowned.

"No. No. He died. He really died."

"Then people do come back from the dead?"

"Ah . . . Jesus did. Yes."

"Wasn't there a man called—" He paused. "His name begins with an L."

"Oh. You mean Lazarus?"

"Yup. That's it. Didn't he come back from the dead?"

"Jesus resurrected him. Yes."

"Then people can come back from the dead?"

"We all come back from the dead, Jimmy. Jesus conquered death for us. We all will exist in a life beyond this life."

"When Jesus came back from the dead—was he the Holy Ghost?"

"With a white sheet?" I shook my head. "No. The Holy Ghost is different from the ghosts in your horror books. It's not Jesus."

"What is it?"

"It's part of the Trinity. God the Father, Jesus His Son and the Holy Ghost. The Holy Ghost is the spirit of God. You might call it God's breath. It's through the Holy Spirit that God works. That he inspires us. It's very difficult to explain. You have to believe in it."

"Oh," said Jimmy, nodding. "I believe in it."

"Good."

"But . . ."

"Yes?"

"But if Jesus and Lazarus came back from the dead. Can't someone else come back from the dead?"

"No," I said.

"Not even maybe?"

"No."

"Why not, Mister Belknap?"

"Because . . . It's— It's different, that's all. Take my word for it."

"You're awful tired, Mister Belknap. I better go back to my bed." I gestured a denial, but he was right. I was dreaming even before Jimmy had reached his bed.

Michael didn't come that afternoon. In some corner of the city he was cowering—certain now that he had been exiled forever from my presence. I felt sorry for Michael. I felt sorry for myself. Pious . . . Michael would never find him. Only a man of imagination could intuit a cat's devious ways. I slept and wakened and slept again. My legs and arms lay, hour after hour, fixed in the same position. I didn't dare mold the heat into another configuration. I think I was afraid it would assume my place in the void; I was afraid I'd be trapped outside the real world.

The real world: that was heat and hunger; vague fear and even vaguer guilt. But, as I lay in perfect stillness, I found myself becoming profoundly contented with my resignation. I had been released from all responsibility beyond the minimal responsibility of enduring. All else lay in Dr. Snow's hands, and his hands, finally, were God's. Only the thought of Pious— which involved love beyond my own ego—hadn't yet succumbed. But it would.

The heat intensified. I welcomed it. The pain in my temple answered, beat for beat, the rhythm of my pulse, and yet I wasn't dismayed. I thought of hunger as a grand thing—of wide and barren deserts, determination, ineffable courage. My incapacity

in things most basic seemed now only an inevitable elaboration
of my surrender of moral responsibility. There was no longer
anything I could do for myself. Dr. Snow would determine—he
would determine. There was time yet to think of policies to be
acted upon, books to be written, ambitions to be resumed. And
so I tried to sleep.

"Hey, Whit? Whit? Huh? You awake?"

I simulated sleep: deep, guttural breaths, upthrust chin, open
mouth, half-opened fists. Artie was silent for a moment. I
knew he was watching; I knew he could see through my pre-
tense. And so, in time, the unnatural natural position I had assumed became intolerable. I moved my legs and, by the rules of
our game, Artie fell at once upon me.

"Hey, Whit?"

"Yes, Art?"

"What's he got there? In his hand?"

"Who?"

"The old guy. Him. What's that thing he's always wavin'?"

"It's a picture."

"Yeah. Yeah, I can see that. But what's it a picture of?" He
paused—Mr. Farbstein had begun to move mechanically in his
sleep. We waited. His hand flexed and unflexed around the picture, as a sleeping child might reaffirm the presence of a familiar
toy. His eyes opened, but they were without sense or coordination, and soon they closed again. Artie repeated his question.

"Its—picture from a plumbing catalogue. Pipes and valves.
Things like that."

"Plumbing catalogue? Yeah? You sure? Why the hell'd he
hold onto that? Like it's his life. I swear he never puts the
friggin' thing down. No. Must be a picture of his kids or somethin'."

"Plumbing catalogue. I saw it myself."

"Yeah? That's crazy."

"He's in the plumbing line. Had a valve put in his heart. I think he's preoccupied with machinery."

"No kiddin'? Then the old bastard's really nuts. No wonder he keeps lookin' at me. Thinks he's a ballcock from a crapper, does he? Ha! That takes the gold ass wipe, by God." He laughed. Then he spat heavily into a tissue. "Son of a bitchin' heat. When's it gonna break?" I didn't care to comment on the heat. "Hey, Whit? That kid, Maureen. Jimmy's sister. How old'd you say she was?"

"I don't know. Sixteen maybe." Sixteen, I said. Yes, sixteen, curse your rotten, degenerate soul. I knew what Artie was thinking, and anger formed in ripples on my forehead and around my mouth. The heat had induced an artificial sensuality in the room. In touching the warm air everything was touched: Mr. Farbstein's square mustache; Artie's thin, yellowed legs; Maureen's nipples, softer still beneath the soft materials of her blouse and bra. And Artie was touching out in every direction, with every part of his body.

"Sixteen. Yeah, that's about what I figured, too. My niece's about the same age, only Ginny ain't so developed yet. No— but she's gonna be real good lookin' some day. Different from Maureen. You'd like her, Whit. Saw her dressed up one Easter —it made my heart jump. Y'know, she looked just like a picture I have of my mother when she was young. Not just like her, of course. But you could tell. Ginny's the one who gave me this." He leaned over to his bed table. A black Bible lay beneath a pile of gaudy paperbacks. "But I haven't started it yet," he said.

"Has your niece been here?"

"No," he said quickly. "No. I guess I'd hoped she'd come,

but Albert wouldn't let her. No, I knew that. Albert's my big
brother. Maybe you've heard of him—Albert Carson? Carson,
Hatcher and Fein? Corporation lawyers? The biggest. He lives
on Seventy-Third Street, right off Park Avenue. No? Quite a
set-up they have. I been twice to Al's apartment—guess you
wouldn't be so impressed, Whit—but it's pretty hot stuff for a
guy whose father was a Brooklyn barkeep. I was only ten when
he died. My father, that is. Albert was twelve or so, and Ma had
to work after that. Strong as an ox she was. She died only coupla
years ago. Seventy-eight years old. Al sent her to one of those
posh nursin' homes. I hear the place was a real gas—like the
Waldorf. Pretty far out in the country, though, and I didn't
have a car . . ."

Artie went on in the rambling, yet intense tones of the confes-
sional, and I listened, as I had learned long before, without really
hearing. Artie cleared his throat, and I was startled momentarily
into consciousness. His lips popped together moistly whenever
he began a sentence. As he spoke, a frog would appear gradually
in his throat, and his voice would begin to get deeper and
farther away. My attention would fade with it—until again he
cleared his throat.

". . . guess that was the wackiest job I ever had. Charlie'd
make up a case full of roaches—male and female—a whole
week's supply. They'd be in little, empty match boxes, so's I
could slide them open and drop 'em in bathrooms or behind
lunch counters. Then I'd hop in my old Ford and go from one
motel or hotel to the other. The newest, fanciest ones, see.
Ones that'd be shocked and horrified if a roach turned up in
the kitchen. I'd eat dinner in some swank place, then I'd drop
a match box on the floor. The roaches'd be pretty hungry by
then, and they'd make a bee-line for the kitchen. Nothing stops
a hungry roach, and they breed like bastards. I'd give my list to

Charlie and in two, three weeks he'd call up and ask if the hotel
or restaurant needed a real professional, hush-hush extermina-
tor. Picked up one hell of a lotta business that way. I lived
high on the pig for about six months—longest job I ever had.
Then I got drunk one night in a brand new motel near Albany.
I knocked my case over, I guess—I don't know. It was Monday,
and I had the whole friggin' week's supply with me. Next thing
I knew, the maid was screamin', and I was layin' stark naked on
the bed with roaches swarmin' over me like I was a corpse in the
sun. There was one hell of a stink, and Charlie dumped me
quick. Yeah, Whit—I was a real stumblebum in my heyday. 1
can remember times—maybe whole weeks—when breakfast,
lunch and dinner come out of a bottle. You wouldn't believe
it, but I swear it's true. Y'know, when I first come in here,
they had to feed me alcohol intravenously. No bull. I'm not
puttin' you on. Bottle of gin hangin' right up there—right
where his bottles are. I started gettin' th' DT's, almost shook
myself outa bed. Intravenously. What a bum. Ha! Hadda
little trouble gettin' the ice cubes through, though." He
laughed.

"But it's been weeks since I swallowed a real one, Whit.
That's God's honest truth. I ain't on the wagon—hell, not by a
long shot—but I'm tryin'. Albert's layin' out so much cash for
these treatments, I figure it's the least I can do. Believe me, he
don't have t'do all this. But he's a great guy. Put Ma in a
nursin' home 'n all. Least I can do—though, if y'want my
opinion, it's a waste of time. My guts're through for good, but,
thanks, you can spare me the gory details. Anyway, I won't be
bothering Al much longer."

"How sad. I notice you're talking as much as ever."

"Sure," he laughed. "Sure. I'll be talkin' even when I'm
dead. I'll greet people at my own damn funeral." He laughed

again. "Hey, Whit—you know what? I like you. You're cool.
If all the priests I'd met in my time were like you—hell, I might
even be a Christian."

"Then, I take it, you're not a Christian?"

"Well, I'm not a Jew, if that's what you mean. But otherwise, no, I'm not much of a Christian. Not practicin', as they
say. Matter of fact, I don't think much about it. Maybe I
should. What d'you think?"

"I think you should."

"Yeah. But, let's face it, you're prejudiced. There's lots of
guys think different, Whit. I mean—I don't wanna be disrespectful or anythin'—I just wanna get your views. What about
this science stuff, for instance? Darwin and Galileo and all that
—didn't think old Artie knew about those guys, huh? Hell. I'm
not all that dumb. I watch television. Educational shows, things
like that. Way I figure it, science can put religion out of business
but good. If we were all apes to start with, what's that make
Adam and Eve? Coupla baboons? Few months ago on Channel
Thirteen, a bunch of scientists had a real case against God. Look
at it this way, Whit. Man is progressin' an progressin'. Every
day he discovers somethin' new. Tomorrow he'll be on the
moon. Next day people'll be livin' to a hundred and fifty. I
mean, we're movin' ahead. We're leavin' old superstitions behind. Every day man's gettin' better and better. He's evolutin'.
He's progressin'. What d'you think, Whit?"

"Take a good look at yourself," I said. "Ask me then." I
turned away from him and onto my side. Artie said nothing. I
waited for a few moments, and then, without turning toward
him, I said, "Sorry Artie."

"It's okay, Whit," he said. "It's only the truth. Get yourself
some sleep."

*

Six-thirty. A cup of tea sat, misting, on my table. An old
Negro woman had brought it. Not Sarah. I knew then that she
had been fired, that the whole ugly incident had been my fault.
I forced my head into the steam that rose from the cup. Tears
ran from my eyes—condensation, irritation. I sipped hastily,
letting the tea scorch the soft inside of my lower lip. I would
get Sarah's address. I would write her a nice, long letter. I would
invite her home to dinner. No. That would embarrass her.
Samson's church. I would make a pilgrimage to Samson's
church.

The Lopopulos came. Mr. Lopopulo smelled very bad that
evening: Mrs. Lopopulo's thick perfume puffed and heaved as
it fought his body odor to a noisome standstill. When Maureen
came into the room, Artie propped himself up and began, pa-
thetically enough, to run his fingers back through his oily hair.
Staring defiance at him, Mrs. Lopopulo slipped a game from
Jimmy's pile and marched her family out of the room. Artie
waved innocently—as he did so, he leaned far forward to
examine Maureen's calves and ankles. When the Lopopulos had
gone, he looked once apologetically toward me and then
dropped back onto his pillow.

I dozed and, in sleeping, met alone with Sarah. She was naked,
basking in the immensity of her proportions, waving a tiny,
yellow fan before her face. "Are you free now, Sarah?" I asked.
"Yes sir," she said. "Yes sir, Mr. Lincoln. You done it. The
devil's let me go. I don't wear his libbery no more. See." She
began to sing, "Let My People Go," dancing slowly toward me,
her buttocks swinging, swinging like twin metronomes. I waited
for her. Then, when she was near enough, Sarah bent and
kissed me deeply on the mouth. Her lips encircled my nose
and the tip of my chin at once. "This is a white man's dream,"
I said. "Yes sir," she said. "That's just what it is. You let me

go, an' you can take one each of what you want." She stroked
the hair of my neck behind my ear, and her breath was lovely
like rich, dark tobacco. My face rose, unresisting, to meet hers,
and then I was awake. Someone had been touching my shoulder.
It was Maureen Lopopulo.

"May I speak to you, Bishop Belknap?"

"Yes. Certainly. Pull up a chair." I tried to seem alert. With
immense effort, I pushed myself up onto my elbows and then
fell immediately prone again. Somehow I was nervous, embarrassed, as though Maureen had been a witness to my dream. I
noticed that Artie had turned his body toward my bed; Maureen
must have noticed at the same time. She moved her chair to the
far side of my bed, away from Artie and against the windowsill.
I inched nearer to her and found myself panting from the exertion.

"You all right, Bishop Belknap?"

"Yes. Yes. Just a little weak."

"Maybe I shouldn't bother you."

"No, please. I'm fine. Tell me what's on your mind." But
now that the preliminary courtesies were done with, Maureen
seemed reluctant to speak. She found a spot on her blouse and,
wetting her finger, began to smooth it away. I watched her
finger, as it accidentally caressed her body beneath her blouse.
Together, we concentrated on the spot—now no longer recog-
nizable—and then, as if by prearranged signal, our eyes met. I
saw that Maureen was very sensual, indeed. There was neither
beauty nor delicacy; there was only subtle emphasis. Maureen's
mouth and lips were a little too large; her breasts were a little
too big for her upper torso; the moisture on her neck made her
skin seem just a little too much like skin. And, with all that, her
youth and innocence lent her a curious, implicit license.

"Go ahead. Something's worrying you. Is it Jimmy? Well,

I wouldn't worry about him. Dr. Snow is a wonderful surgeon."
But, judging from her hesitation, I could tell it wasn't Jimmy.

"Yes sir. I'm awful worried about Jimmy. But, well—you'll
think I'm terrible, talking about things like this when Jimmy's
operation is just Thursday. I guess I'm pretty selfish . . . But,
your honor, I just don't know what to do. I'm so desperate." She
looked to me for encouragement, and so I nodded, smiling, ex-
onerating her on the count of selfishness. "It's Sidney Kaplan,
sir. I'm in love with him."

"Yes," I said. "I thought as much."

"He's wonderful, Bishop Belknap. He's got a hundred-forty-
three I.Q. He's first string on the basketball team, and he writes
beautiful poetry. He's so sensitive, your honor. My father
doesn't understand these things. I don't like to say it, Bishop
Belknap, but my father is boor-jus." She nodded once firmly, as
though she had just told a terrible truth, but one that desperately needed telling.

"Bourgeois? Well now, I don't know. I'm bourgeois myself
—always have been. And I'm afraid you're bourgeois, too,
Maureen."

"I know, your honor. You don't have to tell me that. But
I'm different—I don't want to stay that way. There's no law,
is there? I don't have to be satisfied with second best. I want
to rise above my virement. I want to know things that only a
true artist knows. Okay, maybe I don't have what it takes—but,
if I marry Sidney, at least I'll have half a chance to see the mys-
teries of life. Some of them, maybe."

"Marry. Good grief. How old can you be?"

"I'm young. I know that, too. I'm not even sixteen yet. My
father rubs it in all the time. But, don't you see, Sidney and I
know we can't get married right away. I'm not crazy. I've got to

get a good high school education, so's I can be a mature sexual partner for Sidney."

"I see."

"Yes. I knew you would. You're not like my father." She winked and nodded, as though she had found, in me, a secret sharer. "I've got to train myself to get a good job. After all, I'll have to support Sidney while he writes. Society mistrusts the poet. Sidney doesn't want material things to enslave him."

"But Sidney isn't Catholic."

"No, he's not." She was silent for a moment, her reverie broken. "That's the trouble, of course. You've put your finger on it, Bishop Belknap. My father won't even let me see Sidney any more. Not even see him. But," she smiled, then she frowned, "you won't tell him? Sidney takes three buses so he can meet me after school. And he has to take three buses back."

"Six buses? That's . . . well, that's very impressive."

"Isn't it? I'm going to summer school for the first time. Sidney persuaded me. I'm taking courses in English and classical music appreciation. Bishop Belknap, I'm beginning to realize all that I've missed."

It was a fault, I knew that, but I just couldn't feel sorry for Maureen Lopopulo. I even found it rather satisfying, I'm afraid, to know beforehand what awaited her. Soon Maureen would come to understand, very intimately, the pathetic limit of her own abilities. And then there was the matter of Sidney Kaplan and the quality of his affection . . . In view of that, I didn't think there was anything I could add—anything more authoritative than Maureen's own inevitable and bitter experience. Besides, I was very tired.

"And now—now Sidney says I've got to make a decision. God, I'm so afraid of losing him, your honor. If I lose him, where

will I be? I'll tell you where. I'll be back with boys my father
understands. Like his friend, Mr. Spinelli's son. Bobby Spinelli.
He only failed his department of sanitation test three times.
That's all. I need your help. Please, Bishop Belknap. Why, why
did God make religions?"

I closed my eyes for a moment, wondering whether it was
time, once again, to brush the cobwebs off Naomi Moses. In
that way I might possibly tell Maureen the unpleasant truth,
without alienating her at once and forever. But I had gone
over that story too often before. Another Christian and another
Jew in love . . . I was exhausted and, frankly, bored by the
whole business. I could say, "Love conquers everything." After
all, it sometimes did—when the love was subtle and possessed
of complex resources. But Maureen Lopopulo's love? I'd have
to tell her the truth, though a more outrageous waste of time I
could not conceive of. Hopeless. Hopeless. Hopeless. I wanted
her to go away, to leave me to the stern comfort of the heat and
my hunger.

"Maureen," I said. "Do you want me to tell you what you'd
like to hear? Or what I really believe?"

Maureen said, "What you really believe, sir. Of course." But,
for all practical purposes, the conversation had ended there. I
wasn't on her side. I would repeat, monotonously, arguments
that had certainly been used before to no great advantage. And
she would say, "But I love him." That would be that. Then I'd
have only to make a gracious retreat before matters became
really unpleasant.

"All right then. Let's get a few things straight right off. First,
I'm three times as old as you are. I don't mean to pull rank on
you, far from it. But one of the things I've learned—and, for all
I know, it may be the very essence of human tragedy—one

thing I've learned is that no person can ever really communicate
his experience to another. So much misery might be avoided
if that weren't so. So much. But I guess it just isn't to be. I'm
afraid you've already stopped listening to me. I know you've
resolved to do what you think you must. In a sense, it's inevitable—perhaps, it's even for the best. But, then again, I'd hate
to see you suffer unnecessarily." I thought I'd pass out then—
I hadn't said so many words at one time in days. I heard Artie's
heavy breathing, and my sense of hopelessness joined allegiance
with his very different sense of hopelessness. I knew that Maureen's intensity, her more vital life force, was about to make me
seem ridiculous. And yet, for all that, it was I who was right.

"I don't have to tell you these things—but still . . . You
must know, Maureen, that a marriage involves, at the very least,
terrific problems of balance and compensation. If you marry
Sidney, the disparity between your religions will grow in importance as the first, all-absorbing joys of love fade. When
you're no longer so afraid of losing Sidney, you may wish he
were a bit different. But, if he's the man you say he is, you
won't be able to change him, and, in time, a chasm may grow
between you. A chasm that will bring an end to your happiness." I paused to recover my breath. Maureen said nothing.
After all, I hadn't made a very original disclosure. "Tell me,
honey," I said finally. "Do you think you're a good Catholic?"

"I'm okay. Pretty good—I guess. I believe in God and Christ
and the Virgin Mary, if that's what you mean."

"It is. And Catholicism has been part and parcel of your
whole life. Hasn't it?" She nodded. "Can you honestly say now
—honestly—that you wouldn't mind bringing your children up
as Jews?"

"I don't know. We'll cross that bridge when we come to it."

"No. That's not right, Maureen. Now you're not playing fair. I agreed not to use your age against you. And now, instead, you're pleading youth. Maureen, you've come to that bridge already. You must decide—decide now—whether it's fair to have children, despite the religious chasm that'll always separate you and Sidney."

"What's a chasm, your honor?"

I put my hands to the sides of my face and rubbed them there. Hopeless. Hopeless. And now the very words were being taken from me. I looked at Maureen. I knew that any appeal to her intellect would, of necessity, have a very limited effect. She had found a cause. She was determined to resist anything that threatened the sanctity of that cause. And with good reason. Causeless, what was she?

"A chasm is—well, in this sense, it's an emptiness that separates, a difference that sets people apart. Your children won't know what to believe. Probably they'll reject religion entirely. But that's only one consideration. Your parents—Sidney's parents, too, no matter what he may say—both families would be deeply hurt. You'd be separated, at least in part, from all that's been most familiar to you. Maureen. I'm sorry. I'm afraid your chance of happiness will be very small, indeed."

"But I love Sidney." It had come. I was stymied; confused, frustrated, infuriated by my own helplessness.

"I know you love him. Perhaps you always will—"

"He loves me, too." She understood what I was implying. "We love each other."

"All right. I'll grant you that. I'm sure you both love each other. But, still, there are things that love shouldn't be made to undergo. Things before which even the greatest love is helpless."

And then she fell on me. I think she'd been waiting for me to say something like that, for me to indict myself. Certainly, from the first, she interpreted it as an absolute triumph. I never expected it of her—that was the whole thing, of course. Not of her. From the moment Maureen said it, I knew she'd maneuvered me into an untenable position.

"Love is helpless? That's not what you said in your book."

"My book?"

"*A God For Our Time.* That's your book, isn't it? It's got your picture on the back."

"You've read it?"

"Four times. My brother told me about it. It's the most wonderful book I've ever read, your honor. I'm going to get my parents to read it—my mother at least. I cried when you said those beautiful things about Christian love—about loving people of other religions."

"You—you've read my book?"

"Yes. So, you see, you'll have to talk straight to me." She smiled. "I know all your secrets. I know what you really believe. On page one hundred nine you said, 'Christian love must rise above—' "

"Maureen. Christian love isn't sexual love."

"Sexual. We're not sexual."

"I mean—well, love between a man and a woman isn't always the truest sort of love. Often it's the most selfish emotion we ever know. You love Sidney because he's handsome and clever, and because he shows you new things. That's what we call *eros* —selfish love. There's nothing wrong with it really, but it's different from Christian love, what we'd call *agape*—"

"What you'd call what?"

"No. Forget that. All I'm saying is—you probably love Sidney for selfish reasons. Because he makes you happy, because—"

"You said love, Bishop Belknap. Don't tell me what I read. You said love. And I love Sidney."

"Now don't get upset. Let's try to understand this thing if we can. Let's take an example."

"Okay."

"Good. Well, now. Let's suppose—let's suppose there's a boy and a girl who are deeply in love. Like you and Sidney. Let's suppose, too, that this boy and this girl—well, they're not sure if they should have sexual intercourse with each other."

"What's that got to do with me and Sidney?"

"Please, honey. Give me a chance. I'm not trying to imply anything—it's just an example. Now . . . What was I saying? Yes. Selfish love says, 'We want to share everything. We'll go to bed with each other.' But true love is more responsible, more mature. It says, 'My girl's reputation will be endangered. There's always a chance she might get pregnant. No, I won't hurt her. I won't jeopardize her happiness.' Now, if Sidney and you really felt love for each other, what I'd call unselfish, Christian love, then you wouldn't make yourselves, your parents —and, in the future—your children, as miserable as you're bound to make them."

"I see. You mean we'd just give up. We wouldn't see each other any more."

"Well, no. You could see each other. Of course . . ."

"See each other? Do you know what my father's like?" She shook her head. "And I trusted you. I didn't think you'd put all sorts of sneaky meanings in your book. I thought you meant what you said. But you're no different from the rest. In fact, I think you're worse."

"Please, Maureen. You're being very hard on me. You asked

my opinion, and I gave it to you. If I told you to go ahead and
marry Sidney—I could never forgive myself. There are certain
things we just have to accept. I think I made it perfectly clear
in my book—"

"No, you didn't."

"Well. Perhaps you didn't understand. Some of the writing
is rather complex."

"You mean, I'm too stupid. Too stupid to read books. Well,
your book didn't say 'Adults only' on it."

"No. But maybe if you read it again—"

"I'm not going to read it again. There's a time for reading
and a time for doing things." She stood up.

"Maureen, honey. Life isn't fair. It wasn't meant to be. Believe me, there are things we just have to accept. Sidney and
you—even I once loved a—"

"I'm disappointed in you, Bishop Belknap. I thought you
were a bigger man." She stared at me, and the tears poured
down her cheeks. "I should have known better. It was my
fault." She touched my arm lightly. "We're still friends. Sorry
I took up so much of your time. Good night."

I fell back. The ceiling swelled pregnantly; then it slowly
subsided. I began to hiccup. The vision in my left eye was shot
through with little, colorful dancing lights. Maureen Lopopulo,
aged almost sixteen, had read *A God For Our Time*. And she
had garnered from it such pleasant flowers as she had determined, previously, to find there. That was wrong. Yet *A God
For Our Time* was a thing perfectly right—even, one might
have said, a holy thing. I wondered if I were too exhausted now
to act as a valid instrument of God's word. I wondered. And
then I hiccuped again.

"Pretty smooth. Pretty smooth, I'd say. Man, have you got

her snowed. Poor little-tits. Tears and everything, the whole friggin' works. You clever bastard, you. 'Course, you've had more time than me—yeah, and you sure haven't let the grass grow under your ass. That's for damn sure."

"What—what was that?"

"Maureen, honey. Maureen, honey. Whit, you're a bishop after my own heart. Look at him. Can't even stand up without takin' a pratt-fall—still he's got the little pieces of tail right where he wants them. Under his big, nasty old thumb. What a man."

I laughed out loud for the first time in days. "Either you have it or you don't," I said.

Night fell, bringing with it a cessation of sound. I lay motionless and perfectly flat. Now the heat was a companion curled in familiar closeness against all my sides; hunger emptiness I knew better than any fullness. The weakness of my body, the acquiescence of my will, were at last a relief to me. I had come to know resignation. No longer was there any need to strive.

Artie slept quietly, his arms spread birdlike, his calves straddling the sides of the mattress. Jimmy slept in a bow, his cupped hand near his mouth. Mr. Farbstein sat sternly upright in a posture of attentiveness, but he, too, was asleep. The silence seemed to register in decibels. I acknowledged it and smiled at the ceiling. Then, as a challenge to my complacency, I began thinking of Pious and of Michael, of Maureen, of the things upon things that once I had expected to achieve. But they passed through my consciousness, as water over the flat edge of a tile. And I smiled at the ceiling again.

Miss Black moved noiselessly through the door and into my room. I was surprised. It was the first time I'd seen her since

my angiogram. Even in that terrible heat she seemed cool; as
though cast entirely of some dark, impervious alloy. Miss Black
came to a halt beside my bed—a glass of grapefruit juice held
straight out in one hand, a white envelope held straight out in
the other. The right hand lowered itself, and the glass found
the surface of my table with a hollow click. Then she placed
the envelope beside it.

"Good evening, Bishop Belknap. I have some grapefruit juice
for you. And a letter. Is there anything else you need?" I shook
my head. She turned, her hands pressed flat at her sides, and
moved unerringly toward the door.

The envelope lay, a white rectangle, on the table above and
before me. I made no attempt to bring it down. I mistrusted
it. I think it reminded me of other things, of other envelopes.
Envelopes unopened, too, and suggesting a simple sort of truth
that was beyond me. I watched it for nearly a quarter of an
hour. By that time, I suppose, the envelope had come to belong
within the order that was now my order. I rose up and pulled
it down from the table. It was glued very tightly. For some
time I couldn't introduce the tip of my little finger beneath the
flap. But I worked stubbornly, my breath coming in louder,
more separate gasps, and finally it was open.

There was one sheet of white paper inside, and, on that, only
one typewritten line. I read it once and then again. The line
said, "An operation has been scheduled for you at ten o'clock
Friday morning, August twenty-fifth." It was signed, Terrence
F. Snow. The signature was thick and involved, with large, un-
essential flourishes. Nowhere, not on the envelope, not on the
note, had he mentioned my name.

But what did that matter? Happiness and exultation chased
their tails inside my stomach. I hugged the little piece of paper

to my chest, feeling its glossiness against my hairs. This was my reward. The vindication of my faith, of my willing resignation before God and his instruments. I was so full of joy that a big, moist lump began to swell near my larynx. I wanted to tell Artie; I wanted to tell Jimmy. But they were asleep. And so I said to the ceiling, "I'm going to have it—I'm going to have my operation."

Lord God my Father, Thou, indeed, art the Author of all mercy. I thank Thee. I thank Thee for this new hope of life. I thank Thee for Thy great and loving kindness unto me. Forgive me my terrible moments of doubt and defiance. In the name of Thy great Son, accept now my penitence and my gratitude. Oh my Father, I have not deserved this, Thy mercy towards me.

Rededicate me, my God, to my holy mission. Help me in this new time to love as Thou lovest. For Thou, Lord, art the Holiest of Holies, the Light of the World, the Author of all Being. Forgive me what is past and help me to live in Thee, for Thee and with Thee, now and forever more. In the name of Thy Son Jesus Christ, I ask that Thou accept my thanks. Accept my rededication. Accept me.

I lay back, exhausted, on my pillow. As I did so, a lovely breath of cool air—like an answer—swept in through the window. It blew my sheet of paper to the floor.

The heat had broken.

SUNDAY, AUGUST 20TH—

THE SEVENTH DAY

I SAW IT. It was an egg. Softly boiled and warm, it lay before
me, oozing orange-yellow from a white wound. There was toast,
too—and on it, butter and brown crumbs. Desire gurgled
within me. My hand rose. I sunk my spoon into the egg's middle, and the yoke seeped with an inaudible sigh to the round
edges of my plate. I ate ferociously. And when there was nothing left to eat, I found myself more ravenous than I had been in
days. Now, its memory reawakened, my hunger was obsessed
with taunting and very specific desires—other eggs, other pieces
of toast.

Artie and Jimmy watched, without exhaling, as I encountered
the egg. It wouldn't have surprised them, I think, had I caught
the egg in my fist and squeezed its yellow heart into an upthrust
mouth. Disappointed, Artie offered me his own egg to rape, but
the white and yellow breakfast nurse said, "Go easy. You've got
time. Plenty of time." And so I refused him. Rewards came
only from obedience. Directly from that. There was lunch
just ahead and dinner; and, beyond those, whole days with meals
set in them like rare jewels. I had come out of the wilderness.

"Shut that God-damn window. It's cold as a witch's mound in here."

It was cold, though perhaps not as cold as a witch's mound—whatever that was. The air was an autumnal, clear crystal. Objects seemed to ring when they were touched. Fingernails felt cold on fingertips; sheets were numbing; little metal things gave burn-like, icy shocks. Measured against the preceding afternoon, this day was very cold indeed. Artie had wrapped himself to the throat in blankets. Only Mr. Farbstein seemed not to notice, but, then, he hadn't seemed to notice the heat.

I sat up. I squinted out, over the river for the first time since Thursday. I felt exhilarated, even dizzy. The atmosphere had become transparent once again. The New Jersey shoreline was no longer tinged with brown. The slips, the buildings—even individual people—were visible. There was activity in the private boat basin at 78th Street. Outboard motors gurgled and roared and snapped peevishly at their owners. A breeze ruffled the treetops, baring modestly the paler undersides of leaves. I thought I heard the sound of church bells, and I remembered that—throughout the morning—congregation after congregation had met to pray for the health of all Christian bishops. Joyfully, I read the collect, epistle and gospel for the day.

It was Sunday, and the sick were being visited. Outside our room hesitant pairs of people came and went. Excited whispers rose to speech and were whispered down again. Men tottered behind huge flowers sprays; women's heels begged a moment's attention; cigarette butts lay crushed just beyond each doorway. Relatives, bored with their own sick, peered in to speculate on our misfortunes. And one would have to explain, each time, about the nasty, little probe on Tuesday, the violent attack of a

week before, the pitiful state of one's bowels. Flowers; Agatha
Christies; boxes of candy; flasks of Scotch; trips out for coffee
and a butt while they slept; get-well cards from the satiric to
the sexual to the grain of mustard seed sort; jokes and backslaps;
smiles and soft encouragement; tears suppressed as fingers encircled wasted wrists; hours in the semi-darkness passed just
waiting. It was Sunday. The sick were being visited.

More Lopopulos appeared than ever before. Uncontrollable
younger cousins; aged, sleepy women in buns and heavy black
shoes. Maureen waved at me; she was determined to be "still
friends." Mrs. Lopopulo brought me a small box of candy,
"For being so nice to our Jimmy. The least we could do." And
I had to let all the Lopopulos have "just a taste." But I was in
very good spirits and not to be depressed. I told Mrs. Lopopulo
about my operation, and all the Lopopulos agreed that it was
"just great," and that now there was nothing to worry about.
Artie alone seemed disturbed. He said he was sorry to hear it,
and Mrs. Lopopulo presented him with a baleful grimace for
his pains. Then they left the room. Mrs. Lopopulo was right.
There was nothing to worry about. Nothing. Whatever his
opinion of me, Dr. Snow would, at the very least, save my heart
for the sake of his own greater glory.

After lunch I walked unsteadily, but proudly alone, to the
lavatory. When I'd returned, I stood beside my bed and began,
methodically, to rearrange my things. I pushed my books from
one side of the table to the other, finally settling on an arrange-
ment that was symmetrical and necessarily inconvenient. I
whistled silently as I worked. I opened the drawer and scooped
all my loose change into one corner. I tossed *Fun In The Hospital* onto Jimmy's bed. Then I put my toothbrush and toothpaste together, as is only proper. Hair brush and hair tonic.

Paper and pens. Wallet and handkerchief, because they are both squares. Two envelopes . . .

I had two envelopes in my hand. At first I didn't know what they were, for my mind was filled with the enthusiasm of new resolution. Two envelopes, square and white, but used. Addressed not to me, but to Dr. Terrence F. Snow. On top of the wallet? Under the pens? And then I remembered what they were, and the envelopes slipped, in no exact order, out of my hand and into the drawer. Strength poured down the backs of my heels. My knees gave, and I sat on the edge of my bed.

Letters from the dead. It came back to me then: dying members of unacceptable minority groups, referred to me for distant unction. I closed the drawer. I remembered the green pen scrawl on one envelope—a child's handwriting. My renewed existence was a meretricious sham; Dr. Snow knew very well the quality of my courage. But . . . But someday, on some pretext, I'd make two more pilgrimages. When I was well, not until then, I would read the letters. Even so, guilt appeared, in its turn, to oppress me; when she spoke, I thought at first that the voice had come from within my own head.

"Hello. My name is Myra Farbstein."

The only Myra I'd ever known had been tall and blond and very sensual. She'd run her hand playfully between the insides of my thighs. But this was another Myra. Scarcely as high as my bed; white skin, white hair, white-rimmed glasses; bony shins covered with purplish, raised splotches. And called Myra for the sake of irony.

"Yes?" I asked. Harshly.

"I'm Mrs. Farbstein. Mr. Farbstein's wife?" She pointed toward his bed. I nodded. "My husband's just dropped off to sleep, and I thought—well, you know, we've been neighbors

here all week—I thought I'd come over and introduce myself.
I think it's good we all get to know each other." She spoke shyly,
yet with a certain determination.

"Yes," I said, lying easily. "I was thinking the very same
thing. Why don't you pull up a chair, Mrs. Farbstein?" We
shook hands. "Whitney Belknap."

"Belknap? Could it be? There was a Henry Belknap—we
knew him through the business. Belknap and Collins Hardware? But it's a common name, isn't it? Like Farbstein, only
different." She smiled.

"Henry Belknap was my father."

"You don't say? Isn't that something?" She'd found our
lowest common denominator, and she seemed pleased, relieved.
"It's a small world. We're Farbstein Plumbing Supply, Third
Avenue, Bronx. You don't say? Wait'll I tell David." I had
known Davids in my time. Mr. Farbstein wasn't a David.

"Farbstein Plumbing? Yes, I think the name is familiar."

"A small world. Belknap and Collins, Warren Street . . .
That's a place you got. What's it, four stories? We have
a good trade, I'm not complaining. But nothing like Belknap and Collins. Maybe, who knows, we get to talk a
little business while we're here? A little business maybe give
David some interest." She looked down into her lap for a moment, and then she began fumbling at her purse. As though her
own thoughts had become unsettling. "Have a Life Saver?
Peppermint?"

"No. No thank you. Actually, as far as B & C goes—I own a
controlling interest—but I'm not really involved in the business. Never was, I'm afraid. B & C's been in the hands of managers for nine or ten years now. Since George Collins died."

"Managers? You'd leave Belknap and Collins with managers?

Such a business as that. But you keep a good eye on things, no?"

"No. Can't say that I do. I see financial reports now and then, of course. But that's about all." Mrs. Farbstein was disappointed. Our lowest common denominator had turned out to be not low enough. I tentatively fingered the *New York Times* Magazine Section, but there was no response to my suggestion. Mrs. Farbstein needed to talk; she had chosen me, and I would have to listen.

"So. No big business deal? Not even a few nuts and bolts? Couple washers, maybe?" She smiled, and I returned her smile.

"Afraid not."

"I'm sorry for that. Don't get me wrong—it's not I'm looking for a big bargain. I just thought—well, I hoped I could get David interested in something else. He's got so much time here yet. At least another month."

"He's improved tremendously in just a few days. Even I can see that."

"Yes. Yes, he has. What Dr. Snow did, I couldn't tell you. He's a genius. A God. I was so grateful I—I would have kissed his hands." She blushed when she said that, or made the gestures of a blushing person, for no blood suffused her aged skin. And then I remembered what P. Crecy had told me. She'd done it on her knees. Mrs. Farbstein had crawled across the floor to kiss his feet. It must have been, I thought, a very terrible sight.

"You give me hope. Dr. Snow's operating on my heart next Friday. I found out just last night."

"God protect you. It's terrible. So many sick people. But he's a genius, don't you worry a minute. Not a minute." Mr. Farbstein moved. Asleep, he bent his head and brought the picture up. He looked and smiled. But his eyes were closed, and the movement was merely the acquired habit of many hours.

"Poor David. Sometimes I think . . ." She shook her head. "I don't know what to think."

"Is something wrong?"

"Yes and no. He's coming along so nicely, I feel I'm an ungrateful fool to worry." She paused and then she said it. "But, no. He's not the same man. He's not my David."

"Not the same man. How could that be?" I spoke calmly, but, even so, her words had had their effect. Things began crawling in a vaguely spiral motion over the back of my neck.

"That's it. A stupid remark. Of course he's my husband. Who else would he be? But still, it's there—what, I don't know —and you don't fool a wife of forty years so easy." She hesitated, as if wondering whether or not I could be trusted. Then she leaned close to my face. "Mr. Belknap, my husband is a wonderful man. I want you to know that. A kind man. We had two boys, God rest their souls, they were both killed in the war. In the same week. A terrible thing. David loved them so —so, it made my own love a shameful, silly thing. Hard times, good times, it was always the same—he thought of me and the boys. But now, when I know he needs me—it's as if . . ." She paused; I didn't find it a pleasant pause. "I tell you. It's as if, while he was asleep, while he was under the anaesthetic, he —he saw something that frightened all the life out of him. He's alive, yes. But that's all." I sat up, each hand fisted. I wanted her to go away. When I spoke, I spoke loudly, hoping Mr. Farbstein would awaken.

"Come now. You're just trying to upset yourself." She looked at me strangely.

"You think so? Maybe. Maybe you're right. But still—do you see that picture in his hand?"

"Yes," I said, shamming innocence. "Is it a picture?"

"A picture. You know what it's a picture of?"

"No," I said. I dreaded what was coming. It horrified me as, sometimes, children's marionette shows horrified me.

"It's a picture of valves, Mr. Belknap. Armstrong valves to be exact. Plumbing valves."

"Well, that's a good sign. He's probably thinking of business again."

"Business?" She laughed impatiently. "No, Mr. Belknap, you don't understand. He's not thinking of business. You know what he said to me yesterday?" She leaned forward again. "He said, 'I'm a machine now, Myra. I'm a machine.'" She imitated her husband's thin voice exactly. My forehead furrowed as though a tiny, unfamiliar pain had penetrated into some vital part of my body. It was her affair; I wanted no part of it.

"Please, Mrs. Farbstein. Try to understand. An operation as serious as the one your husband has had—well, it's bound to have a certain harmless effect on his way of thinking. He's a bit preoccupied, that's all. What does Dr. Snow say?"

"Dr. Snow?" She sat back, as though I had caught her in some act of disloyalty. "Dr. Snow? How could I ask Dr. Snow?"

"Well then. If Dr. Snow isn't worried—if he isn't worried, then I don't think you should be." Again Mrs. Farbstein looked strangely at me. For just a moment I thought that she was afraid of me. But she only nodded, as though I'd confirmed a resolution of her own.

"I'd better go back to my husband, Mr. Belknap. Maybe I could come over again?"

"Certainly. Please do. Any time."

*

Late that afternoon I drew a chair up to the windowsill and
sat with Augustine's *City of God* balanced on my lap. Below, a strong breeze had mottled the river in the rough tex-
tures of a Rodin bronze. A Negro man and woman sat, fishing,
at either end of an anchored motor rowboat. First he, then she,
would rise slightly as little rollers passed the length of the boat
—as though they were bowing politely to each other. The
woman took something from a basket and leaned forward. The
man put it to his mouth. From where I sat, so far from them,
so very far above them, I supposed contentment and understanding and peace. I was very happy.

I leaned forward, my chest supported on the windowsill's
rim. Directly, yet far below, I saw a little square garden surrounded by hedges. There was a tile walk in the garden; on
the walk were four scalloped green benches. I leaned farther
out. The middle of the square formed yet another square. In
it, a single waterspout pushed erratically, busily against the
wind. At one time the water had come from a statue's mouth,
but the statue's head was gone. Now the water spurted up from
a pipe in the ragged neck.

I thought the garden very wonderful and mysterious, nestled
as it was between the uncompromising gray giants of Cavendish. No people walked amongst the hedges. It was as secret
and as lonely as any Wordsworthian vale in the lake country. I
wanted to be in that garden. And I thought, when I was well,
I would find my way to it; from that little square within the
square, I'd look up on what had passed, and I'd find it distant
and no longer frightening.

Even as I speculated, a door opened into the garden. A nurse
appeared. Behind her, two lines of men and women—six in a
line—evolved slowly from the doorway. Another nurse followed. I was sorry to find that my garden had been violated,

but I liked to see those twelve walking so resolutely there. They
walked very quickly in a circle in the square. They walked with
determination. They ran. One man's arms moved like pistons
at his sides; his eyes were fixed on the statue in the middle. I
was glad to see them walk. I would have been glad to walk with
them there.

But they didn't walk for very long. One by one, like balls in
a roulette wheel, their momentum faded, and they fell gradually from their orbits to the little square within the square.
And when they had fallen inward, a curious, confused despair
seemed to take hold of them. One man stood with his face to
the inner hedge, stymied. Another put his hands on the slats of
a bench and held them tightly, as though, but for them, there
was only oblivion. A third man urinated. Then the nurses
came in from their positions at the outside of the square; they
hurled the distracted balls back into orbit. But their momentum never sufficed for very long, and, centrifugal force gone,
they dropped inward again.

I watched for half an hour—half an hour after I'd realized
what they were. Then they left, and the statue, expending its
essence from the neck, was the only moving thing in the little
garden. I looked back out to the river. The motor rowboat
was gone. Voices came from somewhere behind me. There was
a man beside Artie's bed. He was stocky and very well dressed.
He had a neatly clipped gray mustache, iron gray hair, and a
wonderfully shiny Phi Beta Kappa key that dangled, sparkling,
on a long chain. He was explaining something to Artie, but, for
all the intensity of his tone, I could see that his attention was
distracted. Artie, for his part, seemed to be disagreeing.
I heard him say, "No," once and then "No, no," in quick suc-
cession. I turned back to the window, for it was none of my
concern.

There were faces at the windows of Cavendish. Old faces, waxen faces, patient faces—faces that looked but not to see. All faces, I thought, very much like mine. Boys in shorts and lettered T-shirts ran a foot race on a path near the river. Toddlers on leashes bent to pick and taste things. But no face followed them. Then the door by the little square garden began to open again. I took my book and backed away toward my bed —from my bed, I was compelled to watch only the river and what lay indistinctly beyond it.

"Whit? Whit? Could you come over here?"

I put my Bible down and slipped a piece of tissue between the pages. I hesitated, then I sat up. I kicked my slippers out in front of me. Pushed my feet into them. Took my bathrobe from the foot of my bed. Then and only then, did I look at Artie. He was watching me. His toothless mouth was half open, as the mouth of a child before it cries. There was sweat on his forehead, in the creases on his neck. His ankles flexed and un-flexed, raising little tents in the sheet, collapsing them.

"Did you want me?" Artie nodded. He continued to nod for some time. There was nothing to do; I would have to go over. I put my bathrobe on. Then I shoved a chair to his bed with the side of my foot.

"What can I do you for?" I asked.

"I'm in trouble, Whit. Bad trouble." The tone of his voice was ominous with fear, and that irritated me. Bad trouble . . . I suspected the whole business was a gross imposition on his part. I wasn't about to be drawn in.

"You've been drafted," I said.

"Whit. It's serious. Please." I sobered, but kept aloof.

"Tell me then."

"I'm gonna die, Whit."

"Nonsense."

"Whit, for God's sake, listen to me. It happens, you know. People die. I'm gonna die. I only got four months left. I'm gonna die before Christmas."

I stared at Artie's sunken, sweat-flecked face, and I knew that he might very well be telling the truth. But I hadn't crossed the room prepared to think of death. Artie stretched his hand out toward me. I think he actually imagined I'd take it. I put both hands in the pockets of my bathrobe, indicating, with a gesture, that they were cold.

"Where d'you get this?"

"Albert. My brother. He was just here. Dirty bastard Snow told him to tell me. That son of a bitch—he'd take your wallet soon's he'd take your pulse."

"Now hold on. Dr. Snow's a great surgeon. We're damn lucky to have him."

"In the pig's asshole. I don't care how great he is. He said it's better I know about it. It ain't better. It ain't better at all. Why'd he have to do that?"

"Well, what's wrong? Why can't they do something? Operate?"

"Operate? Good Jesus God—don't you understand? Whit, wake up—there's nothin' left to operate on. Nothin'. They'd have to take all my insides out. It's eatin' me alive. I'm gonna die."

"Quiet," I hissed. "That doesn't help. Think of Jimmy."

"Oh, yeah. I know that line. Be brave, Artie. Be a martyr. No! Damn it, no! I'm scared to death— Oh God . . . Save me. Jesus, Mary and Joseph, save me. Save me, Whit." He went on like that for a considerable time. I said nothing, and, after a while, he subsided. We looked at each other. Artie was surprised, I think, to find no pity in my eyes.

"Whit, tell me. Where do I go from here?"

"I wouldn't worry about it. Dr. Snow'll think of something."

"For Christ's sake. I don't get it. I really don't. You talk like he was God or somethin'. Get it straight, will you? I'm gonna die. There's nothin' nobody can do. Nothin'."

"Well. All right. Have it your way. Let's suppose it is true—"

"It is." He made a sudden move toward his bed table. Three or four books fell to the floor with muffled slaps, but finally Artie managed to pull the black Bible toward him. "What do I read? Tell me what it's all about." I looked at the Bible. Then I looked at him. Artie saw my hesitation. "It's no good, huh? Too damn late for that."

"No. Never too late. Just give me a minute. I'm a little confused."

"What do I do?"

"It's not what you do. It's what you believe."

"Okay. I know you think it's because I'm sick. I know. I know it looks phony. But, honest—I do believe in God, Whit. I wasn't thinkin' before. I didn't mean all those things I said. I believe."

"And you're repentant?"

"God, yes. Yes, I'm repentant."

"Hmmmm. Let's see your Bible." I thumbed through the pages, until I was certain he wouldn't be reading a useless, colloquial translation. As I closed the cover, I saw two lines of childish handwriting on the flyleaf. "For my only uncle, from his only niece. Ginny." That was something to remember. I handed the Bible back.

"Is it all right?"

"Fine. Start on the Gospels. Read St. Matthew tonight—as

much as you can. We'll talk about it tomorrow." He held the
Bible to his throat.

"Whit. Can a frightened man ask a stupid question? Huh?
When you die, what is there?"

"There's a heaven and there's a hell. Just like they say. One
is with God and it's good. One is without God and it's terrible.
Heaven is for those who believe in Christ, and in His saving
Grace—only those." Artie was silent. "Well, you asked me,"
I said.

"I gotta believe you," he said finally. "The way you say it, I
gotta believe you."

"Were you baptized and confirmed?"

"Yeah. But that was a long time ago."

"It lasts." Suddenly Artie smiled.

"Hell. I oughta have it made—what with a bishop layin'
right next to me."

"Lying," I said.

Now there was something else. It irritated me like an insistent voice pitched just beyond comprehension. At first I
thought it was Artie. He was reading: a pair of heavy, brown
horn-rimmed glasses superimposed awkwardly on his face—I
thought it was the sound of the pages turning. The waiting.
It distracted my thinking, made me look up, pause to listen.
But it wasn't Artie. It was an influence actively and in-
tentionally imposing on my consciousness; I couldn't place it.
Artie flipped his Bible quickly back to the flyleaf and smiled.
After a moment he returned, doggedly, to his reading.

"How's it coming?"

"Not so good, Whit. I ain't thinkin' too clear."

"Relax. Take your time. Don't pressure yourself."

"Okay."

And so, very suddenly, God had dawned on Artie Carson. I thought it all very timely and convenient. But my suspicions were irrelevant. God may have his special ways of saving the heathen—I think probably he does. But that, too, is irrelevant. We can only think, in cases such as these, that those who cannot or will not accept Christ are surely damned. Damned in the worst, the most traditional sense of the word. It's the duty of a Christian to proselytize, not to speculate idly on God's plan for the unbeliever. Artie might yet come around. A very unpleasant responsibility faced me; I'd have to plan strategy with a careful imagination.

Yet, if truth were told, I suppose I didn't really believe Artie was dying. I fancied I might still speak to Dr. Snow. Probably, until this moment, Dr. Snow hadn't been sufficiently interested. I could understand that: Artie wasn't a very satisfactory patient. The next chance I had, I'd put in a word for Artie, and, in time, everything would straighten itself out. Dr. Snow would do something. I don't know but that I was more certain of my influence with Dr. Snow to save Artie's body than of my own influence with God to save his soul.

When his dinner arrived, Artie made a determined effort to eat. "Looks good," he said with contrived enthusiasm. "I could eat a horse." Then he jammed several forkfuls quickly into his mouth. His cheeks swelled as the food began to accumulate there. Soon he had to lie back—great, round pouches at the sides of his face. They subsided very gradually, but that was as far as he could go. "Dirty mother," he said. He pushed the table away. Then he took up his Bible again, cradling it against his hip; his stomach, I knew, could no longer tolerate the weight.

It happened again. I looked to the window. Then I waited,

listening, my nostrils dilated. Nothing at the window. Slowly I let my eyes play over the full width and height of the room. I stopped. Then I saw it. Mr. Farbstein was sitting upright, his body twisted uncomfortably. And he was staring at me just as, hardly an hour before, he had stared at Artie. Surprise communicated itself to my body: I smiled reflexively. Mr. Farbstein smiled back. He had many tiny teeth, and his smile was sinuous and terrible. Reptilian.

"Mister Belknap?" I looked away. But, behind my eyes, the influence persisted, and I knew Mr. Farbstein was still watching.

"Yes, Jimmy?"

"If you're feelin' better now, sir—why don't you come play with us? My mother says it'll do you good. We're out in the solarium."

"Better, yes. But not that well yet. Thank your mother for me. Tell her I certainly will—soon's I feel up to it."

"Okay. Yanks won two from the Red Sox today."

"Good news."

"That's five in a row." I nodded. Jimmy was silent for a moment. "I tried not to hear," he whispered. "But I couldn't help it. Mr. Carson's not too good, is he?"

"What makes you say that?" It surprised me. Jimmy was very upset.

"I heard—I heard he couldn't even live 'til Christmas."

"Well . . . That's not exactly right. That's what his brother said. We don't know what Dr. Snow thinks yet."

"Then Dr. Snow can do something?"

"Oh, yes. I think so. Don't worry about it. Everything's not settled by a long shot. I'll speak to Dr. Snow tomorrow." Jimmy grinned.

"I knew you would. Mr. Carson's a real nice man."

"A nice man? Yes. Yes, he certainly is. Well, you run along now. There's nothing to worry about." Jimmy patted me on the arm almost gaily. Then he ran, defective heart and all, out into the corridor. I think Jimmy, too, had some crazy notion of my great influence with Dr. Snow. I looked up. Across the room, Mr. Farbstein's eyes on me were the eyes of a man who had died in laughter.

Night came, making uniform the surfaces of the river. All along our corridor people were saying their good-byes: voices rose as the prospect of going once again into the real world became tangible. Nurse MacArthur appeared in our room. I waved at her, and she hesitated, uncertain, as though she didn't know me. Then she waved once vaguely. Artie tried not to notice Nurse MacArthur: at least he didn't lean far to the side of his bed in order to examine her calves. He remained intent on his reading. "What's chaff?" he'd ask. "What exactly is a beatitude? I used to know." Then, more or less predictably, he'd say, "Hey, that's good. Interesting. Pretty damn interesting, Whit." The reviews, evidently, would be good.

I looked across the room. Mr. Farbstein's eyes met my eyes, engaged them and registered no emotion. He had lost all interest in Artie. Now he had settled his whole upper torso, the better to keep me under surveillance. I smiled pleasantly. But Mr. Farbstein knew I was trying to compromise his austerity— he didn't return my smile. Judging from the position of his body, he was well content to watch me forever.

Nurse MacArthur came to give Artie an injection; he made a show of reading throughout. When Nurse MacArthur saw his Bible, she looked quickly toward me. Then she spoke quite pleasantly to Artie. I sensed that she, too, knew he had little

time left. But Artie basked in her attention; he didn't feel it
was ominous. He sat up, smiled, talked feverishly, in order to
hold her interest. But it wavered. When she left him to come
to my bed, he was still talking.

"How are you this evening?"

"Well," I said. "This is a surprise. I thought you'd forgotten
me." She frowned while she was smiling: it was something I'd
have thought a human face couldn't do.

"I don't forget patients. It's my job."

"I'm a job now."

"Well, no . . . No. I know what you're going through. I've
seen it before. But what can I do?" She put her hands out in
order to show how helpless she was. I thought perhaps
she hadn't been listening to me. Her answer was strange—it
was barely pertinent in its content and not at all in tone.

"Nothing," I said. "Just smile now and again." She nodded
and then, perversely, she frowned.

"I see you're eating."

"Yes. Everything's coming along fine. Your friend, Dr. Snow
—he's scheduled my operation for Friday."

Nurse MacArthur dropped Artie's empty hypodermic. I
heard it roll against the leg of my bed. She bent to pick it up.
When she stood upright again, she borrowed a piece of tissue to
wipe it off with. That seemed odd to me: surely, I thought,
the thing would have to be sterilized. And then Nurse Mac-
Arthur began to scrape under her thumbnail with the needle's
point. She looked at me curiously all the while—rather as an
armless phrenologist might. My scalp began to itch along the
temples.

"Friday?"

"Yes," I said. "I think it's wonderful news."

"You're not afraid?"

"Oh, yes. Don't get me wrong. I'm afraid. But I'd be more afraid if I thought nothing could be done. Dr. Snow's a great man. If he thinks an operation will solve my problems—whatever they are—well, naturally, I'm cheered."

"You'll have to sign a paper, you know."

"What d'you mean. A release?"

"Yes. That way they have no responsibility."

"Yes . . ."

"They can't operate otherwise. You'll have to sign it."

"That's understandable. They have to protect themselves." I nodded. I couldn't see where the conversation was leading. Most of the time, Nurse MacArthur seemed barely to be addressing me. Once I even glanced over to the window. But, of course, no one was there.

"No," she said. "It's all up to you. You see—Dr. Snow's really got nothing to say about it." She paused. "I've got to go now. I've got other patients."

"Miss MacArthur?" She hesitated with obvious reluctance. "What happened to Sarah Samson?"

"Oh," she said. She seemed relieved. "Sarah was fired. It was a long time coming. She wasn't much use. Besides, she got too involved with the patients. That's not good, you know."

"Could you get me her address?"

"Well, I'll see. Perhaps when you're better. I've got to go now." She turned and walked quickly out into the corridor.

After Nurse MacArthur left, I watched the lights of Palisades Park—busy and joyous on an August Sunday night. I liked to watch the lights. It amused me to think that each light represented a soul for which I was ultimately responsible. Ultimately—distantly, impersonally. Nurse MacArthur had made me thoughtful. As for the release: well, I thought, if that's the

last remnant of my volition, we can't get it over with soon
enough.

Another light burned nearer to my bed. Artie was pressing
on through the New Testament. It wasn't easy for him, God
knows. The Bible shimmered in front of his eyes: he had to
hold it above his stomach, and his arms, I could see, were shaking from the strain. His too heavy glasses had left red scars on
the sides of his nose and along his temples. But he read coura-
geously. Sometimes he would shape words silently with his lips.
Then, when he finally understood them, he would nod
vigorously, as though to encourage himself. Another light.
Another responsibility. But this not ultimate, not distant, not
impersonal.

Lord God my Father, grant me strength. Grant me wisdom.
Let my tongue be Thy tongue. Let it not be bound by pride or
selfishness or fear. I pray Thee, in the name of Thy Son, Jesus
Christ, look down in mercy on Artie Carson. Grant unto him,
at the moment of death, a new vision of mortality—that he may
know, at the last, Thy peace which passeth all understanding.
And let the Word of Christ come upon every troubled soul in
this place—that, by the urging of their sickly bodies, they may
see through life unto Thee.

I have disappointed Thee, My God. I have not loved my
fellow man; I fear I have not spoken of Thee, as Thou wouldst
have had me speak. Annex my soul, annex my mind, my God,
that I may just this once be perfectly Thy Instrument. I have
been close to death. Thou hast seen fit, through Thy surrogate,
to grant me time yet on this earth. Let me be, in that time, a
pure and unclouded glass through which Thy Word may shine
beautifully, eloquently, urgently. And, whatever my fate, let
not my weakness prejudice the salvation of any human soul . . .

THE EIGHTH DAY

ARTIE SNORED as though he were weeping. His Bible lay where it had fallen, in the join of his throat and shoulder. His glasses dangled crazily from one ear. Gray blankets were draped from the mattress in two somber, scalloped loops that reached just above the floor. Artie had clasped his sheet tightly under his chin, but, even so, only a thin V opening out from his groin was covered. A spasm stilled: like the charred, frantic bodies of Pompeii victims. Death that was never quite acknowledged; movement, the momentum of which had carried into another world. But, for now, Artie was alive. He had read until he could read no more. Reading seemed, in him, a terrible thing.

It was still cool. The thin crack under my window surrendered sound to the wind as an Aeolian harp might. I gave it my attention. The sky was blue-white and uniform. The wind scooped troughs in the water; then it fluffed their edges into little white-caps. A tanker, moving clumsily against the current, dug fingers of spray back over its bow. Trees gesticulated, throwing off early, still-green leaves. It was a vital morning with unbounded energy to expend. A day to emulate. A day to appall the spiritless. A day just four days before my operation.

Artie's state of grace had bothered me in the night. I had dreamed of incoherent arguments, incoherently refuted; of unapt quotations and incommunicable statements of faith. As so often happens in dreams, he to whom I spoke displayed every imaginable form of grotesque inattention. He rode the adjustable table like a scooter; he caught flies on my nose; he was a fly; he asked me to hand him a rag as he sat outside the window, licking at its surface with his tongue—but the glass was still blurred, and I was afraid, as I leaned forward to smash it with my fist, that I might knock him backward into the little, square garden below.

Across the room Mr. Farbstein was shaking his head in slow, long arcs. He had a spoon in one hand, and he was waving it rhythmically, as though conducting music that only he could hear. Artie's snoring became a series of interrogatives. Mr. Farbstein overturned his spoon, and egg-white, like sputum, extruded itself to his tray in a long, clouded strand. He smiled, as if, by doing that, he had proven his point. Artie's Bible fell to the floor. He sat up and clawed the dangling glasses from his face.

"God damn," he said. "God damn. It's all the same." He coughed and spat into a piece of tissue. Then he leaned over the edge of the bed to retrieve his fallen Bible. But it was too far from him, and, in reaching down, his body slipped forward. He had to dig his nails into the mattress. I heard their scraping pops.

"Hold it," I said. I leaped out of bed. Artie watched as I picked up the Bible and laid it on his bed table.

"I read all night, Whit," he said. "Honest. But it didn't go too good. I didn't get too much out of it."

"I don't wonder. That was a damned stupid thing to do—reading all night. Well . . . Clean yourself up, then we'll talk for a while."

I walked over to the window. Below, in the little square garden, a sheet of newspaper flexed and unflexed in the wind like a giant, colorless butterfly. Flowers peered forward and then leaped backward in surprise. Little whirlwinds organized dirt and bits of refuse into spirals, while hordes of sparrows channeled the wind along their wings—until it catapulted them through the trees. Someone tapped me lightly on the shoulder.

"Big hurricane's comin' up. It's maybe gonna hit right here. I just heard on th'radio." Jimmy seemed one with the morning. He stood before me on tiptoe, tossing his radio easily from one hand to the other. Now, out of consideration for Mr. Farbstein, Jimmy listened only in the solarium.

"How're you this morning?"

"Great." He pounded himself on the chest.

"Careful," I said. "Careful. You and I, we've got to be careful. We've got to watch our hearts."

"Yes sir," he said. "But I don't feel sick. It's funny. Mister Belknap, is God punishing me for my sins?"

"Your sins?" I smiled: Jimmy's sins. "Nonsense. God doesn't punish people for their sins—not in this world, anyway. He doesn't reward them if they're good either. God's not Santa Claus, Jimmy. Remember that. But—whatever happens—it happens for a darned good reason. Try to learn from it. Just think: how many boys your age have had such an important experience as this? Right now you may think it's not fair. But, later on, it's bound to make you a wiser, more mature person.

You'll be bigger for it." Jimmy thought about that. Then he smiled.

"Gee, Mister Belknap," he said. "Maybe someday I'll be like you. Must be great to know everythin' for sure." I laughed. "My mother says I oughta listen to everythin' you say. She says you shoulda been my father, then I'd learn somethin' every day. I guess she's right."

"Well, now . . . Your mother's very kind. But you have a fine father already."

"Yup. He's okay. I gotta go brush my teeth now. That old lady down the hall gave me a piece of chocolate." Jimmy went over to his drawer. He took out a small pair of binoculars, his toothbrush and paste. He hung the binoculars around his neck; then he put the toothbrush in his mouth and ran, buzzing and broooming, out into the corridor. Artie watched him go. He shook his head, his hope confounded by Jimmy's exuberance.

Lord God above, let the thoughts of my mind and the desires of my heart, as now they are manifested in words, be at this moment wholly Thine—to the honor and glory of Thy Name, through Jesus Christ our Lord. Artie had made ready for my coming. I walked toward his bed. As I did so, I sensed that Mr. Farbstein's eyes were following me diligently across the room.

"Look, Whit," he said nervously, "if you got somethin' else to do, I can wait." I sat down. "Look. Serious—I don't think I'm ready. I didn't understand all that stuff right off. I gotta have more time. I ain't used to thinkin' like this."

"Calm down. Don't have a fit. You're not on trial." I opened my Bible to Matthew One. "Just tell me how far you read— what you think you understand. What you'd like me to explain."

Artie sat up as straight as he dared. He put his glasses on.

He adjusted them. Then he took up his Bible and began fumbling awkwardly for the place. He was stalling, and, at first, I
couldn't understand why. Something had gone wrong. At last
Artie closed the Bible and laid it across his stomach, as though
it were some secret form of therapy. For several minutes he
stared at the ceiling. I began to sense that he was slipping away
from me, and so I put out my hand and touched him—lightly,
only very lightly—on the arm.

"Forget it," he said. "I'm wastin' your time."

"What's the matter? Tell me." He laughed.

"What's the matter? Y'mean you don't know? No? That's
funny. I thought you did it on purpose—like a coupla days ago,
when you told me t'take a good, long look at myself. Whit, this
is insanity. It's pretty damn strong stuff—what's it say? Who-
ever lusts after a woman with his mind, he's already screwed
her up. Good God. D'you know how many broads I've laid
by those standards?"

"And me?" I said. "What about Mr. Farbstein? Your
brother? Jimmy in a couple of years? You think you're a special case? No, friend. You're not. But that's not the point. The
point is knowing it. Admit it and—" I clicked my fingers—
"no more pride. No more self-sufficiency. You've got to despair
before you can hope. In fact, I think you understand only too
well."

"Despair? I could laugh. I'm such a mess I could laugh."

"But you're not laughing." I turned to Romans Seven.
"Okay. You've brought up an important point. I'm going to
read you what St. Paul said about it. I want you to listen carefully—Paul's not always as clear as I'd like him to be. Now, 'Is
the law sin? God forbid. Nay I had not known lust, except the
law had said, Thou shalt not covet. But sin, taking occasion by
the commandment, wrought in me all manner of concupiscence'

that is, lust, sin—'for without the law sin was dead.' For, without the law, sin was dead. Do you see what he's getting at? No? Say no, if you don't."

"No."

"Well . . . It's simple really. 'For without the law sin was dead.' That is, without morality—without someone or something to say this is good and that is bad—there is no sin. Without standards there can be no failure. St. Paul realizes—and this is one of the great insights in history—he realizes that sin is the product of religious or social morality. D'you see now?"

"Yeah. Maybe. You mean, if we didn't think murder was wrong—it wouldn't be."

"Right. Right. Now you're cooking with gas."

"But, Whit. That can't mean that murder and all the rest—it don't mean they're right, does it?"

"Good. That's the next step. Sin is a product of the law—but the law is still the law. In Paul's case, my case, the law is given by God. By Christ 'Whosoever looketh on a woman to lust after her, hath committed adultery with her already in his heart.' It's impossible. Impossible. Every man is an adulterer. Every man is incapable before the law."

"Yeah? Everybody? D'you get excited when you see a woman?"

"Well. Yes. I've been known to."

"Have you ever—I mean . . . you're not married, are you?"

"No. I'm not married."

"Well . . . Have you—have you ever done it with a woman?"

"We're getting off the subject. Personal revelations—even those of a bishop—aren't to the point here." I paused. Artie seemed disappointed. "But, if it'll comfort you . . . Yes, I

have done it with a woman. Not—I might add—not since I
realized there were more important things in life."

"Yeah? How d' you—I mean . . . That must be a long
time now. How d'you keep from bein' frustrated? Do you—"
He made a gesture.

"That's enough, Artie."

"Sorry, Whit. Real sorry. I always go too far."

"All right. Now where were we?"

"Uh—St. Paul was sayin', it's the law that makes us sinful."

"Not makes—shows us that we're sinful. All right. You were
upset by what Christ said about adultery. That's good. That's
the law speaking. That's the law saying—watch it. You need
help. But last night you must have read other things. Things
like, 'The Son of Man hath power on earth to forgive sins.' "

"I know that." Artie sat up. "Christ was God's son. He came
to earth and got crucified. When He died, it made up for all
our sins. So the law don't really matter."

"Right and wrong. Right, that Christ's sacrifice can, does
absolve those who believe in Him. Wrong, that the law doesn't
mean anything. It means a great deal. More than we'd like to
think. And here I'm talking about Christ's law—the law you
read about last night. Remember? 'Turn the other cheek . . .'
'If thy right eye offend thee . . .' 'Love your enemies, bless
them that curse you, do good to them that hate you.' It's a strict
law. They don't come any stricter."

"Yeah?" He fell back onto his pillow. "Well, that's what worried me in the first place. What if—what if I haven't done all
those things either?"

"Artie. The two most important things in this world are
Faith and Love—or, as some would have it, Faith and Loveful Works. But these two things aren't separate, they're com-

plementary parts of a single whole. No man—I know this from my own sinfulness, and I think you know it the same way—no man can be saved by good works alone. We've too many strikes against us. But anyone—you, I, anyone—anyone who has faith in Christ and in his redemptive Grace can be saved."

"I could have faith. I think I could."

"You could. But it's not all that simple. I said Love and Faith were parts of a whole. Okay. That means that one can't exist without the other.

"Faith, which is our only hope, is based finally on Love. Faith is based on Love, and Love, in its turn, is derived from Faith. It's like a circle. I don't think Faith can exist alone. Nor do I think that any man can love—love truly, unselfishly—without coming that much closer to a faith in God. Faith and Love. Faith and Love expressed in loving works. Which comes first? I don't know. Sometimes one, sometimes the other, I suppose. But, whichever, they work together—they strengthen each other; together they lead to hope. No man's love is perfect, nor no man's faith. But together they're sufficient for our needs."

"Okay. I got that, Whit."

"Good. I'll read a bit more. 'For what the law could not do, in that it was weak through the flesh, God sending His own Son in the likeness of sinful flesh and for sin, condemned sin in the flesh.' Sounds confusing, but it's very simple. The law is a product of sin—just as surely as sin is a product of the law. And we men pay a penalty for that—for being subject to both sin and law. The penalty? Well, in a word, the penalty is death." Artie's fists closed tight. "Death and fear of death. Death and a short, fitful, frustrated life lived in slavery to death. What do they call us? Mortals—those who die. That's our greatest distinction, our greatest limitation, the definition of our being. No law can change that, for law, too, is subject to death. But—"

"But," Artie said quietly. "But. But. Come quick with the buts, Whit. I don't like this talk."

"Hold on. But. But Christ came to earth and was a man—a mortal. And, like all mortals, He died. Died. But Jesus Christ was resurrected, Artie. He rose from the dead. You've heard it all before. You've heard it on Easter radio programs. You've read it in little tracts crumpled on the seats of subway cars. You've heard it before—now, know it. Know it. Let the immensity of it fill your mind. Christ rose from the dead and Death, once and for all, was vanquished. There is no more death. The ancient, futile systems of law and sin against law, of temporal reward and temporal punishment—all those are superseded. Now there's a new law—of the spirit. And a new life—of the spirit. This is your hope. My hope. May that hope never be taken from us."

"You believe that, huh?"

"You're God-damned right I do." He smiled. He smiled at me. Me, as witness; me, as Christian. A second-hand thing, his faith—but, perhaps, a thing after all.

"And you're a college man, huh?"

"I'm a college man."

"You write books. You gotta have a big I.Q. You gotta know about science and evolution and things like that." He was silent for a moment. Then he said, "That's good. That's better than I thought it'd be."

"What?"

"Nothing. Just thinkin' out loud. Tell me, Whit. Suppose there's some guy who's very good. Real good. And he loves peopel. You know. But he don't know nothin' about Christ and God. He's just a real good guy. What then—is that enough?"

"No," I said. And, as I said so, my head gestured involuntarily back toward my own bed. My copy of *A God For Our Time* lay, propped on its side, on my bed table. I shook my head. Then I said, "No," once again. And that second time I didn't know who or what I was denying.

"Why not?"

"Because love's a damn tricky business. That's why. A lot more tricky than faith, I think. You see, Artie, there's love and there's love. And it isn't easy, my friend, to distinguish between one and the other. Often—most often, let's face it—love is no more than a form of—well, externalized narcissism. We love because we want others to love us; because we've selfish yearnings that need reciprocation; because we're proud of our goodness; because, simply, love is gratifying emotionally, sensually. That's human love, and, while it's a damn sight better than human hate, it's just not the genuine article."

"What's the genuine article, then?"

"It isn't easy to explain. But . . . Well, I'm afraid the genuine article is a gift. A gift of God's grace. What's it like? What's it like . . . The supreme example, of course, was—is —Christ's love toward man. Unselfish; spontaneous; gratifying nothing; unnecessary, in fact. A giving—a pure outflowing of the spirit, untarnished by selfishness. You can see: it's not something that you or I, stuck in these bodies, driven by these minds, could ever achieve. It's a perfect thing. And it can only be ours through the arbitrary, the forceful intervention of God's Grace. That's what love is. And there's nothing we can do, of our own wills, to attain it."

"Then—"

"Then why bother about it? I told you it wasn't easy to explain. Why bother, since there's nothing we can do about it?

Well, I'll tell you. Because it's the most significant thing in the whole of the universe—when it comes to man, that man is God —insofar as it comes to him. That's reason number one. The other is that we can—yes, after all, we can—do something about it. Oh, we can't create it or attain to it, but we can make ourselves ready for it. Try to, anyway. And the best way, the only certain way, is Faith; especially Faith through prayer. Another way—a less certain way—lies through Love. Ordinary, garden variety, selfish, sensual love. It's not much. Of itself it's nothing—often it's even dangerous. But it shows a willingness. And God's quality is always to have mercy where there is the least justification. And so we've got to keep trying. Trying. It's pathetic. But it's all we know. I have to laugh at people who say we Christians believe in God because it's the easy way out. It's not. It's the hard way in. The responsibility is immense and it's unremitting. But it's worth it. Without God's Grace there is no love."

"Yeah. I think you're right, Whit. Anyway, I know what you mean by ordinary human love. It don't mean crap. Not the kind I've seen. Let me read some more."

"Do you feel like praying with me?"

"Uh— Maybe I'm not ready for that."

"Open to chapter six." He did, and we read the Lord's Prayer together. Artie tried to bow his head, but his glasses kept slipping from his nose. When we'd finished, I extemporized a prayer for understanding and hope and dedication.

"That was nice, Whit."

"Artie. Don't ever be afraid to pray. That's stupid. Even if you should doubt your own faith in God—even then, especially then—pray. Pray. God's there. He listens. He knows more

about it than you do. And he's only asking that you meet him
half way. Now," I said, "I think you'd better take a nap."

"Thanks, Whit. Really. Thanks." I got up to go. "One
thing else. About praying."

"What's that?"

"It says here that Christ cured all kinds of sick people."

"Yes?"

"If I pray—can I pray to get better? God could do that,
couldn't he?"

"He could. But that's none of your business. Artie, everybody's got to die—sooner or later. You know that. It may not
be God's will that you get better. If you pray to get well, and
you don't—you'll become angry, you'll be disappointed in God.
And you've no right to be. God never promised you, anyone,
happiness here on earth. Even Christ suffered unspeakable
torments. But God did promise us life eternal after this life.
Pray for courage; pray for faith; pray for love; pray for forgiveness. I know you're afraid. But I don't dare promise you anything that I'm not myself perfectly certain of. Look ahead.
Prepare yourself. It may be God's will that you walk out of
here a healthy man. I don't know. But if you pray for what I've
told you—for courage and faith and love and forgiveness—
then I promise, you'll never be disappointed."

I said nothing further, and Artie, too, seemed inclined to
leave it at that. As I left his bed, I thought, without pride, that
I had spoken well, that the certainty of my own faith had lent
a persuasiveness to what I'd said. I went over to my table. Pen-
sively, I drew a tissue over the cover of my book. Then I took
it up and blew my nose. I could be forgiven: this was a special
happening; one that required special methods. And it was
time I left Artie alone. In order not to distract him, I took up

the *New York Times,* and went out and down the hall, to the
men's room. I felt actively hopeful then, and a little afraid.

I must've been thinking about Artie. I say that because my
heart seized up, and my hands slapped together in front of my
chest when he appeared. I'd been walking slowly back from the
men's bathroom, my left hand fingering the wooden bar on the
wall. I remember seeing a woman with a tremendous goiter.
She was knitting something blue: I remember thinking she was
strangely pregnant and that, whatever it was, it'd be a boy. The
bar ended at the pantry and began again to the other side of the
door. Another room with four beds, and then a door opened—
it opened inwards; I heard the friction of the hinges—but no
one emerged. I walked toward it, my fingers tapping a senseless rhythm on the bar.

"Come in, Bishop Belknap."

"Aaaah-oh!" I gasped. P. Crecy stood in the doorway. He
smiled when he saw how terribly my body had contorted itself.
My fingers clawed at the air; then some of them became caught
in the pocket of my pajama tops. My knees and hips had given
way together, and, when I tried to straighten, a convulsive pain
rose from amongst the vertebrae of my lower spine, up into the
area between my shoulders. I might have gone to my knees
then, but P. Crecy's smile lent me a perverse sort of courage.

"I've startled you."

"A bit. Yes." I put my hands on my hips and inhaled deeply.
A colored mist closed over my vision.

"Come in," he said. "I've wonderful news for you."

I literally fell through the half-opened door of the consultation room. Inside, the darkness appeared impenetrable. I
stood bewildered, afraid to move, until P. Crecy led me by the

hand to a wooden armchair. There was an acid, oppressive odor in the room—the odor of many snuffed candles. Light came half-heartedly in through a single, obstructed window. As my eyes became accustomed to the half light, I saw that the room was longer than it was wide, and that the floors, the desk, the chairs were covered with tall, tottering piles of books. Two filing cabinets jutted out, blocking, on either side, the lower quarters of the window. Above the cabinets there was a clear space in which the full width of the window was apparent; but, immediately above on either side, pieces of cardboard had, for some reason, been pasted against the right- and left-hand portions of the entire upper half of the window. The morning sun must have been directly behind the glass; I think I remember one area of intense brightness. But the light that penetrated through the yellow, opaque glass buttered surfaces with no more than a ghastly and dull semi-phosphorescence.

P. Crecy's face was one of the surfaces. Now he was perched on a double pile of books, the balls of his feet planted on another, lower pile. He held a long pointer in his hand. At the pointer's end, on the wall above the desk, was an illuminated X-ray viewer. Someone's chest was shadowed there. P. Crecy prodded the chest with his pointer, prying at it between the clouded ribs. He smiled; then he frowned; then he smiled. His expressions didn't evolve one out of the other; they were sudden and complete—like transparencies superimposed one after the other on the same face. The odor became a tactile substance. It insinuated itself between, under the lids of my eyes. I watched his pointer as it tapped at the chest. My chest. My chest, of course.

"Next Friday. Next Friday, Dr. Snow will operate." Unconsciously, afraid perhaps that I'd lose the significance of his

words, I began to repeat what P. Crecy said with my lips. Next
Friday Dr. Snow will operate . . . He spoke slowly, as though
some interference in the silent room threatened the sense of
what he said. And on each level of my mind, to its extremities
in my physical body, there came a response.

"We want you to know—"

To know . . .

"Exactly what will happen."

What will happen . . . And when he said that, all things
passed back into the present, and I saw what I was hearing.
Perhaps it was the odor, perhaps it was the agitated state of my
mind, but people seemed to come and go within the room, and
the light from the window rose to a blinding intensity without
once dispelling the darkness. There were metallic sounds and
sounds of heavy cloth. A sound, too, of regular breathing which
came from me and yet from beyond me. Now it was no longer
difficult to sit upright. I felt a kind of ease throughout my body.

"You will be wheeled—"

Whee—wheeled . . .

"Into the operating rooms on the twelfth floor."

The twelfth floor . . .

"It will be hot. Very hot."

Very hot . . . It was very hot.

"Operations within the thorax require high temperatures.
The organs of the chest are very sensitive to cold."

Very sensitive to cold . . . And I was glad that it was hot,
for I was terribly afraid of the cold.

"Dr. Snow will enter—"

Enter . . . I saw him enter.

"He is surrounded by figures in white, but he stands
tall above them."

Tall above them . . . He did. He stood very tall above them.

"They wash him. They robe him. It is a solemn, a wonderful ritual. No one speaks."

No one speaks . . . I was afraid to open my lips.

"Dr. Snow wears neither mask nor cap. His hands are bare. Dr. Snow never wears gloves."

Dr. Snow never wears gloves . . . No, I thought. Dr. Snow wouldn't wear gloves.

"Now Dr. Snow stands above you."

Stands above you . . . Above me.

"He closes his eyes. His powers of concentration are magnificent, absolute. He says a few words, but we cannot hear. We wait."

We wait . . .

"Dr. Snow stretches out his right hand. A scalpel is placed in his palm. He takes it."

He takes it . . .

"He raises it—"

He raises it . . .

"He makes the incision—"

Incision . . . Incision. Cision. Buzzing, slicing word. I expelled breath and didn't know where it would out. Suddenly in the heat of the room there was a special place of coldness— an icy current in a warm lake. And I began to be afraid.

"Quickly, with precision, he slices through the skin, the muscles of your chest."

The muscles of your chest . . .

"A flap is made. It is turned over to the right."

To the right . . . I am afraid. I am a dog-eared page.

"There is some bleeding. Forceps are applied."

Applied . . .

"Ligatures are tied above the forceps. The flap is covered with sterile cloth."

With sterile cloth . . . Cloth, warm and rough and trustworthy. There was a second breathing now within my chest. Not mine.

"Your ribs begin now to appear. They are very pale. The muscles show pink between them."

Pink between them . . .

"With short, straight incisions, Dr. Snow detaches three of your ribs from their pleura."

From their pleura . . . Three ribs. And the Lord God caused a deep sleep to fall upon Adam . . . Three women, I thought. Three times God.

"Pieces of your ribs are removed at the sternum, outward to the right."

Outward to the right . . . Snapping sounds. Branches bent over shins on bitter autumn days. The coolness seeped deeper into me. Exploring, searching.

"Dr. Snow applies the costal dilator. He turns the handle to open the blades. Pressure is applied within the thorax. The wound in your chest is open, it gapes."

It gapes . . . I gape. I was afraid—a little child bent precariously over bottomless, black wells.

"Now Dr. Snow can approach the throax. He nods once. Yes! Yes, there it is."

There it is . . . I saw as they saw, and I was horrified.

"The aorta is distended grotesquely. Dangerously. An aneurysm. Clearly an aneurysm."

An aneurysm . . . Disgust touched my lips as though in a dollop of bitter phlegm. There it was . . . I saw the big, snaking artery near the heart. On the right side, down three or four inches from the arch, my poor aorta was ballooned out in a sagging D. I thought of putrefaction, and then I smelled something. The pulse across my temples shook through my body, shook my aorta—and, where it ballooned, the shaking seemed a perilous thing.

"Time is passing. Dr. Snow works quickly. He selects the frozen, dried aorta of a two hundred fifty pound hog—"

A two hundred fifty pound hog . . . A surrogate for my diseased and useless body. A hog.

"Great, teethed clamps are screwed into place. Dr. Snow makes incision in the left atrium. Again in the femoral artery. His hands move swiftly, magnificently—like the allegro from a great symphony. The pig's aorta is stitched—"

Stitched . . . Stit-stit-stit-stit-stit-stitched.

"—into place. Clamps are removed. The bypass begins to take up the flow of blood. Your aneurysm subsides."

"Sub—sssides . . ."

"Now clamps are screwed into the aorta."

Into the aorta . . . Things chewed at me, and I gave way pliantly beneath them. My heart, outraged now, pumped furiously into the pig, missed a beat, pumped again. I saw the many vivid reds of my inner self and the lithe fingers that violated, entwined themselves about, my most secret organs.

"One. Two. Dr. Snow has detached your aorta from its surrounding tissue. He holds it loose in his hands."

Loose in his hands . . . I was held. High and uncertain. A long, thin, distorted tube.

"He slices through."

Through . . . I screamed. Not from pain, but from bitter helplessness. And the hose was in halves; a half in each of Dr. Snow's hands.

"Dissecting! Dissecting! Dr. Snow is vindicated. A dissecting aneurysm of the aorta."

Of the aorta . . . Vindicated. Vindicated. I became wonderfully excited. Joyful. Triumphant in Dr. Snow's triumph.

Swiftly, Dr. Snow obliterates the false passage. He stitches the outer and inner layers together. Then, delicately—so very delicately—he cuts a small V-shaped segment in the inner intimal layer above. To provide re-entry. The dissecting passage is closed. The aorta will function normally. You have been healed.

Healed . . . I am healed. *Lord God above, I thank—*

"Wait! Wait—something has happened. Your heart. It's rippling, twitching convulsively—a heart torn from some living thing. Fibrillation. The heart is dying."

"No!" I screamed. "No!" I screamed it aloud in the tiny room.

"Yes. The heart is dying. We look at Dr. Snow, but he seems unmoved. He orders our fibrillator brought to the table. Your pulse has disappeared entirely now. Dr. Snow orders a breathing tube put into your trachea. One hundred percent oxygen. Still the heart is shuddering. Madly, suicidally. Shuddering."

Shuddering . . . I grabbed the arm of my chair, and a pile of books fell to the floor with a violent slamming sound. My heart —my hearts—leaped fitfully and then hung, poised uncertainly, lifelessly, above nothing at all. I had seen it dancing, shivering itself to death. My heart. My life. Prayer, fluent always in my mouth, became a sputter of ejaculations. I was terrified; thoughts of death reached out before the fact itself. They paralyzed my mind.

"Dr. Snow takes the handles of the fibrillator. He places one metal disc above the heart. He slides the other beneath. Current. The undulations of the heart muscle become more violent.

Current. Current again. A tremendous convulsion shakes the length of your body. Your heart lies still. Flat. Collapsed. Dead."

Dead . . . Dead. Dead. The parts of my body were stilled in the chair, responsive to the dread sound of the world. Dead.

"Adrenalin. The needle plunges in. Into the wall of your heart."

Into the wall of my heart . . . Dead muscle. Lying on the sand. Smelling of sea water and rottenness. Deadest of things. Dead.

"Massage. Yes. Dr. Snow is going to massage the heart. He takes it between his hands. Compress. Relax. One hundred— no, one hundred twenty times a minute. Compress. Relax. Compress. Relax. Your heart is buried deep in Dr. Snow's life-giving hands. One minute. Two minutes now."

Two minutes now . . . Masss . . . Massaging. Lovely, soft, active word. Massaging. Word of hope.

"Three minutes. Five minutes. The heart remains slack, inert. Seven minutes now—Dr. Snow's hands work urgently. The heavy muscles of the heart are thick, sluggish—they re-sist. The tension is unendurable. Eight minutes. Dr. Snow's eyes have become glazed. His mind, his soul are in his hands. Nine minutes now."

Nine minutes now . . . My fingers and toes begin to itch. My sinews become expectant as though before some demand-ing reflex action—some sneeze, some desperate choking.

"Ten minutes. Hopeless. Even Dr. Snow cannot continue much longer. One thousand, more than a thousand contrac-tions. Eleven minutes. Our breathing becomes more regular; we acknowledge the inevitable. Only Dr. Snow remains un-affected. He alone is confident. Twelve minutes now. Wait! Wait. Yes. A pulse."

Pulse . . .
"Another."
Another . . .
"Another."
Another . . .
"The heart is beating. See! See it twitch. Again. See how red
it is. I feel a pulse in the arm. Now the first breaths come. A
miracle. A miracle. Brought back to life. Dead and now alive.
Alive."
Alive . . . My body sang in the chair, urgent once more with
the rhythm of life. And then a great fear came upon me. I tried
to move, but my feet and hands were wrapped in the sheets; my
head was held tightly by the anaesthetist's towel. And I remembered—"And his hands and legs were bound with grave-
clothes, and his face was bound with a napkin . . ."

I was walking—walking on a slack, rubber diaphragm that
resisted and then gave insanely. The bones of my knees rapped
against each other. My hand was knotted, white on the wooden
support bar. The odors of the room were embedded in tiny
crystals in the hairs of my nostrils; there was an image in my
mind of a shiny, maroon calf's liver. Saliva ran from the corners
of my mouth, but I didn't dare tongue it in for fear I'd vomit.
Then the wooden support bar ended, and I was projected un-
ceremoniously into a familiar limbo. Artie sat upright in limbo
in bed. His bed like a hammock, swinging. I swung. I slid
slowly down the doorjamb to the floor—holding to a single
hinge with both my hands.
"Whit? Good God—what's wrong? Whit? You all right?" I
nodded, and, on each downstroke, my mouth flew stupidly open.
Artie was trying to rise; the Bible fluttered in the air like a wire-

walker's umbrella as he sought his balance. But he couldn't manage. Instead he leaned toward the nurse's bell.

"No," I said hastily, my voice becoming thin. "No. Nothing the matter. On my feet too long, that's all."

"You sure? You're only gone a few seconds. Let me get a nurse—"

"Only a few seconds . . . No. No, I'm okay." I put the back of my shoulder to the door jamb and extruded my body to its full height. My pajama pocket caught on the hinge and ripped downward. It hung loose from one corner. I touched it. Then I pushed myself off from the wall, across the room to my bed. For several seconds I sat on the edge, feigning calmness. My slippers wouldn't come off; a disgusting, clammy sweat glued them to the soles of my feet.

"God almighty, Whit. You give me the you-know-whats. My heart's goin' like a drum." Artie's stomach was heaving. He seemed upset. "I can't take seein' you fall down. God knows— should be used to it by now. You must be real sick, Whit."

"Nonsense. I always—" I inhaled awkwardly—"always fall down when I get tired walking."

"Yeah?"

"Sure . . ." Then I could sit up no longer. I went down, my slippers hanging from my toes, directly through Mr. Farbstein's line of gaze. One, two, three . . . One, two, three . . . The wind threw combinations at the glass. I started to count, and unconsciousness, earnest and insistent, buttonholed me. Dreams came. A man stood over a table. I couldn't see what was on the table, but the man was very tall and dressed entirely in white. Two little boys in red stood holding bulky things on either side of him. Behind me, a droning litany told of the Blood and the Flesh. I wasn't at ease. I wanted to see what was before them on the table.

Searing shocks shredded the tissue of my chest. I went to my knees, my hands clasped in front of me. The tall man's right hand and elbow were bent now above his shoulder, as though he were preparing clumsily to put a shot. But in his fist there was only a yellow, grainy substance. Shapeless. Fluttering. Then not fluttering. I cried out in anguish. I sobbed. But, after only a while, the tears came less frequently, and I saw that, as they fell on the floor, each tear turned to metallic gray solder. I looked at them. Now there was no anguish, no fear, no pain. I wanted to smile, but there was no smile either. The tall man turned toward me—

"Mr. Belknap?" It was Jimmy. I was so relieved to see him that I wrapped my left arm around the back of his waist, and drew him to my side. I camouflaged my distress by throwing little jabs at his stomach with my right hand. Jimmy squirmed, delighted.

"Mr. Belknap—you're all right, aren't you? Mr. Carson said you fell down again."

"I didn't fall down. I sat down. It looked funny because there wasn't any chair." I grinned at his sober expression. "Sure. I'm okay."

"Yes sir. I was just thinkin'—y'don't feel good enough t'play Monopoly, do you?"

"Monopoly? Of course, I do. In fact, that's just exactly what I feel like doing." It was. I wanted nothing better than to retreat into the little, square world with its mindless, circling tokens.

"Swell. Why don't you and me and Mr. Carson play? Three's better."

"Mr. Carson?"

"Sure. He knows how to play. Don't you, Mr. Carson?"

"What say, kid?" Artie put down his Bible.

"Play Monopoly with us?" Artie hesitated. He looked at me.

"I don't know, kid. Might not be right." He pointed to the Bible. I knew Artie wanted to play, and the realization irritated me. Ostensibly, I wanted to spare Jimmy his language, the smells of his body. But, in reality, I knew I was just jealous of Jimmy's attentions.

"It's all right," I said.

"See?" said Jimmy.

"Okay, Whit. You're the doctor." Artie began making his bed ready with an eagerness that I found pathetic. Embarrassed, I turned to the window. A tugboat cutting through the water seemed to hesitate, arrested in the full force of its momentum, spray suspended like a veil over its bow. Instinctively, I said, "Lord God, protect me." Jimmy called. The tug moved forward powerfully through the water.

I had only Park Place left when we saw Dr. Snow standing amongst us. I shouldn't have noticed even then, but for the sound of the dice gritting together in Artie's fist. Our game was over. Jimmy began arranging the money in neat, little piles. Artie sat up as best he could and pushed desultorily at his token. We had reacted as professional mourners might, surprised in an act of levity. I stood up to receive Dr. Snow.

"It's good to see you," I said.

"Shall we step outside a moment?" I nodded. When we were standing shoulder to shoulder, I realized that Dr. Snow was exactly the same height as I. That surprised me; I slouched deferentially. Dr. Snow smiled. "You seem better," he said.

"Yes. I feel better. Thanks to you." He nodded, acknowledging, without embarrassment, his part in my recovery. As we walked toward the solarium, I remembered that Dr. Snow and

I hadn't spoken since the ordeal of the letters. The God-cursed letters. Dr. Snow knew very well I hadn't read them; probably he had planned another exercise in casuistry. I tried to prod my mind into alertness. But it was too late. Dr. Snow was waiting patiently for me, holding the solarium door open with one hand. One of the hands that had—would—hold the two halves of my aorta, squeeze life into my heart, appraise the inner health of my body.

The solarium was empty. Sunlight had been compelled to thread a tedious way between the high buildings, through the soot-filled air; it had arrived as pale and exhausted as an ancient man. I hadn't been in the solarium before. Copies of the *Saturday Evening Post* lay on the floor, their covers streaked with creases. Two empty wheelchairs faced each other in silent converse. A potted plant with one huge, yellow leaf convalesced mournfully in the shadows. I fell into a low chair. Dr. Snow stood over me. He seemed impatient to leave now, as though he were no longer interested in me.

"You got my note?" His lips parted only slightly when he spoke. His voice was clear and deep, and yet it seemed to emanate from some other thing.

"Yes. I'm very grateful."

"You understand what this is all about? The nature of the operation?"

"I think so. Dr. Crecy was kind enough to—to explain this morning. An aneurysm, I think he said."

"Well. There are aneurysms and there are aneurysms. Some of my colleagues think it's saccular—I must admit it looks that way. On the surface. But I have a hunch they're wrong. I think it's a dissecting aneurysm."

"Dissecting? Is that serious?"

"Quite. No aneurysm is a laughing matter."

"What—what exactly is a dissecting aneurysm?"

"Well. Let's see—you had an automobile accident a few months ago. Am I right?"

"Yes. Nothing serious—fortunately I had a seat belt on."

"Nonetheless—there was a shock to the upper torso. A considerable shock, I imagine. I'm afraid the shock split, peeled away the layers of the aorta wall. Blood poured into the false channel formed by the split. Blood flows very forcefully—in time it enlarged the original tear, as one might peel a banana. Gradually the tear became longer, deeper. Then, for some reason, it stopped."

"Is that dangerous?"

"It's exquisitely dangerous, Whitney. Understand that the false passage—the one that has tunneled into the covering of the aorta—well, as you'd expect, it has a much thinner outer wall. Probably only half as thick—perhaps even less. The pressure of the blood has caused the thin layer to balloon out. It's rubbery and elastic—you can be thankful for that. But it won't remain elastic forever. It's my job to close the false passage. To provide re-entry."

"The operation is—it's absolutely necessary, of course." Dr. Snow's eyes narrowed. He frowned.

"There are plenty of doctors here. Would you care to try another?"

"No. No, please. Don't get me wrong. I've complete faith in you. I was . . . I guess you know. I was afraid."

"You can see how weak you are. You're short of breath. You should have more pain than you do. I admit that. But the angiogram doesn't lie. If that thin outer covering—overtaxed as it already is—should haemorrhage into the thorax . . .

Well, Whitney, you'd die in a wink. In a gasp, in a fraction of a second. I'm afraid it's only a matter of time. In fact, I'm surprised you're alive now."

A chilly breeze blew in through a crack where the window wasn't quite closed. It rustled the plant's one yellow leaf. It crossed the room to wrap itself around my bared ankles. And then I was aware of a secret that, hitherto, I had scrupulously kept from myself: I wasn't prepared for death. Not afraid exactly, not afraid. More surprised, indignant. I had so many things left to do. And now Dr. Snow had made an off-hand gesture of farewell. He was leaving.

"Dr. Snow? Before you go, could I ask a question?"

"Yes?"

"It's about Artie Carson—the patient in the bed next to mine. Someone thought he had only a short time left to live and . . . Well, unfortunately, they told him. He's terribly upset. I thought maybe—"

"What did you think?"

"I . . ."

"Had you another diagnosis in mind? No? I'd say three months at the outside. Mr. Carson is riddled with cancer. Stomach. Pancreas. Spleen. What have you? I expect the brain next."

"But . . . I mean—surely there's something you can do to save him?" Then Dr. Snow laughed. He laughed out loud for the first time. A laugh, I think, of surpassing satisfaction.

"Nonsense," he said. "Nonsense. Mr. Carson doesn't in the least need saving. Have you taken a good look at him? Mr. Carson saved himself a long time ago."

"I don't understand. Why d'you laugh?"

"Your wonderful naïveté, Whitney. Only that. Of course he's dying. Anyone could see that."

"I couldn't," I said, hurt by his derision. "I couldn't."

"Come," he said almost kindly. He took my hand and helped me out of the chair. I was stunned. Not, I know, because of Artie. I simply didn't care to see death uncoiling itself irresistibly and so very close to my own body. And then Dr. Snow was trying to get my attention. He had turned me by the elbow. Now he was pointing out the window. After a moment he said, "Beautiful, isn't it?"

He meant the city. Through a gap between two tall build-ings, more than three miles of the city south to its heart were visible. Myriad windows facing west had caught the last, golden rays of the sun—the reflection, in their panes, shim-mered like candle flames. Above, steeple-like, the Empire State Building dominated all the huge, squared shapes, the skeletal girders, the tufted penthouse tops. There seemed to be missing only the sound—an incomprehensible and mighty sound—that should accompany such rich activity. And, implicit there, was all the life of the world.

"Yes," I said. "Beautiful." Dr. Snow nodded.

"I'll give it all back to you," he said.

Dead, I said. He's dead. Get that straight once and for all. Dead. Then Artie would yawn or belch or clean his glasses, and somber death, in the face of such homely gestures, diminished to bathos. I tried to use words that would make the concept palpable. He's riddled—riddled with cancer. With little can-cers. Roaches infesting a greasy stove. Growing like the scales of a fish; growing like spores on a moist piece of bread. Rid-dled. And then Artie would bring his foot up and scratch, with satisfaction, between his toes.

I took Pious' picture down from the table. This, too, is death, I said. But I didn't believe that either. I could far more read-

ily believe that Pious had never existed, than that now he was
dead. I put the picture in my drawer. The letters were still
there. I took them up, one in each hand. Read them, I said.
Read. Read at least about the possible death of someone only
remotely involved with your life. But no . . . It was quite all
right to consider death in metaphors, in abstractions, in con-
cretions of a certain sort. I was afraid that from one of those
envelopes might come a sense not of Artie's death, not of an unknown Negro's death, but of my death. And then, perhaps, I
should really know fear: an unchristian fear that would deprive
me of my dignity.

There was yet time. Time to understand both the obverse
and the reverse, life and death. Time yet to be a Christian. Dr.
Snow was with me by God's Grace. Artie ran his tongue over
his gums. For me, at least, death was not so imminent.
Now there was still time to watch boats waking the river; still
time to anticipate other boats, other rivers, yet to be watched
and enjoyed. An aneurysm was a terrible thing, but it need not
be the last terrible thing. I put the envelopes back in my
drawer.

There was a man—he smiled at me—a man who would yet
live . . . An influence beyond simple mortal time. I took the
book and propped it against another book on the table, just
where Pious' picture had been. An existence now so tenuously
strong, so undeniable, that it could not betray me by dying. An
existence, me. The me that would last beyond the me that
could not last. It stared down at me, self-sufficient, supremely
confident, patronizing.

Patronizing . . . The man on the back of the book smiled
in celebration of his autonomy. I was that. That book. And
that book—child, creation, thing—had grown enormously out-

size. It couldn't die; nothing could destroy it. And I was no
longer even certain that it was good. This thing that would be
me in libraries, while libraries were; this thing that fused all
the intricacies of me—the evil and the mitigating good—into
an exhausted, circumscribed few ideas. Now, surely, it was beyond me—free of me—me. I opened the drawer and, with
stubborn perversity, I dropped my eternity in amongst the dying and the already dead.

And, across the room, Mr. Farbstein dozed in what seemed a
very contrived pose of sleep. His wife squatted on her chair,
watching with a sort of reverent sadness. Mr. Farbstein never
looked toward me in his wife's presence. Yet, at other times,
even in the undiluted black of night, I knew that he was staring.
I looked up from having closed the drawer, and Mrs. Farbstein
raised her hand timidly, as a child in query. I nodded. She
picked up her black bag, dropped it once in her haste, and then
hobbled toward me.

"Hello," I said. "How're you today?"

"Yes. Fine."

"And Mr. Farbstein?"

"Better. But the same. But better. And yourself?" She sat,
contrapposto, her right foot dangling above the floor. Her right
shoe dropped off—as though she were a deciduous thing, and
its time had come. Her ankles were swollen; certainly her feet
hurt. Still, I wished she'd kept it on.

"Not so bad. This morning I had a blow by blow account of
my operation. Now I ache all over. But then, I always was a
coward."

"Of course—it's worrying. Do you sleep good at night?"

"Yes. I've no trouble there."

"Good. We can't live without sleep. I worry David can't get

to sleep here. He hardly keeps his eyes open when I come. Tell me—do they wake him a lot at night?"

"No. No, I don't think so. Of course, I'm asleep most of the time." She nodded.

"Would you mind if I smoked?"

"No. Go right ahead."

Mrs. Farbstein brought out a pack of Marlboros and knocked a cigarette into her hand. She cocked it in the corner of her mouth. She squinted in anticipation, as she drew a heavy, bronze lighter out of her purse. Mrs. Farbstein flicked it lit with a practiced, easy movement of her thumb. Then she inhaled appreciatively. I was perplexed—a little, old woman with a Marlboro hanging from her dry, lower lip. Strength, I said to myself. I wondered how her husband lit cigarettes.

"Dr. Snow was here today. He spoke to you." I realized then that the cigarette was only a prop.

"Yes," I said. "We chatted for a while in the solarium."

"Maybe he said something about David?" She inhaled; then she looked into the stream of smoke driven upward from her nostrils.

"No. No, he didn't. I don't think Dr. Snow'd talk about other patients just like that—privileged information, you know. Did you want to ask him something?"

"No. What could I ask? I'm satisfied, believe me. What more could he do?"

"Still, something's wrong."

"Sure. Sure, there's something wrong. I'm an old fool, that's what's wrong. Impatient. And, while I'm at it, I want also to apologize to you. I got no one to talk to, and, Mr. Belknap, last time I talked too much. I said crazy things, for which now I'm apologizing."

"Please, Mrs. Farbstein. Don't feel you have to say that. I—
well . . . You know, I felt like apologizing yesterday myself.
I thought maybe I'd been a bit short with you. If so, I want you
to know I didn't mean it."

"You're a good man. There's an empathy in you. I feel it."

"You're very kind."

"Nonsense. And you, you mustn't worry. Take it from me,
I've read everything Dr. Snow has written—everything, books,
articles, lectures. Other doctors, let me tell you, they think he's
a God. Everything will go off fine. I promise you." She smiled
conspiratorially. "I could tell you something about Dr. Snow
—something I bet you'd never guess."

"Tell me."

"Maybe I shouldn't."

"That's not fair. Now you're teasing me."

"No. It's not that. But promise you'll keep it under your hat.
I think—I'm not sure—I think he'd be embarrassed."

"Mum's the word." I put my right hand over my heart.

"You'll excuse me—I can't help feeling a little proud. It's
silly, but I do." She looked back toward the corridor. Then she
leaned close to me.

"The suspense is killing," I said.

"All right. I've got to tell you." She smiled. "Would you believe it? Dr. Terrence F. Snow is Jewish. Jewish." She brought
her palms down on her thighs. "I thought you'd be surprised."

I blurted something out—it began with a B, but it came out
only as a distorted sound. I imagine I stared at her as though
she were mad. I certainly thought she was. Jewish . . . I remember sitting up, trying to discover some suggestion of humor
in the old woman's eyes. But it wasn't a joke—in no sense of
the word was it that.

"Big surprise?"

"Yes. Are you certain? It—it hardly seems possible. Who told you this?"

"Nobody had to—you can see it. When David and I first came to his office. When he was convincing David to have the operation. He's a cold fish, you'd say. He is—but I think he liked David. We talked a few minutes. This will kill you: David thinks his father and David's father lived just a few blocks away. Avenue D. Dr. Snow's father was Isaac Snofski—David remembers him. A rabbi."

"A rabbi."

"Sure. Tell me—you're not Jewish?"

"No. No, I'm not."

"Belknap—no, of course not. Stupid of me. Now he's a big man, it's better not to be so Jewish. It's Snow, not Snofski. I can understand—but I wonder what poor Mr. Issac Snofski thought. A genius, of course. Graduated two years ahead in the same public high school David went to. A long time after David, naturally."

"Public high school? Did you say, public—public high school?"

"Yes. But, I tell you, it's not that gets me. It's something else. My son Joel, may he rest in peace. I can't tell you, Mr. Belknap —it's amazing. The resemblance, I mean. It takes my breath away. The eyes, the mouth. I can't believe it. Mr. Belknap, they even talk the same. And Joel—Joel was studying to be a surgeon, too . . ."

I don't know how long she talked. I think she spoke of her dead sons Joel and Seth. But, to my paralyzed mentality, Mrs. Farbstein could say only, "Dr. Terrence F. Snow is Jewish. Same public high school. Jewish. On both sides. Jewish." And then

there was a roar of cheering, and I was number twenty-eight
again. I put my knuckles into the cold turf and listened as the
quarterback called out the count. We went off at four. I brush-
blocked the man in front of me and cut between the end and
the tackle, toward the middle of the field. I saw the cornerback
pick me up, running in hard from the right to cover me. And,
when he got close enough, I did what I had planned to do—
I took two steps into him. For one fatal moment, his body followed my fake, and by then it was too late. I cut back to the
left and down the middle. At the thirty yard line I looked back.
The ball was leading me perfectly in a high, flabby arc. At the
forty, I cradled it gracefully between my shoulder and my cheek.
That was that. But, before I put my head down for the final
sprint, I took one quick glance back over my shoulder. Number
thirty-seven was beaten. He was running desperately, his head
up, his arms flying out. He was running desperately—but there
was no face inside his helmet.

"Well . . . Hold onto it. We'll talk after dinner." Artie's
head bobbed enthusiastically; then he saluted me and slapped
his heels together under the sheets. I smiled. But, behind me,
the wind pushed a question at the glass. Huh? Huh? it asked.
What're you going to do? And I had no answer. I walked toward the window, as though my physical presence alone might
satisfy it. But the bed intervened, counseling temporization,
and I fell gratefully onto it instead.

I had blundered into the sanctuary. There was no question
of that. Across the room, Mr. Farbstein nodded, seconding my
suspicions. He and Dr. Snow were Jews. Jews. And yet it was
impossible. A Jew couldn't have stood, his shoulders heaving,
his head bowed, in that end zone of thirty years before. I knew

that. No. That wasn't an end zone for Jews—not twenty-five
years ago, whatever it was now. Nurse MacArthur hurried
along the corridor. I groaned. I would have to ask her. That
was that. I had three days left and I would have to trouble
them. A madman. God above, I thought, please let him be a
madman. But the pass patterns—he had known them all. He
had played in that game, Snofski son of a rabbi. No, not Snofski.
I brought my palms together, straining each against the other,
until my biceps ached and sweat covered my temples. Please—
a madman. Let it be nothing more. But already I knew it was
much more than that.

"I'll beat you yet," I said. Jimmy was climbing into bed, but,
when I said that, he trotted promptly over.

"No, you won't," he said.

"No?"

"Nope. You're too nice, Mr. Belknap. You're not tough
enough." Then, very soberly, he said, "I don't think bishops
can play Monopoly."

"That so?"

"Yup. Mr. Carson's easy to beat, too. What's he do?"

"For a living, you mean? I don't know. I think he's between
jobs."

"I bet he's a Good Humor man."

"A Good Humor man?" I laughed. "Why ever that?"

"I dunno. Most Good Humor men don't have teeth. From
eatin' too much ice cream, I guess. But still, kids like them—
even if they're kinda funny lookin', most of them."

"And they can't play Monopoly either, huh?"

"No." He thought for a moment. "Dr. Snow. I bet he'd be
a great Monopoly player. But he wouldn't play, would he?"

"I guess not," I said.

"Did you ask him?"

"What? Who?"

"Dr. Snow. About Mr. Carson." Jimmy came closer to my bed. "Did you find out what's really wrong? He's all right, isn't he?"

"Well, yes . . . . Yes, of course. Just as we thought, it was all a stupid mistake. He'll be all right. It'll take a while but, don't you worry, he'll be all right."

"Great stuff. Did you tell him? Huh?"

"Artie? No. Not yet."

"Want me to?" I put my hand quickly on Jimmy's shoulder.

"No. I'll tell him about it tonight."

"Okay." He grinned at me. "You're pretty cool. Even if you can't play Monopoly."

"Enough. Get back to bed. Your dinner's coming. You wait, I'll show no mercy. I'll cheat."

"Nope. You can't cheat." He laughed, ducked out from beneath my arm, and raced back to his bed. I watched him run. And now Jimmy had only two days left. Whatever I feared, I swore I wouldn't trouble Jimmy's last two days.

"So. What've you learned about Christ?" Artie squeezed his mouth between thumb and forefinger, forcing out the thick, pink insides of his lips. He cleared his throat. Then he picked up a soiled scrap of paper on which, I suppose, he had made notes. But the notes consisted only of unrelated single words scrawled at odd angles. After a moment Artie realized that he no longer knew what they referred to.

"Well, ah . . . It says lots of things here. Like—like, for instance . . . Hypocrites. Oh, yeah. Hypocrites are—" He peered at the piece of paper. He scraped at the word with his nail, as though it might have been obscured by some gummy, opaque substance. "Blessed? Hypocrites are blessed?"

"No," I said.

"Guess not. That couldn't be right, could it? You better tell me, Whit—I'm pretty stupid." He lay there; his Bible pressed to one side of his chest; an orange hot water bottle pressed to the other. He was watching me. Under the heavy glasses, I saw, or imagined I saw, an intensity that hadn't been in his eyes before. I was, for Artie, the outward and visible manifestation of God's Word. He was watching to see which way I'd jump.

"No," I said. "You tell me. Not so much about the Bible— I know about that. Tell me about yourself."

"You—you want me to confess?" He swallowed so violently and deeply that his Adam's apple became entangled in his pajama collar. I laughed.

"No. That's none of my business. Just talk to me. Well— tell me about someone you love."

"You mean—like a woman?"

"Not necessarily. Could be. But there're other relationships."

"Love? I tell you, Whit—women, well . . . Tell truth, women never made much of a fuss over me. See, I didn't have teeth when I was a kid. All the front ones—tops and bottoms —got smashed out when I was about thirteen. I didn't look too pretty, and Ma didn't feel like buyin' me false ones. Said it served me right. Probably did. So I didn't push myself on women much. I remember once—it was at one of those make-out parties—a girl kissed me and got all sick. She screamed. No kiddin', screamed. Said my mouth fell all apart when she leaned on it. So I stayed clear pretty much. You don't go far with women, not without teeth."

"Forget about women then. Who else is there?"

"Who else?" He seemed genuinely confused. "Who else? How d'you mean?"

"Well—tell me about Ginny, for instance."

"Ginny?" He sat up, surprised; both the Bible and the hot water bottle fell away from his sides. "I tell you about her? Sure, I must've. Else how'd you know? Ginny? She's . . . I mean, I never was an uncle before. You know, Whit? Like, if I got a job—sure's hell I'd quit or get fired after a while. It was always like that. But when Albert made me an uncle—it was like gettin' a degree. Like Sergeant Artie, Doctor Artie, Sir Artie. You know—a title, that's what it was. I was Ginny's only uncle, and it was a thing I couldn't get fired from. Couldn't even quit. So I figured I'd do it up right."

"What'd you do?"

"Oh, lots of things. It's funny—maybe you wouldn't believe it—but I'm pretty good with kids. Honest. They like me. Beats me why, the mess I am."

"You ever a Good Humor man?"

"Huh? Why'd you ask that? No—not Good Humor. Did push a cart for Eskimo Pie couple of times."

"I'll be damned."

"Why's that?"

"Nothing. Eat a lot of ice cream?"

"Yeah. Used to, anyway. What's all this about?" He smiled.

"Sorry. Tell me more about Uncle Artie." He thought for a moment.

"I didn't have it too easy—Al didn't want t'have me around. You know how it is. I kinda embarrassed him. It was Al bought me these damned teeth, and I'd have t'wear 'em any time he saw me. I could understand the way he felt. Hell, I'm no buddin' rose. So I stayed away most of the time. But I'd send Ginny all sorts of Uncle presents. You know. For the craziest reasons.

The crazier, the better. Y'see, nobody forgot Ginny's birthday or Christmas. My cheap, little things got lost in the crowd then. But how many people remembered her three-eighths birthday or National Pickle Week? Things like that? Not many. Even once . . . Hell, that was a crazy thing t'do. Even now I get nervous thinkin' about it. Know what I did?"

"No. Tell me."

"Well. Al told me Ginny's gonna be in a play at school. Boy, now I think, I must've been crazy in those days. A real nut. Anyway, I got this 'lectrician's outfit from a friend of mine, and I walked right into the school and up to the auditorium. Christ, was I scared. All those little kids around, and me lookin' like a dirty old man. But I made out I was real busy, right up 'til the show started. Then I found a place up in the light bridge and waited—I hadda lift one of the covers off the roof and lay down in the insulation, right in behind a rack of lights. Whit, she was beautiful. I don't remember what the show was about. I couldn't hear so good, but she had one of those big hooped dresses—like from *Gone With the Wind*. You know?" I nodded "She didn't have a big part, but, by God, she was still the best lookin' kid there. Christ, I musta been outa my mind. I knew, see, that they had a big, fancy automatic light board out in the wings. So I figured—the whole show's lit, see. They ain't gonna come lookin' out in the light bridge if anythin' goes wrong. So long's it ain't too big a thing . . . Crazy. There's three lights in this rack in fronta me. So I took the middle one, pulled out the gel and loosened up the clamps. Then, whenever Ginny'd come on, I'd hit her with this big, bright spot. Whit, she looked like an angel with a halo. I followed her all over the stage—all over." He started to laugh nervously. I smiled.

"Pretty clever," I said.

"Clever? Crazy, that's all. If Al'd found out, he'da cut my balls off. But there's more. This's what really got me. All them big muck-a-muck parents with ties and tails and what-not on —I couldn't get over it. All those muck-a-mucks, like I said, and only Ginny gets flowers. From her stumblebum Uncle Artie. I could laugh. I could laugh." But, instead, he began to cry. "I'm a stupid, useless bastard. Stupid, useless bastard and now I'm gonna die."

You ask them about the things they've loved, not about the things they've hated and defiled. And penitence comes—for just a moment—when, by that little light, they see the depthless blackness of the void. It's a cruel business, but it's very much to the point. It has the virtue of being a self-revelation. If they listen, and, when they're dying, they're inclined to listen, they hear damnation in their own throats. Then it's time to speak of hope. It's a cruel business—I know, I've done it to myself a hundred times.

"I'm gonna die, Whit. I know it now. I lay here at night, and I hear funny sounds, sad like, comin' from my stomach. I put my fingers in my ears, and then I feel them instead. Funny, little sounds. Sayin' goodbye, that's what they're doing. Sayin' goodbye." I said nothing. But, by then, I believed it; somehow, I think, I was trying to learn from him. "You know it, too—doncha, Whit? You're kinda quiet about it now. Like you're embarrassed. You ever go bowlin'? You ever take a ball and let it loose at a full set of pins— let it loose hard? The friggin' ball barrels down the alley—you think you're gonna smash the whole works—and then the ball hooks or somethin' and falls in the stupid gutter. The pins're still standin' there. All you hoped for turns out to be a big, stupid thud. That's all. That's it. That's all."

"It's not all."

"No? Maybe not. But it's all I can see. And it ain't enough, Whit. It just ain't enough."

"No, you're right. It isn't. It's nothing. Listen. D'you hear the wind, Artie? Outside. Listen. It's free. That's the way you want to be—that's the way you will be. Not bound, entombed in this thing." I took his forearm in my hand and shook it. "Free. Your mind, your soul—they want to be everywhere. But you can't go with them—not in this body. You're bound in a straitjacket. Bound. If death is coming, Artie—if it is— then, by God, freedom is coming, too."

"Oh, God." He put his face in his hands.

" 'But as many as received Him—to them gave He power to be the Sons of God, even to them that believe on His Name.' You believe, Artie—you've got to. Because you've known love. Because of the love you felt—up there—up on the light bridge and in a thousand little corners of your life before. Artie, listen to me. Listen. When I speak to you, I'm speaking as well to myself. I'm as dead as you think you are. You and me, the whole world—we know that fact somehow, even if we've shoved it to the very backs of our minds. But now you—because of this terrible illness—you see the handwriting on the wall. You see it clearly, unmistakably. You're terrified. Yes. But I beg you, Artie—be thankful, too. Now you know, as few of us can ever know, what the very worst is. You're ready; you're ripe. You can change everything." I gripped the edge of his mattress with both my hands. The whole of my body was rigid with emphasis.

"God loves you, Artie. He loves you as you loved Ginny that night—beautifully and from afar. And He's following you, too —all over the stage. His light is shining on you. He knows you're ashamed to call on Him—He knows and He understands.

And for you, Artie, He allowed His Son, His only Child, to be sacrificed, to suffer terrible pain. As Ginny is to Albert, as Jimmy is to his father, so—only a million times more intensely —so Christ is to God. He sacrificed His Son so that you might be free some day. Artie, you've sinned beyond human forgiveness. I couldn't forgive you. I probably wouldn't even want to. Nor can you forgive yourself. But what can we know of forgiveness? To despair is to insult God's glorious mercy. All you have to do is come to Him—now, even after all that has passed. That's all. That's all you have to do.

"Believe in Him. Don't be afraid. In Matthew—last night —Christ said that every sparrow is under his care, every hair of your head is numbered. If that is so—and it is so—then you can never be lost. The past flows by like the river out there. It's gone. And the world is new again."

"Whit, the way you talk, you make my hair stand on end."

"They're standing up to be counted. You stand up, too."

"You think so, Whit?"

"I know so."

Nurse MacArthur came in. Suddenly I was embarrassed to be discovered bent, tense and insistent, over Artie's bed. God forgive me, at that moment my own terrible fears returned, and I forgot all about the conversion of Artie Carson. I made a further few cursory remarks that I cannot now remember— then I turned away from him. And when I'd done so, Artie reached out and caught the hem of my bathrobe in his hand.

"Don't go far, Whit. You go, everything goes." I turned back, irritated.

"It's not me," I said. "Don't mistake Him for me. That'd be a bad mistake. Read a bit and then get to sleep. I'm not going anywhere."

But I did leave his bedside. Without looking back, I made

my way slowly to the window. In the distance, a tug was hauling six empty barges upstream. The wind—I could just see past the glass's reflection—was throwing up a hard wall of water against the barges. Yet, imperceptibly, the squat, massive determination of the tug drew the yawning barges through the current. Behind me, Nurse MacArthur had arrived at Jimmy's bed. I leaned my forehead against the pane: by then the pulse in my throat was throbbing so heavily that I fought unconsciously to swallow it down. And when her whiteness in the glass slipped away from the whiteness of Jimmy's bed, I turned quickly around.

"When you've a moment," I said, "come over here. I'd like to speak to you."

She was startled. But I turned back to the window, as though to indicate that I could wait. I tightened the belt of my bathrobe and found my hands awkward and preoccupied. A star materialized out of the blue-black and, when I was easily able to see it, I was able to see others. The wind ran its back against the window, begging to be let in. It struck me then that life was very beautiful indeed. And I knew quite well why now it seemed like that to me.

"Yes, Mr. Belknap?" She had come quickly. I moved a step back from the window, but I didn't turn to look at her. I watched her dark reflection in the window pane.

"What's it like out?"

"Is that . . . It's windy. Hurricane off Cape Hatteras now, I think. May reach here by tomorrow. May go out to sea. I don't think you should be standing here. You should be in bed."

"The stars are out."

"Yes . . . Yes, the stars are out. Look, Mr. Belknap—"

"How long have you known Dr. Snow?" She didn't speak, but

she did move away from me. Just one step, but away. And still
I didn't look at her. I couldn't see her expression in the glass;
anyway, it didn't matter.

"Four or five years," she said.

"Tell me something about him."

"What would you like to know? I haven't much time. There
are other patients."

"Nothing in particular. Where does he come from?"

"Come from? Near Des Moines. In fact, just about a hundred miles from where I was born."

"Des Moines— Good God, that's Iowa."

"Of course it is. You can't miss his accent. A boy I used to
know—"

"Looked just like Dr. Snow. Talked just like him."

"Yes. But how did you know? I never told anyone that."

I pressed both my palms hard against the glass. *Lord God
above. Don't do this to me. Not to me. Not this. I'm not strong
enough.* My fingernails dug into the panes as though they might
scrape away the night's blackness. Shrill squeaking sounds upset the silence. Behind me, Nurse MacArthur took an uncertain
step backward. And another.

"Where does he live now? What—" My voice broke. "What
does he do?" I turned around—when I did, I knew at once that
Nurse MacArthur was as frightened as I. She waved a protective
hand in front of her face.

"Why ask me?" she said harshly. "Why pick on me? I don't
want any trouble. Why won't you let me alone?"

"Tell me. Please, you must."

"No," she said. "No, I won't. Good night, Mr. Belknap."

She was gone. All the surfaces of my senses were as though
subtly distorted. The room, the beds, Artie, Mr. Farbstein, even

Jimmy—they were unfamiliar. And, indeed, now nothing was the same. A water glass swelled under my gaze, and the cracks in the ceiling were suddenly each a crinkled demon. I could no longer bear to see, and yet I was afraid to close my eyes.

Though I walk through the valley of the shadow—I shall fear . . . I shall fear . . . Lord God above, be with me now. Without Thee I have no hope. But with Thee—

The wind nudged the glass.

Oh, God, not me. Oh, my God, ask not this of Thy weakest. Ask not this of me. I shall disappoint Thee. I shall surely disappoint Thee. And then what will I be?

TUESDAY, AUGUST 22ND—

THE NINTH DAY

". . . And I will utter my judgments against them touching all their wickedness, who have forsaken me and have burned incense unto other Gods and worshipped the works of their own hands. Thou, therefore, gird up thy loins and arise and speak unto them all that I command thee: be not dismayed at their faces, lest I confound thee before them . . ."

. . . Be not dismayed at their faces, lest I confound thee before them . . . I sat, huddled over the windowsill, as the unpromising rays of dawn light touched tentatively, then illuminated, those disturbing verses of Jeremiah. I didn't care to sleep —sleep was too prolific of terrible and transparent imagery. A cross. A caduceus. My body racked between terrific, oxymoronic opposites: my right arm and leg wrenched violently upward; my left arm and leg slithering, flopping on the ground. Then running my head off, my breath blowing out in cloudy spurts, running to sanctuary in the little, square garden. I hadn't prayed since. What I didn't want was strength.

". . . This little book asks whether that terminology and that world view are a necessary part of Christianity. It asks whether,

in fact, they only succeed in rendering Christianity incredible
to anyone who possesses the common sense and the scientific
prejudice of the twentieth century." . . . And I will utter
my judgments against them touching all their wickedness . . .
". . . They have probed the heavens and the innermost recesses
of men's bodies. They know very well where God can be and
where He cannot be." . . . who have forsaken me and burned
incense unto other Gods and worshipped the works of their
own hands . . .

Mr. Farbstein, too, was awake. He had been with me during
the whole of my dark vigil. In the course of the night, an odd
urgency had articulated itself throughout his body. Mr. Farbstein sat upright now, his mouth open; it was as though he expected momentarily to shriek. The valve picture lay on his lap,
but Mr. Farbstein was no longer interested in it. He stared
only at me, and his stare was uncompromising and obsessive. I
judged, from the tension that eddied in visible spasms over the
backs of his hands, that some significant climax was impending. Neither of us, I suspected, knew what that climax would
be. But now I, too, watched.

Jimmy . . . The light had reached across his pillow. His
smallest finger was in his mouth, and, where it raised his upper
lip, there was a puckish smile which dissolved into a wistful
smile, which became finally a smile of sleep. Tuesday. On
Thursday Jimmy's turn would come—the whole thing taking
place with benefit of my fullest sanction. It was too late now:
even if I'd known what there was to fear, or what to offer in its
stead. My own will to live was, by then, a matter of the sheer-
est presumption. Soon, I suspected, it would be a sin.

And the morning. It overwhelmed me when I saw it. Everything that could move or be moved seemed frantic, harassed.
In the great, gray buildings there was implicit no more stability

than in a little child's set of blocks. I felt that the whole of God's natural order was, at the very best, purely provisional. The revolutions of the earth on its own axis, of the earth around the sun, of the sun around a still more terrific body—these were as momentary as the shapeless wave heads that battered against the retaining wall. I remembered the much less substantial wall of my aneurysm. Death, I supposed, was only the ultimate spasm in this aimless agitation. Indefinite; undignified; unresolved. Certainly not an acceptance.

"Lest . . ." I read it out loud. "Lest I confound thee before them . . ."

"Whit. Hey, Whit. I had a real good night last night. Slept like a log. I'm crazy maybe, but I think I'm gettin' better. I ate this morning—y'see me? The egg and the coffee, and I didn't feel like barfin' after. That's the thing. Whit, I think I'm gettin' better."

He coughed, and I turned my head away while he squeezed the phlegm into a tissue. I was annoyed. Artie had begun to expect a miracle. And, all the while, little strands of cancer were proliferating, drawing tiny, stifling webs around and round his vital organs. Soon, when the miracle failed to materialize, he would be angry with God. Artie tilted his lenses down coquetishly. His eyes were frank and undoubting. Man, I thought, is a hoping animal.

"But you think different, huh? You think I shouldn't talk like that?" I shook my head.

"No. I don't think you should. Mind you, it's not that I don't want to see you well again. I do. I'd just hate to see you disappointed—with yourself, with God. But you can't help it. I know that."

"Hell, cheer up." Artie smiled. "Look, Whit—I mean, it's

been so long since I felt halfway good. Up here or down there.
I just can't pass up the chance. You know?"

"I know."

"Matter of fact, Whit—it's not really my body. It's you. Honest. Okay. Okay. I didn't mean that. It's this." He squeezed
the Bible. Then he held it up, as though I were unfamiliar with
such things. "I'm not fightin' anymore. I didn't fight the egg
this morning. I didn't fight myself to sleep last night. No, and
I had real nice dreams. Nice. Man, were they nice. I'd tell
you but—" Artie winked. He stared down the length of his
body. He moved his right foot under the blanket. He moved
his left foot. "You're right. I guess I'm no better. Not really.
Look, Whit—I'm not so dumb as you think. I know if I start
hopin' t'get better, I'll be right back where I started from. Only
I'll be lustin' after my own body for a change."

"Well, anyway," I said. "You're right about one thing. I
tend to underestimate people—when it comes to intelligence or
to faith. It's a sort of intolerance, I suppose."

"You intolerant? Not damn likely, I'd say. Someone like
Snow now. That piss-cutter. He's intolerant with a capital I.
He spits on me, and he don't bother to hide it. And he's like
that with everybody. If you ask me, his bedside manner is from
dung."

"What d'you think of him?" I asked. I found something
wrong with my thumb cuticle and began to scrape at it. But
my question had been so exquisitely off-hand that Artie hadn't
even heard me. I repeated it. I watched Artie, as though by
the reflection in my thumbnail.

"Snow? I think he's a grade A phony. I think everybody
builds him up big—but really he ain't such hot stuff."

"Personally, though. What d'you think of him personally?"

"Well. He's a bigot like I said. A snob. And—and . . ."
Artie smashed the flat of his hand down on the mattress. "He's
a real son of a bitch, that's all. The worst. I hate him, but—like
everybody here—I'm too afraid to say anything. Everybody but
you, Whit. He respects you."

"Yes, but—I mean, isn't there something familiar about him?"

"Familiar? How d'you mean?"

"Nothing. Forget it." I got out of bed and draped my bathrobe over my shoulders. Then I began pacing up and down between the two beds.

"Familiar? He's a real bastard, if that's what you mean. I've
known plenty of that kind in my day. Real familiar they are.
What other doctor'd make poor Albert tell me that? Huh? Most
doctors don't tell you nothin'." He smiled. "Hey, Whit.
Maybe I'm crazy. What d'you think? See—this'll kill you—I
figure it's God made him do it. All that stuff about the sparrows
—you know. If Snow hadn't told me, I'd've laid here feelin' piss
sorry for myself and doin' nothing but nothing about it. I'd
never've asked you t'help. Never in a billion years. Look at it
this way—ain't it kind of a magic coincidence, a bishop bein'
right here just when I need one? Someone I'd really learned to
like. Someone who likes me. Trouble with me is—I forget
this's your job. You don't do it because it's me."

"That's nice talk."

"No. I don't mean it that way. Sit here, Whit. You're givin'
me a tennis neck." I sat obediently. "You're bigger'n me—
that's the whole point. If it was just because you liked me . . .
Well, what'd you do if somebody come along you didn't like?
Huh? It's like Snow in a way. Only you love everybody equal.
He hates everybody equal. Except for you—he's met his match
there and he knows it. I bet he talks nice and polite t'you."

I concentrated on the yellow-pink of Artie's gums, the nicotine stains between his first and second fingers. But contempt
breeds familiarity—now, no matter how shrewdly I catered to
my revulsion, I could, at worst, manage only an anaemic disdain.
I leaned forward in order that his odors might reach me. Then
I sat back. After what I had learned the night before, it seemed
ludicrous now still to be titillating my petty disgusts. And I
thought then that all the revulsion I'd ever felt—all the faint-
nesses, the repulsive fantasies—was as artificial as a young girl's
first rejection of her lover. Mortifications set within mortifications—like Chinese boxes.

"Only one thing worries me, Whit—time. We gotta have time
enough. You're goin' Friday. It's on your mind already. I can
see that. Since last night you been kind of far away. And after
that—hell, even if it's the greatest job old phony's ever pulled
off—even then you'll be pretty sick. We won't be in the same
room. If you ain't here—I tell you, Whit—I'm scared. I'm
afraid it'll go away. I'm afraid I'll lose it." He shook his head.
"I—we gotta find some way to speed things up."

"We can still see each other—after. After this."

"Yeah? I hoped you'd say that. That's real swell, Whit. Hey.
Look somewhere else, you old bastard. I don't like him, Whit.
Why'd we get stuck with a nut like that?"

"Haven't you noticed—he isn't looking at you. He doesn't
anymore. He just looks at me."

"That's right. Why the hell is that, I wonder?" A gust of
wind struck the window a sharp blow that startled us both. For
a while we talked about hurricanes and tornadoes. Then we
discussed Christ's calming of the storm on the sea of Galilee.
Artie said he wished he'd been there. He talked of the other
miracles, the healings, and I let him talk.

"Man. I'd like t've seen that bastard Pilate's face. Would I just. You know—when he hears the tomb's empty. I'd like t've seen all them Jews' faces. That must've started them thinkin'. But good. It's no wonder the disciples believed in God, what with miracles goin' off left and right like fireworks on the Fourth of July. They'd've been nuts not to."

"I suppose they had it easy—in that sense. God was always there; always manifested in real things. But, then again, they needed it—most of them were treated pretty terribly. Martyred."

"Today—I mean, today there ain't no miracles, huh? I don't mean me, Whit. But, the way you talk, it's like all that stuff's gone outa style."

"Well," I said, "God works differently in different worlds. In the twentieth century, scientists are the miracle workers."

As I said the words, their sound elicited a shadowy intimation of something I'd heard before. A quotation, a reference —the text of a sermon, perhaps. It passed quickly through my mind, like the remembering of places where one has never been before. Differently . . . The memory carried with it an assertion of its own importance. I tried to recreate the moment of association, but the chain—if such a chain there had been— faded with the arrival of an orderly. He brought Artie's lunch tray.

"Hell," he said, "it can't be time to eat. Not already." He sat forward, looking cautiously from one item of food to another. It was a pathetic meal: broth and stewed peaches and a cup of tea. But it seemed to overwhelm him.

"Don't let it get you down," I said. "You've already eaten a lot." But Artie had stopped looking at his tray.

"Whit, you remember—I said we hadda speed up the process? I just thought of something. Something t'do just that."

"What?"

"Yesterday. When you were out with Snow, Jimmy and I were cleaning up the Monopoly things. Jimmy said you'd written a book. He said it was real good. His sister or something'd read it. Whit, could I maybe have a look at it?"

"No," I said.

"No?" He was startled. "Why not, Whit? If it's hard to understand—hell, I'll concentrate real hard. And with you right here—"

"I said no. It's not for you. It wouldn't do you any good."

"But, Whit—if you wrote it, it's gotta be good. Let me try. It couldn't hurt, could it?" I laughed at that.

"Forget it," I said. And I walked away.

An orderly opened our window. He patted a dust mop on the wall beyond, and the wind flooded in, bringing the dust back with it. I had imagined—some moments before—that there was a faint, pink outline, very like a letter D, in amongst the gray hairs of my chest. Friday. And if not Friday or before Friday, yet soon enough. By now some were already dead. The mother of the green-ink girl, perhaps. By now her daughter was back in school, back running around park benches, back growing up to her special sort of womanhood. Forgetting . . . Perhaps, in her hurry to let the dead bury the dead, she would understand why I hadn't read her letter. Pious must have understood. Soon, I thought, it would be my turn to understand.

"Hi," said Artie.

"H—hi . . . hi," said someone else.

Michael's head and upper torso appeared at the doorjamb. One hand was stretched behind him. I knew Michael was holding onto the wooden bar, hanging down into our room like a cautious human fly. He had a brown paper bag, roughly square, in his visible hand. His collar was too big, a ring carelessly tossed on a peg. He had been watching me. His thin hair, tousled by the wind, stood up in a disordered spray.

"Come on in," said Artie. "He's been hoping you'd come. He's missed you."

"He has?"

"I have."

"See? Come on in."

I smiled. Michael smiled. Then he spread his elbows wide and flew figuratively toward me. But, before he reached halfway, Michael's knee struck the foot of Artie's bed. He yelped and dropped the bag. Then he began walking in circles, bending to rub his shin, and rising quickly when his balance became imperiled. Artie giggled. Michael played it up. He began putting his left leg forward tentatively—as a prim, fat ballet dancer might. I laughed. Jimmy, whose sense of decorum was the most austere, finally allowed himself to join in.

"That's what's happened all weekend," Michael said. He sighed. "If it's higher than the ground, I fall off it. If it sticks out, I get caught on it. The wind out there—you wouldn't believe it—it's tremendous." He smoothed down his hair. "I'm exhausted. I think I give it too much surface. I almost didn't get here."

"I'm glad you did. Pull up a seat. I was beginning to think you'd abandoned me." Michael sat. He retrieved the bag and put it in his lap. Then he turned around and smiled at Artie. Artie waved back. Encouraged, he smiled at Jimmy and at Mr. Farbstein. Mr. Farbstein ignored him, but Michael didn't notice that. Then he put his hand on mine. His hand was cold and damp.

"How are you?" he asked.

"Fine. Fine," I said. There was a silence. "Just fine. I'm
eating solids since Sunday morning. But the best news is my
operation. They've set it for Friday morning."

"No."

"Yes."

"They're going to operate?"

"Now don't get your bowels in an uproar. I'm quite calm
about the whole thing. Perfectly calm. Dr. Snow thinks it's an
aneurysm."

"An—an . . . ?"

"Well, it's very technical. Just don't worry about it."

"Are you sure?" Michael didn't believe me. I thought then
that my fear must really have been showing; ordinarily Michael
believed anything I wanted him to. Michael got up and waddled
over to the window. He was thinking what he'd do if I died on
Friday—thinking about the whole thing quite selfishly. And
yet I was glad that someone would be affected—even in the
least of ways—by my death. Michael came back.

"I brought you a present."

"So I see." It was a book of cat pictures. On the cover a great,
bored tabby had been captured in mid-yawn. Its eyes were
crossed and its tongue was unfurling languidly in its mouth.
Michael wasn't being tactless; he was purposely testing me. I
knew that. The cat on the cover—the cat yawning and not bothering to cover its mouth—might have been Pious. But I evinced
only interest as I thumbed the pages. Michael huddled over me.
Whenever they seemed appropriate, he made long vowel sounds
of admiration.

"I tried," he said finally.

"What did you try?"

"I couldn't find him anywhere. I went to the ASPCA. I went

to the Bide A Wee. I went to that smelly place down in the Vil-
lage. I put ads in all the papers—the *Times* and the *Post*.
Even in the Wall Street *Journal*. I hope you don't mind, I—I
offered a thousand-dollar reward."

"A thousand dollars? No, I don't mind."

"I knew you wouldn't. But I couldn't leave the house. I think
I got two, three hundred calls. People wanted me to take all
kinds of things. Toy poodles and boxers—even a turtle. And
when I said no, they got very excited. Angry. Some of them
said very vulgar things. I don't think anybody read the ad—just
the part about the thousand dollars." He ran his fingers through
his hair and then had difficulty extracting them. A tuft of hair
came out between his first and second fingers. He placed it
thriftily over a bare spot on his wrist.

"Forget it, Mike."

"Every night after the phone stopped ringing—every night
I'd go out and set traps in alleys and doorways. I'd put chopped
meat and liver and herring on little paper plates. Then I'd
hide where I could watch. But it was no good. So many cats. So
many. I didn't know there were so many cats . . . Saturday
nights was the worst. Three little boys held me up in an alley.
They took my wallet. Then they threw my shoes into a sewer
so I couldn't follow them. I walked seven blocks to your place.
In my socks. I stepped in something—ugh. I had to take a bath
in your tub. And I had to throw out two towels. It was terrible."

"Mike. It's all over. Please forget it. It wasn't your fault.
It's very complicated, and I can't really explain it to you, but I
know now it had to be. And I'm sorry—I could kick myself
—I'm so sorry I carried on the way I did. I'm ashamed of myself."

"It's okay. I know he meant a lot to you. He—he was a nice

cat. Even if he didn't like me. I was going to get you a kitten,
but I didn't know what kind you'd like."

"A kitten. Yes. Perhaps when I'm well again."

We discussed diocese business for half an hour. Michael
asked me three times if I'd done any writing, and I adroitly
changed the subject each time he brought it up. After a while
Artie asked Michael to push a pillow up behind his shoulders.
Michael followed his instructions expertly and without the
slightest apparent hesitation. Then Artie said something that
Michael must have thought very funny. Michael laughed so
hard he had difficulty straightening up. He was still giggling
when he came back to my bed.

"He's a funny man."

"Oh?"

"He told me a dirty joke." Michael giggled and put his hand
up over his mouth. "About priests and nuns. I didn't understand it, but I laughed anyway. What's a douche bag?"

"It's very dirty, Michael."

"I thought so. Don't tell me." Michael put his middle finger
in his mouth. "You know. I thought I saw a Bible in his lap."

"You did."

"You mean he's religious? With all those—bags and things?"

"It's rather recent, I'm afraid."

"A conversion. Oh, good." Michael clapped his hands. "He's
lucky to have you here."

"I hope you're right. I don't know. I'm pretty preoccupied
these days."

"The operation." He pointed an accusing forefinger at me.
"You are worried. You're worried about the anana-thing."

"No," I said. "It's not that. I've had to do some thinking.
I've had to reevaluate certain ideas, that's all."

"For your book?"

"Yes. As a matter of fact. For my book."

"You're not worried?"

"No."

"You're happy?"

"Yes," I said. "I'm very happy." And Michael was happy, too.

"Come to the window! Quick!" Jimmy raced past the foot of my bed and threw himself against the windowsill. I jumped out of bed, my bathrobe trailing behind me in one hand. Jimmy held his binoculars to his eyes; he was looking out, over the Hudson.

"What is it, Whit? Huh? What's going on?"

"See?" Jimmy's finger tapped against the glass in the urgency of his pointing. "It was alongside the barge. Pulling it upstream. Then the wind blew real hard, and the rope on the back just snapped. I saw it go. It went flying up in the air. See, part of it's floating in the water." Jimmy handed me his binoculars. I put them to my eyes.

"What is it, Whit? Jimmy? Someone tell me, for God's sake."

"A big, empty barge," I said. "The tug must've been alongside of it. Then the wind broke one of the ropes—looks like the barge swung free on the bow rope and got in front of the tug. Now the current's pushing the barge downstream on top of it. Water's very rough."

"Lookit her heave. They're tryin' t'get another rope on the barge. No. They can't do it."

"No. Now they're backing, trying to get out from under the barge. So they can pull it, I think. But they're having trouble."

"Man. The wind's blowin' so hard, it's like the trees're on fire."

"Oh, God. Why'm I stuck in this miserable coffin? What's happening now? Huh?"

The tug was backing down the current, trying to put distance between its bow and the avalanche of the barge. One rope, slack and bent in a U, drooped from the barge to the tug's nose, but it seemed very insubstantial placed against those two great weights. The Hudson, a docile leviathan had gone into musk. The two unequal decks rose and fell insanely on the water. The barge, with immense surfaces and no engine, tossed and shook itself as the wind and the current put their shoulders to its flank. But now the tug was clear: the barge had slid across the tug's bow; it began to move downstream with the current. The rope quickly lost slack. I handed Jimmy his binoculars.

"She's clear," Jimmy yelled. The rope went taut as the barge hurled itself past the now almost motionless tug. "It broke! It broke!"

"What? What? What broke?"

"The bow rope," said Jimmy. "Now the barge's heading down the river. Gee. I bet it'll crash."

"Anybody on it?"

"Can't see," I said. "No. It's gone behind a building. The tug's turning. It's heading after it."

"Hurricane's coming tomorrow," Jimmy turned away from the window. "Eighty-mile-an-hour winds. Sure glad I won't miss it."

I smiled at Jimmy. His head was tilted forward on his neck, as though set against some dreadful gale. A shapeless, hurried mist, more like gray factory smoke than a natural emanation, had begun to lower the already overcast sky, and with it had come a premature evening. Jimmy touched my sleeve.

"Someone to see you, Mr. Belknap."

Dr. Snow stood at the foot of Artie's bed. Artie and Mr. Farb-

stein stared up at him, as though Dr. Snow's head were the apex
of a triangle formed within their sight lines and the plane of
their prone bodies. Jimmy hurried out of the room, pressing
against the foot of Mr. Farbstein's bed as he passed Dr. Snow.
I walked toward my bed. Artie buried his face, almost his whole
upper body, in the crotch of his opened Bible. Dr. Snow seemed
impatient. Ostensibly he seemed serene, but I could tell that
his purpose, whatever it might be, was urgent and irresistible.
I met Dr. Snow near the foot of my bed. In deference to his
height, I sat on the mattress' edge.

"Whitney," he said. "I've come to say good-bye."

"Good-bye?" I thought I saw a sneer, very like an embryonic
sneeze, wrinkling his nose and mouth. He was looking at my bed
table. "Good-bye?" I asked again. "What d'you mean?"

"You haven't read my letters . . ."

"Have you written?"

"No," he smiled. "No. Things've gotten a bit out of hand.
I see that now. The letters—you know, the ones I gave you a
while ago. Have you read them?" I looked at my feet. And
there, in my well-formed but vestigial toes, I found my own sort
of patient calm. I moved them and they moved. I draped my
bathrobe on the bed. I stroked it. At last, I thought, at last it's
my turn to seem deliberate. I flexed my toes again. Near my
feet were Dr. Snow's white legs and shoes.

"No," I said.

"A shame," he said. "I'd have thought you—you'd make a
better go of it. Well . . . I suppose it's not too easy. Not in
your condition." He removed a hand from deep inside one of
his abdominal pockets. Then he scratched near a cleft in his
chin. A cleft we both had. "Anyhow, back to the matter at
hand." Dr. Snow said it as though our affair had almost reached
an end. I suppose then he had every reason to think it had.

"I have a conference tomorrow, Whitney. In Boston. I'll have to leave tonight. And Thursday promises to be a very busy day. Very busy. I'm afraid I won't see you until after the operation. So, if you have any questions, now's the time to ask."

I said nothing.

"No? No questions? About the operation? No questions about after-effects? No . . . Whitney? Did you hear me?"

"Loud and clear," I said. "Loud and clear. After-effects. No questions."

"Well . . . good. I'm glad you have such undoubting faith. By this time Friday—believe me—by this time you'll be a new man." Dr. Snow meant to leave: certainly he'd lost all interest in me by then. He made an amiable, perfunctory gesture of farewell. Then he stopped. I didn't know why, for I hadn't been watching him—but I knew he hadn't left. I was watching my toes. Dr. Snow's legs appeared again before me. He stood in front of my feet: he forced himself into my line of vision.

"What's your friend reading?" he asked

"Who?"

"Mr. Carson. The man who's dying."

"The Bible," I said.

"Is that your idea?"

"No. As a matter of fact, it's his. I'm only helping where I can."

"I see. Why don't you . . . ?" He looked at my bed table again. "Where's your little book?"

"It's in the drawer," I said. "With your letters."

Dr. Snow said, I see, once again, but he didn't say it very loudly. He did things with his lips, as though they'd become strangely sensitive. After a moment he walked over to the window. Then he took both hands out of their pockets, interlocked

them, placed them very near his right ear. He nodded his
head in rhythmic meditation.

"You've no questions?" I smiled at him. He turned his eyes
back to the window. "Weather's getting worse. Perhaps I'd
better not travel."

"Were you flying?"

"No," he said. "I couldn't."

"I thought you could." He looked at me.

"Are you mad? Fly? In this weather?"

"In any weather," I said. And I smiled.

"You all right, Whitney? D'you feel clear-headed?"

"I'm fine. Just making a point—in an old theology. But
planes are the same thing. Aren't they? When you come to
think of it. Fly is fly. So it isn't broomsticks. So what?"

"Maybe," he said, "maybe you'd better have a tranquillizer.
I'd say you were overwrought."

"No," I said. "Don't do that. I am overwrought. Yes. But
it'd cloud the issue."

"Issue? Well . . . if you say so. Whatever you say, Whitney."

"You're not going then?"

"No," he said casually. "Don't think I will. So, if you have
any questions tomorrow—anything at all—just ask one of the
nurses to call me. I'll be in all day."

I nodded. Then he had to leave. Dr. Snow made a very impressive exit, I'm quite certain of that. But I was staring at my
toes, and so, you see, I couldn't watch him leave.

"Too much. Too friggin' much. Soup and bread and meat.
Lousy lime Jello. Too friggin' much . . . You're right, Whit
—stupid t'hope for anything in this stinkin' world." Artie
shoved his table away, but it caught on the bed leg and rolled

obstinately back. He shoved at it with both hands. It careened away; then it smashed into the wall.

"Cheer up," I said. I was sitting near the head of Artie's bed. When I heard it hit the wall, I reached my hand out absently to calm him. But I wasn't looking, and all I touched were the bed clothes.

"I thought I's goin' great guns. I mean, I really went after that creamed spinach. It even smelled good. I swear, Whit— there's times I really wanna eat. But I can't. I can't. I can't. Two damned forkfuls of creamed spinach. How long can I live on that? Intern said—lousy bastard, what's he care—intern said I'd probably have t'go back on the bottle. I'll die in here, that's what. I'll never get outa this bed. All I need's that damned needle in my arm."

"Cheer up," I said.

"Big, prissy bitch saunters in here. You see her? 'No evacuation today?' she says. Evacuation. With what? She said it just like that. Like she din't know I had terminus cancer."

"Terminal," I said. Then, as an afterthought, I said, "Cheer up."

"Terminal. Yeah, that's it. End of the line cancer. All off, last stop." He waved. "So long now. Whit? What's the weather out?"

"Sorry. What'd you say?"

"Nothin'. Forget it." Then he sat up. "Hey, did old Snow Job scare you? Did he say somethin' about the operation?"

"Everything's all right. How'd you lose your ear?"

"My ear?" He put his fingers up to the side of his face. "Hell. I just lost a piece. Just a little bit. You think it spoils my beauty?" He smiled effeminately. "Happened in the subway. Puerto Rican bastard got me with a switchblade. Ten,

twelve years ago now. I was stoned blind, real easy pickin's. He
knocks me on the floor, then he jumps on me. Plants his knees
right in my gut. Big gold teeth he had. Anyway, he grins and
takes my ear in his hand. Sliced the top right off. Object lesson like." Artie tilted his head, shook it, as though there were
water in the ear. "Crazy. Ain't that right, y'old geezer?" But
Mr. Farbstein, if he heard him, took no notice. He had chosen
me. And nothing could induce him to change allegiance.

"Should've put it in your mouth," I said.

"What's that?"

"Your ear. In your mouth. Then they could've sewn it back
on."

"Yeah? That so? No kiddin'?"

"They do it all the time now. Arms, legs even. Someone
slices off an ear—so they put it in their mouths or in a bucket of
ice, and next time round they sew it on. Happens every day.
Medical science is wonderful."

"Ain't that something?" He pondered that for a moment.
"Just put it in your mouth, eh? I'll remember next time. Too
late now—ear's still on the train for all I know . . . Maybe he
ate it. Think they could've done it back then?"

"I don't know. They can do it now."

"Yeah. Science is wonderful. I'll give you that. But it can't
do everything. Lookit me. Science drew the line right here."
He traced over his operation scar with the tip of his finger. "Or
maybe science just don't give a damn."

Again. They can do it now . . . It had come again. The
intimation. The quotation, the reference, whatever; it was there.
Unarticulated, unformed, but there in my mind. Nurse Mac-
Arthur approached Mr. Farbstein's bed, and my mind struggled against the distraction. To no avail. The links of the chain

had come apart again. Nurse MacArthur plumped Mr. Farbstein's pillow; he lowered his head to stare through the arch of
her armpit. They can do it now . . . From Matthew? Perhaps something, some phrase, I'd read that morning? I shook
my head. Nurse MacArthur walked quickly out of our room.

"That's a cool one. Real cool. Sometimes she's feelin' good,
and then she's all over you. Next minute, the damn room's
empty for all she cares. Hey, Whit? Those Lopopulo people—
what's with them? They go out—one, two, three. Every time.
Just grab the kid's game and leave. They could play in here.
On the kid's bed." He thought that over. "Y'know, Whit? I
bet it's the old guy makes 'em nervous. Damn evil eye of his.
What's he expect t'see anyway? Don't he need t'sleep? Say,
Whit? Jimmy know I'm— I'm this way?"

"Can't tell. He suspected at first—it was only natural the way
you carried on. But I told him you'd be all right. Thought he
believed me, but . . . I don't know now. He seems to know a
lot of things—things I didn't know myself."

"Yeah. That's kids. Wish I could remember bein' a kid. Inside, I mean." He plucked at the sheet with his thumb and first
two fingers. "Y'don't think Jimmy asked me t'play Monopoly
because—because he feels sorry for me?"

"No. He likes you. Don't ask me why, but he does."

"See. What'd I tell you? Kids like me—crazy ain't it?" He
stared at the back of his hand. Then he shrugged his shoulders.
"Uh . . . His sister say anything about me?"

I looked at him; I kept on looking. Artie's hands began to
slide quickly, more quickly, along the edge of the bed cover. He
took off his glasses, and found he had no place to put them. He
allowed a sound in the corridor to distract him, but, when he
turned back, I was still staring at him. Staring, willing him to

change the subject. He began to pull at his knuckles one after
the other. Still, he had to know. He had to know if Maureen
had said anything.

"Huh, Whit?"

"No, Artie," I said quietly. "No. Maureen didn't say one
damn thing about you. Why in God's name should she?"

Artie turned onto his side, away from me. The sheet showed
lines of tension: it rippled out from where he'd crushed it in
his fist. He curled his legs up behind him. Very slowly his
breathing changed, becoming, at the last, a sort of embarrassed
panting. I remembered how once the bed had danced to his fantasies. Then, without turning toward me, Artie began to speak.
His voice was small, as though filtered, dilute.

"Don't say it, Whit. Don't say it. I had a dream last night—
it's no good, if you're sick and dirty, you're sick and dirty. I
tried, honest to God, I did. But when I woke up it was all different. It's like she came and snuggled down with me. I can
smell her. I know how her body feels. It's all I can see. It's all
I can think about. Whit, damn it, I'm insane about her. Okay.
You don't have to tell me. I know it's sick. I know she's just
a kid and I'm a lonely, filthy old man. I know it. But what the
hell can I do?"

"Am I to believe," I said evenly, "after all this—am I to
believe you'd want something done about it?" He turned to
me then, angrily.

"God damn it, Whit. You think I'm out of my mind? I'm
old. I'm dead. I don't want these things eatin' at me—not now,
not any more. I want some peace. Just a little peace." He put
his hands to his face. He rubbed his eyes with the tips of his
fingers. Then he looked at the tips. "Listen to me, Whit. The
last couple of days—since you've been talkin' to me—I've felt

new all over. I thought I's gonna be a better man for once. And
then this comes up, this lousy business, and I'm right back to
go. I can't read. I can't think. It's God damn heartbreaking,
that's what it is."

"Well . . . I warned you—I warned you; I said, don't hope
for miracles."

"I didn't, Whit."

"No? I don't believe you. For a while there you hoped God'd
make you better. I know that. Probably, too, you started thinking a bit of Bible reading, a little elbow rubbing with a real
bishop, and—poof—you'd be an immaculate Christian gentleman. It doesn't work that way. Sorry, brother. If you start
thinking it does, then, my friend—then you'll only first go crazy.
You've got gall—really you do. You think it's easier for me, for
anyone? I used to get so mad I'd spit, just because I'd remember to pick up my laundry or something while I was celebrating
communion. If you try to beat that sort of thing by force, you
play right into its hands. Let it take its course. Be patient."

Artie nodded. But, before he could answer, he was overcome
by an attack of coughing. The attack lasted for some
time. He'd cough, and then his hand would go to his stomach
—but it was a stillborn gesture: he didn't dare touch it. Every
spasm wrenched at, twisted the tender muscles in his abdomen;
the little, frightened sounds he made in anticipation of each
cough were pitiable. I stood up. When again he seemed comfortable, I sat on the edge of his bed. Artie was surprised. He
shifted away from me until one of his legs hung suspended over
the side of the bed.

"So," I said. "Let me tell you a little story. About myself, of
all people. Yes?" Artie nodded. "All right. I was nineteen at
the time. Let's see. What was I? Good looking. Very intel-

ligent. First or second in my class. All that and a three letter
man. Matter of fact, I still hold the school scoring record in
basketball. President of the dramatics club—no, that was the
next year. Three stories published in one edition of the lit-
erary magazine. Women. Yes, women. All I could eat and then
some. Pride? Good God," I laughed. "I was really something.
I didn't think there was anything in the world I couldn't do. It
was just about true, I guess. I was brillant and disciplined to
boot. Just so much time for writing, for acting, for practice, for
fun—for my religious devotions. I was religious even then.
Everything in its time, in its place. I guess I was a bit like my
father. But that's another story . . .

"Anyway. It was springtime, late winter. Ash Wednesday
came around. I decided, as I always did, to give up something
for the forty days. I won't tell you what it was. That isn't important. Just let me assure you that it wasn't anything to speak
of. In fact, Artie, it was so trivial—so stupid—that now I'd
consider the whole business an insult to God. A meaningless
vow if ever there was one. I made it without thinking.

"Artie. I couldn't believe it. Before a week was out—before
five days had gone by—I was on my hands and knees, grovel-
ing, crippled for lack of that little thing. The knowledge that
I could not—yet, of course, could—have it, absorbed all my
thoughts. I couldn't read. I couldn't think. I couldn't sleep
because, in the dead of night with no distractions, the temptation became unbearable. It grew and it grew and it grew. On
the second Thursday of my vow, I collapsed. Utterly. Shamelessly. I had the thing. And again. And again. And again.

"I was mortified. It was my first defeat in a matter of will. I
was so utterly ashamed that I stopped praying. I toyed with a
hundred fantasies of suicide. You see, Artie, in those days I

worshiped heroism. Men put to torture—religious martyrs,
political martyrs—men who, for an idea, endured the most intolerable of torments. Greatness. The superhuman powers that
inhabit the secret springs of the soul. You know the story. And
my trial? My great trial? I was humiliated. Everything I did
suffered. Each discipline, I think, had fed the next. One hole—
just one—in the dike, and the whole damned flood poured in.

"It was hell on earth, believe me. I began to feel that all my
talent—such as it was, had been—was merely the result of some
artificial ritual. I imagined that mediocrity was devouring me,
swallowing me up. A form of madness? I know that now. I
had a paper to write, and I refused to write it. Never had anything like that happened. I didn't attend class. I began smok-
ing, even though I was in training and didn't in the least like to
smoke. I did what were, in my mind, the most degenerate
things a man can do. I ate candy and went to the movies for
eight or ten hours at a time. And all this for a silly vow that
should never have been made.

"Anyhow. Late winter became April. Nothing had changed.
I went on the road with the baseball team. I remember now
it was a beautiful evening—one of those evenings when spring
is still a novelty. I was assigned to a little oblong box of a
dormitory room: one or two privileged athletes were allowed
to bunk alone. I couldn't sleep. I read a detective novel—
another degenerate habit—until there was no more to read.
Still I couldn't sleep. I poked around the room. Someone had
left a Bible in the desk drawer. I took it out and walked over
to the open window. I began reading out loud. Like from a
pulpit. It made me feel good, mostly because I'm one hell of
a reader. But, after a while, even the sound of my own voice
became tiresome. I sat in a chair by the window and looked out

through the new budding branches of a tree—out over the quiet lawns of the university. Then I dozed off.

"Three little knocks—taps more like—woke me up. I was dazed from sleep, and I guess it took me a few seconds to open the door. No one was there. I stood at the door for a while. But there was no sound in the hall. I went back in. As I locked the door, I remembered Gilly. Gilly was the freshman manager. I don't recall his last name, just the things they used to call him. Silly Gilly. Girly Gilly. Gilly the Filly. Blue Tits. A little kid. Thick glasses. Dead acne all over his face like a landscape of extinct volcanoes. Purple. I remember he always wore his underpants right up to the moment he got into the shower. He was ridiculously underdeveloped. Inevitably, someone would hide his underpants and towel. His glasses, too, if they could get them. And he'd come, sopping wet and cold, out of the shower. He'd dance tiptoe between the lockers squealing, 'Come on, fellers. Come on.' Sometimes he'd get them back. Only sometimes. After a while Gilly always carried extras. It was pretty pathetic watching him dance like that— short-sighted, short-winded, short where it counted. His baby fat bluish and jiggling all over his body. It was pathetic because I sensed—maybe the others did, too—that Gilly was enjoying it. Then the sadists came out. Rat-tail towels snapping at his fat backside until it was bright red. It hurt. Nothing hurts as much as a wet rat-tail. But he took it. And he took it. And he took it.

"I guess I treated him differently. Don't get me wrong. I wasn't crazy about Gilly or anything approaching it. I never stopped anyone from snapping his fat ass with a rat-tail. But, still, the bus rides were long and Gilly, ridiculous as he was, well—he was really a sensitive little kid. So I didn't make him move when he sat next to me in the bus. I listened to him. In time, of course, he told me all his problems. There was a thing he called It, which I supposed was homosexuality. He asked me if It bothered me. I said no. I suppose the other guys wondered about our relationship. But, since I never bothered to defend Gilly—since, too, I could handle myself in a locker room —they kept their opinions to themselves.

"It came to me then. Those knocks, they'd been Gilly's. Lately he'd been taking liberties. He'd touch me. If I'd make an error, he'd squeeze my thigh in the dugout and say it was all right. He had begun carrying my duffel bag. I had meant to talk to him but—preoccupied as I was then—I'd never gotten around to it. I remembered those three hesitant taps. I saw him standing at the door, his heart leaping in his chest. I saw him running hastily, clumsily when resolution failed him. Artie. Those three knocks seemed terribly poignant to me then. Poignant and suddenly very important—like the three knocks before a curtain goes up.

"For a moment I knew—knew—what it was like to be Gilly. Someone like Gilly. Then I thought of my own self and I was ashamed. Artie. God is gracious. Generous. He had given me so many things—I saw them all in a shadow cast by Gilly's slope-shouldered, fat body. The Bible still lay open on the window-sill. I walked, numb, to the window and slapped the flat of my palm down on the open page. I picked it up and read. This is what I read, Artie." I took his Bible. "This is what I read. 'And one of the malefactors which were hanged railed on him, saying, If thou be Christ save thyself and us. But the other answering rebuked him, saying, Dost thou not fear God, seeing thou art in the same condemnation? And we justly; for we receive the due reward of our deeds. But this man hath done

nothing amiss.' " I looked up to the ceiling then; it had become difficult for me to read. Tears welled up in my eyes, as
they have done ever since that first time. " 'And he said unto
Jesus, Lord, remember me when thou comest into thy kingdom.
And Jesus said unto him, Verily I say unto thee, To-day shalt
thou be with me in Paradise.' "

"Artie. Artie," I said. Artie was afraid: he put his hand to
his mouth. "That's it. Don't you see? This—this that I've just
read you—this is God's Graciousness. Off-hand. Uncompli-
cated. Absolute. So absolute. 'Lord, Remember me when thou
comest into thy Kingdom.' And then—no buts, no qualifica-
tions, no reservations. Today. Today. Now. That moment.
This moment. 'Today shalt thou be with me in Paradise.'
That's all, Artie. And it's here. For you, Artie. For you, damn
it. For you."

"I believe you, Whit."

Artie began to cough. Three times his wretched stomach
heaved, and then a long, low scream of a cough would come. He
turned on his side, holding frantically to the sheets, his elbows
bent outward. He coughed and it would not come up. He
coughed and my own throat constricted. He coughed and the
walls of the room were rubber, trembling with his cough—
from the palm of my hand on the mattress, through my body
to the very ceiling, the room reverberated with Artie's coughing.

Then the tone of his coughing changed. Sounds echoed now
in his throat, no longer in the depths of his chest. I watched
as a fat wad of sputum and saliva slid from his mouth. It hung
down over the side of the bed. Artie's left hand clenched and
unclenched in front of my face. He wanted a tissue. I tore one
from the box.

It thinned and new substance poured from his mouth
to thicken it. I watched. Now there were colored motes of matter in the solution. Suspended there. The light from above his
bed shone down through the stream, and, for just a second, I
saw blues and reds and greens. Such greens. And then they
flowed together, and all the color was gone. Just the tiniest of
strings hanging there—a gossamer spider web reaching out,
floating on the breeze. It moved; it spiraled in the air. It
seemed glad.

I held the tissue. Artie's hand groped, imploring, in front
of me. His head still hung over the bed's edge. I put the tissue
in his hand. Artie took it; he tried to bring it to his mouth. But
my hand would not let his go. I held tightly, the tissue white
between our joined knuckles. Artie's hand alone could not
comprehend. He shook it. He pulled it. Then, with saliva
running down over his chin, Artie turned his eyes up to me.
He looked at my face. And then his hand tightened, too.

THE TENTH DAY

THE PANE BECAME pock-marked, shattered with rain. The wind followed, blowing it clear again and almost dry. Under my breath I hummed of rain and walkers in it. I was waiting. I was listening for the sounds of a bed—a bed being rolled to an assignation. Below, the river flung its hip against the bulwark and then leaped quickly, its gray head appearing momentarily over the edge. Already, on the far lane of the West Side Highway, cars were moving, ornamental fountains. In the distance I could see another blanket of hard rain contracting, distending as it made its way toward my window. The pane became pock-marked, shattered with rain. I tapped out an agitated rhythm, such as impatient lovers tap. The wind followed, blowing the pane clear again and almost dry.

I had awakened early that morning. For perhaps fifteen minutes, I had compelled myself to lie quietly—my eyes only on the ceiling—savoring remembrances of the night before, dreading the ordinariness of a further encounter. Then, when my impatience had become intolerable, I closed my eyes and turned toward Arrie. I inhaled and held my breath. Slowly, with deliberate slowness, I spread the bars of my eyelashes. But Artie wasn't there. I jumped to my elbows. His bed was gone. The table was bare, without books, glasses, teeth. Where the leg of the bed had been there was only a piece of damp, crumpled tissue. Now it was nearly three hours since I'd discovered Artie was gone.

Below, the statue's watery head had been blown out by the wind, the copper wick perpendicular, dead. I rapped my fingernails against the glass. It had rained, too, on the night of Carol's eighteenth birthday. Afterward we'd sat in the kitchen with cups of tea, and it was there that I'd exacted the first deep kiss of my life at the point of a carving knife. She was four and a half years older than I, seeming both beautiful and wise. With the first breasts whose shape and texture I'd been permitted to know. I had embraced her fiercely until, at last, she had said it hurt. Then I was kind.

I turned cartwheels in the rain that night. I remember urinating in the service entrance of her apartment building— as a dog will when he wants to stake the limits of his property. That night lingered with me, undiminished, until we met for coffee two days later. It lingers with me now. I think I understood its significance even then, for I stood straight, my hat off, reverencing the smells of the night, the taste-impregnated soreness of my inner lip, the light in her bathroom window five stories above. But I don't often remember coffee two days later.

"Mornin' Mr. Farbstein. Mr. Belknap. Isn't it great? Huh? An' it's only just started. Gonna hit us head on—seventy, eighty miles an hour by tonight. Lookit the river."

"Calm down a minute," I said. "How long've you been up?"

"Hours an' hours. Since way before breakfast. Minute I

heard the wind slammin' like that—see, there goes a garbage can lid."

"Jimmy. Were you here when they came for Mr. Carson?"

"No sir. He's gone when I got up. Think there'll be any boats on the river today? Wonder what happened to th'barge— bet it crashed someplace. Bet. My father's not working today 'cause of it. An' he works Saturdays and Sundays sometimes."

"You're sure of that? Mr. Carson wasn't here when you got up?" Jimmy nodded, his nose flat on the glass. That meant five or six in the morning at the latest. Something, I thought, something serious had happened to him. Across the room Mr. Farbstein persevered. The skin around his eyes seemed pink and raw. He, certainly, must have seen them come. I left Jimmy at the window and walked slowly toward Mr. Farbstein's bed. As I approached, Mr. Farbstein's lids stretched until his eyes were perfect circles. Then he pulled his picture over his stomach, as though to shield it from some anticipated blow. I stood over him. A nervous tick twittered in his upper left cheek. He turned his head away from me, but his eyes never left mine.

"Did you see when they took Mr. Carson?" Mr. Farbstein's lips moved. "Excuse me? Did you see when they took him out?"

I pointed toward the bed in front of him. Mr. Farbstein smiled. He lifted the catalogue picture up to where my eyes were. I shook my head; patiently, I repeated the question. Mr. Farbstein seemed to comprehend: he drew back his upper lip and chuckled. A barely audible, a halting, staccato sound, whirring up from inside him, as though from the works of some unbearably over-wound mechanical toy. Jimmy called me. I

backed away from the bed. Mr. Farbstein's body righted itself
as though to follow me. It whirred. Then I turned away.

Jimmy seemed disheveled. I tied the belt of his bathrobe
and smoothed his hair between the fingers of my flattened hand.
As I did so, Jimmy told me about the wind in the trees, on the
surface of the water; the wind as it worried hapless bits of de-
bris. I stood behind him, my hands cupped firmly on his
shoulders: a bulwark, I suppose, firm against Mr. Farbstein's
appalling eyes. Jimmy begged me to open the window just
once.

"Bet I could stand up in it," he said, squaring his feet. "Wish
I could go out. Never get a chance like this again. Hurricanes
don't come up here much. Not real big ones."

"I wonder. What d'you think's happened to Artie?"

"You think he died?" Jimmy looked at me thoughtfully.
"Could be, y'know. They don't like t'let the other patients find
out. They burn the sheets and the mattress. Everything.
That's the way they do it."

"That so?" I smiled. "No, Artie wouldn't have died. Not
that way. Not so suddenly."

"But he's gonna die. That's for sure." Jimmy breathed a
circle on the glass, then he wiped it away with his fingers.

"How can you know that? No one knows. I thought I told
you that before."

"Yes sir, I know. But Dr. Snow said different. I figured you
told me that just so's I wouldn't get worried. Like my father
does."

"But why—what made you ask Dr. Snow?"

"I didn't ask him." Jimmy scraped at the pane with his
nail. "It was in a dream. He told me in a dream."

"In a dream?"

"Lookit that car go through. Wheee! Bet the water's risin'
all over. There's a big pond near my house—"

"In a dream?" He didn't answer. "Jimmy. I'm speaking to
you." He stepped away from the window, his fingertips still
on the glass.

"Sure," he said. "I dream about him a lot. Most nights, I
guess. It's scary. Sometimes it's nice, though. Sometimes it's
real swell." I put my arm around his shoulders. Then, per-
suasively, I drew him away toward his bed. I needed to sit: my
knees had begun to give warning. Jimmy jumped up onto the
mattress next to me. We huddled, bent shoulder touching
bent shoulder, for the length of two or three full minutes—our
backs noncommittal against the insistent questioning of the
eyes behind us.

"Tell me," I said. "These dreams—what're they like?"

"They're all different. All kinds. Sometimes my mother's
there. Sometimes my father and Uncle Joe. Sometimes kids
from my school. But still, I know they're not. They talk just
like them. But they're not."

"What do they say?"

"Oh," he shrugged. "Mostly how much they'll miss me if I
don't get better. Ma cries and Pop looks all funny, like he swallowed something. It's just like them, but it isn't. They're all
Dr. Snow. One night I even dreamed about my operation. I
saw my heart and my bladder. Like a football inside. Black.
You know—all those things." He was remembering. "It was
real—real interesting."

"All Dr. Snow? What d'you mean?" He shrugged again.

"It just is. Yeah. That's right—one night he was Mr.
Murphy, our baseball coach. I think we were playin' the
Hawks. They're in first place. I was pitchin' real strong, too—

for maybe three, four innings. Musta fanned ten guys. Then
—next inning—when I come out on the mound . . ." He blew
his cheeks out. "Gosh. I got this real awful pain in my chest.
Right down t'my belly button. My arms went all heavy.
I started pushin' the ball. Aimin' it. Then it—the ball, I mean
—it started gettin' bigger an' bigger. Big as a volley ball. You
know how crazy dreams get. The Hawks started hittin' it all
over. Got a million runs off me. I felt awful. Sick like. I even
started crying." He laughed shyly. "But then Mr. Murphy
came out on the mound. Right off, I thought—he's gonna
take me out now. But he's a real great guy. You'd like him Mr.
Belknap. Everybody likes him—even the guys on the bench.
Even Johnny Cahill when he got kicked off the team for
smokin'. Mr. Murphy's great. He talked real nice t'me. He
made me put my hand straight up in the air—like this."
Jimmy raised his arm as high as it would go. "Then he put his
hands on me, one in front and one in back. Right away the pain
was gone. I pitched for five, six innings after that—'til I woke
up. I was real fast." He shook his head. " 'Course, it wasn't
Mr. Murphy. It was Dr. Snow. I knew that right off."

"Jimmy." I placed the flat of my hand on the back of his
neck. Grinning, he tossed his head as he pushed his neck back
against my palm. "Do these dreams—do they worry you?"

"No sir. They're just dreams, aren't they? There's nothin'
in dreams. You told me that yourself."

"Yes," I said. "Yes, I suppose I did. And it's the truth."

"Somethin's comin'. Maybe it's Mr. Carson."

There was a banging of casters in the hall. Almost at once
the square, gray foot of a bed straddled our doorway. I leaped
to my feet. But the bed was empty, sheet-less. A heavy Negro
orderly—barrel torsoed, narrow shouldered—rolled it into

Artie's space. He raised his hand, as if to indicate that more was yet to come. Then, assured of our interest, he disappeared into the corridor. He returned with a little, wheeled table; he pushed it into the middle of the room. Then he stood for a moment, measuring me—bent at the waist, his hands flat on the little table's top. He was grotesque. His upper body was so cylindrical, continuous, that abdomen, chest, stomach coalesced without definition. Tiny ears had been thumbed into either side of his head, yet with dangling, spoon-hollowed lobes. A bushy, uneven mustache that moved with his breath; a mocha-cream complexion that suggested taste to my eyes. At the back of his skull, a forehead of overlapping flesh-folds—as though he were in perpetual indignation at what passed behind him. And eyes, tiny and close, yet open in a sort of flippant suspiciousness—like an elephant's, I thought. After a moment he pointed his forefinger at me.

"You James Lopopulo?"

"No," I said. "That's him."

"Wouldn't you just know it?" He shook his head. "They're nuts down there. If he's got hair on his chest, I got fuzzy palms." He flapped his arms. He had muscular biceps and the thin wrists and forearms of a woman. With a shiny, green watch. Jimmy laughed.

"Excuse me," I said. "That bed—where's the man that was in it?" He peered at the bare mattress.

"Not there, is he?" he said. "Took his sheet with him, too." He pursed his lips.

"But there was a man here yesterday. Right there. Arthur Carson. Have you seen him?"

"No sir. Haven't had the pleasure. Name's Brown. Not Dr. Brown, just Brown. Certain suitability to it, don't you think?

Flunked outa Harvard Med. School, otherwise I wouldn't be in
this sad state. The one in Mississippi. The famous one. But
medicine's in my blood. The stamp of the healer. Unmistakable. So, t'make a long story more repulsive, I become the
official chest and other parts shaver at this great metropolitan
hospital. Just bidin' my time, so t'speak. Someday—sure
enough—someday a well-known Southern surgeon goes spastic
yellow smack in the middle of a big operation." He made flam-
boyant gestures with his hands and arms. "Then Paul Brown
—who just happened t'be wheelin' his shave cart in the neigh-
borhood—Paul Brown steps right in, sizes up the situation
in a second, sews the patient's upper septricle to his gonads and
saves the day. Thereby provin' the equality of the races in general, and the superiority of Paul Brown in particular." He
nodded in approval. Then he nipped one corner of his mustache between thumb and forefinger.

"But the bed?"

"Got your own problems, huh?" He frowned; the wrinkles
at the back of his head disappeared. "The bed . . . Well, as
I was sayin'—until my time comes—I'm just plain Brown,
comma, Paul. Shaver. And, brother, nobody but nobody's
gonna tell me nothin' but nothin' about what goes on here.
Sorry. That's the sad truth. Never heard of your Mr. Carson.
Probably never will. Nurse just asked me t'shove it down here."
He turned to Jimmy. "James Lopopulo. Says here I gotta shave
your chest. Do you or do you not got anything to shave?"

"Sure," said Jimmy. He threw open his pajama top.

"Well, now," said Paul. He adjusted an imaginary jeweler's
lens. "Look at that. Seven, eight, nine follicles. Phenomenal.
Have t'get the razor—that's all there is to it. You play baseball?" He picked up Jimmy's glove. "Klock. There it goes—a
long drive t'deep, deep left center. Way out there. Brown goes

back, back. He's still goin'. He's got it! Man alive, what a
catch." He caught it leaning over the foot of Mr. Farbstein's
bed. Mr. Farbstein continued, undistracted, to stare at me.
Paul shook his head. "A four-hunnert-fifty footer that was.
Brown hit it. Same man—case you hadn't guessed. Good
pocket y'got here. What you use on it?"

"Neat's-foot oil."

"Uh-huh. You just lay down, while I get my razor an' cheap,
men's room smellin' soap."

"You gonna shave Mr. Belknap?"

"That Mr. Belknap?"

"Yes. He's gonna have an operation, too. Friday."

"Chest operation?" I nodded. "Let's see. Thursday. Thursday . . . Chests. Whitney Belknap. Well, it ain't exactly
Kosher . . . Save me a trip up here. You wanna get shaved,
too?"

"Please, Mr. Belknap."

"Well . . ."

"Please. You'll have to do it anyway. Won't he?"

"That's right. Do you and the boy together. Two for the
price of one." Jimmy ran over to Mr. Farbstein's bed. He
stood in front of him, his chest bared, unaware that Mr. Farbstein was ignoring him.

"Me an' Mr. Belknap," he said. "We're gonna get our chests
shaved. Okay, Mr. Belknap?"

"All right." I put my hand on Paul's shoulder. "You think
the nurses know?"

"Well, Lord knows, they should, shouldn't they? But this
place—y'could be dead two days before anybody'd be impolite
enough t'mention it. They know what they're doin' here. I
give 'em that. It's just they don't want nobody else t'know."

"Listen," I said. "Could you—could you make some in-

quiries? It's very important. I've asked a few people, but no
one seems t'know."

"Me? It's gotta be me? Me? Why pick the busiest guy in the
place?"

"Please."

"Oh, well. Okay. My girl friend's sister works in information. I'll see what I can see. Ready, James?"

"Yup. Wait'll I tell that Mike Santora. Wait'll I tell
him."

We were shaved. Jimmy first, then I. Paul whistled through
his mustache. I saw that he was powerful: the brown-
black veins in his biceps slithered gently over thick muscles.
Yet his fingers were fine and delicate—gentle against the skin
of my chest. Jimmy sat beside him in awed reverence. He was
disappointed, I think, that his own shaving had taken such a
short time. I found the pleasant scratch of the razor and the
soft, searching balls of his fingers wonderfully soothing. The
wind slapped at the glass in an effort to disconcert me; but it
succeeded only the first few times. Paul cocked his head to one
side. Then he mowed a graceful figure S with his razor.

"You are there. A historical moment. The great sculptor—
Michelangelo Brown—putting a few final touches on his famous Sistine Chapel Statue." He looked at my body. "Such
delicacy. Such grace. Such moxie. The very figure of a reclining
god. Glorious. Brown has outdone himself again." He buried
his tongue in the corner of his lips and shaved at the edges of my
rib cage. "All the peers of the realm is lookin' on. But Brown
is imperturbable. What he carves seems almost to live. To
breathe." He peered into my eyes. "Almost, but not quite."
Jimmy laughed. "Now. Only a few more strokes and . . . Immortality. The audience sighs. Brown steps back. The good
Lord in His most creative mood couldn't've done better. Not in

the Garden of Eden." I stared down the length of my body. Pink, not gray.

"You look all funny, Mr. Belknap."

"So I do."

"Hmmph," grunted Paul. "A Brown original never looks all funny. You know what?"

"What?"

"You look young with that gray stuff gone. That's what James means by all funny."

"Perhaps I do. Once—you may not believe it—once I wasn't a bad figure of a man."

"I give you the benefit." He stood up. "Now me—I's always a bad figure of a man. My girl says I look like a fat man sittin' in a steam cabinet. But she loves me anyway. That's the proof of the pudding." He poked himself in the stomach. Then he looked at his green watch. "Gotta go now. Brown is in demand."

"You won't forget?"

"Oh, man. You don't let a guy alone." He stuck one palm out flat, as though testing for rain. "No. I won't forget. What's the name?" He took a ball-point pen from his vest pocket.

"Artie Carson. Arthur, I guess."

"Arthur. Carson. That's ess-oh-en?" I nodded. "He'll probably be back before I am. I worked in some hospitals in my time—but for information this's the worst. Ho Chi Minh'd learn more, quicker, on a guided tour of the Pentagon. When exactly'd he make his—ah, untimely exit?"

"I don't know. Before Jimmy got up. In the middle of the night, I guess."

"Middle of the night? What was his trouble?"

"He was dying of stomach cancer—but he had time yet. I'm sure of that."

"Man. I hate to mention it—but none of us's sure. Not about the time we got left. Well, let's see—" He looked at the green watch. "Eleven o'clock now. I see her on my lunch hour. Stop back up here one, one-thirty. Okay?"

"Fine. Fine. I appreciate it."

"No sweat. Just tell anyone who asks—tell 'em where y'got your chest shaved. Paul Brown's place. James. Let's see your curve." Jimmy wound up in slow motion; then he released an imaginary ball into the corridor. "Hey. Pretty good. Right off the table. Only—you should follow through more. Like that. Okay. No more foolin' around. See you boys."

Paul flipped his towel onto the little table and pushed it easily out through the door. His legs were thin and bowed, as though wasted by the weight of his upper body. He seemed to walk only on the outsides of his feet. As he passed Mr. Farbstein's bed, he saluted once, ironically. We could hear his whistle for a long while after he left. Jimmy stood watching the door, his pajama shirt still open.

"You better button up."

"He's nice."

"Yes. He's nice." I stared down at my pink chest. Then, while Jimmy's back was turned, I flexed my arms, hardening my pectoral muscles. Almost the chest of a young man; almost, but for tiny crystalline facets in the skin. Somehow at that moment—even with the association so obviously before me—I didn't think of my heart. I breathed deeply and walked over to the window. After a while Jimmy and I pulled up chairs. The storm continued to perpetrate acts of violence on the city, but, by now, even its violence was possessed of a certain familiarity. I kept my arm around Jimmy's shoulders. Soon, wearied by his long morning storm watch, he fell asleep; his head was nestled against the pit of my arm.

*

Michael puddled into our room just after lunch. He was dressed in a yellow slicker and a yellow rain helmet. In one hand he carried a tiny, pink umbrella. The umbrella was inside-out. Under his left arm Michael held a large and very damp bundle of letters. I told him to take the letters back. Disappointed, Michael picked out one or two of the more attractive letters and tried to interest me in them. But Artie hadn't returned, and I had no intention of being consoled just then. By lunch time I had realized that, whatever the reason, Artie wasn't coming back.

"Here's the best one."

"Mike, will you—well, what is it?"

"From your publishers." Announcing the eleventh edition of *A God For Our Time*. I considered telling Michael that there would be no eleventh edition, but, after a moment, I decided to deny myself that small satisfaction. I put the letter aside. "Everybody's talking about you. Someone in Saint John's said you were very sick. He said you had cancer." Michael paused. "You don't have cancer, do you?" I shook my head. "He said you had cancer of the prostate." I laughed.

"In Saint John's? It figures. Cancer of the prostate, no less. Wait'll I get my hands on him."

"You couldn't—I mean, you couldn't have cancer of the heart, could you?"

"Good God protect us. There's no such thing."

"No? I just wanted to be sure. Bishop Nelson and Bishop Parker called last night. Bishop Nelson—you know how he is —he got very angry when I said you weren't seeing anyone. He called me a stupid foul-up. I don't mind, but diocese business is piling up. You were supposed to speak at the Peace Convention in Washington next week. Then there's the Youth League Banquet, they've postponed it twice now."

"I know."

"If you could just dictate—"

"Mike. No. Things are pretty confused right now. I'll—I'll be home soon."

"You will? When?"

"I don't know. But maybe sooner than you think."

"Oh, good. I can hardly wait. Everything's been so hectic—" He looked at his fingers. There were what seemed to be orange nicotine stains between the tips. But Michael never smoked. "I got a postcard yesterday. From Mrs. Bolt. She's in Florida now."

"Already? I thought she was only thinking of going."

"Already. It must be beautiful down there. The card had water skiers on it. And those funny trees with big roots—"

"Cypress."

"Yes. And Spanish moss. The card said, 'Love, Mrs. B.' It doesn't seem right, though. Why go to Florida in this weather? You don't think—I mean, you don't think she's taking a vacation from me?"

"Of course not."

"Really? I don't know. Her husband—I've seen pictures of him—he was big. Muscles all over. On his arms and his stomach. He was a tennis instructor. That's how she met him —on a tennis court." He almost whispered. "In Florida."

"Nonsense. Besides, isn't she a little old for tennis?"

"She's very strong. Very. She can beat me in arm-wrestling." He locked grips with the air for an indecisive few seconds. Then he took a crumpled piece of paper from his inside pocket.

"No," I said.

"Please. I wrote it last night. Just look it over—then maybe you can add a few nice touches. Light things. Things I wouldn't think of."

"But now."

"Please."

"You don't let a guy alone, do you? All right. Give me the thing." He handed it to me. I opened the paper very slowly, allowing my impatience to dissipate in deliberateness. There was God's love, *agape,* and there was man's love, *eros.* And then there was Michael's love. The Greeks hadn't bothered to coin a word for that.

"What d'you think of it?"

"Hold on. 'Dearest Mrs. Bolt. I have not been . . .' Mike, after all these years, d'you still call her Mrs. Bolt? What's her first name?"

"Hilda. I think."

"All right then. Give me your pen. 'Dearest Hilda.' " Michael grimaced in spite of himself. I became annoyed. " 'Dearest Hilda. I have not been able to eat or drink since you left.' Why not just 'eat'?" I wrote. " 'I have not—haven't—been able to eat since you left.' That sounds better. Not much better, but better."

"Drink, too. She makes me delicious chocolate sodas. With whipped cream. Michael specials we call them."

"Do we? I see. I see now. You really haven't been able to drink. Excuse my stupidity. I thought it was love. But it's just your stomach. As usual."

I put the letter down. Michael made fists, digging his thumbnails into the upper joints of each forefinger. Then he took the letter and folded it neatly. He returned it to his inner coat pocket. He was very hurt. I was furious with myself for having hurt him—so very furious that I had difficulty not compounding the injury. Finally he spoke.

"What's the matter? What's wrong? You've never been like this before." I think Michael had decided to ask Artie about me. And, for the first time, he noticed that Artie wasn't there.

"He's gone," I said. "I don't know where. If you must know —I'm worried about him. What time d'you have?"

"Twelve-thirty. Twenty to one. Why?"

"Nothing. Read me some more of your letter . . ." But I had already stopped listening. I was thinking of love and of a sermon I had delivered many years before . . .

". . . Three days ago Mary Ellen Lister—a little girl we all knew—was killed instantly by a speeding car. It happened just here. Just outside this church. Loveliness and joy and innocence were with her when she died. Now all that is gone. And the rest of us? The rest of us are faced with a bitter, an appalling question. An ugly question. A question that places the very roots of our faith in grave doubt: the justice and benevolence of our Almighty God.

"Once a great Chinese was asked to define Beauty. He thought and then he said, 'Beauty is love touched by death.' Love touched by death. I think he was right. There seems to be—in the very act of love—a mysterious, irresistible yearning toward self-consumption. Death, rather than being the arch enemy of love, is, instead, the test of it—the aging that matures the wine to its most superb taste. The fire that burns the dross from golden ore. Love is not love until it has shown its willingness to reach beyond life. Beyond selfishness and materialism and vanity. Beyond to the place whence all love springs—the very heart of God.

"Christ, too, was young and beautiful and full of joy. Surely, if the word has meaning at all, He was innocent. God loved Christ when first He begat Him. God loved Christ when he saw that His Son waxed in virtue. But never, I think, never did

God love Christ as He loved Him on the Hill of Calvary. For
there God's love—even God's—was burned free of dross in the
terrific fire of the crucifixion. Why do even the most primitive
peoples know this—that in the sacrifice of a pure virgin, of an
unspotted animal, lies the salvation of a whole race? Because
the love, the willing acceptance of the innocent, passes beyond.
It annihilates our petty egoisms; it enables us for once—perhaps
the only once—to partake of God's absolute Glory. Joying, sor-
rowing, but feeling as God Himself feels. Then and only then
do we stand as tall as God in God's own great Kingdom.

"Mary Ellen is dead. If you have wept because of that or, in
bitterness, clenched your fists; if even you have come to question God's goodness because she died—if even that, you are a
better man. She's shaken you. She and God. She's struck you
to the soul. And you lie astonished, ripped from complacent
bodies, brutally goaded into recognizing what we all must recognize—death. And the insignificance, the pettiness, of that
death before God's overwhelming love. Do you see what she's
done? She's cleansed you just a bit. You ought to be thankful.
I, for one, intend to be . . ."

"'. . . endless and undying affection—' One or the other.
No, neither. Just affection. 'Affection, your Noodles . . .'
Noodles? Is that what she calls you? Noodles?" Michael
nodded; he hadn't even the decency to blush.

"Yes. You see, when I first moved into One-twenty-five—the
first Sunday—she made me a big pot of noodles. For me and
her and three friends who were coming. The friends never
got there, but I ate every bit. The whole big pot. With sweet,
brown gravy. Ever since then she's called me Noodles: it's—
it's affectionate, isn't it?"

"Well, yes . . . I suppose it could be." I handed him the
letter. "There you are. Pretty good, if I do say so myself."

"Thanks. Thanks." He held it in the air like a torch. "I'll
type it up tonight. Then I can send it tomorrow."

"Write it long hand. It's more personal."

"No. It's too personal. My hand sweats. Then it smudges up
the paper. My ball point won't write in sweat." He looked out
the window. "I wish I could stay here. I heard there were
electric wires down all over. But I didn't see them anywhere."

"They're underground—here in the city, anyway."

"Are you sure?" I nodded. "Should they be?" I nodded
again. "Well," he said, "I guess that's all right. But now Mrs.
B's umbrella is ruined. Do I have to carry all those letters
back?"

"Please."

"Friday, is that when it is? In the morning?"

"Yes. Look, Mike—whatever you do—be sure to drop in
tomorrow. I may need you. Don't fail me now."

"I won't."

"What time is it?"

"One-thirty."

"Damn. Where is he? Mike, how many people have you told
—about the operation, I mean?"

"Just a few. Bishop Nelson, of course. Bishop Parker, too.
Dean Thomas. Mrs. Childs. The elevator man. That's all, I
guess."

"Okay. Don't tell anyone else. Not until after Friday. You
better run along now. Looks like it's getting worse."

Michael began putting his yellow slicker on. When he had
snapped the rain helmet under his jaw, he walked—two un-
supported chins dangling—over to the windowsill. Jimmy
smiled. I realized, in the midst of all my preoccupations, just

how ludicrous Michael looked. He was really nervous now. The wind snapped at the glass in an effort to intimidate him. Michael jumped back, but not immediately—even in a state of panic, his reflexes were none too good. He kept straightening up and sighing, as if resolved to leave. But, soon again, he would sag and press his stomach up against the windowsill. He tried to fix Mrs. B's umbrella and succeeded only in pouring a handful of rainwater inside his open boot. Then he sat down, all squeaking rubber, and tugged the boot off. His sock, of course, had absorbed all the water. He shook his boot in the air. A single dollar bill floated out. Michael picked it up. Then he folded it neatly and slipped it into his pocket.

"Hi, Paul."

"Hi, Jimmy." I sat up.

"Mike. I think you better go. It's not going to clear up." Michael looked longingly at me, and, I think, at my comfortable bed as well. Then he tramped out—a bullet-headed, heavy, yellow thing. He looked, I suppose, like a man playing the part of a canary. I smiled vacantly. I was very fond of Michael.

"I have returned." Paul stood at my bedside, his hands behind his back. He puckered his lips and then opened his eyes as far as they would go. He cleared his throat.

"Where is he?"

"Well now . . ." He began tucking his shirt down under his belt. "Did I get that name right? Arthur Carson. Spelt with a C, not a K or something?"

"Yes. Carson."

"In that case, Agent Brown's got nothin' much t'say. He ain't here."

"What? That can't be."

"Can't it? Couldn't find nothin'. It's like he never was here."

"Well, he was. Right there. Until the middle of last night."

"That so? That a fact? They take all his things out?" Paul went over to Artie's locker and opened it. "Pretty dusty," he said. He opened the bed table drawer. Then he walked back to my bed very slowly. He took a deep breath and let it out in a low slushing "aaaah." "Mr. Belknap," he said. "I don't wanna say nothin', but—"

"He was here," said Jimmy.

Paul looked at him. Then he nodded and looked at me. He seemed embarrassed. He stuck his thumbs under his armpits and let his fingers fall over his chest. For a long moment he stared down at his tiny feet. The feet, disconcerted, began to make little movements.

"Okay. So he was here. This is a big place. They've probably moved him to another ward."

"But, I mean—aren't there any records?"

"Don't ask me. I just work here—why, I don't know. This place gets on my wick. It really does."

"I've got to talk to him. He shouldn't be alone. Not now."

"Yes sir? Well, I done what I could. Can't squeeze him outa thin air. You can't expect me t'do that."

"No . . ." I said. But by then I was thinking of the knob on the men's bathroom door. The knob stuck. Not very badly, I suppose. And yet I had stood for a long minute, sweat in my eyes, my knees uncertain beneath me, while I struggled that morning to turn it. Afterward all control had gone from my fingers, from the muscles in my palm. I couldn't crumple tissue paper. Now I stared at the heavy muscles above Paul's elbow. If the mind were to be willing, I thought—even then there might be impediments.

"Good luck," said Paul. He was waving good-bye. Content with that. "Good luck, Jimmy. Keep followin' through."

"Paul," I said. "Wait. I'll have to ask you another favor."

"Jesus God," he said. "Not again." Paul brought his hand up suddenly—I think as a prologue to some absolute gesture of denial. But he seemed content to roughen the texture of one eyebrow. He counted ten with wiggling ears; the furrows at the back of his head expressed bewilderment and understanding, bewilderment, understanding. He looked at his watch. Then, hands clasped at his belt, he walked in the manner of a child—awkward, pigeon-toed—to the head of my bed. I smiled.

"Why—why d'you wear that green watch?" Paul examined the watch. Then he brought the dial close to my face.

"Captain Cobra watch. Genuine. That's what it is." A green, hooded cobra with ruby eyes bleared out from the face, one eye obscured by the minute hand. The watch was cheap and very worn. The second hand lay loose at the bottom of the face. The numbers had faded; only the zero in the ten remained.

"Cobra?"

"My third kid brother's. Was. Now it's mine. Television show—lasted about two months, just long enough t'sell some watches. Eyes glow in the dark. Not the numbers, though." He put it to his ear. "So? Man's gotta know the time. Only watch in existence tells the zero hour. Seven, eight, nine, nothin'—all gone."

"The snake is green, too."

"Yes, it is. Yes sir. The snake is green. Green, that's what it is. Mister, I know this ain't the loony locker, I know that—but it'll do fine 'til the real thing comes along. You feelin' okay?" I nodded. I felt very well. A thick clot of satisfaction rose in my throat. "Listen, Sahib. If you got any favors—tell 'em off. Make it fast. Paul gotta say no, sorry, and the sooner, the bet-

ter. I need a little time t'make excuses that'll sound good.
My mother's gettin' sicker by the minute. Lethal sick. An' my
sister—well, she's went an' got pregnant while I'm talkin'.
Now she's twelve months gone."

"Okay," I said. "Friday—Friday morning—they're going to
operate on me. Paul. Will you promise me one thing? Will
you come to this room early Friday morning? If I've already
gone up—then you can forget the whole thing. If I haven't—
will you help me to leave here?" Paul wrapped his arms over
his bulging chest. Then he bent slightly at the waist.

"Let me get this straight. This operation thing—d'you need
it or don't you?"

"Well . . ." I hesitated. "Yes. I guess I do."

"Uh-huh. You need it, brother, you better have it. Who's
your doctor?"

"Snow." Paul was silent. I thought he had recalled something. "Will you help me?"

"No," he said. "No. No, I won't." I started to speak. "No,"
he said. He stiffened his right forefinger. "No. No. And no
again. And just for good measure—no. No . . . No. First of
all, who d'you think I am? Good God Almighty. Snow don't
like nobody—least of all my shade of nobody. You think I wear
Cap'n Cobra watches because I like to? I got people t'take care
of. This ain't much've a job, no it ain't. But, thank you, it's
better'n nothing."

"It's not asking much. All—"

"It's enough, brother. I can see it now. Boy, can I just." He
spread his arms wide. "Okay. I walk up to Snow and I say, 'Colleague—' That's what I call him. 'Colleague,' I say. 'In my
opinion the patient don't need no operation.' I can see it." He
ran his fingers over his hair. Then, for a moment, he mimicked

Dr. Snow's indignation. "There's Snow edgin' away from me
all the while—like he's gonna catch a case of the bad brownies.
He stands back. He looks at me, an' poof! He blows me out
like a kid blows out a birthday candle. Poof! No more Paul
Brown. No more shavin'. No nothin'. Mister. You think, just
because I'm a big mouth talker—you think I'm all crazy? I'm
bidin' my time, friend. Waitin'. Yeah, an' this ain't the magic
moment. No sir and no sir." He shook his head in exaggerated
long arcs. "You scared? That's it, huh?"

"No. Yes . . . But it's not what you think. It's something
else. I can't explain it."

"I see." He puckered his lips. "You take my advice. These
doctors here—you don't hafta like 'em, but they know their
business. If they say you gotta have an operation—don't fool
around. Have it. Get the damn thing over with. You'll be better off—no matter how you feel now. Well. Sorry I can't help
you." He started to back off. "S'long, Jimmy. S'long, Mister—
ah . . . Belknap. Good-bye all."

"Paul," I said. He spun around at the doorway. I smiled at
him, and again that clot of satisfaction rose in my throat. "See
you on Friday."

"See you in hell first," he said. Then he waved and was gone.

Paul didn't shut the door behind him. Yet, as he left, I remembered a door's closing many years before. It closed in our
old, rambling summer house in Southampton. I wasn't more
than five years old at the time, and yet, unwisely, I had contrived to infuriate my father. He and I were alone in the great,
bare attic. I was watching him, wondering how his anger
would manifest itself. With a terrible insuck of air, my father
raised his hand to strike me. Then he thought better of it. Instead, he turned and walked out—locking the tall, mouldering,

cracked-paint door behind him. Loudly, so that I knew it was
locked. And when his footsteps were no longer on the stairs,
when there were no sounds beyond the room, I realized suddenly the enormousness of what he had done. There were no
lights in the huge loft. The paling sunlight was fast running out
through cracks in the four boarded-over windows. I ran and
pressed my hands to the cracks, as to a drain. But darkness
closed down over me nonetheless, and, the heat drawn out of its
walls, the old room began to stretch and contract like a waking
night beast. I ran to a corner and pressed my face into the angle
of the walls: to circumscribe the hugeness of the dark. But in
vain. The back of me was exposed and unprotected; the skin
on my calves and buttocks and kidneys, the nape of my neck,
ached with horrid anticipation. A long finger touched me. I
screamed. I screamed. And I ran, smashing my forehead against
a boarded window in blinded panic, grasping for unconsciousness, but yet aware. I screamed again. And again. I screamed
until my diaphragm became paralyzed with terror. Then I
screamed in silence. And now, instead of screaming, I rang for
the nurse.

Miss Black came in. That—no more, no less—was what she
did. She came in with such impeccable precision that I felt
constrained to watch her. Miss Black moved only in straight
lines, and those lines, in their turn, were soldered to other
straight lines at ninety-degree angles. I had to suppose that—
by standards that apply to classical statuary and to bookends
and andirons—she was a very beautiful woman. Her face, her
body, even the configurations of her clothing, were charac-
terized by an undeviating symmetry: from the part in her hair,
through the dimples in her upper lip and chin, down through
the row of buttons on her uniform—everything was either

twinned or halved exactly. She might have been her own mirror image. There were no moles, no scars, no identifying marks of any sort. Miss Black stood beside my bed, peering down at me with an intense concentration typical of the very unimaginative.

"Yes?"

"I want some information. I want to know where Mr. Carson is. Him. The man who was in that bed."

"Sorry," she said. "I just came on. You'll have to ask the night nurse."

"And where is she?"

"She's off this evening. She'll be in tomorrow." I spat then. I actually spat. Toward the floor, not at her—but I spat.

"No," I hissed. "No. That's not good enough. Not by a long shot. I want to know now, this minute. All those damn forms of yours—find one that says where he is."

"Sorry. I can't do that. They're collected in the morning." I stared at her for a long moment, massing the fullness of my once considerable presence behind my forehead and eyes. But Miss Black was neither impressed nor disturbed.

"All right," I said, nodding. "All right. Have it your way. If you don't know, Dr. Snow will. He's in the office now. Call him."

"Sorry. I can't do that. Dr. Snow is very busy and I doubt—" She infuriated me. I sat up, driven beyond restraint by her impertinence.

"Don't bother to doubt—just you call him. That's all. Dr. Snow'll see me. Don't you worry your big, black head about it." I hesitated, shocked. I hadn't meant to use that ugly word. I awaited her reaction, cowed by my own intemperance. But Miss Black said nothing. She only shrugged—her shoulders rising in perfect tandem. It was as if, in fact, she weren't black.

"If you insist. But it's not wise. I warn you—Dr. Snow doesn't like interruptions."

"I'll take the responsibility, thank you. Just call him. Tell him, if he's not down here in half an hour—in half an hour— I'm getting up out of this bed, and I'm going home. Tell him that." Miss Black inflated her nostrils in a dispassionate sneer. Then she turned and left me.

I stood out of bed and hurled my bathrobe over my shoulders. I missed. I bent to pick it up. Angrily I strode backward and forward past the foot of my bed—pounding hand into fist, growling, delighted with outward, senseless manifestations. Mr. Farbstein belched, a long, sad sound, and healthy bathos descended on the room, on my self-conscious fury, on the whole of the conflict we were engaged in. But I ignored it. I crossed to the window. There, my fingertips pressed to the glass, I felt for the storm's pulse—determined to let its unpurposed energy augment my resolution. A dangerous thing to do. I knew it even then.

He appeared almost at once. I had expected that. He was waiting in the doorway long before I was aware of his presence. I had expected that as well. Mr. Farbstein went limp. His eyes fell away from my body; his head arched backward onto his pillow, as though the bones in his neck had become grotesquely hinged. Dr. Snow was smiling. His hands were out, nudging and caressing themselves with tiny, quick touches. His eyes were nowhere and everywhere at once, undefined in their multiplicity as are the eyes of a fly. Dr. Snow began to walk toward me, but I walked toward him more quickly. We met at the foot of Artie's bed.

"You wanted to see me?" he said.

"Where is he?"

"Where is whom?"

"Artie Carson." I pointed to the bed. Dr. Snow sighed. Then he slid his hands into his front abdominal pockets. "Don't tell me he's dead. He isn't. I know that."

"You know nothing," he said. "Not the very least of things. But it's true—you're right about that. Mr. Carson's not dead, not yet. His condition has deteriorated. I'm sure you'll be sorry to hear that. Last night he suffered a painful bladder failure—very painful. We had to put a catheter in. It seemed best to move him to another ward. The nurses there specialize in terminal cases." I stood to my left: I tried to position myself directly in the line of his gaze. But it was like searching for thin slivers of glass in clear water.

"That was a mistake," I said. "Careless. Not what I'd expected from you."

"A mistake? The catheter, you mean?"

"A botch. A first class botch. Had you been willing to grant me that—God knows, it was little enough—had you been willing . . . Who knows? Who knows, I might even have capitulated." He shrugged.

"Well. I can't understand you. That's all there is to it. It's too complicated for me."

"Let me see him."

"No. No, Whitney. I can't allow it. You'll only upset him. He needs rest now."

"I demand to see that man!" I screamed it. Dr. Snow moved quickly; he forced me down onto Artie's bed. Then he stood over me. He spoke urgently, credibly.

"Don't be insane, Whitney. Get excited like this and you'll ruin everything. Good grief, man—don't you know what's going on in there?" He touched my chest. "Your heart's hang-ing on by a thread. No more than that."

"I demand to see Artie Carson."

"All right." He backed away from the bed. "T'hell with you. If you won't listen to reason—then you can just forget the whole thing."

"Me? Me forget the whole thing? You may find yourself without a patient."

"And you—you may find yourself dead." Mr. Farbstein groaned. Somewhere along the corridor glass shattered. I pressed my nails into the bare mattress edge.

"If it's to be. Then it's to be," I said. Dr. Snow took several steps backward. Then he nodded, as though some familiar thing had become again apparent. He shrugged.

"I'd be surprised. That's the truth. Tell me, Whitney—have you read the letters yet?"

"I don't have to."

"No? Don't be so sure. First things first, I should think." He shook his head. "Hell bent for martyrdom, eh? You men of the cloth—this poor world's never enough for you. Spoiled, that's what you are. Ungrateful—disgustingly ungrateful. Still, it's up to you. There's nothing I can do."

"No. Nothing," I said.

"I hope you change your mind. There's time yet, you know. Time to remember what life is about—what comfort is. Hap-piness. Fame." He paused. When I didn't reply, he went on. "We have an appointment Friday morning. That's the only appointment we have. You've already taken up a lot of val-uable time—very irresponsibly, it seems. But enough. It's use-less talking. I can see that. You're angry about Mr. Carson—I can almost understand how you feel. But good medicine transcends sentiment. That's all there is to it. I have to go now. I won't see you again."

"Let me send him a note." Dr. Snow shook his head. He turned to go. At the doorway he swung around to face me.

"Whitney. These things are a lot subtler than you imagine. Subtler than the decalogue; subtler than all that nonsense. Right and wrong—they were always hopelessly confused. But now . . . The Golden Rule, for instance. D'you remember that archaic thing? Do unto others as you would have them do unto you. Morally unexceptionable that, wouldn't you think? Yet, just imagine, Whitney—to a masochist it can offer such fascinating possibilities. Fascinating." He shrugged. "But then it's no longer valid. Is it?" Dr. Snow smiled when he said that. Then he was gone.

The tea treatment again: one cup—a dinner. No solid food, she said. In major surgery the metabolic balance of the gastroint—gastrointestinal tract becomes a critical factor. She had difficulty saying that, and she smiled when it was finished. I said something ironic, something about the excision of souls, and, as I did so, the hurricane blew a Wagnerian coda to my disappointment. At times the ebb of the wind was as great as its headlong rush; we held to mattresses, expecting bodies, beds, walls to be sucked out under windows. A cup of tea. Not very subtle, I thought. Not very subtle, after all. And patiently, un-subtly, too, I gnawed the cup's smooth lip.

Jimmy's people had gone to the solarium—from force of habit; perhaps, too, because Artie's presence was still heavily distinct in our room. Maureen had appeared for the first time in days. The Lopopulo's were sad and worried. Mr. Lopopulo put his son's slippers on, kneeling beside his bed—then he bent and softly pressed his lips against the boy's instep. Jimmy laughed and said it tickled. Little people—people for whom all death's euphemisms were coined. People for whom trouble and entertainment, striving and satisfaction—all the paraphernalia of life—existed solely to disguise their uninterruptible progress to mortality.

Mr. Farbstein had begun to pant, as though watching were some tiring, manual exertion. Nurse MacArthur came over to him, but Mr. Farbstein refused to notice her. He knew his vigil was fast approaching its end—that the bridegroom, the thief, whatever, had almost come. I felt his agitation: a vibration with tiny amplitude and terrific frequency. I pitied him, for I, too, was tired of watching. Nurse MacArthur arranged his pillow. She poured him water. She murmured to him and looked deeply into his empty eyes. And then I realized that her motions had become superfluous, purposeless in themselves. She was doing to do. After a moment, she turned, hands on hips, and looked toward me. Unembarrassed, I joined my glance to hers, and then I diverted both to the place where Artie had been. Nurse MacArthur inhaled, her lower lip shuddering in with the force of her breath. Then she came over to me.

"He's gone," I said when she was close to me.

"Yes. He's gone."

"Can you tell me where?"

"No." She shook her head. "I don't know."

"It's not fair, you know. Not fair at all. What can I do?"

"Nothing. You did too much—that was it, I think." She looked toward the window. "Perhaps it'll be enough."

"I'm helpless here," I said. Nurse MacArthur hesitated. She looked at Mr. Farbstein, and he smiled—at her, at us, there was no certain way of telling. Then she turned back. She put her

hand on my wrist: her nails bit into my flesh. I started with the
pain.

"I'm going to tell you something," she said. "Please listen,
Mr. Belknap."

"Yes—"

"Remember—when you first came in here—you mentioned
a doctor, an assistant of Dr. Snow's?"

"Yes. Dr. Crecy."

"Well. That's just it, Mr. Belknap. I've checked through our
records. There's no such doctor registered here."

"You must be wrong," I said. I sat forward, my fingers working nervously at the fringe of my blanket. "That can't be."

"But it is. His name just isn't anywhere. Not even on the
day charts."

"But, it was just a couple of days ago—he took me into that
little consultation room, the one down the corridor. He talked
to me for . . . Well, it must have been at least half an hour.
He explained about my operation. All the gory details. How
they cut away the ribs and tie things off. How my aneurysm
would look. Why, he even told me what Dr. Snow would do
if—" I paused. I remembered my pseudo-death and it terrified me. "If my heart stopped while I was on the table. It
was very frightening."

"He did that?" Nurse MacArthur brought her hand up to
her breast as though involuntarily. "No doctor ever does that
—not unless he's a sadist or a madman. Not here. Not in any
hospital."

"But he did. I can describe the room. So, you see, I didn't
dream it."

"I know you didn't," she said. My chest began to rise and fall
in sudden, painful lurches.

"Then—"

"She's another one. Miss Black. I don't understand. I just don't understand." She shook her head. I thought for a moment she was going to fall.

"What do you mean? What about Miss Black?"

"Her name's not down anywhere either. I asked one of my friends about it but she only laughed. She said they must be Dr. Snow's special assistants. But I've never heard of such a thing. Hospitals can't be run that way."

"Why don't you ask Dr. Snow? He must know." She laughed and her laughter was nervous and unpleasant.

"That's just it, Mr. Belknap. He does know. I couldn't ask him. I'd be afraid. I should report this. I know it. But I don't want any trouble."

And things, things that go bump in the night. I scratched the side of my head, hurting myself. So it's not up there, I thought. Not all in my head. It's a habit we have. To blame our own minds for anything that isn't simply explainable. To prefer madness rather than acknowledge one unscientific, one irrational event. We've been intimidated and that's just the way they wanted it. I looked up. Nurse MacArthur had begun speaking in a very loud voice.

"The blood has to go somewhere. After it leaves the ventricle—"

"What?" I looked up again. Miss Black was standing in the doorway, exactly at the midpoint of the arch. Nurse MacArthur said something about heart surgery. Then she turned her back on me and walked past Miss Black out the door and into the corridor. That was the last I ever saw of her. And, across the room, Mr. Farbstein sat upright, his little teeth grinding audibly against each other. He held the call bell tightly between his hands.

*

"Say a prayer for him. Please."

"I will. I have, Mrs. Lopopulo."

"I want to thank you now—now, no matter what happens tomorrow. You've been wonderful." She cried easily as she leaned over my bed.

"Nonsense. Jimmy's been pretty patient with me, too. It's been give and take. He's quite a gentleman."

"A wonderful boy. I'm the mother—I know I'm prejudiced —but I'll say it anyway. A wonderful boy. Why? Oh, why?" She sat down in the chair she had refused just a moment before. Jimmy was saying good-bye to the others. Maureen stared out the window; she seemed bored. Jimmy's aunt knelt in prayer at the foot of his bed, her garters and the pocked fat of her upper thighs were clearly visible.

"He'll be all right."

"Yes. Yes, I know." She smiled; then she sobbed. Then she smiled and sobbed simultaneously. "Dr. Snow is a wonderful doctor. I know. But still, strange isn't it? It's you makes the difference. You. You've got the right connections. It's your word that counts. Alfonse promised me—today—he promised me he'd go to church every Sunday if things come out all right. He went this morning."

"I'm very glad. Christ loved the young and the innocent. He was one of them."

"Yes. Yes. I knew it—I knew God wouldn't punish the innocent. Oh, you're wonderful." Mrs. Lopopulo hoisted her great bosom up over my chest. Suddenly it was very dark. Then Mrs. Lopopulo kissed me—on the mouth. I hadn't expected that. There was no breath in my lungs when her lips covered mine: for a short moment I thought I would suffocate. "Thank you," she said. She smoothed the hair back on my graying temples. Then she blushed—Maureen had been watching us. She

turned back to the window. Mrs. Lopopulo stood up and pulled
her dress down.

"Good luck," I said. "Good luck to you all. Take care of
yourselves—make this time a cause for rededication."

"Yes. Yes," said Mrs. Lopopulo. "Maybe I—we all could
come hear you preach. Where is your church?"

"I preach very seldom these days. There's so much adminis-
tration."

"A shame. A shame. Your voice is so beautiful. Well. I must
go—can't bear saying good-byes. What is it Shakespeare says?
'Parting is so sad!' Something like that. A wonderful writer."
She paused. "When . . . ?"

"Friday."

"Terrible. But don't you worry—" She looked up at the
ceiling. "He takes care of His own."

"He does. Yes. Pray for me, will you?"

"May I?" I nodded. "May I, really? Maureen tells me you're
quite a famous person. Maybe—maybe you could visit us someday. I'm president of a small ladies' group in Brooklyn. I'm
sure we'd all love to hear you speak. Anything you'd want to
say. Of course, we're mostly Catholics—but everyone's so
ecumenial these days. Well. We're in the Brooklyn book. Alfonse Lopopulo. Drop in any time, pot luck."

"I may just do that."

"Promise. Well. I really must go now. I bet Maureen thinks
we're carrying on." She giggled and brought her shoulders up
quickly, almost to her ear lobes. Then she looked toward
Artie's bed. "I'm certainly glad he's gone. I told Alfonse—if
he's there one more day, I said, I'm going to complain. I know
this is semi-private. I know. But there're things a boy Jimmy's
age shouldn't have to see. And hear." She straightened her

dress again: running her palms slowly from beneath her
breasts to the upper part of her thighs. "Come along,
Maureen." She spoke impatiently, as though Maureen had
purposely detained her. "Good-bye. Good luck. God bless you.
We'll never forget what you've done." She ran over and kissed
Jimmy on the forehead. Then she left, waving a good-bye to
'Mr. Firestone' as she passed out the door. The others left more
slowly—no one wanted to be last in the room. Jimmy bounced
on the edge of his bed three or four times after they'd gone.
Then he came over to me.

"I got a sleeping pill. First one I've ever had." It was yellow; he held it between his thumb and forefinger. "I gotta take
it now. So I'm gonna say good-bye."

"Jimmy," I said. That was all. I lifted him almost from the
floor in my embrace. I held him against my chest, and he suffered my doing it—for a long time. Innocence, I thought, innocence courts sleep. I set him free again. I put my hand on
his arm.

"Jimmy," I said. "I held you then, not because I'm afraid
for you. Remember that. But—but because I love you as my
own child. You're right—we're right—there's nothing in
a dream that can do us harm. Nothing. We can wake up. We
can always do that."

"Mr. Belknap? Why don't you have any children? You'd
make a swell father."

"Because—never mind." I smiled. "Thanks, anyway. Take
your sleeping pill. Then I'll come over and we'll pray
together."

We prayed, and Jimmy slept even as I finished speaking. I
got to my feet. Then I bent and put his two little slippers together, toe to toe, beneath his bed. Outside, the storm raised a

hoarse voice once again. I walked to my bed—knowing, even then, that the hunger-fatigue had returned to my body. I sat beside my bed. Distanced beyond myself—as though keeping watch over my own body's passing. And then I prayed.

Lord God, my heavenly Father, however it may be Thy plan to test me, I pray—let not the life of even one of Thy innocents depend on my strength. Protect these—Jimmy Lopopulo and Artie Carson—from evils that are my concern alone. Whatever my fate, let it be a separate thing, let it be mine only.

Know—my God—that there is no bitterness in me. Thou hast granted me what only I desired—one touch of Thine eternal Grace. If I fail—as may well happen, for there is great weariness in my body—if I fail, I fail in glory. However Thou hast determined for me, I will be always Thy faithful witness.

THURSDAY, AUGUST 24TH—

THE ELEVENTH DAY

His bed had been stripped. It yawned at me. They had
pounded the pillow and then set it on its small end against the
headboard. A grave with a stone—the stone bent double in
mourning. Jimmy was gone, as I had known he would be. But
the bed was the goneness, the thing in itself. Blank, ciphered.
Another empty rectangle stood diagonally across from it.
Artie's. I looked toward Mr. Farbstein, and then I thought of
bishops—black and red—and how they moved on a chess
board. Diagonals, parallel and contiguous—intersecting con-
tinually—yet, at every point, absolute and impenetrable.

The rain had become a simple torrent. Deprived of the
wind's vitality and momentum, it fell in a monolithic perpendicular. The morning's half-light had caught the pattern of
rain globules on the window and projected it—hugely magnified, blurred—onto the wall above Mr. Farbstein's bed. The
great, hazy drops ran down his wall, as, in miniature, they ran
down the pane: slowly at first, their mass barely overbalancing
friction; faster then, as they gathered substance from water
around them; plunging down at last, irresistible. Below, demi-

god of the blackness into which they vanished, Mr. Farbstein
sat upright. Wizened. The least of living things. His vigil now
a hideous exhibition of endurance. The magic lantern imposed
an enormous and allegoric Chinese water treatment on his
head. And still Mr. Farbstein sat, staring at me.

I was weak and feverish. My fingers hung from their palms
on strengthless hinges. A viscid, excremental sweat infested
my armpits and groin; it glossed my new, pink chest. The bed
clothes lay tortuously braided about my body: from their torment I could infer the nature of my dreams the night before.
As I lay, an association—I thought of it then as the association,
for it had plagued me since before Artie had disappeared—
struggled to express itself in inanimate objects. It flowed from
the metal water pitcher, to my gooseneck lamp, to the valve on
the radiator; it shook them, intensified and stressed them in its
frenzy. But they resisted the passage of communication.
Throughout the rest of that long day, it remained muted, obstinate.

We were alone—frightened, terribly bored, almost innocent.
He and I: surrogates for plodding, oxymoronic forces in furious
stalemate. We waited, superficial things without volition or
knowledge, and we watched—each hoping to discover some sudden relevance in the other. Now even our hard, mutual abhor-
rence was without significance. We waited. Dullness dis-
seminated itself in regular sounds, regular shadows. The
radiator began to speak, psss-tick, sss-tick, sss-tick. The thing
was yet inarticulate. And morning became early afternoon.

I prayed for Jimmy. Instrument after instrument—brittle
metal and sickly plastic—the apparatus of his torment evolved
out of my subconscious. I felt fear for Jimmy: fear for his body.
It was a realizable thing, compounded out of an empathetic

horror. But for Artie—my man, my special God-given man—I felt something else again. Loneliness befriended only iron- ically by pain. An irresistible descent into nothingness, as, around him, the real world became first soft, and then as sub- stantial only as the air. I remembered his very real joy in Christ. I remembered his moment of seeing into. And I prayed for Artie.

The sounds of the rain had become monotonous: a hissing rush indistinguishable now from real silence. Within the room there was only a breathing, very regular and assumed to be our own. Miss Black alone violated our specialness. She, too, was silent. No one passed along the corridor. When I staggered to the bathroom, silence followed me down the hall, mitigating the harsh sounds of my feet on the floor. In bed, I snapped my fingers against the dense onrush of soundlessness. It seemed as though we two were being isolated, sterilized. An intense and very artificial environment closed over our little diagonal. Ob- jectified. Abstracted from all contexts. Understood.

I was hungry, exhausted. I lay for hours, my wrist balanced on my forehead, conscious thought circumscribed within my watch dial's tiny round. I learned how minutes were doled out —one after the other—by the imperturbable bureaucracy of time. Early afternoon became late afternoon. No one arrived. Without sound, without movement to differentiate one moment from another, the day, if such it was, unfolded with the senile preoccupation of an old man unbuttoning his shirt. Only light and thought remained: light was suspect and thought—thought was no longer even that.

I knew by four o'clock that Michael had deserted me. I knew, and yet I knew that he had not. Now nothing could participate in our specialness but by supernatural fiat. I saw from my win-

dow that the river still flowed and that boats still traveled it.
I wasn't comforted. Though the hands of my watch insisted
that this specialness was yet within time, I began—at one level
of my consciousness—to doubt the river, the boats, the sun that
made them visible. I lay. I waited. I allowed myself to become
totally known and experienced. And I prayed for those I loved.

"Sign this," she said.
Reluctantly, I diverted my attention away from the watch
dial. I had been practicing: I knew the smaller parts of time almost by heart. Fifteen second, thirty seconds, the precise dura-
tion of a minute. Good things to know. Miss Black spoke again.
The angles of her elbows were each inverted quarters-to-five.
In one hand she held a piece of paper; in the other, a ball-
point pen. Her skin was as eager to reflect light as dark, oiled
metal. It seemed as though Mr. Farbstein had begun humming
a high-pitched, formless song: the wind strained through a mesh
of high telephone wires. I sat up awkwardly and cleared my
throat.
"What time is it?"
"Ten to five."
"Ten to five? I'm a little slow." I bent to adjust my watch,
but Miss Black intercepted my hand.
"Sign this, please."
"What is it?"
"The release. You'll have to sign it."
She turned on the light. The paper, heat-white in the sudden
illumination, blinded me. Miss Black pushed the table roughly
up to my chest. Then she put the paper in front of me. I knew
what it was, and yet the implications of the thing were beyond
my comprehension. The whiteness of the paper stretched past

the table, melding into the whiteness of my sheet. Black spots hurtled at the vulnerable, seeing parts of my eyes. I knew that my wrist was being manipulated. Mr. Farbstein's song split in two—a low, dissonant polyphony. I had a pen in my hand.

"Could I wait? I—I want to ask someone about it."

"No. You'll have to sign now. We can't start things until you do."

"You can't make me sign," I said.

"No . . ." said Miss Black. But she must have suspected, for she brought the lamp down then—it hung over my shoulder; I could feel the warmth of the bulb. The light became unbearable. I put my hand up to shield my eyes, but the light lodged between my fingers, glowing there. Miss Black stood over me. I won't sign, I said. But I said it to myself, and already I could feel my fingers preparing themselves. The paper was an open pit of light; it seemed blank. I touched my pen to it. Then I stopped.

"What's my name?" I asked.

She answered without hesitation. I nodded. I wrote. I found the familiar lines fascinating. Whitney Belknap: called that for convenience sake. Instead of coward. Instead of betrayer. Judas. Whitney Belknap, I said—Whitney Belknap is a euphemism.

"Excuse me?"

"Nothing. D'you want your pen back?"

"Thank you," she said. She turned the light off. "Would you like something nice to drink?"

"No," I said. "It won't do. It's not that easy."

"Sleep then," she said. "You need sleep. You're very tired."

Mr. Farbstein's song lingered for just a few moments after that. Then it merged with the silence. I sat there, stunned. It had come, and I had signed it. I put my hands flat together in front of me. Then I bent my forehead to touch them. Taken by surprise, I'd given them a terrible encouragement. Mr. Farbstein smiled at me—there could have been affection in his smile. Certainly there was relief. And now I was too mortified to pray. Instead, I did as Miss Black had told me—I fell asleep . . .

. . . The rope stretched from my abdomen to the branch and beyond, by a simple extension, to the pure blue heavens. The sky—just that much of it—had been preordained mine. I could see the three of them above me: there as a matter of course. Now, carelessly prone at boat's bottom, I leaned my soft head against the fragile bulwark and heard the river's lapping just beyond my ear. Stable, sequestered, sure. In subtle elevations it exalted me toward the sky and tossed me down again, encompassing, on the current, the full amplitude of human expectation.

They moved onward down the sky. And I knew, even then, that it was no longer sufficient to lie curled in warm sunlight. I rose unsteadily and pulled the rope down from the branch. The boat rocked with my balance. Instinctfully, I took the oars in my strong wrists and began rowing with the current. The water rushed swiftly beneath me. I passed through a convocation of water-lilies that sucked daintily at my prow.

Arrogant ducks—bourgeois and confident—surrounded me to avoid me, articulating their one sufficient word. A yellow butterfly, oaring the air, coyly teased the water's surface. A frog made a rude remark. I rowed with self-consuming fury down the river. Then the swans passed. Beauty and purity and grace with all their concomitants: black feet and tiny teeth and whip-like, hissing necks. I came close to admire, fearful as admirers should be. The smell of rich cow-things—leathery hides, grass and thick dung—swirled in the air. I rowed to show that my arms, too, were rich: resilient and strong and as new as the spring.

There was a wooded grove. My river inhaled, swelled wide its ribs, and pored sluggishly over the forest's floor. Dead trees sprouted in mid-course. Where they did, the water was dark and untroubled. Morocco-bound branches tapped insistently at my shoulder blades. Distracting, amicable, they blackened the sky in legions: yet, even so, I knew my three were there—now one, now another, now three together they danced through the involved writings of the leaves. I pulled impatiently. Brittle parchment grass slithered over my oar blades. Bits of tin and paper, the records of a human passing, bubbled from the water's depth. I pulled. And then the river was clear again and mine.

Not mine alone. There were people on the banks. At first only an isolated man; a single child sifting the shallow waters. Soon, though, whole groups hurrying toward the river's edge. I rowed with determination, striving to put them behind me, but the river seemed to lead only deeper and then deeper in amongst teeming shoals of people. Now both banks were seething. I could see people arriving at the far rims of the multitude; they were running. Then, at once and with a sort of collective shyness, the mobs began smiling and waving. Silently. They shoved to the water's edge, women and Negroes, little children and heavy, alien-featured men. Once, disconcerted, I waved back at them, but the oars leaped free, striking me dully under the elbows. After that I only smiled.

It was the sound; the sound even then, I think. The rushing of my oars in the water had somehow become hollow, resonant. I slowed for the first time. I listened. The breezes had accumulated; I experienced them now as a single, chill wind. I

stroked once again—and then I stopped. The rushing of my
oars went on, becoming louder. Instinctively, I looked up.
The banks were deserted, but that wasn't it. Above—they were
gone. The sky was pale and empty. I wrenched at the oars,
cursing my body for its inattention. I rowed and I rowed. I
rowed so mightily that my back rose almost erect. And then I
heard it.

A roar. Distant yet, but thunderous and resounding, a colossal
throat in swallow. The sides of my boat vibrated sympathetically. Oars clattered in oar locks. It had become bitterly cold.
I jammed the oars deep into the water, but my hands rebelled:
pieces of white, blistered flesh flaked off in ugly strips. The boat
plunged forward. Boiling water threw up my oar blades, tossing them crazily into the air. The roar had become imminent,
oppressive. I dropped the oars and stood, toppling, in the bow.

I couldn't see anything. The river vanished ominously around
a turning. In the air, above the trees, a white mist floated against
the sky—the sign and residue of terrible cataracts. A rainbow
hovered in the mist, but I was not deceived. I began to panic.
Knees, eager to run, banged against the boat's sides. And then
I saw it. Just ahead and to the left, there was a tiny, tunneled
fork. Barely a stream, but seeming to me like God's glorious
salvation itself. Both arms upraised, I drove my right oar deep
into the water. Desperately I worked my boat to the port side.
Twice the current snatched me around in sickening, twisting
circles. I fell into the bow again and again. Yet I succeeded
—in time I found I'd penetrated the less violent side currents
of the stream. And, impelled by a last urgent stroke, my boat
nosed wearily into the shadowed branch. I dropped, exhausted,
on my knees. The hard prow's point cushioned my forehead.

I was unconscious for some time, for the sluggish current had

had time to carry me some distance forward. I awoke gradually. My right hand had been trailing over the side. Now I pulled it in, and put the fingers to my sweating face. I gagged. My hand was white, coated with a sperm-like, cloudy jelly that hung in strands between my fingers. There was a ponderous, sweet odor in the air—of rotting flowers and sulphur and certain sorts of excrement. I imagined I could see it, for the mist above me was yellow. Layers of scum interpenetrated each other in the water—a thousand different consistencies. The trees above me were ancient, long dead. Branch after branch leaned down in supplication. Moss—not gray, brittle Spanish moss but brownish, wet stuff—oozed from the branches. I sat up suddenly. The boat barely registered my movement.

And then I heard it.

A roar. The same terrible roar. Farther away as yet, still far distant—but inevitable. I stood, an oar swaying uncertainly over my head. "Damn you to hell," I said. "Damn you. Damn you." I struck into the flabby water. A branch grazed my temple. I took it in my hands and wrenched it from its socket. Then I dug into the fetid water and began to pole—up, away from the roar. Back to the roar. I pushed until the branch disintegrated into thin, brown shreds. Then I took an oar and dug it in against the muddy bottom.

I poled maniacally—and yet with a nauseating, inescapable slow-motion. I dared not look back; I dared not measure my progress. The boat's stern made vulgar, sucking sounds, as, stroke after heavy stroke, I pulled it from the ooze. My body's strength had dissipated long before. The oar seemed to buckle on a dozen hinges. The slime made it slip, slither from my hands. Each thrust into the water brought forth smells as from a putrescent stomach. I found the end of my tongue dangling

loose in my mouth. I spat it from me. With deep, pleasant
swallows, I cannibalized my own body.

And then they were there. Three of them. Blazing sureness
in the utter blue of the sky. The sun was warm. The force of
the current was a real thing: alive, vital and murderous. It
swept the boat to it in a brusque embrace. I toppled back: my
shoulders were wedged in the prow's angle. But around me, I
saw—I saw—the deep abundance of existing things, and I hurried to enjoy them. Even the rich terror of the roar behind me.
It came nearer but they were there. The green of the leaves and
the grass. Two cows, tails twitching. Birds maneuvering in
mobile formations. Rainbow-colored darning needles. The
very smell of life and its warmth.

A little girl was playing there—there, so near the end. I saw
her. She waved and ran toward me into the river shallows. I
saw the current flare, in feathers, over her feet. The little girl
bent; she plunged her hands under the stream. Then she rose
and held water out to me in cupped, reverent hands. I waved
and smiled; I remembered to do those things. And the little girl
lifted her hands high over her head. She broke them apart.
And the water cascaded down in greens over her small, nervous
form. The boat began to tremble. The water was a foaming
rumble, the insucked tongue of a leviathan and thundering
mouth. And I saw, clearly through a thousand prismic layers,
the three of them still blazing and mine and with me . . .

A waxing machine ran noisily, roaring. It smashed into something. I pulled two blankets away from my face. Then I lay
back: my left hand trailing over the edge of my bed; my shoulders propped on pillows. The machine stuttered. It waned.
Silence took our room by surprise, yet soon, mastering dismay,

the sounds of our breathing reconstituted themselves. I began
to hum. Eternal Father strong to save. Strong—strong to save
. . . The rain still fell, bringing darkness down in the stark per-
pendiculars of a night shade. Whose arm hath bound . . .
bound the restless wave . . . Mr. Farbstein started forward furiously: I suppose he recognized it long before I did. Answer
when we cry to Thee . . . Thee . . . Thee . . . I toyed with
variations. For those in peril—those, those in peril . . . She
was still there. It had come. An intimation of understanding,
as valid as the understanding itself. Fatigue soothed me now.
Happy with my body, I leaned down to nuzzle my own shoulder.
I sang nervously. For those—for, oh for—for those in peril on
the sea. It had come. Is this the way it is? I wondered. Is this
it? Is this the way it is?

I sat up suddenly and snapped the light on over my bed. Mr.
Farbstein squinted. I twisted the lamp head until it glared directly into his face. Mr. Farbstein retracted his head like a
turtle; it seemed to sprout from his breast bone. Swiftly then, I
opened my bed table drawer. A crossword puzzle book. A handkerchief. A tooth brush. A God—*A God For Our Time*. Two
envelopes. I took them out. Then, with meticulous symmetry,
I placed them edge to edge before me on the bed. There was one
from Maryland; it was written in pencil. One from a little girl;
it was written in green ink. Mr. Farbstein shook his head. I
puckered my lips and blew at him.

"Death," I said. "Reflections on death by Whitney Belknap."
I cleared my throat. Then I glanced patiently from side to side,
gathering the several attentions of my audience. I cupped my
hands and raised them to the level of my chest. "Death." I
paused. "A line drawn, for the sake of argument, between two
realities—a lesser and a greater. A thing referred to as past, a

thing referred to as future, but a thing powerless of itself to vitalize any present. Eternity's one boundary. A striving. An acknowledgment of something else. The only beginning and the beginning only of understanding. The ego's end: the sur-passing synthesis. The one easy humility. Only that.

"If there are no further questions," I said. "We will proceed." I waited, but there were no questions. I nodded. Satisfied, I took up the green-ink envelope. For just a moment, I held it to my cheek. It seemed warm. Then, ceremonially, I took my forefinger and inserted it under the open flap. There was a sheet of paper inside, folded twice. I unfolded it once. I unfolded it a second time . . .

The paper was blank.

I sat stunned, staring at the unblemished whiteness of the thing. Then, with awkward haste, I took up the other envelope. I ripped it open. Nothing. Nothing. Nothing, addressed to Dr. Snow. I laughed self-consciously, and then I began to laugh in earnest. I took one of the blank pages and folded it into a paper airplane. I raised my arm and threw the airplane at Mr. Farb-stein: it caught in the air and looped backward on itself. For just a second, Mr. Farbstein's concentration was surprised; he turned to look at the white thing coming at him through the light's glare. The plane concluded its loop and fell, without any controlling momentum, in a flat dive. It hit the floor with a barely audible tick. It lay there.

And then I wanted to show Artie. I turned spontaneously to my left. The other blank sheet was in my hand. But Artie was gone. This, I had wanted to say, this is all. Blank. Nothing. Be happy. I, too, have been afraid, ashamed, but not now. I re-membered Artie's child-like joy in Christ. His wonderful en-thusiasm for God's miracles. . . . I'd like t'have seen them

Jews' faces. That must've started them thinkin'. But good . . .
And I had said, Miracles—they're different now . . .

Different . . . now . . . And then I remembered. There
it was, the association—jarred from the tip of my tongue. I fell
forward toward my bed table, knocking the metal water pitcher
to the floor. It must have made an awful sound, but I didn't hear
it strike. I picked my Bible up.

"Then if any man shall say to you, Lo here is Christ or there,
believe it not. For there shall arise false Christs and false proph-
ets and shall show great signs and wonders, insomuch that, if
it were possible, they shall deceive the very elect. Behold, I
have told you before: wherefore, if they shall say unto you, Behold he is in the desert, go not forth. Behold he is in the secret
chambers, believe it not. For as the lightning cometh out of the
East and shineth unto the West, so shall also the coming of the
Son of Man be."

I closed my Bible. In most reverent flippancy, I balanced it
by its long end on the tips of my fingers. A long ah-aaah was
working itself loose in my throat. Ah-aaah. I flung my Bible
into the air and caught it tightly to my bosom. Miss Black had
come in. She glided noiselessly to my bedside. The floor was
covered with water, and, in the water, dozens of polygonal ice
bits. Miss Black said something to me. She shook her head;
then she shook her long, hard forefinger. But I knew, at least by
then, that I no longer had to listen. I watched her bend. I
watched her pick up the metal pitcher. Her gleaming, black
hands clasped its gleaming, silvery sides; I saw the texture of
the thing and of the toucher, and I knew they were the same.
Miss Black lowered herself at the hips. I closed my eyes in distress. That most wonderful instrument—the ball and socket
joint—that thing of infinite variation and subtlest movement.

That God-strung creation, source of all human litheness. Body's
kin of thought itself. Oppressed now, involuntary, proscribed.
Without imagination.

"You see," I said. "That's it. What you make your God—
that, in time, you become." That was the real danger, the real
blasphemy of the Golden Calf. And now this graven image—
so subtle, so splendid, so credible—progress. St. Augustine's superb Christian logic, perverted by Descartes, evolving finally into
its own antithesis. "For many shall come in my name saying, I
am Christ: and shall deceive many. Even him whose coming is
after Satan with all power and signs and lying wonders." Unde-
ceived, I lay. I groped about me, as a child who had first learned
that the sensations in his fingertips correspond to the real shapes
of things. I bided my time. I examined everything. For now I
was certain.

Three hours. Four hours and still enthralled by my astonishment. And, all that while, I prayed for Artie and Jimmy. Prayed
without recognizing the thing, prayer. Their essences—undiluted, at last, by my own obtrusive essence—became insistent
and ubiquitous, demanding love. I prayed for them as I lay,
reading the creviced meanings of the ceiling. I prayed for them
while, with my hand, I explored the splintery, dry wooden support bar. I prayed for them as—tottering and cold—I stood before the darkened window. I felt the glass and knew precisely
the nature of its inanimateness. I felt the breeze, and I knew
what its position was in the scale of natural and unnatural
things. I saw a garden down below. A square within a square.
Pavement, hedges, benches—glinting wet in the illumination of
two feeble lamps. A headless marble statue tossed a superfluity
of water into the drenched and sodden air. A garden. Not a
very satisfying garden. But nothing—certainly nothing more
than a garden.

The lights in the garden went out. The lamp over my bed went out. The squares of light in the great squares of Cavendish flickered once and were gone. Something fell—a resilient thing that fell and fell again with diminishing force. Bouncing. Then the lights came on again. They were yellow now and dim. I could see bits of blackness as they alternated with the light. A dull, grinding noise accelerated somewhere within the bowels of the hospital. The light was not the same. It seemed borrowed, derivative. No longer participating directly in the great light that illuminates the world.

And, across the room, a sound of breathing fell gradually into rhythm with mine—then, just as gradually, it fell out again. I turned from the window to look at him. David Farbstein. White. Shriveling. Gone to powder. A dry ember—held in human form by some remembered energy. Unraveling now. I brought my eyes even with his staring eyes. And, though I knew he could neither see nor hear me, I raised my right hand and blessed him with the sign of Christ's holy cross.

Mr. Farbstein fell asleep.

FRIDAY, AUGUST 25TH—

THE TWELFTH DAY

THE OTHER black sock. I rolled it. I stretched it slowly with the thumb and forefinger of each hand—stretched it into an open oval. For half a moment I dared do no more. I waited on the ebb and the flow of my small strength. Then, breath exploding in gasps, I wrenched my right knee up to my chin. I locked it there and patiently, toe by toe, I began to insert my foot. The cursed toes wouldn't go in. The black opening wavered from left to right, down, then up. I could hear the sinews crumbling in my thigh. I began to pant, struggling. But it was too late. The knee joint cracked and gave way; my lower leg jumped forward. The little toe of my right foot caught on the oval's edge—the sock leaped from my hands. Again. I'd have to start again. Again. I lay my cheek on my bared thigh and dozed.

Outside, the sky had come, by imperceptible degrees, up to brightness. An inconsistent drizzle still fell, but it had lost character long before. The storm was over. Mr. Farbstein snored at me: sounds like the crushing of thick fruits. He had slept the whole of the night. Now—now it was eight-thirty. More than an hour had trailed away—in the undressing, the socks. Half an hour—less than that—left. I held my watch hand up. The hand gnarled itself, straining, unable to steady. I was capable now only of hesitant, fragmented actions. The movement of a hand, a few toes, planned for whole moments beforehand. I shook my head. My clothes . . . I knew I'd have to confront them with a *fait accompli*—for the sake of my own morale.

No. I fell away from my foot. I forced my knuckles into each other until they ached. The arch of my foot had given way. Pain swept up my body; the hair on my stomach rose and fell, as though charged with a static electricity. I leaned forward and bent my foot in my hands—into the heart of the pain, through the pain. Then I lay back again, feeling for the first time the little cold nipples of sweat that had formed all over my skin. The sock sat—so far away—a black skier's cap on the tip of my foot. I lunged forward. Then I clawed the sock slowly up the length of my foot. My thumbnail broke as I brought it over my heel's mound. The green diamond clocking slithered up my instep. The sock's heel stood out from my ankle. It looked like a lanced blister. But it was on.

I pulled my shirt up from the floor. I studied it. The right sleeve was a simple matter, but, beyond that, I was stymied. I couldn't bring my strained left shoulder up behind my back. I tried throwing my arm up, swinging it until it arced high enough. But my fingers missed the hole. Once. Twice. A fifth time. I took the shirt off. Carefully, I spread the sides of my left sleeve hole. Then I slid my right arm in. Again. And this time I succeeded on the first try. My fingers caught in the hole; with a sound of ripping, I forced my inflexible left arm deep into the sleeve. But the pad of my thumb ached under the broken nail, and I managed to insert only two buttons—one at the top, one near the bottom. A quarter to nine. Fifteen minutes now.

I saw my black pants. They hung limply by a single leg from

a chair back near the window. Black pants. They might operate on a man in a shirt. They might operate on a man in black
socks with green diamond clocking. But a man wearing black
pants, I thought, surely such a man would be safe. I dragged
my adjustable table up between the bed and the distant chair.
I sat, absolutely inert, on the edge of the mattress. Then, with
a terrific leap, I threw myself onto the wheeled table and, from
it, I fell quickly to the chair. Rebounding, the table crashed
against my bed.

Mr. Farbstein woke—suddenly, as though in a slap's recoil.
We stared at each other. I numbered each successive stage of
comprehension as it appeared on his face. His eyes began slowly
to protrude. And I thought that, for a single moment, they
were once again the repository of his human soul. His upper
body sprang forward. Then his mouth opened wide and, as it
did so, Mr. Farbstein brought his open hand up against his
cheek with a cracking sound. The tattered catalogue sheet
flew from his lap; it fluttered noiselessly to the floor.

"No," he said.

I gasped. To my startled consciousness, it was as though
some wretched animal had suddenly, inexplicably begun to
speak. Mr. Farbstein shook his head. He seemed terrified. He's
mad, I thought. I opened my mouth. I wanted to soothe him.

"No," he said. Quietly at first. Then, "No," again. Louder
this time. Then louder and louder still. "No . . . No. No.
No!" He pointed a finger at me. "No! You can't do it. You
can't. No! No! No!"

He began to scream. The no's ran together. Compounded,
they became a long and agonized howl. Mr. Farbstein hissed.
He gnashed his tiny teeth together. Saliva poured from his
mouth, dribbled down his chin. I was horrified and so startled

that I jumped away from the chair. I fell, half leaning, against
the windowsill. Now Mr. Farbstein's hands were flying uncontrollably about his head. They clawed at his clothes. His hair.
His body trembled in its every part. I remember watching his
little white heel, as it hammered furiously against the foot of
the bed.

"What?" I said. "What is it? What?" I was screaming in
sympathetic terror.

"I woon't. I wooon't let you. I woon't."

Mr. Farbstein threw himself backward. Then, with reptilian
slitherings, he began to maneuver his wizened body up to the
headboard. My eyes closed involuntarily: I knew what he was
going to do, and his satanic determination sickened me. He was
gasping now, squeaking. He had reached the headboard. Prop-
ping his upper body on arms no thicker than mop sticks, Mr.
Farbstein clawed at the wall until he'd caught the call bell in
his hand. "No. No," he said. "Not now. Not. Not. Not.
Not." His little teeth were chattering like a rodent's. His head
bobbed up and down. He caressed the little call bell between
his fingers. Then he held it up.

"Please," I said. "Don't."

Mr. Farbstein pressed the bell.

My legs came undone. I sagged down to my knees before the
window. His laughter flared up behind me in monotonous reports. I squeezed my hands together. I was frightened, as I have
not been frightened since the unreasoned fears of my early childhood. I pressed my forehead to the glass. A film of rain—I could
see each individual mote—hung almost motionless in the air.
The river was calm. Squares of blue showed between great,
brown clouds. I saw cars on the highway, and, for just a moment, I considered trying to break the window. But I couldn't

raise my fist. I was paralyzed. *Lord God—Lord God*—I choked: the tissues in my throat were fat and swollen. They were coming. They were coming. And my legs were still bare.

And then the sky opened. The sun shone brilliantly through a small gap in the clouds. The light caught the still suspended raindrops and shattered itself upon them. From beyond the Soldiers and Sailors monument—stretching up in an arc to the south-west—there rose a magnificent rainbow. It faded momentarily. Then the sun's rays gathered body, and it stood bright above and strong enough to bear the whole world's traffic on its span. Mr. Farbstein's laughter seemed to die; perhaps I was no longer hearing it. For just then I had remembered—remembered the words of my God in the very beginning: "I do set my bow in the clouds and it shall be for a token of a covenant between me and the earth." Something struck me on the shoulder. It struck me again. But I didn't acknowledge it; not until I had said each word under my breath.

"Fool. Stupid fool."

I turned around. My body crumpled, as I did so, in a confused heap below the windowsill. P. Crecy stood over me. The colors of my rainbow were still on my retina, and now they streaked the white front of his coat. Miss Black stood behind P. Crecy. At her side there was a large, wheeled bed.

"You," I stammered. "You don't exist."

"Don't I now?" He raised his eyebrows. "Is that so?" P. Crecy went down to where I was lying. "Not exist?" he said. "Me? Not exist?" He said it with indignation. "Fairy tales, that's what. Miss Black. Please. Help me lend the good bishop a hand."

She came forward. P. Crecy was already lifting me at the armpit. Miss Black took my other arm. Though they were inches shorter than I, they manhandled my body with ease toward the wheeled bed. I struggled. I dragged my legs. I remember trying to use my weight against them. Then I was on my back, my shoulders pressed to the mattress.

"Don't let him go!" Mr. Farbstein was screaming. "Don't let him go-oh!"

"Not exist?" P. Crecy frowned. He pressed his fist against the bones of my chest. "You've got a nerve. Existence—is this what you call existence? Sixty years, seventy if you're lucky. Animal meat rotten from its conception—that's all you are. Think again. Who's more real, you or I?" He smiled and I felt the hard knots of his knuckles between my ribs.

"No," I whispered hoarsely. "I was wrong. You are real. I was being stupid."

"Yes, you were. You certainly were." Crecy clicked his tongue. "And your aneurysm is real, too. Don't think it isn't. As real as death. Isn't that right, Miss Black?"

But Miss Black didn't answer. She was busy removing my socks. I struggled against her; I almost cried in my frustration. My feet hid themselves under each other to no avail—the socks came off. With a perverse show of neatness, Miss Black folded my socks and laid them carefully on my bed. Mr. Farbstein chuckled. Then he screamed like a silly girl on a Coney Island roller coaster. I tried to pull myself up.

"Please," said P. Crecy. "Don't be difficult. It's for your own good. I promise you—before the sun goes down today—before then, you'll be a well man. You'll have twenty—thirty years ahead of you. Time to—"

"No," I said. "No. I won't have it. And you—you don't dare make me."

"Don't we?" said P. Crecy.

"Don't we? Don't we? Don't we? We. We. Wheee—" said Mr. Farbstein.

"Don't be an idiot," said P. Crecy. "You'll die if you don't get help. Believe me. I swear it's true." He put his hand to his heart.

"If I die," I said. "I die."

"I see. A hero. A martyr. It's rather sudden, isn't it?" P. Crecy put his finger to his lower lip. "No, my friend. It doesn't wash. I'm afraid we know you better than that. We know you're scared. You don't want to die. Who does? You've signed the release. Your chest is shaved. You're ready to go. You've been ready all along." I sat up then, shoving against his chest.

"I'm not going anywhere."

"Oh, yes—yes, you are," Crecy hissed. His eyes yellowed; the pupils tightened to pinpoints. He snapped his fingers, and Miss Black handed him a hypodermic. P. Crecy held it poised over my bicep. I tried to squirm away. But Miss Black had thrown the full weight of her upper body onto my chest.

"Relax," said P. Crecy. "Relax." There was sweat in the corners of his eyes. "In a few seconds you'll feel nothing. Not pain. Not anguish. Not responsibility. Nothing." He plunged the needle into the crook of my arm. I screamed. The pain threw my body into convulsions. Miss Black fell on me, smothering my face with her breasts. I bit her there. Then I tore my arm loose—hypodermic and all.

"You blundering ass!" I screamed. I turned onto my side. "Listen to me, Crecy. Listen. I don't want the operation. Understand? I really don't want it. If you push that stuff into my arm, you'll do it against my will. You'll save me, Crecy. For nothing. For absolutely nothing. An act of charity." I laughed at that. I think my laughter was the first thing he believed. He wrenched out the needle, twisting it.

"I don't believe it," he said.

"Yes, you do."

P. Crecy stood away from me. He drew the back of his sleeve across his eyes. He had begun to believe me. I saw confusion in his face, and I rejoiced in it. P. Crecy opened his mouth, as though to speak, but, just then, Mr. Farbstein squealed in terror. Crecy looked up.

It was Paul.

He stood in the doorway. His heavy shoulders were suspended in mid-shrug. He held his palms flat on the enormous surface of his chest. Paul raised his eyebrows and slowly began to shake his head from left to right. In that one instant's distraction, I sat up and swung my legs over the edge of the bed. Paul took a step forward. P. Crecy snarled.

"Paul," I said. "Am I ever glad t'see you. These people want to—"

"I heard," he said. "I heard."

"Miss Black," said Crecy. There was a brutal tension in his voice. "Make Bishop Belknap comfortable. Don't let him get over excited." Crecy walked forward, shoving my bed behind him. "What's your name?" he demanded.

"Paul Brown."

"All right, Mr. Brown. I'll give you just five seconds to turn around and walk out of this room. If you do—I give you my word—I won't mention this to Dr. Snow."

"Who's this guy think he is?" said Paul to me. "Dr. No? Is he serious? That's what I wanna know. Is he for real?"

"Stop this," said Crecy harshly. "Stop it now. This minute. Listen you—whatever your name is—this is a sick man. He's going to die. He knows it. He'll die unless he has an operation. You want that on your conscience? No? Then back off." Crecy turned to me. He put his hand on my shoulder and slowly impelled my body back down onto the bed. Paul began walking toward us. When he reached the bed, he took Crecy's hand in his and wrenched the fingers back until Crecy's knuckles snapped audibly.

"Shut up," he said in a quiet, high voice. "Man's got his rights, sick or not. If he wants t'go home, he'll go home."

"He'll go home. He'll go hooome."

"That will be enough."

Dr. Snow was there. He sat, one leg crossed on the other in a chair near the doorway—a spectator. His hands lay folded in his lap, the fingers limply intertwined. His head was supported at an angle on the chair's back. It was a position, I thought, that only a man sitting some while could assume. There was no urgency in his voice, though—ostensibly—he'd spoken to halt a violent action. And the eyes: they were, by all outward evidence, a blind man's; the eyes of one who had never come to depend on or appreciate sight. His eyes seemed to be wandering in and out amongst the ceiling cracks. Certainly they never once embraced Paul or P. Crecy.

"Let him go," he said. "It's over, Crecy. The bishop's too much for us. Let's give in—let's let him rush to his martyr's death."

Dr. Snow said it quietly, as though he were bored. He continued to sit there—after P. Crecy and Miss Black had left, after Paul, somewhat intimidated, had begun to pack for me. His left foot swung in the air; an easy rhythm, seemingly not a manifestation of despair. There was none of the usual agitation in his hands. As I dressed, I found I couldn't keep my eyes off him. His negligence was intolerable; there was a surfeit to it. He's posing, I thought. He's posing, and I can see through it. As if in answer, Dr. Snow looked toward me for the first time.

"Regrets already?" he asked.

"No," I said. "No regrets. Just exhaustion."

"It'll get worse. This excitement—it's put the seal on your heart. I give you a week."

"I believe you," I said. "But that doesn't signify any more— it's the others. Artie Carson. Jimmy—" Dr. Snow waved his hand.

"No," he said. "You're wrong. Missed the point as usual. They don't signify. Dead or alive. Damned or saved. It's all irrelevant—like Job's cattle or his houses or his children. Now, anyway . . ." He smiled quite pleasantly. "If it's any comfort —though, God knows, I don't owe you any—if it's any comfort, this whole business . . . the whole shooting match—it was special. Different. Unrelated. And now it doesn't matter at all."

"I don't think I believe you," I said.

"Good," said Dr. Snow. "Rescued from another act of charity. It's funny. No one ever does—believe it, that is. Even when it seems to me they have to." He laughed. "Pride, you know. Pride again. Pride still. Get the hell out of here, Whitney. And die. Die soon."

"Paul," I said. "Wait. Don't pack those." I took the manuscripts and my copy of *A God For Our Time*. "Here's a little present for you. I've written something on the flyleaf." I threw the book to Dr. Snow, but it fell short. He got up.

"Very weak," he said. "I take that back. I don't think you'll last to Monday. And on the third day, his heart went pop . . ." He picked up the book and opened the cover. He read out loud. " 'To Dr. Terrence Snow. Without whose inspirations this book could not have been written.' I'm flattered. Really."

"The manuscripts are yours, too. They're not as good—I think I shot my wad the first time." I got off the bed. "Let's

go, Paul. Dr. Snow's a busy man. And looks like I've got even
less time."

Paul picked up my bag. Then he came up beside me and
settled his shoulder under my armpit. I put my arm around him.
Slowly, step by step, we made our way toward the door, toward
Dr. Snow. I stopped when we had come even with the foot of
Mr. Farbstein's bed. I looked down at him. He'd been quiet
for some time. His head drooped between his shoulders, and
his little, white hands were huddled together. As I looked, Mr.
Farbstein raised his head until his eyes were on my face.

"Take me with you," he said.

"You're with me now."

"Balls," said Dr. Snow. "Balls. I suppose there'll be no stop-
ping you now. Die, Whitney. You can't die soon enough."

We stood together on the corner. The sunlight was pleasantly
warm. The smell of grass and earth, brought to a pungent bou-
quet by the rain, was all around us. I realized how wonderful
the merest living was. But there was no yearning, for, then, I
was just born and that was intoxication enough. To live—with
the whole of understanding. To live, no matter how long, in
the light that is the only true light. That alone is living.

A taxi came, and Paul helped me toward it. It was green.
Michael and I had come in a yellow taxi. We'd swerved in
front of a Volkswagen and then between two other taxis—one
yellow, one green. I was amazed at how observant I'd become.
I recalled that I had, after all, a book still to write, and I thought
I might yet be granted time to finish it. But I didn't presume to
hope.